BATTLE
FOR EARTH

Keith Mansfield always wanted to be an astronaut. Rejected by the European Space Agency and ineligible for NASA, he instead publishes mathematics books for Oxford University Press. He has scripted light entertainment shows for ITV and also contributed to 'The Science of Spying' exhibition at London's Science Museum.

His first book, *Johnny Mackintosh and the Spirit of London*, was published in 2008. The Johnny Mackintosh stories are based on childhood daydreams of being captured by aliens and escaping to see the wonders of the Galaxy. In reality, Keith lives in Spitalfields in the East End of London. Every window of his home looks out onto Norman Foster's beautiful Gherkin, the inspiration for the *Spirit of London*, Johnny's spaceship. ✩✩

Praise for
Johnny Macintosh and the Spirit of London

'This book offers excitement all the way as Johnny, stuck in a children's home while his mum's on a life support machine, finds out he has a sister and ends up hurtling through time and space.'

Daily Express

'A great read.'

The Sun

'The story is great . . . the characterization in this book is fantastic and Mansfield paints some exceptionally believable, lovable and fun characters. The writing is engaging and accomplished. It's reminiscent of Rowling, yet still maintains an individual style.'

Bookbag

'Vivid with life and colour . . . brilliantly original and multi-dimensional . . . I recommend wholeheartedly.'

Families Oxford

'A brilliant book, combining fantasy and real places together in one book. I absolutely loved this book and would recommend it to young people and adults alike . . . This is Keith's first book, which he's written superbly, making it totally believable . . . I adored the characters of Johnny and his sister . . . I hope that we shall be seeing more of Keith Mansfield's work because he writes such a brilliant story.'

BFKbooks

Praise for
Johnny Mackintosh Star Blaze

'Full of adventure and excitement.'

Anorak

'If you like stories in space with aliens, other planets and deadly enemies threatening the Earth, this series is going to suit you well . . . definitely a hit for sci-fi fans.'

Chicklish

'Awesome! The book cover just makes you want to pick it up straight away because it is so colourful and looks exciting. Flying around in a spaceship disguised as the London Gherkin! WOW!!! This is the first Johnny Mackintosh book and I hope there will be more to come.'

Bridgend County Council Library Services

'Ever since reading (and being disappointed by) *Charlie and the Great Glass Elevator* I have often felt a little pessimistic before reading sequels to books I had thoroughly enjoyed – will the author manage to recreate the magic with their second book? . . . However, with *Star Blaze* my pessimism was totally unfounded – in the same way that *The Empire Strikes Back* improved on *Star Wars: A New Hope*, so too does *Star Blaze* improve on its predecessor, and that is praise indeed. And the parallels don't end there – like *Empire*, *Star Blaze* is also a much darker book in places than the first in the series.'

The Book Zone

Readers' Reviews

'This was an excellent book filled with fun, action, laughter, sadness, and Johnny's inner struggles. It has something for most young readers. I highly recommend this book for teenagers.'

Courtenay, aged 14

'Personally, I absolutely love *The Spirit of London* . . . On World Book Day, we dressed up as characters from the book, one of my classmates even dressed up as Alf!'

Malaika, aged 11

'I am happily writing this letter to you because you have inspired me to be an author just like you. I like the Gherkin, the stars and the planets you made up.'

Hayrunnisa, aged 11

'I am just writing to say how incredibly interesting your book is, I just cannot think of any improvements at all. Lots of children in other schools will enjoy it . . . even adults!'

Miguel, aged 11

'I am writing to say I am a colossal fan of your books . . . Johnny Mackintosh is an inspiration for me as it makes me look at the stars and even makes me want to go into space myself . . . I cannot wait until the next one.'

Nile

'I love space and I am hypnotized by the details you wrote about space. Your books have inspired me to look at space and to be an astronaut.'

Samantha, aged 11

'I can't believe how good you are at writing books. Your book inspires me to go to space one day.'

Simon

'When the book is being read to me or when I read it, it really sucks me in, it is like having an adventure without leaving your chair.'

Zakariyy, aged 10

'I can assure you that I absolutely love your book. The main characters are just like my friends . . . what I really like about it is the suspense created, like when the asteroid is about to hit the Earth – fantastic!'

Hamsca, aged 10

'I love adventure books and therefore I find this book thrilling and wish to read more of your series . . . it is probably the most exciting and intriguing book I've ever read.'

Eugenie, aged 10

'I absolutely love your fantastic adventures. I think they are mad, clever and funny all at the same time . . . I rate them 110% . . . do you think you could lend me your spaceship sometime?'

Nathan

Books by Keith Mansfield

Johnny Mackintosh
and the Spirit of London

✩ ✩ ✩

Johnny Mackintosh
Star Blaze

✩ ✩ ✩

Johnny Mackintosh
Battle for Earth

JOHNNY MACKINTOSH

BATTLE FOR EARTH

KEITH MANSFIELD

Quercus

First published in Great Britain in 2011 by
Quercus
21 Bloomsbury Square
London
WC1A 2NS

A CIP catalogue reference for this book is available from
the British Library.

ISBN 978 1 84916 329 3

This book is a work of fiction. Names, characters,
businesses, organizations, places and events are
either the product of the author's imagination
or are used fictitiously. Any resemblance to
actual persons, living or dead, events or
locales is entirely coincidental.

3 5 7 9 10 8 6 4

Typeset by Nigel Hazle

Printed and bound in Great Britain by Clays Ltd, St Ives plc

A threefold thanks for this third story

to my mum and dad, who raised me to love books
to all the great friends I've made through this writing
adventure and to Jane, who struggled as soon as Johnny
entered the space elevator, but has steadfastly supported
him on his travels since ✩

The Creature from the Deep ✧✧

A crowd of tourists, most of them Japanese, were looking up at the building they all knew as 'the London Gherkin'. With their cameras and mobile phones they were busily snapping the impressive curved glass and steel structure, and its bands of diamond-shaped windows, all set against a clear summer sky. Strangely, although the people who owned the skyscraper were very proud of it, they weren't keen on just anyone coming here to view it, let alone take photographs. A couple of blue-uniformed security guards were doing their best to shoo the sightseers away. They were already worried they'd be in trouble for allowing a pair of blond teenagers and their Old English sheepdog in through the main doors, and weren't about to make the same mistake again.

One hundred and eighty metres above, Bentley (that very sheepdog) lay curled on a comfortable padded chair, snoring rather loudly. The teenage boy and girl were watching the scenes below from what the tourists might have thought was the very top floor of the building. The boy's name was Johnny Mackintosh and, contrary to appearances, he wasn't standing in the Gherkin at all. Through his dark green eyes, speckled with silver flecks, he was gazing out from the bridge of his very own spaceship.

Called the *Spirit of London*, she was a lookalike for the real Gherkin and had, at this particular moment, replaced it, standing proudly at the address 30 St Mary Axe in the heart of the City, London's financial district. Johnny's sister, Clara, had a rare and very special ability to manipulate the structure of space itself. She was so good at doing this that she was able to take the entire skyscraper and 'fold' it out of the way – into its very own pocket of hyperspace – allowing the spacecraft to take its place unnoticed. Her ability was shared by an unusual alien creature called a Plican, also on the bridge. Looking rather like a squashed octopus, this was currently scrunched up inside a cramped compartment at the top of a clear cylindrical tank beside Bentley.

There were three other living beings on the bridge. One of these, Sol, was the mind of the spaceship herself and was so clever that she was able to project the view of whatever was happening outside onto the windows of the original London Gherkin, now standing in hyperspace, with only a two nanosecond delay. This meant that any workers unknowingly passing in and out of the hyperspatial gateway to the actual building would be very hard-pushed to spot the difference.

A couple of police vans had drawn up in the little square below. Their rear doors were open and the tourists were being ushered inside. One or two looked to be making a fuss, but were forcibly bundled in before the doors slammed shut. At ground level, the security guards were becoming used to this sight and barely shrugged, knowing it made their lives simpler. Up above, Johnny couldn't help feeling a little uneasy. It struck him as odd that the vehicles had no identifying markings on their roofs.

'Finished,' came a voice from behind a copy of *The Times* newspaper which was lowered to reveal a figure in a dark pinstriped suit, topped by a bowler hat. Alf, an artificial life form, had a broad smile etched across his slightly metallic face and was keen to show off his completed crossword. Although extremely knowledgeable and fiendishly intelligent, the android sometimes struggled to complete the puzzle – especially when the clues veered away from the pure logic he loved best.

Johnny and Clara had been planning their first ever visit to Mars, with Johnny telling his sister about all the probes scientists had sent to the red planet, but which had mysteriously failed to arrive. Alf had been itching to join in the conversation, but was struggling with the final clue: 'Her King is a pickled vegetable (7)'. His crossword now finished, the android hurried over but, just then, it was the final member of the crew who spoke.

Kovac was a computer, but so unlike any other computer on Earth it would be akin to comparing a pocket calculator with the entire Internet (or so Kovac, at least, would have you believe). 'I have intercepted communications between the security services about supposed extraterrestrial activity in central London,' said the machine, his transparent casing lighting up in time to the words. 'Apparently a street entertainer – I believe the description was "juggler" – witnessed a green, bug-eyed alien coming out of the River Thames. Quite why you have me monitor all these ridiculous goings-on is beyond me. My time would be far better spent searching for structure within the number pi. I believe that, in base 11 at several trillion decimal places—'

'Kovac,' said Clara, 'exactly where in central London?'

'Does anyone listen to a word I say?' asked the computer. 'If you must know, it was Trafalgar Square. Why you even bothered having this annoying spaceship fit me with a quantum processor . . .'

The computer's grumblings were lost as Johnny, Clara and Alf stepped through an archway that had appeared out of thin air in front of them, wide enough for three people at its base but curving outwards so that twice that number might have fitted higher up. In the same way that Clara could relocate the real London Gherkin, she could take a corner of space in one place (for example, the *Spirit of London's* bridge) and fold it so it was touching a portion of space in another (say, near Trafalgar Square), making it possible to step instantaneously from one to the other.

They found themselves in a little alleyway they'd hoped would be deserted. As it happened, a tramp was sitting on a sleeping bag drinking from a bottle and Alf, whose complex circuitry was unable to cope with the manipulation of space, collapsed right in front of him. Johnny, himself feeling a little sick after unfolding, bent down, pulled out the android's left ear and turned it all the way round, before letting it snap back into position. Successfully rebooted, Alf sat upright and said an enthusiastic hello to the tramp who, having seen three people apparently just walk through the wall in front of him, looked approvingly at the bottle in his hand and took several hearty glugs. Johnny, his sister and the android ran past, out into the late afternoon sunshine and up a busy side street towards the square.

The view looked reassuringly normal, with no aliens or spaceships to be seen. People were gathered around the lions at the base of Nelson's Column while, closer to hand along the southern edge of the square, red double-decker buses and black London taxis wound their way slowly between traffic lights. From the far side, a car-free zone, sunlight reflected off the sparkling windows of imposing stone buildings. Beneath, people streamed one way or the other, heading home after work.

'Over there,' said Clara, pointing in front of the fountains in the centre of the square. A small crowd had formed a semicircle around a suntanned, bare-chested man wearing scruffy trousers and a silly, striped jester's hat. He was juggling three large red skittles.

As Johnny and the others waited to cross the road, two men in dark suits approached the juggler who caught his skittles and took off his hat, bowing to his little audience in one sweeping movement. It looked as though he was about to pass the hat round for a collection, but the men flashed some identification, causing the street performer to drop his skittles and throw his arms up in frustration. Hat firmly planted back on his head, he was led away towards a waiting police van.

'We're too late,' said Johnny.

'I am not so sure, Master Johnny,' said Alf, who was staring into the sky. 'My eyesight covers a broader spectrum than humans' and, if I am not mistaken, something has joined Admiral Lord Nelson atop his column.'

Johnny and his sister followed where the android was pointing. At first all Johnny could see was the statue of the great man with a hand inside his jacket and a sword by his side, wearing a bicorn hat to ward off the pigeons. The sight reminded him of a particularly vivid dream he'd once had of being aboard Nelson's flagship, HMS *Victory*, at the Battle of Trafalgar. A blur of movement brought him back to reality. It was as though someone or something had indeed been standing right beside the admiral. Johnny stared as hard as he could, screwing his eyes right up, but whatever he'd spotted, Nelson now appeared alone.

Clara gasped and put her hand to her mouth. 'There is someone up there . . . I think,' she said, weakly. 'Right at the top.'

Johnny had never understood his sister's absolute terror of heights. If anything, Clara's vertigo had worsened over the past few months and she'd completely stopped using the antigravity lifts on board the *Spirit of London*, instead folding herself between decks. Now she'd turned even whiter than normal as she peered upward towards the granite admiral.

Johnny squinted, trying to focus on the very top of the fifty-metre-high pillar. He still couldn't make anything out. He looked down and, to his horror, saw Alf holding what could only be a little gun.

'Alf!' he hissed as the android squeezed the trigger. There was no sound at all.

'Direct hit,' said Alf, tucking the weapon inside his suit pocket. None of the passers-by looked to have noticed.

'What on Earth are you doing?' asked Clara.

'Do not be alarmed,' said the android. 'It was merely a tracking device. Now we shall be able to follow the creature.'

Able to breathe again, Johnny looked up – this time he was certain he saw something and it wasn't good. For a split second the air behind Nelson shimmered and a black sphere, about ten metres across, appeared from nowhere. Adjusting its cloak, it vanished just as quickly. There *was* a spaceship in Trafalgar Square after all and there was no mistaking it belonged to the evil Krun. Whatever creature was standing on top of the column, it appeared to hate the insect-like aliens every bit as much as Johnny did. It scarpered, scrambling down the vertical pillar at breakneck speed, somehow able to hold on.

'Oh my,' said Clara, grabbing Johnny's arm as though she might faint at the very thought of the descent.

Now it was on the move, the creature was much easier to spot and other people started pointing towards the column. As it reached the base it sprang over the lions and into the Trafalgar Square fountains. A crowd on the far side began taking photographs, barring the thing's escape. It doubled back and fled from them, crossed the road oblivious to the oncoming traffic and ran straight towards, then past, Johnny, Clara and Alf. Up close, hidden behind green slimy skin, strange flaps on its neck and very large webbed hands and feet, it looked oddly like a boy. It set off down a busy street leading away from the square. From behind there was a shallow fin protruding out of its back.

Alf, who could run *very* fast, took off in pursuit, a blur of arms and legs, leaving Johnny and his sister behind as the odd figures streaked away down the pavement.

'Come on,' said Clara as a new archway opened in front of them. She pulled him through and Johnny found himself standing beside the entrance to Downing Street, staring up Whitehall all the way back to Trafalgar Square. There was no sign. For a second he thought they'd lost the alien, until he turned as Clara shouted, 'There!' pointing to a truck heading further along the road. Using its webbed hands and feet the creature had fixed itself onto the back, hitching a ride, while Alf was jogging effortlessly just a little behind it. Again Clara took charge, pushing Johnny through another archway and following behind. They were at one end of Westminster Bridge beneath Big Ben and the Houses of Parliament. Sirens wailed from north and south of the river as police converged from opposite directions.

Clara was off again, this time sprinting across the bridge at full pelt towards the halfway point where Alf, not even out of breath, had the little alien cornered. Johnny followed, overtaking his sister, then slowing down so as not to startle the thing. Clara soon caught up. The green creature stared wide-eyed at them both, its head tilted to one side. It reached out a webbed hand, but when Johnny moved forward the scaly arm was swiftly withdrawn. Johnny again saw the air shimmer overhead. He couldn't be certain, but suspected the same partially cloaked black Krun sphere. At street level, two police vans arrived from either end of the bridge. Their doors opened and more than a dozen armed officers fanned out in a semicircle, pointing their rifles at the unlikely foursome.

A black car with tinted windows drew alongside. Out of the

rear door stepped a dark-haired woman in a smart suit, wearing very high heels. 'Well, this is a surprise,' she said in a drawling American accent. 'Long time no see, Johnny.'

The alien was shaking, clearly terrified as it looked from rifle to rifle. It backed away until it reached the railings lining the bridge – there was nowhere left to go and only a huge drop to the murky waters of the River Thames beneath. Cornered, it turned to Johnny's sister, arms out pleading and, in perfect English and quite a posh accent, said, 'Help me, Clara.'

Before anyone could react, something peculiar began happening to the pavement beneath them, as if it were made of rubber and warping. The next moment, Johnny, his sister and Alf fell through the very ground under their feet. The last thing Johnny saw was the police open fire as the strange creature leapt over the side and into the river far below. Next thing he knew, he was lying beside Clara and an immobile android on deck 18, the garden area of the *Spirit of London*.

'Welcome back,' came the ship's reassuring voice.

'Hi, Sol,' said Johnny, before turning to his sister and asking, 'What happened?'

Clara was busy rebooting the prone android. 'It was weird, wasn't it?' she said, adding, 'What was that thing? How do you think it knew my name? And who was that awful woman who knew yours?'

Alf sat up looking thoroughly confused.

'Colonel Bobbi Hartman,' Johnny replied. 'Sorry I didn't get to introduce you.'

The last time Johnny had seen the colonel, she'd been testifying against him during his trial for High Treason on Melania, the planet most of the spacefaring population of the Milky Way galaxy knew as its capital. Bobbi Hartman worked for the mysterious Corporation, a secret organization prepared to go to any lengths to acquire alien technology.

'I do not think either Colonel Hartman or the amphibious creature is the issue here,' said Alf, fixing Clara with a hard stare.

'What are you talking about?' she asked.

'I suspect you know very well what I am talking about, Miss Clara,' said the android. 'Time and again I have warned you of the dangers of too much folding. You lost control.'

'How dare you?' Clara replied, her face turning pink. 'I've never folded accidentally. It was that thing – the amphibian. It did something to the pavement.'

'And conveniently brought us back to the ship?' said Alf.

'I don't have to listen to this,' said Clara. The silver flecks in her normally pale blue eyes sparkled with power and she disappeared in a point of light, having folded herself elsewhere.

✡ ✡ ✡
✡ ✡

Tossing and turning in the bed that pulled down from a wall in his quarters, Johnny chewed over the strange events of the day. How could the alien creature possibly know Clara? How did Colonel Hartman know about the amphibian? As if running into the colonel hadn't been bad enough, Johnny was far more worried at seeing a Krun shuttlecraft right here, on Earth, bold as brass above the streets of London. These were the parasites who'd killed his dad. He supposed it was too much to hope that the horrible insect-like scavengers from the rim of the galaxy were gone for good, but so much had happened in the last year that anything had seemed possible.

Six months ago, at the time the Krun had gone into hiding, Johnny had destroyed the entire fleet of the aliens' one-time allies, the invaders from the neighbouring Andromeda Galaxy, but there had been a terrible price to pay. General Nymac, the fearsome Andromedan leader, had proved to be none other than Johnny and Clara's much older brother, Nicky Mackintosh, thought dead for ten years. To stop the Andromedans, Johnny had been forced to destroy Nicky's own ship and, almost certainly, Nicky with it.

With 'Nymac' gone, the Emperor of the Milky Way (and Johnny's friend) Bram Khari had returned from self-imposed exile. Bram had been able to restore order, throwing out the corrupt officials who'd been running the galaxy in his absence. A whole century of neglect was being swept aside, but it didn't alter the fact that Nicky had probably been blown up with his ship and Johnny didn't have answers to all Clara's questions about him. She'd changed after that, often picking fights. And Alf accusing her of accidentally folding them away didn't help. Johnny hated the pair arguing – there'd been a bad atmosphere on the ship all evening.

✩ ✩ ✩
✩ ✩

'Wakey wakey, rise and shine. Some of us have been awake for hours, you know – I calculate precisely nine thousand, five hundred and fifteen, as someone didn't bother to programme me so that I could sleep in the first place. I can't think who that might have been.'

'Kovac,' said Johnny sleepily. It was very rare for the quantum computer and not Sol to wake him up. 'What's going on? What time is it?'

'Good morning, Johnny,' said the ship. 'It is 5.38 a.m.'

'What?' said Johnny. 'It's Saturday.'

'I told you he wouldn't like it,' said Sol, presumably to Kovac.

'It's hardly a matter of likes or dislikes,' said the computer. 'I have information I deem important enough to pass on at the earliest opportunity – whatever time it is.'

'What is it then?' said Johnny, his eyes still shut and his quilt held over his head to block out the slowly brightening room that was doing its best to rouse him gradually.

'I have discovered I am not alone in monitoring the security forces for indications of alien activity.' Johnny lowered the quilt. This could be interesting. 'I have detected another tracer program at work – with a rather unexpected origin.' The computer sounded even more self-satisfied than normal.

'Where?' asked Johnny, suddenly awake and alert.

'Halader House itself.'

'Kovac,' said Johnny, frustrated. Halader House was the children's home where he had been brought up and still lived much of the time. It was also where Johnny had first programmed Kovac, and to where the computer's four-dimensional casing was cleverly and continuously linked. 'You woke me up for that? That's the residual echo from your box, durr-brain. Go back to sleep – or at least let me.' With that he pulled the quilt cover over his head and said, 'Lights out.' The room immediately obliged.

As he lay in the dark, drifting back to sleep, Johnny resolved to return to Halader House later that day. If Clara and Alf were still arguing it would be good to be somewhere else, and at least he might be able to get a night's peace. There was another reason to spend time at the children's home. In Johnny's attic bedroom was a Wormhole that linked directly to the Imperial Palace on Melania. Kovac was tasked with monitoring any communications through it, but it made sense for Johnny to have a proper catch-up with Bram. It was only one sphere, but it might be wise to tell the Emperor that the Krun had returned.

☆ ☆ ☆
☆ ☆

When Johnny finally surfaced it was late morning. Straightaway he asked for news reports from the previous night. An alien climbing Nelson's Column before ending up right outside Parliament was surely headline material – the Prime Minister had probably already made a statement. Yet it turned out there had been no mention of the incident anywhere.

At least the arguments from yesterday had stopped. Alf was so engrossed in his efforts to trace the amphibian that he seemed to have forgotten to be cross with Clara. Having gathered together the results, the android had called a meeting in the strategy room on deck 14.

Everyone was standing on the mezzanine level, overlooking the space into which Sol had projected a gigantic map of southern England, a collage of satellite images with other features and labels superimposed. As Bentley dozed against Johnny's feet, Alf traced out the route the creature had taken since yesterday evening, occasional thin streaks of red highlighting its journey west out of London.

'Why can't we follow him all the time?' Johnny asked. Currently no signal was visible and it looked as if the trail had gone cold.

'The tracker only works above ground,' said the android. 'If you observe closely, you will see the absence of a trace occurs when the amphibian is in his natural element, namely water.

Kovac took up the story. 'Within the river systems, the creature's speed is impressive – up to a hundred knots. Several boats were despatched to trawl the Thames yesterday evening, but it would have been long gone.'

'Can we tell where he's going?' Johnny asked.

'Although an extrapolation of the amphibian's movements cannot be a hundred percent accurate,' the computer replied, 'I am certain it is attempting to reach the Severn Estuary and, from there, the open sea.'

'You're wrong,' said Clara.

'Excuse me,' said Kovac. 'I have performed more than forty-seven quintillion calculations on the subject over the last few hours. How many have you done?'

'If he'd wanted to reach the ocean, why didn't he just swim down the Thames?'

'Unhappily, I am shackled within this tedious box and not able to ask him directly. I hypothesize he was afraid the Thames would be blocked in an attempt to capture him. If you're so much cleverer than I've previously been led to conclude, what's your theory?'

'He's not thinking – he's acting on instinct,' Clara replied. 'He's from the Proteus Institute. That's why he recognized me – he wants to go home.'

It was like a lightbulb being switched on inside Johnny's head. The Proteus Institute for the Gifted was the 'school' from where he'd rescued Clara, over a year before. Run by the Krun, and once linked directly to Earth orbit by a secret space elevator, it was an institution where the foul aliens experimented on human children. 'Of course – those things in the tanks,' he said.

'What things? What tanks?' asked Kovac. 'How can I be expected to reach a sensible conclusion if I am not party to all the relevant information? Sometimes I wish I hadn't been cursed with my quantum upgrade – I could have existed quite happily as a humble, extremely crude, operating system.'

Johnny often wished that, though he hardly would have described Kovac's original programming as crude. The letters stood for Keyboard- Or Voice-Activated Computer, which was, in Johnny's opinion, a very impressive piece of coding. It was when Sol designed the quantum processor to enhance Johnny's original design that the personality problems had started.

'Beneath the Proteus Institute we found tanks filled with water,' said Clara. 'There were pupils inside, floating upside down, their bodies turning green. I thought they must be dead. Then one opened his eyes.' Johnny remembered how Clara had fled the horrible room and he'd had to go after her, leaving another girl, Louise, behind. Clara went on, 'The Krun were creating monsters, human–alien hybrids. I might have been next.'

'That's why they were there yesterday,' Johnny added. 'Seeing what had happened to their experiment.'

'The Krun were there, Master Johnny?' Alf sounded apoplectic.

'I saw a Krun sphere in Trafalgar Square,' Johnny replied. 'It followed us down to the river.'

'Why did you not say?'

'You were too busy arguing with Clara,' said Johnny.

'I was making a very important point,' said the android. 'Miss Clara does far too much folding.'

'Can we just drop it?' said Clara. 'We know where he's heading. Let's go to the Proteus Institute and pick him up before anyone else does.'

Just then something started to beep on the map below. Everybody turned and looked for the source of the noise. A thin red line was tracing out a path across the countryside from the end of the River Parrett down towards Yarnton Hill, the town where the Proteus Institute was located. Clara had an 'I told you so' smirk across her face. 'Everybody ready?' she asked as one of her trademark arches began to form beside her.

'Miss Clara – I must insist,' said Alf, 'this time, we are flying.'

☆ ☆ ☆
☆ ☆

Johnny, Alf and Bentley joined a clearly unhappy Clara at the foot of the *Spirit of London*. As Johnny stepped out of the antigrav shaft, he slapped the three-metre-tall statue of the silver alien for luck. The group passed through the revolving doors leading out of the ship and into a little square, where they smiled at the security guards in their blue uniforms, climbed a few steps and entered a London taxi conveniently parked nearby. This was no ordinary black cab.

The *Bakerloo* was one of the *Spirit of London*'s shuttlecraft, small ships capable of short-range and sub-orbital journeys. Located on deck 2 of the main spacecraft was another, larger shuttle called the *Piccadilly*, cleverly disguised as a red double-decker bus and, parked alongside it, glistened an Imperial Starfighter – a special gift from the Emperor. That was Johnny's favourite, partly because it looked so streamlined and perfect, but also because it was lightning quick and highly manoeuvrable, though he was pleased he'd never had to fight a real battle in it. Of course he also loved flying the *Bakerloo*, but it was Alf who reached the pilot's seat first.

The shuttlecraft used advanced mind-control technology – you simply had to think of your intended destination and the ship would respond. Packed full of all manner of sensory apparatus, if you merged your mind fully with the craft, you could see, hear and smell for miles. When he flew it himself, Johnny felt as if he was almost becoming the *Bakerloo*, though he couldn't help thinking the journey was a lot more clunky when Alf was at the helm.

Being a weekend, the City was nearly deserted, but it was still so full of CCTV cameras it took a few minutes before the *Bakerloo* confirmed they were not being observed and Alf could think, *Shields on.* Instantly the sides of the shuttle shimmered and disappeared around them and, just a fraction of a second later, the android, Clara, Bentley and Johnny himself also vanished. Next, Johnny felt his stomach lurch as the now invisible craft shot skyward at tremendous speed and the Old English sheepdog, who loved nothing better than flying, slathered a long, wet invisible tongue all across Johnny's similarly invisible face.

'Let's tell Louise we're coming,' said Clara's disembodied voice from the front. 'We've not seen her for ages.'

'Great idea,' Johnny replied. Louise was the pretty older girl who lived in Yarnton Hill and who'd broken into the Proteus Institute with him. Just as he'd hoped to find Clara, Louise had been looking for her neighbour, Peter Dalrymple. Taken prisoner by the Krun and held on an alien base near Neptune, the poor girl had got more than she'd bargained for. Johnny and Clara had eventually rescued her. Of course he'd invited her to stay on board the *Spirit of London*, but Louise seemed keen to keep her feet on the ground and had returned home.

Clara messaged Louise, hoping to see her (very) soon. Far faster than any supersonic jet, the shuttle was already descending and it wasn't long before they saw the surface of the road coming ever closer, whizzing by directly beneath Johnny's invisible feet. At the very last second, the shuttle reappeared around him (and himself and the other passengers with it), becoming like an ordinary, if slightly out of place, London taxi. It touched down with a slight skid as they passed a road sign indicating that Yarnton Hill village was three miles down a road to the left. When they rounded the next bend a familiar valley came into view.

Perched on one side was the long-since abandoned Proteus Institute for the Gifted, a red-brick, four-storey building dominated by a square central tower. 'Oh dear,' said Alf as they reached the beginning of the tall wire fence that ran along the side of the road, barring entry to the institute's grounds. 'Kovac has asked me to inform Miss Clara that her hypothesis was mistaken.'

'What are you talking about now?' snapped Clara.

'Please do not shoot the messenger,' said the android. 'I have been informed that the amphibian has reached, but then passed, the Proteus Institute and is continuing on his journey.'

'To where?' asked Clara, before the shuttle and its occupants vanished again and Johnny felt himself rise upward, like a bird soaring on the wind.

'That, I suppose,' Alf replied, 'is something we shall have to wait to find out.'

☆ ☆ ☆
☆ ☆

They didn't have to wait long. The tracer signal soon stopped, this time in Yarnton Hill itself, and Alf parked the *Bakerloo* close to the train station at one end of the small town. Trying to home in on the exact location of the trace was difficult, so they split up with Johnny and Bentley going in one direction and Alf and Clara in the other. Using their own wrist-based communicators (or wristcoms), they would soon be able to triangulate a proper fix on the amphibian boy, wherever he was.

Trying to appear inconspicuous – never easy with an Old English sheepdog by your side – Johnny was walking along a parade of shops when he heard another dog bark behind.

'Guess who?' said a girl's voice as a pair of soft hands were placed over his eyes. Johnny spun round and was immediately smothered by the long curly brown hair of a tall girl with lots of matching brown freckles. She kissed him on the cheek before pulling away and saying, 'What are you doing here?' He felt his face going red as Louise dropped to her knees and said, 'And Bentley too.' She started fussing the sheepdog, who was more interested in sniffing Rusty, her red setter.

'Clara sent you a message,' said Johnny, kneeling down beside her and whispering as he stroked Rusty. 'You remember those things we saw at the institute – the ones in the tanks?'

Louise nodded seriously.

'Well, one of them's here,' Johnny went on. 'We've split up to get a fix on its location.'

'Clara's here too?' asked Louise.

Johnny's wristcom beeped. 'That's her now,' he said as his sister's face appeared at the centre of the dial. Quickly Johnny established the details. 'They've got him cornered on Station Street,' he told Louise. 'What's the quickest way?'

'Follow me,' she said, already on her feet and running. 'That's where I live.'

Johnny chased after her and soon drew level, with both dogs bounding along beside them. They turned a corner and saw Clara and Alf up ahead. Sprinting, they joined the others outside a pair of large semidetached houses that shared a drive, ending in a circular section of tarmac before two adjacent front doors. Louise bent forward, panting, her hands on her knees and her cheeks turning very red. 'This is . . . my . . . freakin' . . . house,' she said between gulps of air.

'The creature is standing at the end of the driveway,' said Alf.

'Wow. He can really blend in, like in Trafalgar Square,' said Clara.

Johnny stared very hard, but saw nothing until there was clear movement towards them. A little nervously, the strange amphibian was edging up the drive. Rusty began barking furiously.

'Oh my god, it's Peter,' said Louise. She opened the gate to move towards him when a green bolt of energy zapped from the sky and struck the boy, sending him sprawling to the tarmac unconscious. Louise screamed as a black sphere landed in the very centre of the driveway, firing in her direction.

Johnny dragged her to the ground just in time and looked up to see the energy beams pass overhead and slice a nearby tree in two. He shouted, 'Clara, get us out of here.'

An archway opened right behind Peter's slimy green body. Johnny could see the *Spirit of London*'s bridge on the other side. He got to his feet, pulling Louise up with him and with

Alf and Clara not far behind, but the fold closed before any of them could reach it. The garden wall and tarmac drive began to distort, bending impossibly, sending him and Louise crashing to the ground. Four figures, men dressed in the dark suits typical of the Krun in human form, emerged from the sphere. Two of them collected the amphibian's limp body and started back to their shuttle while Johnny lay helpless. The other two pointed powerful blasters at him and Louise. Instantly Bentley and Rusty leapt through the air, knocking both Krun to the ground and clamping their jaws around the aliens' arms. The other Krun disappeared inside their ship, taking Peter with them.

'Master Johnny,' Alf shouted, 'Miss Clara has fainted. We must return to the *Bakerloo*.' The android picked Clara up as though she weighed less than a feather and ran down the street towards the parked shuttle.

The black sphere lifted into the air without its remaining two crew, who looked up horrified while still trying to ward off the dogs. More bolts of energy shot from the Krun ship, silhouetting the aliens in an aura of glowing energy. Bentley and Rusty jumped away as, for a fleeting second, the abandoned Kruns' true form was revealed – long fly-like snouts topped by huge insects' eyes, and each with four elongated arms, flailing wildly as though trying to stop the firing. Then their bodies vanished. The Krun never left traces behind, even if it meant killing their own.

Johnny knew he and Louise would be next – there was no cover to hide behind – but then the *Bakerloo* materialized, hovering between him and the alien sphere, its doors open. He practically threw Louise inside, and Bentley and Rusty jumped in after her. As an energy bolt sailed just past him, Johnny dived through the open door and the black London taxi wheeled away into the air, fading from sight and taking them out of danger.

2

No Entry ✧✧

Having witnessed what had happened to her former next-door neighbour, Louise was anything but her normal breezy self. The signal from Peter's tracker had vanished, which didn't help. Meanwhile Clara lay unconscious in sickbay, running a frighteningly high temperature. With Alf and Louise taking it in turns to look after her Johnny felt surplus to requirements, but he couldn't bear being elsewhere in the ship, not knowing what was going on. He sat out of the way, watching his sister tossing from side to side and listening to her delirious ramblings about the Twyfords, the couple who'd raised her. He wondered what it must have been like to grow up not knowing a thing about your proper family.

It was several hours before her fever began to ease and she opened her eyes. Louise was mopping her forehead, but Clara called her brother over to the bedside. Her eyes appeared darker than normal and a fleeting look of desperation flickered across her face.

'What went wrong?' she asked.

'It was when you tried folding,' said Johnny. 'You passed out.'

'You're saying I can't control my folds?' Clara snorted, lifting her head and trying to force a laugh.

He didn't know how to respond. 'Look – maybe Alf's right,' was the best he could do. 'Take a break from it. Have a rest.'

'It's Sunday night,' said Clara, sounding exasperated. 'I've got to get you to Halader House.' At the end of every weekend Johnny's sister would open a gateway direct to his attic bedroom in the children's home so he could prepare for school the next day.

'It's all right,' said Johnny. 'I think it's best if I stay here and keep an eye on my little sister. I'm sure Alf will write me a note.'

'Don't you dare,' said Clara. 'It's football practice on Mondays – you've got that big tournament coming up. If you miss training you'll be moaning all week.'

Johnny was relieved his sister was beginning to sound a little more like her normal self. 'OK,' he said, smiling. She knew his timetable better than he did. 'I'll go, but I'll take the *Bakerloo*. No more folding space for the next few days . . . promise?'

'We'll see,' she said, turning away. The conversation seemed to have sapped her strength. Clara put her head back down and fell instantly asleep.

'Don't worry, she'll be fine,' said Louise, whose own mind looked to be on other things.

'You mustn't worry either,' Johnny replied. 'We're going to find Peter.' He knew neither of them could be certain they were telling the truth.

☆ ☆ ☆
☆ ☆

Johnny hadn't the heart to separate Bentley and Rusty when they were so pleased to see each other again. He left the two dogs on the garden deck, stepped into the lift shaft, said, 'Deck zero,' and floated on air all the way to the foot of the *Spirit of London*. It was dark outside, but the ship looked magnificent lit up as a pretend skyscraper. Nearby, another van was about to take more apparently over-eager tourists away. Johnny saw a policeman slam the rear door and then look up surprised to see him standing alone in the little square. Not wanting to be arrested, he turned away and walked quickly up the steps into the waiting *Bakerloo*.

Halader House stood at 33 Barnard Way in Castle Dudbury, a grim new town to the northeast of London that remained permanently grey, whether from the constant rain or ubiquitous concrete. The children's home itself was across the carpark from the local train station, so Johnny left the shuttlecraft in the taxi rank beside a telephone box and marched across the tarmac towards the back gate.

Away from the big city at least the stars were brighter, and he smiled to see the wonky 'W' of Cassiopeia twinkling above – it had always been Johnny's special constellation. Although his skin was unusually pale and blemish free, along the inside of his left forearm were five large freckles that mirrored the pattern in the sky above. The Emperor had told Johnny that this was his Starmark, an imprint from the Milky Way itself. The constellation indicated where he was born – the number of stars it contained revealed how many others like him there were in the galaxy, with special gifts.

Johnny had never felt very special. Growing up, the only things that distinguished him from other people were not living with his parents and the weird effect he had on most things electrical. No one wanted to talk to him about his mum and dad, which was fine as far as Johnny was concerned, but occasionally he was with someone else when a streetlight went out as he walked underneath and, however often the music system in his bedroom was repaired or replaced, it never worked for more than a few days. Things like that used to be a pain, but in the last year he'd gained some control and begun to understand how he was making them happen. It wasn't as cool as Clara's ability to fold space – something he'd managed to do only once, to save his life when in a blind panic – but being able to direct electric currents at will did sometimes come in handy.

Halader House had recently fitted keyless locks, opened by electronic RFID (Radio Frequency Identification) tags. As Johnny entered the backyard he passed the wooden kennel where Bentley was occasionally forced to sleep and reached a wood-framed glass door. Hardly even having to think about it, he waved his hand to send the electrons inside the lock whizzing to their new locations before turning the handle and letting himself in.

Of course Johnny had been given his own key fob, but the system was programmed not to allow fourteen-year-old residents to come and go as they pleased at this time on a Sunday night. If following procedures, he'd have had to walk round to the main entrance, ring the doorbell and explain his late arrival to Mrs Irvine. From past experience, he knew the Scottish Manager of the home would be distinctly unimpressed to be woken up in the middle of the night. He could still picture her in her tartan dressing gown giving him a severe tongue-lashing the only time he'd done it. This way worked better and Kovac could hack the Halader House records to show Johnny had been safely inside all day.

The lights were out, but having lived in the children's home since he was two Johnny could have walked its corridors blindfold. Silently, he made his way past the computer room, Kovac's original home, and the kitchen–diner. Happily there was no sign of the huge cook, Mr Wilkins, whose favourite pastime seemed to revolve around making Johnny's life as miserable as possible. He climbed the main staircase to the first floor, tiptoed along the entire length of the corridor, turned a corner and came to the small spiral staircase that led only to Johnny's attic bedroom. At the top he pulled down the trapdoor onto which he'd screwed a 'No Entry' sign a year or so earlier and carried on up inside.

Johnny hated being away from the *Spirit of London*, but there was something here in this pokey room in deepest Essex that made it all worthwhile. He sat down on his bed and stared at two twinkling patches of light in front of him. It looked as though dust was glinting in moonlight, but tonight there was no Moon – only stars were visible through the big box window. Johnny leaned forward and placed his head into one of these hazy splodges; when he opened his eyes he found himself staring at a bustling scene at the heart of the Imperial Palace on Melania.

It was the middle of the day on this world at the centre of the galaxy, and the two red giant suns, Arros and Deynar, were both high in the sky. Self-propelled containers, brimful of exotic-looking contents and overseen by four-winged, near-transparent, slender aliens known as Hapchicks, were flying this way and that. Johnny had never seen the central courtyard so busy.

An elegant woman, golden robes flowing behind her, appeared to glide towards Johnny. As she came closer, he saw her eyes, beneath close-cropped dark hair, were huge and she was smiling warmly in his direction – she must have spotted his floating head in the midst of all the activity.

'Johnny Mackintosh, I presume,' she said in perfect English.

Taken aback not to hear Universal (the standard language for interspecies communication within the Imperial Court and across most of the spacefaring galaxy), Johnny was momentarily flummoxed. 'You speak English? How? Sorry – I don't know who you are.' He could feel his face turning redder and redder.

The woman smiled and let out a beautiful, gentle laugh. 'My name is Ophia,' she said, 'and I believe we have something in common – I speak all languages.'

Dotted throughout the Milky Way were ancient creatures called Hundra who worked as intergalactic interpreters, ingesting the words of one speaker and excreting the language of the listener. The very first time Johnny had encountered one it had splintered off a tiny fragment of its own soul and placed it within him. Effectively it meant he could speak or translate anything, but he'd believed this was a secret known only to himself and the Emperor. The woman standing before Johnny couldn't be a Hundra – they looked like floating, slightly flat, footballs. Warily he said, 'I'm not sure I know what you mean.'

The woman laughed again – it was impossible not to warm to her. 'I apologize if what I said made you uncomfortable, Johnny Mackintosh. Sometimes I forget myself. Why don't I fetch Bram to speak with you?'

'That'd be great,' Johnny replied. 'If you don't mind . . . thanks.'

'Please remember that the Emperor is especially busy, today of all days,' said Ophia. 'Try not to detain him long.'

It was good to hear someone else on Melania refer to the Emperor as 'Bram'. Normally they'd use some ridiculous title like 'His Divine Imperial Majesty'. As the tall woman turned and glided away, Johnny couldn't help thinking there was something more than a little odd about her – it might have been that he didn't remember seeing her blink once.

'Johnny – it's good to see you face to face. That is, if a Cornicula Wormhole really counts.' Close up, the Emperor's face looked worn and lined, as though a spider had woven its web directly onto it, but his blue eyes were as piercing and alert as ever, and his silver hair still sparkled with a life of its own. 'Is this a purely social call, or is something troubling you?'

'Well,' said Johnny, not sure where to begin. He didn't want to make Bram think he was frightened by diving straight into a story about one Krun sphere. After all, he'd been in far worse situations and survived. Deciding to build up to that slowly, he said, 'Social, I suppose. Clara's not very well, but I'm sure she'll be fine.'

25

'Perhaps it is good, then, that I am coming to see you,' said the Emperor. 'I had thought of making it a surprise visit, but I'd hate you to be out gallivanting and have us end up missing each other.'

'Great,' said Johnny, buoyed by this unexpected news. 'When are you coming?'

'I was wondering about Tuesday.' Bram laughed at the evident shock written across Johnny's face. 'I hope you can fit me into your busy schedule.'

'Of course . . . yeah . . . that'll be great.'

'Then it is decided,' said the Emperor. 'If you will excuse me, you'll be aware I have preparations to make.' Bram stepped back and bowed, allowing Johnny to glimpse the activity going on around him.

'Bye,' shouted Johnny. 'See you soon.' With a faint plop he pulled his head out of the Wormhole and caught sight of his reflection in the window, blond hair sticking up all over the place – he'd have to wash it before Bram arrived. He could tell the Emperor about the Krun then. He fell asleep under twinkling starlight – the streetlamp beneath Johnny's window had long ago stopped working.

☆　☆　☆
☆　☆

Breakfast at Halader House was to be endured rather than enjoyed. It made Johnny long for the kippers or bacon and eggs that Alf would rustle up in the *Spirit of London*'s galley. Mr Wilkins's porridge was watery and full of salt, and included the odd crunchy black bit he didn't dare think about. The huge bearded man ladled an especially large portion into Johnny's bowl, as though relishing extra suffering he could inflict. It was too much to expect the cook's beady black eyes to look anywhere else before Johnny had scraped every last spoonful of the grey sludge into his mouth.

To make matters worse, Miss Harutunian, Johnny's red-haired social worker, came over to sit beside him. He liked the American, who always seemed genuinely interested in him, but found it impossible to speak to anyone so early in the morning.

'Everything OK, Johnny?' she asked, beaming at him and showing off two rows of dazzling white teeth.

'Fine,' he grunted.

'I've been having a think about your care plan,' she said, clearly not about to be put off. 'Remember when we last went to see your mum at St Catharine's?' Johnny froze, his spoon halfway between bowl and mouth. This didn't sound good. 'There was that nice doctor at the hospital . . . tall guy . . . Carrington, wasn't it?' Johnny nodded. 'Well, he phoned yesterday asking to come and talk to you. But I've been thinking – it's so long since you last went to see your mum, why don't we go there instead?'

Johnny shook his head, probably a little too violently. He had no desire whatsoever to see the mysterious Dr Carrington, the man who'd performed Colonel Hartman's DNA tests on him and Clara. They'd surprised everyone, not least Johnny, when the results showed he and his sister were only half human. At least Johnny didn't think for a moment that the doctor realized his mum had been the Diaquant of Atlantis, perhaps the most powerful alien in the whole galaxy. It was true that Carrington had helped them escape the Corporation's clutches, but Johnny was keen to keep him at a very safe distance.

Miss Harutunian, on the other hand, still thought Johnny's mum was in a coma at St Catharine's Hospital for the Criminally Insane, and there were so many things wrong with that belief he hardly knew where to begin.

For one, it turned out that there wasn't even any such place. The supposed mental hospital had been a secret Krun base, accessed through a portal into hyperspace. Now that portal was sealed, creating a self-contained 'Klein fold'. The Krun trapped inside were cut off from their queen and stranded forever. Before the gateway had closed, Johnny and Clara's dad had died there, as had their mum, at least in her human form. However, given that she was some kind of trans-dimensional alien superbeing, she had shortly reappeared from another place and time, revealing her true identity to Johnny and Clara and reviving their dead father, transforming him, like her, into a creature of pure energy. But they left together to 'go on', with seemingly no prospect of ever being able to return.

At this time of morning it made Johnny's brain hurt just thinking about it, but one thing was clear – taking his social worker to this fictitious place to visit his kind-of dead alien mother would be an especially bad idea. 'I think it's better if Dr Carrington came here,' he said, forcing down the last mouthful of porridge.

'Well, if you're sure, said the American, 'but we'll have to visit your mum soon. Your care plan says at least twice a year.'

'Gotta go,' said Johnny, pushing the thankfully empty bowl away from him. 'Sorry, but I'll be late for school.' He walked quickly away from the table before Miss Harutunian could call him back.

☆ ☆ ☆
☆ ☆

While Johnny found school more than a little boring, especially since Alf had downloaded the entire National Curriculum directly into his brain (the android wanted to be sure Johnny wasn't missing any of his education), it was great to be able to play football with his friends. There was a time when decks 20 through 22 on the *Spirit of London* had been a five-a-side arena, but since a weapons upgrade a few months ago the pitch was no longer there. Johnny didn't miss it too much – Alf and

Clara were pretty rubbish opponents – but he had used the space to practise free kicks and corners and it was especially handy having Sol ping the ball straight back to him each time. Johnny was keen to retain his place as the school team's set-piece specialist.

So it was exciting when the bell rang for the end of double chemistry and Johnny could make his way out of Miss Hewitt's laboratory and down to the school playing fields for games, the final lesson of the day. They spent most of their time playing two-touch six-a-side within quite a small area. Mr Davenport, their coach and PE teacher, was emphasizing the importance of close control and moving the ball quickly, with the qualifiers for the National Schools Trophy fast approaching. It was a good session and, as Johnny jogged in the early evening sunshine, warming down on the way to the changing rooms, he was joined on either side by Dave Spedding and Ashvin Gupta, his two best mates in the team.

'We've been thinking,' said Dave a little nervously.

'Not something Dave's especially used to,' Ashvin added.

Johnny had the feeling this was some kind of prepared speech.

'Why you never have us back to your place after school,' said Dave, cutting to the chase.

'Have you ever *been* to a children's home?' asked Johnny.

'Well, no,' said Dave, looking a little awkward.

'But that's kind of the point,' said Ash, who wasn't going to be put off quite so easily. 'We could come back now . . . for tea.'

'If you'd ever eaten our cook's food, you wouldn't be saying that,' said Johnny.

'Cool – we'll get chips on the way,' said Ash.

Johnny had planned to check up on Clara and make sure she was OK, but he'd never had friends come back to Halader House. He also reminded himself that it was important to spend more time there. He'd neglected the home to his cost a few months ago, allowing Nicky – or rather his alter ego Nymac – to clone him and have the double take Johnny's place. It was a very close call and Johnny had nearly been killed. He'd resolved from then on to make more regular appearances at the home, just in case. Having friends with him might also stop his social worker re-raising the thorny question of maternal visits.

'You're on,' said Johnny, 'but it's definitely got to be fish and chips.'

☆ ☆ ☆
☆ ☆

As they walked through the main Halader House doors, reeking of vinegar, Johnny caught sight of Miss Harutunian smiling at him, but she didn't come over. He led Ash and Dave up the stairs and along the corridor and laughed at their reaction when they stopped in front of his very own spiral staircase.

'Very cool,' said Dave, admiring the official looking 'No Entry' sign screwed into the trapdoor. 'Where'd you get it?'

'In the basement,' Johnny replied. 'I took it off some door down there.'

'What was behind it?' Ash asked, clearly hoping for an exciting mystery.

'I don't know, do I?' Johnny replied. 'It was locked. I just thought the sign would look good up here. Come on.' He pulled down the trapdoor and led the way inside. The bedroom was messy, but not too bad and his two friends didn't bat an eyelid. Instead they were drawn straight to the space posters covering every square centimetre of the attic room's sloping walls.

'Where'd you get these?' Ash asked, particularly admiring the picture of Sagittarius A*, the black hole at the very centre of the galaxy that Johnny had snapped himself. The others had been a Christmas present from Alf, reprinted from the android's memory circuits.

'You know . . . around,' said Johnny.

'Wow – this is all yours?' said Dave, as though amazed someone could have their own room. 'It must be great not having people bossing you around . . . always telling you what to do.'

'I think I'd rather still have my parents,' said Johnny matter of factly.

'Yeah, but your dad was a murderer, wasn't he?' asked Dave. 'Didn't he kill your brother or something?' He ignored Ash elbowing him in the ribs. 'He in the nick somewhere?'

'I don't see him any more,' said Johnny. Dave or his parents must have read the story in the papers. Johnny didn't remember much about the night twelve years ago when the Krun had come to their house in Derby. He knew he'd been hidden under the bed with Bentley, and sometimes now he had the idea that he'd seen someone else there watching but not helping. The aliens had taken Nicky, faking his brother's murder and framing Johnny's parents. After they were found guilty, Johnny's dad had been taken away for a decade of Krun torture while his mum, pregnant with Clara and apparently traumatized by the shock of it all, had been imprisoned in St Catharine's.

Twice, a year ago, Johnny had met his mum. Once, journeying into the distant past, he'd rescued her as Atlantis sank beneath the waves; the other time was in St Catharine's Hospital when the Krun had killed his dad. Both times she'd been wonderful and seemed to care deeply for him. He just couldn't understand why she'd allowed the aliens to rip her family apart without lifting a finger to stop them.

Changing the subject, Ash asked, 'What d'ya do up here, Johnny? Got any good games?'

Johnny spent so little time in Halader House nowadays that there wasn't much, but he did keep a handheld console in the box under his bed, which also contained some of his dad's old stuff. Soon they were taking it in turns to play *Starfighter 3D*. Johnny got the top score, but the other two were pretty good. He couldn't help thinking they might make good pilots. After a while Johnny slipped out on the pretext of going to feed (the absent) Bentley, and called Sol on his wristcom, telling the ship that Bram would be coming to visit and making sure Clara was OK. She was still in sickbay, at Alf's insistence, but said she was feeling better and sounded bored out of her skull.

By the time he got back, Dave and Ash had had enough of the game and were itching for something else to do. 'We've got a plan,' said Dave, a wicked gleam in his eyes. 'Let's explore your basement – see what's behind the mystery door.'

'There's nothing there,' said Johnny. 'And it's out of bounds.'

'Are you scared?' asked Dave.

'Of course I'm not scared,' Johnny replied. 'It's just rubbish – there's nothing to see.'

'Definitely scared,' said Ash, nodding sagely at Dave.

'There isn't anything to be frightened of,' said Johnny. 'All right – I'll show you.'

The other two smiled, but Johnny didn't mind. Checking the basement would hardly take long. Then he could say goodbye to his friends, show his face in the common room and take the *Bakerloo* back to the *Spirit of London*.

The wooden stairs to the basement were through a doorway right next to the common room. Johnny led the way, shining a torch taken from the box underneath his bed, while the other two made exaggerated shushing noises. In the gloom they took turns placing the beam underneath their chins, making the most gruesome faces they could to scare the others. The place smelt of damp and, apart from some old bookshelves and leftover rolls of beige carpet that matched the bland corridors, there was nothing of any note. A new 'No Entry' sign had been screwed onto a large cupboard built into the wall near a corner.

'What do you think's in there?' asked Dave, trying the handle, which was locked.

'Secret alien technology, I expect,' said Johnny for a laugh. 'Probably taken from Roswell.'

'Let's find out, shall we?' said Ash. He rummaged through his pockets and, with a flourish, produced a metal hairgrip.

'As if,' said Johnny.

'Ye of little faith,' Ash replied. He knelt down and pushed it into the lock, wiggling it about.

'Should've brought the game with us,' said Dave. 'We could be here be here for hours.'

There was a metallic click and Ashvin stood up smiling.

'Let's see if it was worth the effort,' said Johnny, walking forward and turning the handle. The door opened to reveal a dumping ground for old blankets and coats, plus a bucket, mop and two old brooms. 'Definitely,' he added, as Ash and Dave's faces both fell. 'Seen enough, boys?' Johnny asked.

Dave looked at his watch and said, 'I should be getting back anyway. My mum'll kill me if I'm out too late.' When Ash elbowed him in the ribs, he added, 'Sorry . . . I didn't mean . . .'

'Don't be daft,' said Johnny, laughing as he closed the cupboard door.

Ash was leading the way through the darkness towards the stairs when he stopped suddenly, causing Dave to bump into him and swear loudly. Ignoring him, Ash asked, 'What's that noise?'

'I can't hear anything,' said Johnny.

'Shhh!' hissed Ashvin.

As they all quietened, Johnny noticed it too – the whining of some sort of motor. Next moment there was banging coming from inside the broom cupboard. He shouted, 'Hide!' and the three boys desperately dived for cover. The cupboard door opened and out stepped a huge, hulking shape. It reached upward and pressed something on the wall. Lights flickered on throughout the basement, revealing Johnny, Dave and Ash crouched beside an old bookcase as Mr Wilkins glowered down at them, tears streaming down his bearded face.

'Manager's office . . . now,' said the cook.

✦ ✦ ✦

Mr Wilkins rapped hard on the wooden door and a woman's voice on the other side said, 'Enter.' Johnny, Ash and Dave were pushed inside, the big cook following.

'Mr Wilkins,' said Mrs Irvine in her broad Glaswegian accent. 'To what do I owe the pleasure?' Wearing a tweed jacket, she was sitting behind a large wooden desk in front of a floor-to-ceiling window that looked across the carpark to the train station. The desk was flanked either side by tall bookcases containing huge dusty tomes that no one could possibly want to read. Through her large, pointed glasses, the Manager surveyed the three of them standing in front of her.

'It's the boy, ma'am,' said the bearded cook. 'Found him and his good-for-nothing friends in the basement.'

The Manager fixed her owl-like eyes on Johnny. He felt about a foot tall and wished the floor would open and swallow him up. 'These are friends of yours from school, Jonathan?' she asked, indicating Dave and Ash.

'From football,' Johnny said, nodding.

To the other two Mrs Irvine said, 'Ben Halader House is a happy home.' She was the only person who always bothered to use the children's home's full name. 'We have very few rules, but one is that our little basement should remain out of bounds.

34

You may leave, but remember, these are dangerous times and it bears no profit to be looking for trouble.'

Ashvin and Dave turned to go, Ash mouthing a silent 'sorry' while Dave rolled his eyes to indicate that the Manager was clearly off her rocker. Once the door had closed behind the others, Mrs Irvine turned to the cook and asked, 'Are you all right, Mr Wilkins?'

Johnny dared to look up from his trainers. Tear tracks glistened all the way down the big man's cheeks, disappearing into the bushy black beard.

'I'd been in . . . in the broom cupboard, ma'am. It was . . . upsetting.'

'Yes, of course,' replied the Manager. 'Quite understandable. Perhaps you should leave too and sort yourself out. I'll deal with Jonathan.'

Johnny couldn't see what was understandable at all. The whole thing made no sense whatsoever and he'd very much like to know how the cook came to be stepping out of a deserted broom cupboard, but now probably wasn't the time to ask. Had he been buried under the coats? As Mr Wilkins closed the office door behind him, Mrs Irvine focused on Johnny again and said, 'Well, Jonathan?'

He knew his face was as red as a traffic light. 'I'm sorry,' he mumbled. 'We didn't mean any harm.'

'What, exactly, did you see, young man?'

'It was dark – we couldn't find the light switch and we only had one torch,' said Johnny, waving it in the air. 'We'd just gone down to have a look round and Mr Wilkins came out of the cupboard in the corner.' It didn't seem wise to tell her Ashvin had picked the lock first and that there hadn't been the slightest hint of the giant cook.

It felt as if the Manager was X-raying him. She stared in silence, her lips pencil thin. Johnny couldn't bear it for long.

Compelled to talk, he asked, 'Is Mr Wilkins . . . Gilbey, OK?' He'd discovered the cook's hilarious first name a few months before.

'Mr Wilkins will be fine,' said Mrs Irvine, the tone of her voice making clear there would be no further discussion on that particular matter. 'And this is everything that happened in the basement?' Johnny nodded. 'Let us hope so,' the Manager continued. 'Have you heard the story of Pandora, Jonathan?' He shook his head, wondering where, what or who Pandora might be. 'There are some boxes that are better left unopened. Once they are unlocked, it may be impossible to close the lid.'

Perhaps Dave was right and Mrs Irvine was going mad.

The Manager continued, 'Other than school, you shall divide your time between your bedroom and the dining room for the next fortnight. You will not set foot in the common room and on no account will you go anywhere near the basement. Do I make myself clear?'

Johnny nodded again. He'd never been grounded before – it seemed completely unfair.

'Someone will be checking on you later, so there will be no sneaking away to meet your friends. If, for any reason, you fail to follow these instructions,' said Mrs Irvine, 'I shall have no choice but to inform the school you are unable to participate in extracurricular activities . . . namely football. There will be no second chances.'

Johnny gulped and nodded again.

'Very well, Jonathan. You may go.'

☆ ☆ ☆
☆ ☆

It was ridiculous. Johnny paced the floor of his bedroom wondering exactly when someone's face would pop through the trapdoor and it would be safe for him to leave. He'd called Sol on his wristcom and also spoken to Alf. Remarkably, the trace on Peter had briefly resurfaced on an island called Santorini, somewhere in the Mediterranean. Johnny knew he'd heard of it, but couldn't think why. Louise was desperate to go after him, but the android had refused, saying they couldn't afford to be without any shuttles in case of emergency. It sounded as though Louise thought this certainly qualified, but Alf had stood his ground. Johnny promised he'd be returning with the *Bakerloo* the instant it was safe to get away.

For something to do he poked his head into the second Cornicula Wormhole. This one led to Pluto Base where the few surviving Tolimi, very short aliens rescued from the recent Alpha Centauri supernova, had set up home. Nicky had caused the cataclysm while acting as Nymac, under the control of a being known only as the Nameless One.

Now, for the first time ever, the base was deserted. Instead of the usual hive of activity, everything he could see (admittedly not much as the Wormhole made it very hard to look anywhere other than straight ahead) had been tidied away and turned off.

Fed up, he pulled his head out and collapsed on his bed, looking at the stars. There was the Plough – the seven stars that looked like a saucepan and handle and were duplicated as large freckles on his sister's left calf. These formed Clara's Starmark and meant she was one of seven who the Milky Way had given certain special gifts to. Johnny started thinking about the others.

Erin, son of Marin, and Zeta, daughter of Zola, were brother and sister too, a king and princess on the faraway planet Novolis, orbiting a blue giant star. Then there was Nicky. Johnny had told Clara that their older brother might still be alive, but he didn't really believe it. The more he thought about the time a few months ago when their brother's spaceship had blown up, the less likely it seemed that Nicky could possibly have survived. Bram might have heard something – it would be good to see the Emperor tomorrow.

All those with Starmarks had powers they had no right to expect. Bram had explained it by saying the life force in them was more concentrated than in the galaxy's other inhabitants. He'd said they were a little like the original first ones, the initial life bearers who appeared and spread across the cosmos. The Nameless One had only a single Starmark. As he drifted towards sleep, Johnny couldn't help wondering if he was *the* first one, all alone with no one to christen him. It made sense that he was more powerful than all the others put together.

✧ ✧ ✧
✧ ✧

Johnny awoke with a start. Outside was pitch black – surely no one would be checking on him now? It was the sort of clever thing Mrs Irvine did, knowing that if someone had come earlier he would have been tempted to sneak out straight afterwards. He should probably get up and make his way to the *Bakerloo*. He rolled over. Outside the window, the stars had moved, rotating about the Pole. Orion the Hunter was low above the horizon. Johnny realized that Nicky had worn an insignia of three stars together, nearly in a line but not quite straight. For the first time, he knew that Orion's Belt had been his brother's Starmark. He stared at the little band running across the sky – the leftmost, Alnitak, was Zcta and Erin's giant sun. He closed his eyes . . .

Johnny was in a long corridor stretching far into the distance, with hundreds of different doors of varying shapes and sizes arranged right and left. He knew this place – he'd been here before, if only in his dreams. He'd met Princess Zeta through one of the doorways, some sort of mental gateway to her homeworld. He turned round, looking for the way, and saw he was not alone. King Erin, even younger than Johnny, was attaching something to a door Johnny recognized. The boy king's tufty orange hair was sticking up between two stubby horns of hardened skin surrounded by pale lizard-like scales.

Erin turned to face Johnny, revealing the six dark scabs in a perfect hexagon that surrounded his face. 'You shall not come here again,' he hissed, a forked tongue poking out as he spoke. 'I have forbidden my sister from talking with you – her place is by my side.'

Only now did Johnny notice that it was a 'No Entry' sign that Erin had been screwing to the wooden door. He stared at it, wondering where the boy might have found such a thing, and then the door opened. Framed by it, against the background of a blue giant star sinking quickly into a calm ocean, stood a pale girl covered in scales, with long purple hair and bright orange cat-like eyes.

'Please, my brother,' said Princess Zeta. 'Let me speak with Johnny. He will have need of me.'

'I am Erin, Son of Marin, King and Ruler of the Alnitak Hegemony,' roared the orange-haired boy. 'I forbid it.' He slammed the door in his sister's face, turned to Johnny raising an open palm and shouted, 'I deny you entry to this realm.'

Johnny found himself flying backwards through another doorway. He fell out of bed with a loud thud and landed on the floor of his attic bedroom. Getting shakily to his feet, he looked out of the window and saw it was already morning.

3 ✿

Armada ✿

As soon as he could after breakfast (four slices of burnt toast that Mr Wilkins had spread thickly with Marmite, which Johnny hated) he snuck away and took the *Bakerloo* straight back to the City. The *Spirit of London* wasn't a happy ship. Apparently Clara had snuck out of sickbay to fold Louise and Rusty to Santorini and collapsed immediately afterwards. Alf had brought her back and she was now lying on one of the beds. Her eyes were filled with oily black splodges and she was running a fever. She told Johnny it was nothing, that she felt completely fine and if Alf didn't give her the all-clear soon she'd simply fold herself to her quarters – or anywhere else she wanted to go for that matter. When he dared to suggest that might not be such a good idea, his sister practically bit his head off, accusing him of always ganging up on her with 'that annoying android' and never letting her make her own decisions about anything.

Meanwhile, when Alf wasn't fussing over Clara or telling her off in equal measure, the android was frantically zooming all over the ship, cleaning and polishing places that already looked spotless to Johnny, which was really annoying Sol. Bentley was moping around because Rusty had disappeared as quickly as she'd arrived and, to make matters worse, Kovac kept banging on about evidence for a complex surveillance operation apparently being mounted from Halader House.

'I don't have time for this,' Johnny told the quantum

computer, which seemed to have forgotten that, thanks to his four-dimensional casing, Kovac really was in two places at once and his other location *was* the children's home. 'The Emperor's going to be here any minute now.'

The computer had never met Bram and finally fell silent, not wanting to find himself stowed away on the cargo deck for the duration of the Imperial visit.

Johnny was in his quarters changing into his Melanian clothes when Sol announced that the *Calida Lucia*, the Imperial Starcruiser, had unfolded close to Saturn and was asking them to rendezvous there. He flung on his white tunic top with the five golden stars of Cassiopeia across the front, stepped into his black trousers with the matching gold stripe down the sides and went to collect Bentley from the garden. As he walked along the corridor he messaged Alf to say that they were about to fold to meet the Emperor, which sent the android into a blind panic – in his opinion the ship was nowhere near tidy enough for an Imperial visit.

Johnny practically had to drag the Old English sheepdog to the antigrav lifts, but once they were inside and floating, bobbing up and down ever so slightly, Bentley's mood lifted and the sheepdog began wagging his tail. Johnny said, 'Bridge,' and the pair of them flew upward to the very top of the *Spirit of London*. They stepped out and Johnny walked across to the captain's chair, placing three fingers on the armrest. Three capsules rose through the floor at the back of the bridge, the gel pods that would make any long-distance fold that much more bearable and far less life-threatening. Johnny tapped the side of the Plican's tank, trying to indicate to the strange creature squashed inside that it wouldn't be long now before it would be released into the main cylinder and able to unfurl its long tentacles. Normally Clara kept the Plican company throughout long journeys while each of the alien's eight limbs took hold of different pieces of space and conveyed the *Spirit of London* between them. Today, however, it was probably best his sister stayed in sickbay.

Johnny said, 'Ten seconds, Alf,' and, roughly nine and three-quarters seconds later, the android emerged from the lift shaft, still holding a duster in each hand.

Once Bentley and Alf were safely sealed inside their gel pods, Johnny took a last look around his bridge as morning sunlight reflected off the River Thames far below. He said, 'Whenever you're ready, Sol,' and stepped into the remaining open capsule. As the door closed he lay down and warm orange goo, smelling of petrol, flooded the chamber. Almost at once it was over his chest and he opened his mouth to allow the unearthly gel to slide down his throat without touching the sides. As the liquid level rose over his head, he watched his hands and feet inflate, followed shortly by the rest of his body, all through an orange haze.

Cocooned and cushioned, he was dimly aware of the fold beginning and the *Spirit of London* leaving Earth. The walls of the chamber and then the ship herself flew through him without effect. Briefly, he saw the Moon, before travelling ninety degrees in another direction as the distant stars became lines of light in the background. He was pulled another way – the stars changed course – and finally in a different direction again. The walls of the ship and then the gel pod rushed through him into their right positions. On Earth, in London town, the original Gherkin would have sprung instantly back into real space to occupy the void, taking its proper place without anybody noticing.

Quickly the chamber began to drain. As the level dropped below Johnny's chest, fluid oozed out of him and a hoover like an elephant's trunk descended to suck up the remaining gloop. He couldn't help feeling a pang. Whenever he'd used to travel this way, he'd had to hold onto the locket his mum had given him, to stop it disappearing up into the tube and away. Before Bram reassumed power, the mad Regent and scheming Chancellor Gronack had tried to have Johnny executed by firing squad. He would have died had the locket not proved to be a personal shield, saving him and turning the weapon's fire on those shooting at him. Now it no longer hung around his neck, stolen by his clone and lost forever. It was sad that he no longer had such protection, but he didn't miss it for that – until then he hadn't even known what it was. What he craved were the pictures inside: one half showing his mum and dad smiling, with a very young Bentley; the other of Johnny, Clara and Nicky, together in a line. Occasionally he would still look at the pictures in Clara's locket, but it wasn't the same as having them with him all the time.

Sol announced the return to normal space and Johnny swapped the capsule for his captain's chair at the very centre of the bridge. They had unfolded to just beyond the asteroid belt, the band of failed planets between the orbits of Mars and Jupiter. Outside, in the distance, Johnny could see one of the irregularly shaped rocks tumbling along its path around the Sun. Sol switched to her powerful dark energy drive and the ship was soon speeding towards the rendezvous. Alf emerged from his pod, placing his bowler hat carefully in position, and then Bentley appeared, shaking out his coat and showering orange goo across the deck. The android chased the Old English sheepdog around the bridge, which looked the most fun Bentley had enjoyed all day.

After all Alf's hard work making the ship spotless, Johnny didn't have the heart to tell the android they'd received a request to transport over to the Emperor's ship. Feeling it wise to vacate the scene, he made his way to sickbay to check on Clara, but his sister wasn't there. At Sol's direction he found her sitting on the rocky outcrop near the centre of the garden deck, dressed in an outfit similar to his but with seven lilac stars in the shape of the Plough on her front. Her eyes were nearly entirely black. Open on her lap was a bright pink notebook in which she was writing. Their dad's journal, recounting a trip he'd made long ago, was on the flat rock beside her.

'Are you OK? Can you see to write?' Johnny asked.

His sister looked up, smiling a little manically. 'Never better,' she replied. 'Are we there? Shall I fold us across?'

'We have to take a shuttle,' said Johnny, unnerved by the way Clara was looking. 'You know Alf hates not being able to get through the fold.'

'OK – I'll drop these back in my room and see you over there.'

'No, I think it's better if we all go together.' Johnny left before his sister could argue. He collected Kovac and went down to the shuttle bay, waiting in the pilot's seat of the *Piccadilly* for a couple of minutes, trying to ignore the computer's persistent chatter. Alf joined him with Bentley, both of them clambering on board and taking their places on the lower deck, before Clara unfolded directly onto the back seat.

☆ ☆ ☆

The *Calida Lucia* was vast and flawless, a sparkling ribbon of light stretching for tens of kilometres, looking nearly as magnificent as Saturn's spectacular rings. There were no airlocks on the Imperial Starcruiser so Johnny guided his shuttlecraft to the appointed place where the walls, themselves made from powerful forcefields, opened to allow the London bus inside. Through a succession of these fields, the *Piccadilly* was led into the gigantic central chamber that ran the length of the Emperor's ship.

Once before, Johnny had been here and seen it nearly empty, save for the *Spirit of London* standing alone against one wall. Now there would not have been room for his beautiful craft – the central hold teemed with life and ships. He handed over control to the mind of the *Calida Lucia* herself, who guided the shuttle between giant battleships and medical transports, steering clear of flying maintenance crews and floating platforms carrying the fearsome Imperial Guard. As they went they passed *Cheybora*, the warship he knew best. Johnny thought about the ship's captain, his friend Valdour, who died trying to save him from the Regent's firing squad. It was still hard to believe that the first and best space captain he'd ever met was no longer alive – that his battle-scarred face would never again fill Sol's viewscreen.

The *Piccadilly* settled in the only available space, close to a stack of what looked like hugely magnified dandelion seeds, but which Johnny knew to be the Emperor's own shuttlecraft. Bram stood, his face more lined and wrinkled than Johnny had ever seen it, waiting beside the bus doors, his arms wide apart, a pulsing white sphere the size of a beach ball hovering above each open palm.

'A gift for the people of Earth,' said the Emperor as everyone trooped out. His sparkling eyes lingered over Clara, but he made no comment on the blackness within hers. Johnny came last, carrying Kovac.

'Shield generators?' Johnny asked, remembering when the *Spirit of London*'s had needed replacing.

'Very good,' said Bram. 'Your planet is too close to Alpha Centauri to withstand the gamma-ray bombardment from the Star Blaze.' The Emperor was talking about the recent supernova. 'Humanity needs protecting.'

'But that's not for years yet,' said Johnny.

'Three and a half years is but a twinkling of some cosmic

eyes,' Bram replied. The spheres drifted through the open door and settled softly in the *Piccadilly*'s luggage rack. 'You will come to understand why it must be done now. The generators are to be placed at gravitational wells within the Earth–Moon system, from where they will not drift.'

'L4 and L5 if I am not mistaken, which I very rarely am,' came the voice from the end of Johnny's arm. Kovac's casing glowed in time to the words. 'The stable Lagrangian points.'

'Ah, this must be Kovac,' said the Emperor. 'Welcome to the *Calida Lucia*.'

'It is an honour to be aboard, Your Imperial Majesty,' said the computer. 'I have been looking forward to exploring a proper spaceship.'

'Yet how will that be possible,' said Bram, 'when you are tied to Johnny's arm, and it is my hope that this arm, and the person it is attached to, will accompany me elsewhere?' The Emperor clicked his fingers and Johnny felt a strange lightness at the end of his wrist. He let go of the quantum computer, which remained hovering in mid-air. Then Kovac flew forward of his own accord.

'That seems to have done the trick,' said Bram. 'Alf, my old friend.' The android's face took on a definite pink sheen. 'Several of these engines need to be checked over before we set out and, as you can see, my people appear somewhat behind schedule.' The Emperor pointed to some battleships berthed nearby, many of which looked as if they'd seen better days. 'Perhaps you can show them how it's done?'

'It will be a pleasure to be of assistance,' said the android, bowing and then vanishing in a blur at full speed.

'I'm sure Bentley will be happy to relax nearby,' said Bram, clearly remembering how, the last time he was on board, the grey and white dog enjoyed having his paws massaged by the carpets in the *Calida Lucia*'s corridors. 'And, Kovac – my ship is at your disposal. Go where you wish. Clara and Johnny – I would like you to accompany me to Titan.'

Saturn's largest moon housed a secret. It was called the Fountain of Time and, apparently, had been built by their mother the Diaquant. One of the giant dandelion heads separated from the stack at the end of the Imperial Starcruiser's hold and settled on the ground, so that some of its pointed white quills were close to the Emperor. He blew on the nearest few, which parted, and a walkway extended from the central hub out to where he was standing. 'Follow me,' he said to Johnny and Clara, and then he walked, very slowly, up the ramp.

☆ ☆ ☆
☆ ☆

From the inside, the Emperor's shuttle was completely transparent and they could see Titan's thick orange clouds swirling around them. Clara sat on the floor of the ship, her forehead glistening as her fever became worse. Bram stood in front, hair blowing in a nonexistent breeze, waving his hands over the controls. In very little time they broke through into the lower atmosphere and the landscape below came into view. With its mountains and valleys, oceans and rivers, it looked remarkably like Earth.

They settled on a rocky outcrop beside a large, featureless plain, bounded in the distance by a chain of small hills and all under the heavy orange sky. Bram turned to them both and said, 'We shall not be alone at the Fountain of Time. There are . . . beings who have sought sanctuary here. I urge you to treat them kindly.'

Although the ship's sensors told them there was no oxygen outside, the walls opened and a ramp extended. Bram led the way, walking slowly down before disappearing midway, through an invisible curtain.

47

'I don't feel well,' said Clara. When she looked up her eyes were now totally black. 'I think I'd better stay here.'

Johnny was scared, but tried to sound calm. 'Come on,' he said. 'You love this place – it'll make you feel so much better.' He reached out and pulled her gently to her feet. With his sister leaning heavily on him, they descended the ramp together. At the point where the Emperor had disappeared, everything changed. Sweet smells of heather and honey filled Johnny's nostrils, a sky dominated by Saturn hung overhead and in front was a beautiful lake of liquid gold, filled with chronons – particles of time.

Bram stood by the edge of the lake, but he was not alone. Two dozen figures robed in scarlet hovered around him. The creatures within the flapping cloaks were strangely fuzzy – out of phase with the regular universe, making the bodies inside the cloaks almost invisible. Even so, they were still far clearer than when Johnny had last seen them. These were Owlessan Monks, strange beings who worshipped the galaxy itself. Like Clara and the Plican, they had developed the ability to fold space, but only by working together. One on its own could do next to nothing, but two acting in tandem were twice as strong. Add a third and their abilities doubled again – ditto with a fourth and a fifth. Twenty-four of them in the same place would be immensely powerful.

By now Clara was a deadweight on Johnny's shoulder. As he half carried, half dragged her towards the edge of the lake, the Monks shrank back as though afraid. In the past they'd always seemed curious, wanting to touch him, but sometimes not quite daring.

'It is your sister,' said Bram, in response to Johnny's questioning look. 'She has treated space badly, folding and creasing it too much. They sense she is tainted. I hope that, in this place, time will heal and cleanse.'

Lifting a palm upward, Bram spoke softly and Clara lightened, until she was practically floating beside Johnny. Together, followed at a distance by the flying Monks, they skirted the edge of the lake, arriving on the far side at a grotto of blue crystal pillars, within which a large transparent dome stood on a crystal plinth.

It was here that Johnny had finally come face to face with his clone. He shivered – that day he had been certain he was going to die. While he laid his sister carefully down, the Emperor stepped onto the strange path that led towards the centre of the lake, to the Fountain of Time itself. The scarlet-robed Monks remained by the shoreline. Some of the liquid was defying gravity and spilling up over the sides, where it clumped together, like blobs of golden mercury, before sliding back into the main pool.

Clara opened her eyes – a couple of tiny white spots were visible among the blackness. 'You were right, it's so peaceful here,' she said, sitting up and resting her back against the plinth.

Johnny leaned back, looked up at Saturn hanging in the sky above and felt his whole body tingle with relief. It was as if something of their mother remained here, a secret hub of peace and power hidden from the galaxy. It was a place of renewal and was healing his sister, just as the Emperor must have known it would. Together they watched Bram shuffle to the point on the walkway that triggered the liquid chronons to surge into the sky, a beautiful fountain of gold, hanging like a shimmering curtain of light before slowly falling and engulfing the Emperor. Forty thousand years in the past, Johnny and Clara had met Bram when, a youthful Senator, he visited Atlantis. It was astonishing to think anyone could have lived so long. Now it was only the Fountain of Time that enabled him to keep going.

Bram stood for several minutes, arms aloft, as the liquid fell on him. Slowly the four stars of the Melanian constellation, Portia, began to glow across his chest, and the aura spread until a light was shining from his face and the wavy sparkling hair. Finally the Emperor lowered his arms and began the walk back. The curtain of chronons, hanging in the sky, fell to the ground like the final firework of a spectacular display. Halfway down the invisible path, the Monks crowded round Bram like moths drawn to a new brightly lit flame. He brushed them aside and kept going towards Johnny and Clara. Only a few of the creases across his face had vanished completely and, while walking more normally, he wasn't about to win any medals. Bram, though, clearly thought otherwise.

'Clara – I see you're looking more your normal self.' The blackness in her eyes was definitely fading. 'While you're resting, I hope you don't mind if I challenge your brother to a race?'

'What?' said Johnny.

'First to the far side of the lake wins,' said Bram, a clear twinkle in his eyes. 'On three.'

'Are you sure?' asked Johnny. 'I know you've just been in the fountain, but I don't want to tire you out.'

'One . . .' said Bram, adding, 'Scared you might lose?'

Johnny had briefly considered letting the old Emperor beat him, but not if Bram was going to say things like that.

'Two . . .' The Emperor set himself in the pose of a runner about to spring into action. Johnny did the same. 'Three.'

Johnny sprinted. He was out of the crystal grotto in a shot and soon reached the boundary of the lake. Looking over his shoulder he saw Bram smiling, still frozen in his runner's stance, but now surrounded by swirling Owlessan Monks. Johnny began to slow.

'You'll need to run much faster than that,' shouted the

Emperor. There looked to be a broad smile etched across the lined face. With Monks holding him on either side, Bram was lifted into the air.

Johnny picked up the pace – he was halfway there now. Another glance over his shoulder told him that Bram, although now hovering at the centre of a long line of Monks, was still above the original shore.

'Faster,' cried the Emperor.

Johnny wondered if this was some sort of test of his fitness. He sped up even more. Scarlet cloaks with near-invisible inhabitants began unfolding in front, either side of Johnny's intended destination. As he neared the finish, Bram himself appeared out of thin air, unfolding in the very centre of the line of Monks.

Johnny slowed and came to a halt in front of the Emperor. 'That's . . . cheating,' he said, gasping for air.

'Guilty as charged,' Bram replied, rubbing his arms as if to warm himself up. 'You needed to see for yourself what these creatures can do.' The Monks were rising upward, circling in the air above them. Taking a firm stride forward, the Emperor continued, 'I suggest we walk back.' Johnny nodded and fell in beside him. 'I also wanted to remind you that the fastest runner doesn't always win the race, just as the most powerful fleet needn't win a space battle. Trust me – I would have liked to race you properly – but my time is drawing near. Even the fountain struggles to sustain me now.'

Johnny made to contradict him, but Bram raised his hand and continued speaking. 'I will not be sad when I go beyond – death is not the end. I hope in the time I have left to still be of some use to the galaxy. I had thought that in the halls of Lysentia, the last paradise of the first ones, I might learn the secrets of the Nameless One – how to defeat him – but I have failed in my quest to locate it. I see now it was

51

arrogant to believe I would ever find it, let alone be granted entry.'

As they neared the edge of the lake the Emperor bent and scooped some of the liquid chronons into his hands. They carried on to rejoin Clara, sitting beside her in the crystal grotto. 'As I was saying,' the Emperor went on, 'I needed a new strategy – another way to win this war. With General Nymac dead, the galaxy has been cleansed of the Andromedan invaders. The Nameless One who sent them is weakened and hurting. I know that he intends to come here – to bring the fight again to our door. He must already have left his throne in our sister galaxy, but I will not let him reach here. Now, while he licks his wounds as he travels, is the time to strike.' Bram threw one handful of chronons into the air. The particles of liquid time began to rotate, forming a beautiful swirling spiral in the clear sky above – the galaxy in miniature. As he gazed upward, smiling at the glittering whirlpool, strands of silvery light from his own hair linked with the gold of the galaxy he ruled. 'Inside the *Calida Lucia* you have seen my armada, a great fleet that will sail for Andromeda and meet the Nameless One head on. When the fight is joined, I will not allow our Milky Way to be the battlefield again.'

'You really think Nymac's dead?' asked Clara. Her eyes had almost returned to normal.

'Without a doubt,' Bram replied, still gazing lovingly upward. 'His once great forces have been routed.'

'You know he was our brother?' she said.

The Emperor turned to Johnny, who nodded awkwardly. He'd always assumed Bram knew everything. Now, when the ruler of the galaxy spoke, it was as if choosing his words carefully.

'Clara, Johnny . . . I'm so sorry. I knew Nicky had been taken . . . more than a decade ago. I deeply regret it. There was always the possibility that the Nameless One had turned him. With the success that Nymac had, it seems suddenly obvious.'

'It wasn't his fault – it was that mask,' said Johnny. 'The Nameless One welded it to his face – could see through it – made him do all those things. He tried to break free.'

Bram stood, wrapped his arms around himself and gazed at the spiral above, though the link between him and it was no longer visible. 'The fault was not your brother's – he was a child. The fault was mine.' His face looked so creased it was as if the soaking in the Fountain of Time had never happened. 'Truly, I share your loss and travel to Andromeda to avenge you.'

'But won't that take forever?' Johnny asked, also standing. 'The Andromeda Galaxy's two and a half million light years away.'

The Emperor smiled again, if weakly, and threw his second handful of chronons into the sky. Now there were two spirals swirling above them, the Milky Way joined by her larger sister, the Andromeda Galaxy. 'You ask, yet we have seen Andromedan troops in the Milky Way. How did they come here? Never forget that all of us here are the lawmakers,' said the Emperor. 'You, Clara, can bend the very fabric of space. Johnny – it is nothing for you to command the movement of charge across great distance. The speed of light, too, can be moulded, stretched or, perhaps, even broken. It is we who have allowed it to remain fixed for so long, but now I choose otherwise.' Bram placed his palm in the gap between the two whirlpools of tiny stars. 'In this great void dividing the galaxies, where there is nothing to take hold of to fold space, I shall decree a far faster speed. The journey will still be long, but it will be measured in months – not millions of years.'

'He's still alive,' said Clara, as though she'd stopped listening after Bram's pronouncement about Nicky. 'He has to be.'

53

'Come here, Clara,' said the Emperor, holding both hands out to pick her off the ground and pull her into his arms, where he held her close. It looked to Johnny as though they might both be crying. 'While I can stretch the speed of light, I cannot remake the past. I do not know for certain what fate befell your brother. Use the thought chamber.' He nodded over her head to the transparent dome on the plinth behind. 'It is the truest place to look, although we do not always enjoy what it shows us.'

'But if you go,' said Johnny, keen to change the subject away from Nicky, 'what happens on Melania? What about the Empire?'

At that, Bram's eyes sparkled again and his face once more shone with a little youth. 'At least there I am confident. After the death of the last Regent, Chancellor Gronack fled – the troops loyal to it were not as loyal as it believed. The capital, my homeworld, is at peace. I confess I thought long and hard over someone to entrust it to. Happily, I drew a total blank.'

'And that's a good thing, why?' asked Johnny.

'If you can't find anyone qualified,' said Bram, 'what better way than to make somebody? Someone a hundred percent perfect for the job.'

'Make someone?' said Clara. 'You mean, like an artificial life form?'

'You have your mother's ability to read me, Clara,' said the Emperor. 'I mean *exactly* like an artificial life form. One properly able to step into my shoes and become a good Regent, although I have decided a change of title is in order. She is the Emissary, my mouthpiece to the people. And, Johnny – you two have already met.'

'Ophia,' he replied. It couldn't really be anyone else.

Bram laughed. 'Ophia indeed. The Empire is in safe hands. She will handle my affairs wisely, until another is ready to step forward to take up the reins.' Bram's gaze fell briefly on Johnny who blushed, hoping the Emperor hadn't really meant him. There was no job in the galaxy he'd like less.

Bram sat, Clara following his lead, wiping her now completely clear eyes. The galaxies over their heads faded and the chronons fell to the ground, clumping together and flowing back into the golden lake. In their place, filling the air overhead and swooping in and out like great red bats, were the Owlessan Monks. Before, Johnny had only been able to see skeletons under their cloaks, but now there were muscly sinews and some flaps of skin, as though another layer had been added. With Clara looking like her normal self, they weren't as reluctant to approach. One even reached a bony finger in her direction, but she shrank back and tried to brush it away.

'I saw *Cheybora*,' she said to Bram. 'Is she going with you?'

'And the Tolimi,' said the Emperor explaining the orderliness of Pluto Base. 'And many others who have suffered loss.'

Johnny wondered if Clara was up to something – there was very little to tie her to Earth and a whole universe out there to explore.

As if thinking the same, Bram added, 'Your place is here – within the galaxy that spawned you. Where I am going, you cannot follow. Should you wish to leave the solar system, visit Melania. The Imperial Palace is at your disposal and I have no doubt Alf would like to meet Ophia. You will not thank me for saying it, but you are too young for this fight.'

Johnny didn't think that was fair. Now was probably the time to tell Bram about seeing the Krun sphere on Earth. He tried to interrupt, but the Emperor carried on speaking. 'It is time. Yours may be the finest company in the galaxy, but already I have lingered too long.'

'Can you leave us here?' Clara asked. 'Just for a while.'

'Indeed it is best you remain,' said Bram. 'But I must say

goodbye. In case I do not return, it has been an honour and a privilege to know you both.'

Johnny felt numb at the suddenness of it all. He couldn't believe the one person in the galaxy he knew he could rely on was leaving now. He watched Bram hug his sister. Then it was his turn.

'You'll beat him,' said Johnny. 'I know you will.' Trying to act as grown-up as possible, he offered the Emperor his hand.

Bram took it and shook. 'Johnny Mackintosh, should this prove our last meeting, I have left something for you with Ophia.'

'Don't say that. Of course . . .'

Bram held up a hand and the words in Johnny's throat died. 'Purely a precaution, but one I deem prudent when facing the Nameless One. Do not misunderstand me – I am wedded to the Milky Way and do not intend death to come outside its borders. When I go on, I would like to take the first steps from Melania, the world I love. Tell me, do you recall what I once gave into your safekeeping, on the moon where Sol was born?'

'A piece of your soul?' said Johnny, remembering what he had been asked to carry in his locket.

'Do not speak of it,' said the Emperor. 'Ophia will keep safe what needs to be kept safe. Should you see it, I ask that you will look kindly on me. An old man, I have tried to make amends.'

Inside Johnny's head he could hear a strange wailing – he knew it was the monks crying as the Emperor left them too. He'd lost his mum and dad, Captain Valdour was gone too and now even Bram was leaving. As the Emperor of the Galaxy turned and walked away, a cloud of scarlet whirling above his head, Johnny sank to the ground feeling powerless and alone.

☆ ☆ ☆
☆ ☆

It was hard to know how much time had passed, or if time flowed in the same way, if at all, in the stillness around the golden lake. The Monks slowly dispersed from the place where Bram had disappeared, but they did not approach. Johnny stared at the ground. Where his clone had shot at him in the past, there were now no craters from the blaster fire. Where the pillars of blue crystal had been shattered, they were now whole. After what felt a long while, it was Clara who spoke first. 'I'm sorry I've been mardy.'

'Hey – you've been ill,' Johnny replied. He hated heart-to-heart conversations like this threatened to become – girls seemed to cope with them so much more easily.

'Thanks for making me come. I feel so much better here,' she said. 'Will you help me use the chamber? I don't know how to work it.'

'I think you just look inside,' Johnny replied. Bram had once told him the thought chamber showed you what was happening to people or places that were connected to you. He didn't much care for the strange dome, however impressive it was meant to be. He remembered the many times he'd peered inside and found the Nameless One staring back, eyes filled with such powerful hatred that it had looked as if he might break out of the chamber and kill Johnny on the spot. He didn't think he'd ever look in there again.

'Johnny, come and see. I think it's Nicky.'

'What?' In a flash his thoughts were all forgotten and Johnny was on his feet, staring into the dome. A man lay face down in the snow in the middle of a blizzard. His body was nearly covered by a carpet of white. It was impossible to tell who he was, let alone if he was still alive.

A pair of feet appeared beside the prone figure, feet wearing garish, jewel-encrusted slippers. A long, spindly alien arm reached into the snow and flipped the man onto his side.

The body was mangled, burnt and broken, the face horribly disfigured all down one side.

'It is him,' said Clara. 'Where?' she asked, her nose pressed against the very top of the transparent dome. 'Where is he?'

Now Johnny could see him better, there was no doubt she was right – lying on top of the thick white covering was their brother, eyes and black hair encrusted with ice and frozen solid, looking every bit as dead as Bram had claimed. The alien's hand began digging around, dipping into the snow at various points. It paused at one place, felt around for a few seconds and then scooped furiously, sending snow flying upward. Ice was beginning to form over the long, thin hand when it stopped digging and pulled, from the blanket of snow, a black mask – made to cover one side of Nicky's face.

Clara looked to Johnny, her expression caught somewhere between horror and amazement. 'We have to find him,' she said.

'Clara, he's dead,' said Johnny. 'I'm sorry.'

'You don't know that,' she replied, her eyes blazing. The act of turning away from the chamber had broken the link to her thoughts. When she looked back, Nicky had gone and the ice world with him. Instead, a new image was forming, a swirling vortex of pink, purple and black with a tiny figure almost lost at its centre. Johnny watched with his sister as the view slowly zoomed in on the person, tumbling alone in nothingness – trapped in the void that was hyperspace.

Closer up, he could see her blonde hair. As she fell her body turned towards him and he recognized her face, even though it was contorted in absolute terror. Inside the dome was a second Clara and this one was screaming. The Clara standing beside him began screaming too. He pulled her away so she didn't have to watch herself falling, seemingly forever, trapped inside the horror of a Klein fold. She was breathing heavily, her heart pounding, her eyes wide with fear.

'I don't like it here any more,' she said. 'It's not right. I want to go.' She broke free from him and began running towards the lake. Johnny chased after her. The Monks converged on Clara, trying to block her path and prevent her from leaving. He heard their cries somewhere inside his head. She brushed them aside and ran up the little slope away from the lake, away from the Fountain of Time, and vanished through the invisible wall.

Johnny followed, taking one last look over his shoulder. When he turned away, he found the *Piccadilly* waiting, Alf in the pilot's seat and with Clara already on board.

4 ✩

The Blood-Red Planet ✩

Alf appeared even more confused than Johnny about what was going on, but the android piloted the shuttle up and away through the thick atmosphere. Johnny sat one side of his sister on the back seat of the bus, with Bentley jumping up on the other. Gradually, as the Old English sheepdog snuggled beside her, a tiny amount of colour returned to Clara's face, but she looked too afraid to speak.

By the time they reached the *Spirit of London*, the *Calida Lucia* and her internal armada had already folded away to begin their long journey beyond the rim and away from the galaxy. Bram was out of contact. Johnny wouldn't be able to tell him that Nicky had been found, or his suspicions as to who might have found him. He couldn't be sure about the alien's arm and hand, but was almost certain he recognized the slippers as belonging to Chancellor Gronack. Bram had said that the traitor had fled Melania. If only Johnny had asked the Emperor where the scheming Phasmeer had gone.

The space around Saturn was too unsettled for them to fold straight to Earth. Instead they would have to travel more conventionally, which could only be better for Clara's health. Johnny asked Alf to scan their surroundings and, as luck would have it, Mars was nearly as close as it ever came to Saturn. A detour might cheer Clara up – take her mind off things, especially the image she'd seen of herself in the thought chamber. He decided they would finally visit the red planet.

✧ ✧ ✧
✧ ✧

Early space probes had taken intriguing but inconclusive photographs of the Martian surface, showing what were called the Pyramids of Elysium, next to what appeared to be a gigantic human face gazing upward. Johnny had always meant to visit and see for himself. For his part, Alf was curious to hear about the probes that had gone missing, so Johnny repeated the conversation he'd had with Clara, in a little more detail. Given the great expense of space exploration, the failure rate for Mars was unusually high. It wasn't only *Beagle 2* that had bitten the dust as it neared the planet. Over the years, around half the missions launched had failed for one reason or another.

Alf stayed on the bridge while Johnny asked Sol to locate Clara for him. She was on the garden deck with Bentley. As he went to check in with her he couldn't help remembering Mrs Irvine's warnings to him and wonder if, even now, someone was poking their head through the trapdoor at the top of Halader House and into a deserted bedroom. He joined his sister, sitting on top of the rocky outcrop, and told her about their new destination. She smiled and Johnny noticed it was the first time he'd seen her do that for ages. It was on this very spot that he'd first told her about their brother. He had wondered if she would want to begin searching for Nicky straightaway, but perhaps the two scenes she'd witnessed in the chamber were too closely linked for her to even think about that.

'I have to tell you something,' said Clara. 'I've known for a while, but I didn't want to face up to it.' She sounded resigned but relieved. Johnny didn't know how to respond, but Clara

61

seemed content for him simply to listen while she continued. 'What we saw in the thought chamber . . . after Nicky . . . me in the Klein fold. That's what's going to happen to me.' They were both looking down at their black Melanian boots. 'If I keep folding I'll be sucked into hyperspace and trapped forever. Alf knows, Bram knows . . . even those Monk things know. So I have to stop.'

'OK, then stop,' said Johnny.

Clara laughed. 'It's not that easy,' she replied. 'The thought of never doing it again . . . it's beyond words.'

She slid down off the rock and, for the first time Johnny could remember, set off for the antigrav shaft with Bentley alongside. 'C'mon,' she said, looking back to him. 'We're going to Mars.'

☆ ☆ ☆
☆ ☆

Sol interrupted Johnny as he was gathering his things together. She had disturbing news to report – a low-level dispersion field was operating between certain latitudes on the planet. This was very odd and Johnny went straight to the bridge. It was soon clear that any spaceship attempting to land within a certain area on the surface would have its circuits fried – and that area included the Martian pyramids, from one of which the ship said the field was being generated. It certainly explained some of the probe failures. Sol had automatically increased her hull shielding to maximum and, in high orbit, was safe and likely to be undetectable from the planet's surface, but it wouldn't be possible for her to land without revealing herself and causing considerable damage.

The magnified image of Olympus Mons was being shown on the viewscreen – they were overflying the gigantic volcano, the largest mountain anywhere in the solar system and three times taller than Everest. Still digesting their unexpected discovery of

Martian technology, Johnny stared at the summit crater, itself nearly a hundred kilometres across, imagining the force of the eruption it would have produced. All of a sudden it came to him why he'd heard of Santorini, where Peter had resurfaced. It was the site of a huge volcano on Earth, apparently ending a great early European civilization. Some archaeologists even claimed it was this that had caused the destruction of Atlantis, but as he'd been there, Johnny knew that had been nothing to do with volcanoes. A flash of light inside the caldera caught his eye. He shouted to Sol, who magnified the view still further.

Climbing into the Martian atmosphere the ship identified a Krun Hunter–Killer, Assassin Class. The long black flying cylinder ended with a curved prow and sported needle-like protrusions all along its hull – a mixture of sensors, communications equipment and, of course, weapons. The dispersion field had been briefly switched to stand-by, enabling the craft to reach orbit unimpeded. Johnny asked Sol to project its intended destination – the reply left little doubt that the HK was heading for Earth.

✳ ✳ ✳

In the half-hour they'd been observing from orbit, two more Krun ships had left through the mouth of the volcano. Although all three vessels were on a course that would take them to Earth, Johnny decided not to follow. First he had to discover what was happening directly below. What were the Krun doing on Mars? He'd left Alf in command of the *Spirit of London* and was sitting in the pilot seat of the *Bakerloo*, beside Clara, hovering just above the limit of the dispersion field. Currently invisible, his sister was wearing a spacesuit the same as his, a tight-fitting outfit that served as a second, highly protective skin, topped by a clear bubble helmet. They were hoping for another Krun launch, when the field would be turned off and the shielded shuttle could pass through undetected. They didn't have long to wait.

This time, one of the smaller Krun spheres was coming the other way, in to land. They followed it down through the atmosphere, its trajectory taking it towards the largest pyramid rather than the great volcano – it touched down immediately in front of the pointed structure. Johnny piloted the *Bakerloo* nearby, well hidden (he hoped) within a gulley bounded by a line of smooth-topped boulders. The sensors revealed a lot of methane within the thin atmosphere, normally a strong indicator of life and not at all what he'd expected.

They left the shuttle and poked their bubbled heads over the edge of the rocks, just in time to watch a full complement of Krun exit the sphere and waddle inside the pyramid. Up close, it appeared to Johnny that he and Clara were hiding behind the very top of a vast, ancient wall that had at one time bordered the complex, but was now all but buried by rusty brown Martian soil. The pyramid itself was like pictures he'd seen of Egypt, only on a far grander scale (and with a small spaceship out in front). Though worn by neverending sandstorms, it retained some of the features left behind by the original builders – a great entrance was clearly visible, and the sides were pitted with small black squares, perhaps shafts leading into its interior. It can't have been the Krun who built it – they were scavengers who lived off what others left behind. Something about the structure, perhaps its red coloration, again made Johnny think of Atlantis. Although cruel and terrible, the Atlanteans had built a great spacefaring civilization that spanned half the galaxy. Of course they would have come here – it was right on their doorstep. If Johnny hadn't drowned Atlantis beneath the ocean, Terra (the old name for Earth) and not Melania might now be ruling the Milky Way.

In the low Martian gravity, it was an easy jump down the

far side of the wall. Taking great long strides, they jogged towards the pyramid and, drawing close, began to notice a network of dark red paths leading away from hollows in the ground and towards the towering structure. It was as if some very heavy objects had left their mark and, as they passed the lone sphere, it was clear the depressions were the same size as Krun spaceships.

Johnny and Clara joined one of the paths. It looked as if someone had sloshed red paint over the ground, as well as scattering occasional little white stones and tubes, that made a satisfying crunch when stepped on in their space boots. Like a river network, their path merged with another and widened before joining yet another tributary until they reached the base of the pyramid itself. Here the route onward could have been a vast river delta, running underneath a gigantic door through which the Krun had just entered. The ground was soggy underfoot, as though freshly painted.

'What now?' Clara asked.

When breaking and entering, it didn't seem wise to use the front door and, for once, his sister couldn't fold them inside.

'I think I can get us in – this way.' Johnny had spotted what looked like a side entrance further along. They bounded towards it, feeling terribly exposed, but once they arrived at least the lock turned out to be electronic. Johnny closed his eyes, picturing the way the currents flowed and the magnetic fields they produced. He could feel how it worked – what would open it – and directed the electrons to their appointed places at the right speeds. Very quickly the door shot upward, retracting into a gap above to reveal an airlock with fragments of painted walls. It was hard to tell, but it looked like the picture of an ancient waterway – maybe the stories about canals on Mars were true after all. They stepped inside and Johnny made the door slide closed behind them. The airlock was automatic. A breathable, pressurized atmosphere soon surrounded them and the door at the other side of the narrow chamber opened.

A corridor, supported by ornate pillars carved to look like reeds, led steeply upward. The walls were lined with white stone, on which the elaborate mural continued, only here inside the pyramid it looked nearly as perfect as the day it had been created. It depicted colourful boats being pulled by dolphins. Johnny could almost hear the seagulls and smell the salt air. Now there could be no doubt who built this place – it was like being back in Atlantis.

Johnny's suit told him the air was perfectly breathable, so he touched a button on his collar and his bubble-headed helmet collapsed cleverly into the lining of the suit around his neck.

Clara did the same. 'Yuk . . . What's that smell?' she whispered.

Johnny shook his head. It was like decay, something rotting. 'We'll get used to it,' he replied.

'I'm not so sure,' said his sister, smiling again. 'It's worse than your bedroom.'

They climbed quickly, their way lit by shafts in the roof at regular intervals. Then they rounded a corner and found the way blocked by an organic curtain of sticky yellow mucus. Clara hung back and Johnny could see it was up to him to tear it aside. This wasn't as bad as it looked, largely because of the suit's gloves, but pieces clumped together around his fingers like a thick spider's web. More mucus covered the floor beyond, and organic sacs, their yellow membranes stretched and lined with green veins, hung partway up the walls. Inside every one were a few black blobs, each the size of a marble. Johnny and Clara kept going, but found their boots sticking to the floor, making progress awkward.

The sound of approaching footsteps sent them into a panic. The only way to hide was to press themselves into one of the

66

narrow gaps between the sacs on the wall and pray they weren't seen. The clammy mucus stuck fast to Johnny's spacesuit, making it hard to move at all. Into the corridor, wearing overalls, waddled a line of ugly insect-like creatures with long snouts protruding from their fly-like heads and four hinged arms by their sides. It was a troop of Krun workers. Buzzing around them were a handful of fat flying insects, like little moths, which settled on the sacs and crawled inside. Thankfully, the Krun lined up with their backs to Johnny and Clara, each in front of one of the milky yellow bags of gloop attached to the opposite wall. Then, with one pair of arms, the Krun hoisted a sac each into the air, holding it up to their faces while, with the other arms they squeezed along their snouts, squirting jets of yellow fluid out into the wobbly containers. All the while, the two arms and the snout were making strange clicks. It was one of those times when Johnny wished he didn't have the sliver of the Hundra's soul living within him, translating.

'Who's going to be a big boy . . . that's right – eat it all up . . . a special treat from the Queen.'

Johnny whispered, 'They're birthing eggs.'

His sister slapped a gloved hand over his mouth and gave him a scowl that suggested anyone with even a quarter of a brain cell would have already guessed as much. Happily, the Krun were too busy feeding their young to look round. Then a leftover little bug flew towards Johnny and settled on the tip of his nose. He felt himself going cross-eyed, trying to focus on it, but didn't dare do anything that might make another sound. Leaving a cold trail of slime as it went, it hopped onto his cheek and he felt the patter of the tiniest of feet across his face. He tried to shake his head to get rid of it, but pulling away from the webbed mucus created a slurping noise and he was forced to stop. Whatever the thing was, it had reached his ear. Johnny was willing it, *Don't go inside . . . don't go inside*, but it felt as if the insect had done exactly that. Johnny hoped he'd imagined it – that the creature had taken a quick peek and then flown away. He still daren't move. The Krun workers finished and reattached their sacs to the wall. Once they were done, they waddled away in the direction they'd come. Inside each of the sacs, several of the little black blobs were now moving around within the fluid that held them. It was disgusting.

Johnny tried sticking a gloved finger inside his ear, but removed it to find only wax. Carefully he and Clara followed the retreating Krun to a junction in the corridor, where the aliens disappeared out of sight. As Johnny neared it he began to hear a new, much lower-pitched Krun voice that seemed to be coming from the walls. Over and over again it was whispering, '*Feed me.*'

'Who's that?' he said, running to peer round the corner. There were several metal doors leading off the corridor and he wondered if the strange speaker was behind one of them.

'What are you talking about?' asked Clara, frowning. Johnny pressed his ear to the cold metal of the nearest door, but heard nothing. Clara tugged at his spacesuit as other voices approached. Johnny nodded and, with the subtlest of commands, he sent the metal barrier upward into a recess. They slipped inside and the door closed behind them.

The chamber they'd entered took up nearly one whole side of the pyramid, with great shafts of light from outside criss-crossing the cavernous space. It was a vast vault, with row after row and column upon column made of transparent tanks, linked by tubes, all the same. Floating in the murky waters must have been thousands of the human–alien hybrid amphibians like Peter, their skins glowing faintly green, organic tubes like Krun snouts leading into every tank.

'Why? What are they for?' Clara asked, as she gazed upward, totally horrified.

Johnny shook his head, unable even to guess. The pair walked between rows, wiping the crud off their spacesuits as they went, their footsteps echoing up and down the huge space. The poor things inside were at every stage of development, from babies up to young adults, but they all followed Johnny and Clara with their eyes. Several of the more developed specimens swam to the very edges of their tanks, pressing their faces against the sides. It was horrible – Johnny felt powerless to help and was glad when he reached what looked like an open lift that might take them higher up the vault, hopefully to another level where they could leave this place behind.

It took a lot of effort to coax Clara onto the platform. Finally she crouched on all fours as far from the edges as possible and looked only at the lift floor. As soon as Johnny pressed the 'up' button she grabbed his leg so tightly it almost cut off his circulation, even through the spacesuit. They rose slowly into the air. Clara's eyes were squeezed shut and Johnny was glad she wasn't watching the thousands of sad faces that followed their progress as they went higher.

He decided to take them as close to the top of the pyramid as the lift went, ignoring a few open corridors they passed during the ascent. By working their way down systematically, he hoped they'd discover what the Krun were up to. It made for a long ride. When they finally jerked to a halt Clara's eyes opened in a silent, terrified scream as she took in the huge drop below. She crawled away from it on all fours, beyond their platform and onto the more solid ground of an open corridor at the side, oblivious to the mucus that covered the floor and walls and the flesh-like flaps that dangled from the sloping ceiling. Johnny hoped they'd be able to find another route down – no way would Clara return to the open lift. After scrambling noisily on her hands and knees for several metres, she finally stopped and leaned her back against the wall between a clump of birthing sacs like the ones they'd seen earlier. She was breathing very hard but, as Johnny caught up, she nodded to indicate she was OK. He carried on past to investigate a light at the far end of the corridor.

They were near the very apex of the pyramid. The corridor they'd entered led to an opening above a square chamber, adjoining a walkway that encircled the walls, high above the floor. Clara wouldn't like the drop, but the only way to go was forward. There were voices coming from below, so Johnny lay on his front and peered over the sides. Directly beneath him, a familiar large blue globe was slowly spinning. It was a projection of Earth, semi-transparent, and through it he could see the insect-like faces of several Krun staring up from around a circular table. They were studying the planet so intently he was sure none would have noticed his head poking over the ledge. Another alien floated above the scene, chained to the ground. Brown and grey and shaped like a slightly deflated football, it was a Hundra, one of the galaxy's translators. The creature's leathery hide was covered with glowing red welts.

'Clara – look at this,' he hissed.

Despite clearly being Earth, the globe looked very unusual. North and South America, while clearly marked, were simply blacked out. Instead of properly showing the continents, it was the oceans where the information was mapped in minute detail. Deep trenches, underwater mountain ranges and all manner of other detail about places on the seabed had been highlighted. Nearly three-quarters of Earth's surface was covered by water. Johnny hated to think why the Krun were so interested. It sounded as if an argument was in progress at the foot of the chamber and, now Johnny looked closer, he could see somebody else, wearing a suit, standing before the table of aliens.

'Of course I will find it, and soon. These briefings cause

unnecessary delays – if I could simply merge with the collective . . .' Bizarrely the voice was speaking English, but with every stressed syllable it cracked a fearsome whip into the Hundra, forcing the captive creature to translate into Krun. It was a sickening sight. Johnny recognized the whip wielder instantly. It was Bugface himself, the Krun known as Stevens who had shot dead his dad. He'd once thought that he'd watched this particular alien die, but Stevens later delighted in telling Johnny that he was one of nine, all identical, from the same birthing egg.

The synchronous reply came from all the other Krun around the table. 'We serve the Queen. She deems vital detail may be lost should you transform before giving your reports. Your joining will not be delayed much longer.' These aliens were thought to have a single, hive mind, meaning they thought and spoke as one.

'But it is so inefficient,' said Stevens. 'I loathe it – I loathe them and everything about their stinking human form.' The tips of his whip crackled with electricity over the body of the Hundra.

Johnny winced on each stroke. He scoured the room for anything that might help him stop this, but the only thing he recognized was a DNA shower, the device by which the aliens manifested as human when on Earth.

'Perhaps you have forgotten the importance of your mission,' replied the other Krun. 'Find what we seek and, once Terra is ours, the whole galaxy will be next. Our new fleet will be unstoppable. Fail and you know the consequences – the dead flesh we feed the Queen is not to her liking – she has been asking for live prey.'

Clara had crawled alongside Johnny. As long as she was lying down with no chance of falling, she seemed capable of peering over the edge.

'Then tell her it will not be long now,' said Stevens as he whipped the chained translator. 'I have narrowed the search to a very few sites.'

'See to it that it is not,' replied the Krun. 'The Queen is satisfied. You may transform – we will report directly to her.'

Stevens didn't need telling twice. He practically ran to the cubicle. The other Krun gathered in the middle of the room, linking arms, and the section of floor beneath them began to descend into the pyramid. Once out of sight a replacement piece of flooring slid across. Meanwhile, the globe portraying the slowly rotating Earth vanished.

'Quickly,' said Johnny, jumping to his feet. 'We have to follow them.' He began running around the elevated walkway that bounded the chamber, towards some steps that led down one wall. Clara remained rooted to the spot. 'Come on – they're getting away.' She tried to stand, but was shaking too much to manage it. In reality, it was such a short distance from the walkway down to the floor that Johnny supposed it wouldn't do too much harm. 'OK – just this once, fold yourself down,' he said.

Clara shook her head. 'You don't understand. It might be the end if I did, but I can't anyway – not even if I wanted to. I could never do it when there's a drop. It's stupid, but it's the vertigo.'

If it weren't so serious, Johnny would have laughed. He ran back, took his sister's hand and said, 'Close your eyes and I'll guide you. Quickly . . . Bugface will be out soon.'

Clara nodded, but the process of leading her around the walls and down the stone staircase was far from quick. Finally on the solid floor, they ran over towards the spot where the Krun had exited. Clara stopped beneath the floating Hundra. 'We've got to do something.'

White bubbles still filled the cubicle in the corner as Stevens immersed himself in his original DNA. The process wouldn't take long. Johnny tried to find exactly where the Krun had been standing to take their lift, but the join in the floor was invisible. It had to be there somewhere. Trying to remain calm, he closed his eyes, hoping to sense some special flow of electricity beneath his feet. The room was alive with different currents, but there was one that stood out above all the others, shining like a searchlight inside his skull. The pyramid contained an orichalcum core, the special mineral of the Atlanteans, and Johnny was standing directly above it. Lining a circular shaft, it marked the exact centre of the pyramid. He'd found it. He saw how to work it. With his mind he summoned the lift before turning to his sister. Across the room, foam was beginning to drain from the shower cubicle. Over by the Hundra Clara had pulled the chains, drawing it down to near floor level – the poor creature was badly hurt, the scars in its hide looking deep and raw. For most inhabitants of the galaxy, to touch one of these ancient translators meant instant, painful death, but Johnny had long ago discovered it was otherwise for him. Now, equally impervious to harm, his sister was tenderly stroking the rough hide of the bruised creature while she began unbuckling its harness.

'We have to hurry,' said Johnny as he ran over to help free the tethered alien. A motor whirred beneath the floor in the centre of the room – the lift was coming. Johnny wondered what he'd do if it proved full of Krun. The safety net of having Clara fold them to escape any situation had gone.

Clara was struggling to undo the final buckle, buried within a deep gash in the Hundra's side. The DNA shower in the far corner emptied – out stepped Stevens in his true form.

'You!' said the Krun, running into the centre of the room to block their escape.

Finally the Hundra was released and, despite the danger

they were facing, Johnny felt he could cry with happiness as the tiny piece of another being's soul within him exploded with joy. Stevens made a horrid, chirruping sound as he reached for a blaster. The Hundra lifted into the air and flew towards the Krun.

'Come on,' said Johnny, seeing their chance of escape. He knew the lift had arrived and, with Clara running beside him, followed after the flying creature as it dive-bombed Stevens. The Krun was forced to flee. Johnny pulled Clara onto the right spot and willed the elevator to descend. Stevens was running around the room screaming, pursued by the Hundra. Agonizingly slowly, the floor began to sink as they started their journey down the pyramid. Above their heads the shaft sealed itself shut. They'd escaped for now, but with Stevens linked to the collective, every other Krun on the planet would know Johnny and Clara were on Mars. It was definitely time to leave.

The descent was taking an age, but at least this central shaft was enclosed and free from the Krun crud. Its orichalcum-clad walls hummed with power, and the murals they passed depicted scenes from Atlantis of blue-robed priests, the building of a great tower and even the erection of a huge arch. The images felt like they went on forever, as if they were travelling a very long way down.

They exited into a wide tunnel, irregular patches of light shining dimly from behind the walls and roof. A constant background rumble told Johnny they were near water and, as his eyes adjusted to the gloom, he saw a steep-sided narrow channel running along the centre, carrying a fast-flowing underground river. Johnny knew there used to be surface water on Mars, so he supposed he shouldn't be surprised to see this beneath it. What he didn't like were the spherical black pods lining the far bank. They opened in unison, lights from inside each one silhouetting a single Krun soldier.

Green blaster fire from one of the nearest grazed Johnny's shoulder, burning off a piece of his spacesuit and drawing blood. He ducked, gritting his teeth against the pain and pulling his sister down with him. They took cover behind some sort of hard, resin-covered object on the floor, one of a series of rough cylinders either side of the deep gulley, each a couple of metres long. It didn't feel like it would protect them for long. Behind, the lift rose up and away, leaving them stranded. He looked to Clara to take them out of there, but she shook her head. It was as if the image of his sister trapped within the Klein fold was reflected back at him in her eyes.

The Krun soldiers on the far bank stepped forward, guns blazing. As they reached the edge of the gulley they kicked the objects lining the bank so they rolled down into the river channel. Each shot downstream at high speed. Cowering behind their flimsy defence, Johnny couldn't see any way out. They were pinned down, horribly exposed, and under the barrage of blaster fire their flimsy cover was disintegrating around them. He pointed along the tunnel and crawled, keeping as low as possible until reaching the shelter of the next of the rough cylinders. This one was still intact. Clara tried to follow, but was driven back. Then, as one, the soldiers ceased firing and she scuttled across. Behind, the lift had returned, allowing another Krun to step out on their side of the bank and waddle slowly towards them. Pressed to the ground beside his sister, Johnny looked up at the ugly, six-limbed creature he thought he recognized.

'I can't think of a better way for you to go,' said Stevens. 'She wants live ones – I'll give her live ones.' The Krun cracked a whip into the ground right in front of them, sending sparks flying into the air. Clara tried to back away, causing whatever they'd taken cover behind to start rolling down the steep bank.

'Jump,' shouted Johnny, but Clara was one step ahead. They

landed in the centre of the torrent, grabbing hold of the big float just before it caught the current and shot like a cork out of a bottle, zooming downstream towards a distant point of light.

It was all Johnny could do to hold on. He wasn't sure what they were heading towards, but anything that led away from Stevens and the Krun soldiers had to be good. A constant rumble in the distance was becoming louder all the time, like the cascading of a waterfall. The terrible image of Niagara Falls came into his mind – he had to believe such a thing couldn't exist – not underground – not in this place. He fought to keep his head above the water. Solid objects carried along below the surface kept brushing his legs while, up above, long flaps, like pieces of skin, hung from the tunnel roof and slid over his face.

'*Live ones . . . feed me live ones.*'

Their float was heading towards the same deep voice Johnny had heard earlier. They were also nearing the end of the tunnel. They burst into the light as the cave opened out and the roaring of the river lessened. For the first time Johnny could see that, whatever was carrying them along, it wasn't water. A bright red liquid frothed and bubbled around them, the same colour as at the base of the pyramid.

The float flew into the air as the red torrent gave way beneath them. Johnny thought they were done for, but the drop was quite small – it was only a weir. Even so he couldn't hold on and was dragged below the surface. Eyes closed, tumbling in the strong current, he thrashed out in panic, but a surprisingly strong arm clamped itself around his neck and pulled his face up into the air. Clara kicked out strongly, dragging Johnny backwards into the calmer flow beside the bank. Now he could see the solid objects being carried in the swill. He retched – there were fingers and toes and even half a skull, its eyes part detached but held on by nerve strands. They rounded a bend and passed under several more of the skin-like flaps. Clara grabbed one to stop them being carried further downstream and Johnny followed suit. Taking a handful of the hanging folds he used them to climb up and onto the bank, from where he helped his sister out.

A mass of other solid objects had washed up nearby, including whole arms and legs, and some clothes. This time, Johnny really was sick. After vomiting uncontrollably, he turned to see Clara doing the same. Then he noticed something he was sure he recognized – a silly, jester's hat, just like the juggler had been wearing in Trafalgar Square. He didn't want to think about what had happened to bring it halfway across the solar system to here.

At last they stood together on the bank, spacesuits dripping red. The ground beneath their boots was squidgy and soft. The stench made Johnny want to be sick again.

'*Live ones*,' came the voice from all around, as if inside his head.

'Clara,' said Johnny desperately. 'Are you sure you can't fold us out of here?'

'Please, Johnny. Don't say that. I mustn't,' she replied. 'I can't do it.'

He knew she wasn't meant to be folding *all* the time, but this did seem an emergency. They walked together along the bank beside the frothing river of blood, searching for a way out until they finally came to a gap in the wall beside them. To enter, they had to push through another horrid sticky curtain of mucus. On the other side the space opened out and they stopped. It was hard to believe an underground cave could be so big – like a cathedral, with great bone-like struts lining the walls and ceiling and filled with row upon row of the birthing sacs they'd seen before. Even as they watched, more were appearing, deposited from organic, see-through tubes that moved across the roof before lowering them all the way down to the floor and then planting whole new line after whole new line.

'I've got a really bad feeling about this,' said Clara.

'You and me both,' he replied.

Despite the suit around him, Johnny suddenly felt cold. Then, before he could even begin to think what to do, he was hoisted into the air by one of the crane-like tubes. It held him, dangling upside down, his feet clamped by ugly black pincers as it swung him through the air over the rows of eggs. He saw Clara behind him – exactly the same thing had happened to her. Blood rushed to his head as he passed over thousands of the miniature blobs, some moving within their eggs, all destined to become more Krun. The thing carried him forward to the very end of the cavern until he was hovering above a vat filled with a thick milky batter.

It was instinct. He reached up a hand and pressed the button on his collar just as the tube released him. His bubble helmet encased him a fraction of a second before he hit the surface. He shouted into the microphone, 'Helmet, Clara – use the helmet.'

His body stiffened. He battled to move his arms and legs, but it was like wading through thick mud and in no time at all they were stuck fast – he was being cocooned. The helmet too was almost totally covered, but he could still see through a couple of slivers. Something banged into him. 'Clara, are you OK?' he shouted.

'I mustn't fold, Johnny. I'm sorry, I mustn't. You saw it too.' His sister sounded desperate, but at least they were both still alive.

Johnny was plucked from the vat and dropped into another river of blood flowing slowly but unstoppably forward towards a set of giant, salivating jaws.

'*Live ones,*' said the voice. '*Fresh meat at last.*'

He couldn't move – his body had set rigid. He was about

to become the Queen's next meal. 'Clara!' he yelled from his cocoon. 'It's the Queen – she's going to eat me.'

He reached the mouth . . . he was between the jaws . . . sticky saliva spattered the thin slivers through which he watched, terrified . . . then he found himself sitting, very awkwardly, in the pilot's seat of the *Bakerloo*. He heard Clara's sobs coming from the inside of his helmet but, set rigid, was unable to turn round. 'I owe you big time,' Johnny said to her. His sister's ability to fold space had saved them before, but this had been a really close shave. He heard another voice scream with frustration and wondered where it came from. Though he couldn't move a millimetre, the shuttle shot skyward – it was a wonderful thing that it worked by thought control. He didn't care about the dispersion field – he trusted his little ship to get through it. He was desperate to reach home and the comfort of the *Spirit of London*. His own senses merged with the *Bakerloo*'s and, as they crossed the boundary into the field, the pain became intense. He fought to shut it out.

'Master Johnny – you will be detected. Whatever is going on?'

'Alf,' shouted Johnny, his head screaming as he shared the little black London cab's hurt. 'Open the shuttle bay doors – it's an emergency.'

He couldn't concentrate. He hoped Sol would guide them home. For a minute, the *Bakerloo* felt like it was disintegrating around them. Finally, they entered the ship and skidded to a halt along the deck.

'Alf – help,' he said into his microphone. 'And Sol – get us out of here.' He couldn't even turn his head to see if Clara was OK.

5 ✫

Into the Deep ✫

For what felt like hours after Alf had taken Clara to sickbay, Johnny had sat trapped rigid and awkward, inside his skintight casing within the *Bakerloo*. Extracting his sister from her own vile cocoon while keeping her rising fever under control was proving far from easy. Effectively paralysed, Johnny remained behind, able only to talk and listen as, all the while, the cramp in his muscles grew worse. Periodically, Alf's voice came through Johnny's helmet, apologizing for the time it was taking, but that Clara did appear to be all right, while Johnny kept hearing the deep growling voice of the Krun Queen, as though he couldn't shut out her horrific memory. Johnny kept assuring the android that he was fine, saying he didn't mind the wait and was just glad his sister would be OK. He knew how close to death he'd come and, yet again, Clara had been the one to save him. He also sensed a little of what it had cost her to create the fold, remembering just how much the image in the thought chamber had terrified her.

The Plican hadn't folded them straight home. In their present state, neither Johnny nor Clara was able to go into the gel pods, but that wasn't the main reason. While they'd been underneath the Martian pyramids Sol had detected a five-strong fleet leaving the Olympus Mons crater. She was now following the Krun Hunter–Killers from a discreet distance, hoping to discover their intended destination once the aliens neared Earth. If the Krun still had a base there, they had to find and destroy it once and for all. He thought about that jester's hat in the river of blood, and of the juggler being led away in Trafalgar Square. It was obvious now. The men in suits hadn't been plain-clothes police – they were Krun, disguised using DNA showers. There had been no news reports because there were no witnesses – the Krun had taken them too. He suspected they were even behind the tourists being removed from outside the Gherkin. All to be turned into food to nourish the Krun Queen so she could breed more of the vile aliens. If nobody stopped them, there'd soon be enough Krun to take over Earth.

Finally Alf returned to the shuttle bay and, with great difficulty and repeatedly bashing Johnny's helmet against the roof and sides of the *Bakerloo*, extracted him and carried his rigid body into the lifts and up to sickbay. Clara waited until the android had degunked enough of the helmet for Johnny to see out of. She looked even paler than usual, her forehead glistening with perspiration and her eyes thick with the oily blackness. She rubbed her arms to restore the circulation and smiled sadly at Johnny, before waving goodbye, saying she was going to the garden deck. Johnny was unable to wave back.

Alf was finding it awkward to remove the cocoon – it had solidified with one leg and one arm forward, so Johnny's body wouldn't lie flat. Happily Sol intervened, creating an antigravity harness which the android fastened around Johnny's middle to hold him floating above the bed. It made it far easier for Alf to cut off the Krun skin at a molecular level, using a specially adapted nanoscale scalpel. The android sliced the very last piece away from underneath Johnny's chin, just as the Krun ships were reaching high Earth orbit. Finally Johnny could remove the helmet and extricate himself from the spacesuit. Alf told him that enzymes within the Queen's saliva were designed to begin the digestion process long before anything reached the stomach and the suit had saved his life.

He ached all over, with a terrible stiffness in every muscle he knew and plenty he didn't – it was far worse than after any football match, but there was nothing to be done about it now. Slowly and awkwardly he made his way along the corridor, up the lift and onto the bridge.

'Hello, Johnny,' said Sol, the words coming from everywhere as lights blinked on her voice screen.

'Nice of you to join us,' said Kovac, who was hovering nearby.

'Hi, Sol,' said Johnny, walking stiffly towards the captain's chair at the centre. 'Progress report – have you got a fix on the Krun base?'

'Negative, Johnny,' replied the ship. 'The Krun fleet is dispersing to five separate projected destinations.'

Five bases – it was worse than Johnny had feared. 'Whereabouts?' he asked.

'One near the South Pole, one in the Mediterranean and three in the western hemisphere, latitudes 38.04738219 south, 12.35813 west . . .'

'Stop, Sol,' said Johnny. 'Give me names . . . countries.'

'Antarctica is the only relevant landmass. I believe the Krun Hunter–Killers are subaquatic – the remaining four flight paths are anticipated to finish within the Earth's oceans. The fleet has now separated.'

'Follow the closest,' said Johnny. 'Whichever's easiest.'

'I am capable of shadowing any Krun vessel with ease,' the ship replied.

'Sorry, Sol – I meant just pick one.'

'No offence taken, Johnny,' said the ship. 'We are now on a heading for the region of the Atlantic Ocean known as the Bermuda Rise.'

The *Spirit of London* burst through a thick layer of cloud. Far below, the needled black cylinder that marked one of the Krun vessels was only just above the ocean waves.

'Will you be OK underwater?' Johnny asked the ship.

'It is simply another fluid, albeit slightly denser than the atmosphere I am currently travelling through, and containing more obstacles. I do not anticipate any propulsion problems – however, I will not be able to remain shielded.'

'Had anyone asked me,' said Kovac, 'though evidently that would be far too much to expect, the more obvious choice would have been the Mediterranean. Projected splashdown is close to the signal from Louise's wristcom.'

'Obvious, but less efficient,' Sol replied, noticeably colder than usual. 'My selection affords the opportunity to monitor the three Atlantic splashdown sites. I have messaged Louise informing her of the incoming Krun vessel. With her help, we may identify four out of five.'

Johnny couldn't help thinking there was something to what Kovac had said. Louise was resourceful, but there wasn't much she could do if a Krun HK landed nearby and he had to admit he was worried. He'd hate her to be captured and processed into the Queen's next meal. But there could be no going back now. They were approaching the water frighteningly quickly. Johnny couldn't help it – he grabbed the arms of his chair and braced for impact but, as they broke the surface and continued below, there wasn't the slightest sensation. Somewhere in Johnny's head he sensed the ship's disappointment in his lack of faith in her.

'Sorry, Sol,' he mumbled out loud, before snapping back to the matter at hand. 'Distance to the Krun ship?' he asked.

'Computing . . . 7.0710608 kilometres, approximately,' Sol replied. 'I have detected another vessel in pursuit.'

'Another spaceship?' Johnny asked. 'Can you identify?'

'I believe it is a submarine of Earth origin,' said the ship, 'although some of the technology is extremely advanced.'

'On screen,' said Johnny.

He hadn't been sure what to expect, but was stunned by the image that appeared – like a giant stingray with a beautifully streamlined, wide thin body and capable of keeping pace with the Krun spaceship just a little further beyond. He was gobsmacked. 'No way is that from Earth,' he said.

'The submarine carries no governmental insignia and is running near silent,' Sol replied. 'However, I have analysed all audio communication and determined the commanding officer. She is speaking English.'

'Can I listen?' he asked.

'It is possible to generate a live feed,' Sol replied. 'Relaying... *I'll show them whose jurisdiction it is now. Prepare the depth charges.*'

Johnny choked. He'd recognize that voice anywhere. It was Colonel Hartman.

'Are you all right, Johnny?' the ship asked, turning off the feed.

'Fine . . . thanks . . . I think,' said Johnny, coughing.

'The Krun ship is charging weapons,' said Sol. 'Should I intervene?'

'Er . . .' It was an impossible choice and with no time to decide. Step in and they'd be forced to give themselves away, losing what could be their one chance to follow the Krun. Do nothing and a crew of humans, even if it was the Corporation's people, would almost certainly die. 'No,' said Johnny. The Krun ship fired and the giant artificial ray was lit up by an eerie green halo. 'Yes!' shouted Johnny, instantly changing his mind. He couldn't let this happen. The next moment it was as though a solid wall of water had been shot from the *Spirit of London*, slamming into the black vessel, disabling its weapons.

The Corporation's submarine had survived the Krun attack and, from out of its sides, came a spread of a dozen twinkling balls – in the gloom it was hard to tell what they were. Then flashes of light in quick succession flared around the black Krun cylinder. Cracks began appearing along the needled ship's hull. Johnny couldn't believe Colonel Hartman's sub could cause so much damage – maybe it was a delayed reaction from his own firing? The tail of the black ship broke away, filling the water with a cloud of green specks that seemed to move as one.

'What is that?' asked Johnny. 'Magnify those green bits.'

The viewscreen homed in on a school of familiar-looking half-human, half-alien amphibians, kicking out with their webbed feet and swimming in formation away into the ocean depths.

Nearer at hand there was a blinding flash, then another and another, the last one so close it felt like it was right on the bridge. Johnny felt an incredible force pressing him back in his chair and making it impossible to breathe. The *Spirit of London* shuddered and then she nosedived.

'Sol!' Johnny shouted. 'Are you OK? What happened?'

The ship's voice was far slower and deeper than normal. 'Hyperspatial gravimetric charges,' she said. 'I have lost propulsion.'

'I don't believe it,' said Kovac. 'Finally I'm given the ability to move and I'm going to die before there's any chance to use it.'

'Shut up – nobody's going to die,' snapped Johnny. 'Sol – fold us out of here – into orbit.' If the dark energy drive wasn't working there were many places Johnny would rather be while repairing it than at the bottom of the ocean.

'It's all very well you saying that,' said Kovac, 'but I estimate the probability of everyone on board dying as 98.947%.'

The *Spirit of London* was heading directly into an undersea

85

cliff face, seemingly powerless to change direction. Johnny gripped the arms of his chair. There was a horrible crunch that reverberated all down the spine of the ship, before she rebounded off the rock wall, spiralling down into what must be some sort of trench. Outside the water was quickly becoming black as night.

'Unable . . . to . . . fold,' said Sol, extremely slowly. 'Plican incapacitated . . . by . . . hyperspatial . . . charges . . . Shutting . . . down.'

Johnny spun round in his chair to see the central tank. The ship was right – the strange creature's body was even more scrunched up than normal and parts of it had become transparent.'

'Master Johnny – thank goodness,' said Alf, crawling out of the lift shaft. 'Whatever is going on?'

'Everything's offline,' Johnny shouted. 'Sol's hurt – the Plican too. Have you seen Clara and Bentley?'

'No . . . and we are taking on water.'

'What?' Johnny couldn't believe it.

'Considering there must have been a hull breach, might I suggest emergency bulkheads?' said Kovac. 'My probability for survival requires following an optimal strategy.'

'No,' shouted Johnny. 'Not till we know where the others are. We're not cutting them off.' A trickle of water ran out of the lift shaft and across the bridge. Johnny exchanged a nervous glance with Alf. They both knew the quantum computer had a point, but neither was prepared to take that most drastic of steps.

Alf spoke first. 'Now might be an appropriate time to tell you I cannot swim.'

Johnny grimaced and raised his wristcom to his mouth. 'Clara – can you hear me? Are you OK?' There was no reply. It couldn't get any worse. He went over to the lift shaft and peered inside. The water level was hard to gauge as there was a swell moving up and down the centre of the ship, but it looked well over halfway and rising, even as he watched. He knew there must be air pockets still scattered throughout the *Spirit of London* – he had to hope. 'I'm going in,' he said to Alf. If only he'd still been wearing his spacesuit there'd have been a far better chance of reaching Clara. Johnny was a rubbish swimmer and wasn't sure how long he'd be able to hold his breath, but it was the only option left to him. 'If the water level reaches deck 40, put the bulkheads across. Save yourself and Sol and try to stop the Krun – that's an order.'

'You're not leaving me up here with this dozy tin can of a ship and her dithering mechanoid sidekick, are you?' said Kovac.

Johnny wanted to throw something at the computer. 'Kovac, I'd love to take you with me, but . . .' A thought struck him. 'Kovac – I'd love to take you. You're coming with me. Water's just another fluid – you must be able to fly through that too.'

'Salt water might corrode my casing.'

'Then we'll build you another one,' screamed Johnny, exasperated. 'Alf – take off your jacket. I need your braces. We can make a harness.' He would have Kovac pull him through the water like a miniature submersible.

'A harness? Like a common mule,' said Kovac.

'Exactly,' Johnny replied.

✩ ✩ ✩

Every second counted. The braces weren't as secure as he'd have liked, but they would have to do. Johnny had taken off his boots and was standing, beside the hovering Kovac, holding onto a pair of makeshift reins while peering into the gloomy depths. Alf was looking anxiously at him from across the shaft. If Johnny didn't jump soon, he knew he'd lose all courage.

'On three,' he said to the computer. 'We'll jump together and then you can pull me to deck 18.'

'I fully expect to regret this course of action,' said Kovac, his casing lighting up the gloomy bridge as he spoke.

'One . . .' said Johnny. The water was already around deck 34 and coming up very quickly. 'Two . . .' He took a very, very deep breath and wrapped the ends of the braces round his wrists. 'Three.'

Johnny jumped, pulling Kovac down with him. He hit the water, feet together, and carried on under. Never had he felt such cold. His whole body screamed – any air in his lungs must have frozen. It was like having a million shards of ice jabbing into his forehead. He pivoted as though in zero G, somersaulting to face down the shaft, but there was no blood reaching his legs to drive the muscles to kick out. He hung hopelessly in the dark salty water, miles below the surface of the ocean, tucking his knees into his chest as he desperately tried to warm himself.

The harness jerked. He clung on for all he was worth as a survival instinct kicked in – to let go meant certain death. Kovac plunged into the depths pulling Johnny behind. Once, what seemed a lifetime ago in Atlantis, Johnny had been pulled through an underwater tunnel by a dolphin. Then at least the water had been warm. With his whole body numb, even if he found Clara and Bentley, he wasn't sure he'd be any use.

Down further they went – he couldn't hold his breath much longer. Kovac must surely have missed the turn. He considered simply opening his mouth and welcoming the ocean inside. It would be quick and the pain would stop. Then he pictured another mouth – the Krun Queen's – opening before him. He could still hear her voice in his head. He thought of Clara and how, despite the cost, she'd folded him away to safety. No way was he going to abandon his sister.

Deeper still . . . he could see lights in the darkness as the water pressure squeezed his eyeballs. The reins yanked sideways. Johnny's fingers slid to the very end, but he held on . . . just. He let a little air out of his lungs, or else they would burst, and saw it rise in the direction Kovac was pulling him. They were going upward. He broke the surface. There was an air pocket. He gulped it down, filling his lungs hungrily.

His head above the surface, Johnny's teeth began to chatter uncontrollably, but there was another noise too – the sound of Bentley barking.

'K-K-Kovac,' said Johnny, 't-t-talk to me.'

'Haven't I done enough already without engaging in mindless conversation?' asked the computer. As he spoke, the light from his casing illuminated the garden deck. Almost everything was submerged except the very tops of a couple of trees. It was from one of these that the Old English sheepdog was barking.

'B-B-Bents,' shouted Johnny. 'Here, b-b-boy. K-K-Kovac – k-k-keep t-t-talking.'

'And what, exactly, do you want me to say? Perhaps you would like to question my solution to the Riemann Hypothesis?'

The grey and white dog had seen them. He leapt into the water and paddled for all he was worth, holding a large bundle in his mouth.

'Or it may be that you have a more succinct formulation of my unified field theory?'

Now Bentley was closer, it was clear the 'bundle' was wearing clothes.

'I suppose there is my quite brilliant, if controversial, analysis of the many-worlds hypothesis.'

The Old English sheepdog paddled into the pool of light cast by Kovac, holding Clara by the scruff of her neck. Her eyes were closed. Her body had a blue tinge and felt even colder than his own.

'G-G-Good b-b-boy, g-g-good b-b-boy,' said Johnny as he forced his unresponsive limbs and numb fingers to strap his sister's limp body into the harness. Kovac was still prattling on so at least there was light. Even if Clara was dead, Johnny couldn't leave her sodden, saturated body down here, all alone in the dark, but he had to hope against hope.

Bentley's head sank beneath the water's surface. Johnny's arm darted under and hauled the exhausted sheepdog up by his matted fur. Then Johnny took a trailing end of one of Alf's braces and tied it around the dog's collar, hoping it would be enough.

K-K-K-Kovac,' he said, 't-t-t-take them t-t-t-to the b-b-b-bridge. Then c-c-c-come b-b-b-back.'

He wasn't at all sure the quantum computer had heard the last bit. The lighted casing was already vanishing under the water and soon went out. It was freezing. Johnny kicked his legs to tread water and keep afloat, but his toes and calves were cramping up. Clara's body had looked so cold, worse even than Nicky's, seen through the thought chamber. Bram had said that death was not the end, and Johnny's mum and dad had 'gone beyond', whatever that meant. If he closed his eyes and stopped fighting, maybe he'd join them.

His head banged against the roof of the deck. In the dark he hadn't seen how fast the water was rising. He felt around, found a nearby strut and wrapped his arms around it. There was very little room – soon the air would be gone.

A mighty clang rang out along the *Spirit of London*'s hull as the great ship shook and lurched, continuing its fall down into the trench. Briefly, Johnny found himself dangling in mid-air as the water receded – they were going to be saved. Then it washed over him, all the way to the roof, down his throat and filling his lungs. The wave subsided. There was air again – just. Johnny retched with what little energy he had left, spitting out salt water.

Another bang . . . and another and some scraping, as though the poor ship was bashing rock after rock on her way down. There was a voice. Perhaps his family was calling to him from beyond. He tried to make out the words, but his frozen brain was so slow.

'Clara . . . Johnny . . . coming.' The ship lurched again as she plummeted ever deeper, the water even blacker and colder. Again Johnny was hanging, but this time the swell still came up to his knees. Below the surface his feet were so cold that for all he knew they'd fallen off. This time he was prepared as the wave roared back, closing his mouth to the icy wash. It subsided a little, but remained above chin-level. With all the strength he had he lifted his body higher, keeping his mouth above the water line. There was a light – tiny, but glowing softly, coming from his arm. His brain tried to make sense of it. The luminous dial – his wristcom. Someone had been speaking in his ear. Perhaps Clara was still alive. The gears whirred faster in Johnny's brain.

'I cannot stabilize the ship,' came Alf's voice. 'If only Master Johnny were here.'

'I-I-I-I am h-h-h-here,' he tried to shout. He lowered his mouth as close to his wrist as possible, taking it right down to the water line. 'Where's C-C-C-Clara?' he stammered.

'Johnny!' came his sister's squeal. The wristcom was under water. He couldn't lift it to respond.

'Master Johnny – Kovac must be close to your position,' said Alf. 'Hold on.'

The computer had heard him and was coming back. The *Spirit of London* shook again, but then everything went silent, as though she was away from the canyon wall, still falling – falling forever. There was a light coming closer, as if he was reaching the end of a long tunnel. He'd read that this was what you saw when you were about to die. The water came over his mouth and up to his nostrils. The light was brightening. He didn't want it to be the end – not when he'd heard Clara's voice. Again he lifted himself, pressing his lips against the very ceiling of the deck for one final lungful of air.

'There you are,' said Kovac, bobbing up beside him.

In the computer's glow Johnny saw his own skin was blue with cold.

'Hold on,' said Kovac. 'Let's hope I can find my way back. Of course I expect I will, although any lesser machine . . .'

Johnny's fingers had locked rigid around the roof strut. He stared hopelessly at them. He tried to bite at them, even gnaw them off – it was as if they belonged to someone else. He willed them to move and roared with rage. He wanted to live – he wanted to see his sister again. Finally, slowly, agonizingly painfully, his muscles responded. Johnny twisted a piece of Alf's trailing braces around his wrists.

'Don't let go,' were the quantum computer's final words as it yanked him into the depths.

There was no left or right, up or down. He just held on and went where he was dragged, his lungs all but exhausted of air. Once more, in the distance, he saw a light, shining at the end of a long corridor, only this time it was different. This time it told him there was power on the bridge. Kovac was pulling him to safety. Whatever he did, he mustn't let go. He gripped his makeshift reins as tightly as he could, but even as the bridge loomed large, they fell slack. Something had gone wrong – the harness had slipped off Kovac. He'd come so very close. Johnny tried to kick with his legs, to propel himself the final few metres up the lift shaft, but it was no use. His momentum slowed and then he stopped, hovering agonizingly close to the surface. Then he was sinking, falling away into oblivion.

Something was pushing into the small of his back, bashing the last of the air from his body, sending little bubbles floating past his face. It seemed too soon to have reached the foot of the ship. Then he was moving upward again – being forced through the water. Lights swam before his eyes – he couldn't hold out another millisecond. They broke the surface, Johnny first, then Kovac, shunting him on and into the air, out of the shaft and onto the floor of the bridge. He tried to breathe but his lungs were full of water. Warmth surrounded and engulfed him. A long tongue slopped over his face and he closed his eyes. He felt burning – even his insides were on fire as a hot fluid poured down his throat.

✿ ✿ ✿
✿ ✿

'*Live ones . . .*'

It was so very cold. Johnny tried to curl up into a tight little ball for warmth, but his body was unable to bend. He wondered if somehow none of it had been real – that he remained deep inside the Krun Queen's belly, his chattering teeth the effect of some slow-working poison, freezing his veins and sending him mad. He couldn't see properly, but could still hear her voice. It was so very cold.

✿ ✿ ✿
✿ ✿

Apart from opening his eyes, he still couldn't move. Slowly Johnny was able to focus on the ceiling, not very far above him. Everything looked orange. His eyes might have been damaged after so long in the water. Something about this place felt familiar and reassuring. Now a thick orange glove was in front of his face. He wanted it out of the way and it dropped to his side. Finally Johnny twigged – it was his own hand. He was in a gel pod.

'Sol?' he asked.

'Master Johnny – excellent. You are awake. How do you feel?' Alf, not the ship, had responded.

'Orange,' Johnny replied. 'What happened? Where are we?'

'We are, at least I hope, on the seabed. I do not think I could take another fall down the trench. Kovac has calculated our position as 8724.209 metres below the surface. You may have noticed I placed you in a gel pod. It seemed a wise precaution – the same applied to Bentley and Miss Clara.'

'But they're OK?' Johnny asked.

'You all appear to be making full recoveries,' said the android, 'your sister especially so. I have concluded that being exposed to such sudden, extreme cold, your bodies shut down and have, effectively, rebooted.'

'What about Sol?' Johnny asked.

'It sounds as though you are ready to see for yourself,' Alf replied. 'The emergency bulkheads are holding, but Sol herself is . . . not herself. I hope you will be able to help her. I shall drain the pod manually.'

The orange goo oozed from the chamber, but there was no familiar trunk to hoover the remains off Johnny. Covered in orange gunk and still lightly inflated, he stood up, opened the door and stepped onto the bridge. The ship's clear walls showed the view outside – black as space, only without the stars. It was terrible to think of all those kilometres of water pressing down on them.

'Aha – come to thank your heroic saviour, have you?' said Kovac. The computer's casing was pitted and marked, but glowed with pride as he spoke.

'Thanks,' said Johnny. He sat down in his chair and began checking which systems were still working. There weren't many, but at least, if the gyroscopes were to be believed, the *Spirit of London* had settled vertically upright on the ocean floor.

'Is that all?' asked Kovac. 'I risk everything to go into that water not once, not twice, but three times to save your skins, and all you can say is, "Thanks"?'

Johnny couldn't help smiling. 'Kovac,' he said, 'you were absolutely incredible. Without you, we'd be dead. Thank you.'

'Yes, I was incredible, wasn't I? You know, I rather surprised myself and that's no easy task. When I pushed you up—'

'Kovac,' said Johnny again, 'what would be even more incredible would be for you to think of how we might get out of here . . . quietly.'

'Sadly,' said Alf, 'the Plican does look in rather a bad way.'

Johnny spun round to examine the tank. He could see straight through half the creature's body. He knew very little about the being that propelled his ship through space, but was sure that becoming part transparent couldn't be a good thing. 'We need Clara,' he said simply.

Alf was standing beside the chair, holding his bowler hat which he was twiddling round and round very quickly between his fingers. 'I really do not think it is a good idea to ask your sister to fold us out of here,' said the android, looking at the floor rather than directly at Johnny. 'Clara has only just recovered – such an act could bring about a relapse.'

'Relax, Alf,' said Johnny. 'Clara's not going to be doing any folding, but she can help make the Plican better. I'm sure of it.'

'Let us hope so,' the android replied. 'If that is the case, I shall begin draining her chamber.'

Johnny's checks showed that most of the ship's systems were in emergency hibernation mode. Life support was functioning, which was reassuring, and there was background power in some areas. It was as if Colonel Hartman's charges had knocked Sol out and she needed some sort of stimulus to awake. It had to have been a very lucky shot from the Corporation's submarine, but even so it was a little frightening. He remembered a few months ago, when the Regent's forces had threatened to stop the *Spirit of London* leaving Melania, they'd released hyperspatial gravimetric charges as a warning. It was obvious where the Colonel had acquired them and her other alien technology – presumably as payment for testifying against Johnny at his trial.

One of the gel pods opened and out onto the bridge, blinking and rubbing the remaining orange goo out of her eyes, stepped Clara. Once it had gone, they looked reassuringly back to their normal pale blue with silver flecks. She smiled and said, 'Hi, everyone.' Then she caught sight of the cylindrical tank, and added, 'Oh, the poor Plican,' and rushed over.

'Is there anything you can do?' Johnny asked.

His sister had placed her hands on the tank and was studying the strange, multidimensional creature. 'I think so,' she said. 'It's a matter of coaxing it back into our space, but I'll have to be gentle. It could take a while.' She looked around the bridge and into the blackness outside. 'Are we OK down here?' she asked.

'Miss Clara, take as much time as you need,' said Alf. 'We have life support and emergency power. I daresay Kovac will be more than happy to visit the galley and furnish you with rations as necessary.'

'You do, do you?' said the quantum computer in the corner.

Alf went on, 'We are perfectly safe.'

'Then what's that?' asked Johnny, pointing between his sister and the android to beyond the hull, where the biggest eye he'd ever seen was staring back at him. It blinked and disappeared.

'What's what?' Clara asked, turning to where he'd pointed.

'It was out there,' said Johnny. 'Something was watching us.'

'Master Johnny – are you certain you have fully recovered from your ordeal. No one would think any less of . . .' Alf stopped talking as something scraped along the ship's hull.

Everyone held their breath.

'There!' shouted Clara, pointing behind Johnny. He spun round but there was nothing.

'Oh my goodness,' said Alf, staring transfixed in another direction again.

This time everyone saw the eye staring back.

'There's another,' said Clara.

Johnny looked to his side and spotted a slightly smaller, milkier eye just beyond the windows of the bridge. Then, as all three of them watched in horror, more gigantic eyes emerged from the gloom, along with the faintest outlines of massive, writhing bodies.

'What are they?' Clara whispered.

As if to answer her question, something long and thick slid across the ship's hull – a gigantic tentacle with suckers bigger than dinner plates. Another joined it, and another, planting themselves very firmly on the outside of the ship.

'Giant squid,' Johnny whispered, though he'd never heard of any *this* big. The bridge began to sway, as the massive animals bashed the ship, sending her one way then the other.

'This is not good,' said Alf.

They lurched alarmingly as if the *Spirit of London* herself were about to topple over, but then she was pulled upright again.

'They're playing with us,' said Johnny. 'Like a cat that's caught a mouse and knows it can't get away.'

'One is inside the ship,' shouted Alf, staring at a console. 'What do we do?'

'The bulkheads will keep it out of here,' said Johnny hopefully. 'Clara – the Plican.'

Clara tore herself away from the scene outside and got to work, but then the ship tilted again. They were rocked first one way and then the other, back and forth, each time going further and further. With no artificial gravity, Alf was the only one who could stay on his feet, standing at what looked a very unlikely angle. Johnny was clinging to the Plican's tank, but Clara was sliding from one side of the bridge to the other.

'Alf,' Johnny shouted, 'put Clara in the chair.'

The next time Clara slid by, the android caught her and heaved her into the captain's chair at the centre of the bridge. Quickly she strapped herself in. This time, though, the *Spirit of London* teetered, balancing along her bottom edge one hundred and eighty metres below, but didn't return to her centre. She had passed the point of no return. There was a deathly groan from within as the stresses on the spaceship grew and, very slowly at first, she began to topple.

Not even Alf could stand up through this – he and Johnny were flung towards the far wall while poor Clara was left hanging. They reached the near horizontal. Johnny was sure he was done for and braced for impact but, in the nick of time, air bags inflated from the inner walls. There was an almighty bang as spaceship struck seabed. Johnny bounced and then settled again. Water ran out of the lift shaft and sloshed over him. Thankfully there wasn't much – it appeared the bulkheads were still sound. Johnny breathed a sigh of relief.

Far above him, dangling from the chair, Clara said, 'Will somebody *please* get me out of here?'

Alf was already on his feet. Kovac hovered partway up, oblivious to everyone's discomfort. Then another giant eye appeared outside the hull. Next moment, the suckers had returned and, due to their efforts, the ship began to roll across the ocean floor.

'I . . . don't . . . like . . . this,' said Clara spinning in the chair at the centre of the bridge.

Johnny knew what she meant. He felt like a hamster inside one of those clear plastic balls being rolled across a very bumpy carpet.

He knew it was down to him to act. Johnny forced his arms into the gaps between the cushions to reach through to the inner hull. Just outside was another of the massive inhuman eyes, staring in. The ship rolled backwards, but he didn't let go. He thought about all the atoms there must be between his hands and didn't even have to close his eyes to picture the electrons they contained. He started them moving, while staring at the giant squid just a few metres away as the electricity flowed backwards and forwards between his fingers. The current started small, but doubled in size every time it bounced from one hand to another. For a second the ship stopped rolling and settled. Johnny let the sparks fly. Outside, through the airbags, the ocean was lit up, as if by one lightning strike after another and another. Unexpectedly, in the midst of it all, Johnny saw ruined buildings dotted around the sea floor, ancient and majestic. He also saw more giant squid than he would have believed possible, but none could stay clinging to the hull.

'Ouch,' said a female voice. 'What have I missed?' It was Sol. The main lights came back on and gravity and the bridge's orientation were deftly restored, with Clara now sitting calmly at the very centre of the deck and Johnny sprawled on the floor at her feet.

'That's much better,' said Johnny's sister. He looked beyond her and saw the Plican had become substantial again – as healthy as ever.

'Is everybody all right?' asked Sol. 'Rather a lot appears to have been going on.'

'We're fine if you are,' Johnny replied. 'Please can we fold . . . now.'

A tentacle again slid along the outside of the hull – the squid were returning and Sol didn't need telling twice. A blue light pulsed at the top of the Plican's tank and the creature fell through into the main compartment, unfurling eight tentacles of its own. The rocky wall of an ocean trench came rushing towards and then through Johnny. He was pulled another way, and crossed a barrier between water and air. Then came a jerk upward at great speed into the blackness of space. Finally it was ninety degrees in another direction again. The *Spirit of London*'s hull flew through him and settled into its right place.

The Moon hung bold and bright nearby, dominating the view. Johnny's stomach, though, felt as if it was still on the ocean floor. The horrible thought of all the salt water he'd swallowed over the last few hours returned to him – he simply couldn't help it and was sick all over the deck.

6

The Lady Vanishes

'Are you OK?' asked Clara, walking across with a pitying look in her eyes, but careful to stop far enough away to keep her toes out of trouble.

Johnny nodded, but then was sick one more time.

Politely ignoring this, Clara added, 'Your eyes go all silver when you do that thing with electricity – just like Mum's.'

Johnny had never known – he'd seen it in his sister, but not in himself.

'The Plican folded before I was able to vent the water and additional debris,' said Sol. 'It did appear a good time to leave. If you have no objections, I would like to discharge the detritus.'

'Give me a minute,' said Johnny, getting to his feet and walking across to reboot Alf.

It turned out that, as well as containing around a quarter of a million cubic metres of seawater, there were several very long tentacles now lying at the foot of the ship. They must have been severed when the *Spirit of London* folded but, try as he might, Johnny struggled to feel much sympathy for their previous owners.

He decided it would be a terrible waste to simply send all that water out of an airlock, so they hovered above a crater near to the Moon's South Pole and released the unwanted cargo there. The Sun's rays never penetrated to the foot of the one he'd picked, meaning the water would freeze and stay frozen. There were other ice-filled reservoirs like this, clustered around the satellite's poles. One day, when humanity was ready to take that step further out, their water would be an invaluable resource for a lunar colony. They might even enjoy the deep-frozen squid and it would be funny hearing the scientists argue over where it could possibly have come from.

Although the *Spirit of London* was largely self-cleaning and despite Alf's best additional efforts, it would be a while before the combined smell of salt water and squid went or they became used to it. The garden would have to be completely regrown. The shuttles on deck 2 had been turned upside down and even the statue of the silver alien on deck zero had been washed all the way across from the bottom of the lifts to the main entrance. It took a gravity assist from Sol to return it to its original position.

They had to hope the Emperor's shield generators, somehow still in the *Piccadilly*, remained undamaged, and deposited them as instructed at the two stable points where the Earth's and Moon's gravitational fields cancelled out. All the ferrying around and cleaning up took time, but Johnny knew they couldn't put off forever the moment when a decision had to be made. The *Spirit of London* had only been able to stand in the heart of the City thanks to a complex simultaneous fold. At the exact instant the Plican brought the ship out of orbit, Clara (who always had to travel to Earth in advance by shuttlecraft) would send the original Gherkin building into the hyperspace niche she had built for it. Unless his sister began folding again, they would need to find a new place to land and some hitherto unthought-of way of having two identical and very distinctive 180-metre-tall skyscrapers at different places without anyone noticing.

☆ ☆ ☆
☆ ☆

Alf had called a meeting – he, Clara, Johnny and Bentley were in the strategy room on deck 14. 'I believe the time has come,' said the android, 'to look for a new, better-hidden base for the *Spirit of London* when on Earth. We must search for potential sites, or create a new one, as a matter of urgency.'

'I rather think there are other priorities,' said Clara. 'Like whether Louise is OK.'

'Alf has already requested I attempt to make contact,' said Sol.

'Good,' said Clara. 'So what's wrong with London anyway?'

'I believe,' said Alf, 'that with the renewed Krun activity it is important to be nearer to Johnny in Halader House.' Johnny was a hundred percent certain that the real reason was that Alf didn't want Clara to fold the Gherkin away into hyperspace.

'It takes two minutes to fly to Halader House,' said Clara. 'Surely, with all this "renewed Krun activity", it's more important than ever to be in London?'

'We also know,' said the android, not to be deflected, 'that the Krun have identified the *Spirit of London*'s regular location.' That was true, Johnny thought. When Nicky, in his guise of General Nymac, had cloned Johnny, it was to Stevens he'd turned to train up Johnny's double. One day, the clone had actually come aboard and pretended to be Johnny. 'Another reason,' Alf went on, 'why we need a new landing site – probably underground.'

'Look,' said Clara, 'I'm not stupid. I know you've all been talking about this behind my back. The real reason is that you don't want me to fold, but I'm better now. I've proved it. I folded us off Mars and nothing bad happened. That stuff in the thought chamber . . . it wasn't true. Don't you see I can keep folding? I'm cured.'

'Master Johnny – some help, please.'

Clara and Alf both turned to him, waiting for an answer.

Johnny took a deep breath. 'OK,' he said. 'Clara – you must remember how scared you were by the thought chamber? By the Klein fold.'

'But I'm better now.'

'Just because you folded once . . . it doesn't mean you're cured. Alf's right. We do need a new place for the ship.'

'Thank you, Master Johnny,' said the android.

'Typical,' said Clara. 'I knew you'd side with him. You never let me make my own decisions.' She crossed her arms and looked away.

'I'm not siding with anyone,' said Johnny. He hated the way his sister wouldn't even look at him. 'If you'd let me finish, I was going to say that Alf's right in the long run, but I can't think of any massive unexplored underground caves between London and Essex, so we'll have to build one. And we can't do that from up here.'

'Master Johnny,' said Alf, 'I hope you are not suggesting—'

'Alf,' said Johnny, cutting in. 'What choice do we have? We're not going to stop the Krun from up here, and Clara does seem OK.'

Now the android crossed his arms and looked away. Johnny felt terrible. He stroked the Old English sheepdog's fur underneath his collar and at least Bentley responded by rubbing a wet nose into his chest.

☆ ☆ ☆
☆ ☆

Alf had insisted on accompanying Clara in the *Bakerloo* and looking after her during the simultaneous fold. Of course, Clara was furious at the very thought, saying more than once, 'I'm not a little girl any more.' For Johnny, it was a relief to have them both off the ship. He was watching them now on the viewscreen, using the *Bakerloo*'s cameras. Clara was sitting on a little brick wall that bordered the plaza in which the Gherkin stood. Beyond her, the London skyline was reflected in the beautiful diamond-patterned windows while, at the foot of the building, workers were walking in and out underneath the massive entrance, made from a giant 'M' above a matching 'W'. Johnny liked to think it stood for 'Mackintosh' above the stars of Cassiopeia.

Clara turned towards the camera and said, 'Ready when you are.' Beside her Alf gritted his teeth and gave the agreed signal – raising his bowler hat.

'OK,' Johnny replied. 'Sol – count us down from three.'

Immediately the ship said, 'Three . . .' the gravity generators on the bridge were turned off and Johnny floated into the air. 'Two . . .' the Plican's tank glowed with a strange blue light. 'One . . .' The creature pushed itself out of its cramped compartment into the main cylinder. 'Now.'

Johnny couldn't keep watching the screen because it flew towards and through him and then away into the distance. He felt as if he was falling at incredible speed towards London. At the last moment he was jerked upward and the ship's hull snapped back into position around him. His stomach took a few seconds to catch up, but somehow he managed not to be sick.

Floating in the artificial zero G of the ship, Johnny stared again at the viewscreen. It was as though there were now two London Gherkins, superimposed but not quite in the right place – like the ghosting of a weak TV signal. Sol turned the gravity on and Johnny fell into his chair. When he looked again, the *Spirit of London*'s outline was razor sharp against a beautiful blue sky.

'Hello, Clara,' said Sol.

Johnny spun the chair round and nearly jumped. His sister had unfolded onto the bridge right beside the Plican's tank.

'I feel so much better,' she said, grinning from ear to ear.

A few seconds later, a disgruntled Alf stepped out of the lifts saying, 'Miss Clara – you must only fold when absolutely necessary.'

'Don't be such a bore, Alf,' she replied. 'It's quick, it's fun and I don't have to scare myself half to death by standing in that thing.'

'That thing is a very luxurious antigravity shaft,' the android replied.

'Enough – both of you,' yelled Johnny. 'We've got more important things to worry about, like stopping the Krun.'

'Yet you insist on ignoring one of the few pieces of evidence we have,' said Kovac, who lifted off the floor and floated across.

'What are you talking about?' asked Johnny.

'The enemy of my enemy is my friend,' replied the quantum computer. 'I have persistently informed you that somebody at Halader House is eavesdropping on both the Krun and the Corporation, yet you choose not to investigate.'

'Not this again,' said Johnny. 'There's nothing to investigate.'

'Are you quite certain, Master Johnny?' asked Alf. 'If Kovac believes it to be important . . .'

'Look,' said Johnny. 'There's no reason me even being at Halader House any more. Bram's gone and the Tolimi went with him – the Wormholes are pointless. It's much better for me to be here.'

'I don't know,' said Clara. 'I thought there was something funny about the place.'

'Now who's siding with everyone else?' said Johnny, exasperated. 'OK – first step, Halader House. Let's get it out of the way.'

'I have received an SMS,' said Sol. 'It's from Louise, requesting you go to Santorini.'

'Now that's a much better idea,' said Johnny. 'We can take the *Piccadilly*.'

'As Miss Clara did remind us,' said Alf, 'Halader House is only two minutes away by shuttle. Surely it is more efficient to go there first?'

Johnny threw his hands up in the air in despair and said, 'Sol – tell her we're coming. It'll just take a few minutes.'

✿ ✿ ✿
✿ ✿

Johnny had snuck into Halader House hoping not to be spotted, but glancing down the main corridor that looked near impossible. He stopped just in time to hear Miss Harutunian explaining to his school friends Dave and Ash that he wasn't around right now, but that she wanted to show them something down in the basement. He wondered what on Earth they were thinking of, returning to the scene of their crime, but then he saw Mr Davenport, the football coach, was standing the other side of the main doors checking his watch. Following suit, Johnny saw the date on his wristcom. He hadn't thought – it was the day of the big tournament.

Normally he loved football as much if not more than anything, but right now it was something he could do without. He was considering simply slipping away and out the back door, when the thought was cemented by the arrival of the next person to walk in through the main entrance. Tall and balding, with only a few hairs combed across his pale scalp and with round steel-framed spectacles, it was Dr Carrington. He shuffled in wearing a long mac and carrying a leather case. As Johnny crouched at the corner of the stairs, he heard the doctor greet the red-haired social worker who, very apologetically indeed, especially with the doctor having come all this way from Tunguska, explained again that Johnny was nowhere to be found.

It was definitely time to go. Johnny backed away, desperate to stay out of sight, when a voice behind him boomed,

'Sneaking out the way you came in are you, sonny? I don't think so.'

A thick hand was placed in the small of Johnny's back as Mr Wilkins pushed him forward into the open. He could feel the hairs of the cook's bushy beard tickling the back of his neck – it wasn't pleasant. He was guided towards the little gathering in front of the main doors.

'Look what the cat dragged in,' said the cook.

'Jonathan – good to see you, yes . . . very good,' said Dr Carrington as Johnny was pushed centre stage. 'Miss Harutunian here told me you'd gone missing. I was worried. Missing . . . yes.'

'Er . . . hi,' said Johnny, desperately wishing he was anywhere else. The only reason Dr Carrington could have for coming here was to perform tests on Johnny, which were very unlikely to be pleasant. Right now, a few football matches sounded a far better option. 'I'm sorry if you've come a long way, but I've got this really big football tournament I can't miss. I was just going to get my kit.'

'Johnny's our star player,' said Ash. Johnny wanted to kick him. He needed the doctor to think he was as ordinary as possible. Outside, Mr Davenport had caught sight of them all and was tapping his watch, urging them to hurry.

'How very interesting . . . indeed,' said Dr Carrington. 'A chance to witness your sporting prowess at first hand . . . first hand, yes. Why don't we go to the match, Miss Harutunian?' he asked.

'Well, Johnny,' said his social worker, a slight twinkle in her eye. 'You heard the good doctor – go and get your boots.'

Behind, Mr Wilkins growled with annoyance. Johnny turned and ran up the stairs, trying to put as much distance between him and the strange group in the hallway as possible. At the end of the corridor he climbed the spiral staircase, pulled down his trapdoor and flung himself onto the bed. He raised the wristcom to his mouth and began trying to explain what was happening.

'Master Johnny – we do not have time for this,' came Alf's voice in his ear. 'You are meant to be checking for a hidden surveillance network, not going out to play with your friends.'

'Alf – it's not like that. It isn't up to me,' said Johnny.

'I like watching Johnny's football,' he heard Clara say in the background. 'I think I'll go – I'll bring Bentley.'

Wonderful, thought Johnny. Everyone and their dog would be at the game. He collected his boots and the rest of his kit from the bottom of the wardrobe and jogged down the stairs to the others, following Ash and Dave into the minibus.

'That place you live in is seriously weird,' said Dave, as Johnny sat down beside him. 'They were telling us you weren't there.'

'I'd been grounded,' said Johnny, 'after we were caught in the basement.' He knew neither Dave nor Ash were likely to have forgotten their talking-to from Mrs Irvine. Besides, it was a better explanation than that he'd been saying goodbye to the Emperor of the Galaxy, visiting pyramids on Mars, narrowly escaped being eaten by a horrid alien bug, arrived home to be shot at by a futuristic submarine using alien technology and finally fought off an attack by giant squid.

'Even from school? Must have been really dull,' said Ashvin.

'Was,' Johnny replied.

'I was worried you'd gone missing like those other kids,' said Dave. Johnny didn't have the slightest idea what his friend was talking about, a fact that was clearly etched across his face. 'Of course, you won't know,' Dave went on. 'The whole tournament's been rejigged as some schools couldn't field a team. We're not playing Home Counties qualifiers any more – it's East of England. And if we win, it's straight through into the final.'

'These kids – what happened to them?' asked Johnny.

'Who cares?' said Ash.

'Listen up, you lot,' shouted Mr Davenport from the driver's seat. The coach began barking instructions as he drove the team north.

⁂ ⁂ ⁂

The tournament was taking place at Northampton Town's training complex, which was even less glamorous than it sounded. There were eight teams, divided into two mini-leagues of four. The league matches would each last half an hour, after which the winner of one group would play the runner-up of the other in hour-long semifinals. Johnny's Castle Dudbury Comprehensive team were representing Essex, having won the County Cup the previous year. Wearing white shirts and black shorts, they were first out of the changing rooms. Captain, Micky Elliot, and coach, Mr Davenport, led them on a warm-up jog towards the pitches, with a few stretching exercises along the way.

The sky was blue, but with clumps of white cloud racing each other across. As the wind howled over the exposed playing fields, Johnny huddled with his teammates between the two pitches being used for their half of the draw. It was hard to concentrate on what Mr Davenport was saying. Their first opponents, St Edwards from Suffolk, had arrived and were warming up on the very far touchline, in front of a row of poplar trees where little Miss Harutunian was deep in conversation with the towering Dr Carrington. Johnny wondered what they could possibly have to talk about that was so interesting, before realizing it was probably him.

Out from behind the trees came Clara, tugging at Bentley's lead. Not surprisingly, the sheepdog always struggled after folding. Johnny's sister walked to the edge of the far pitch, quite close to Miss Harutunian, and looked to be scouring the playing fields for Johnny. He daren't wave with Mr Davenport in full flow, telling them that this was what they'd trained so hard for. Failing to spot him, Clara turned to the couple by her side at the very instant that Dr Carrington glanced over the head of Miss Harutunian directly at her.

Each froze, staring at the other. Then, bold as brass, in full view of anyone who might be watching, Clara opened a fold and stepped through, dragging Bentley behind her. Dr Carrington jumped, clearly startled, and the social worker turned towards where he'd been looking, only to see nothing.

Throughout the time Clara had spent at the Proteus Institute for the Gifted, the Krun had employed Dr Carrington to monitor her for evidence of unusual abilities. The doctor claimed he'd done his utmost to protect her, not experimenting on her and preventing at all cost the types of procedure that had been carried out on Louise's friend Peter. Even so, Johnny could understand his sister loathing the very sight of this strange man who appeared to have a finger in every alien pie, but that didn't excuse Clara folding in plain sight. She shouldn't have folded at all. He began rehearsing the argument he knew he'd have to have about it, when he was plucked from his imaginary row by Mr Davenport saying, 'Johnny, are you with us?'

'What? . . . Sorry,' said Johnny.

'I was just saying,' the coach went on, 'that it's good to have our mascot here, but Bentley won't be much use if your mind's elsewhere . . . focus.'

Clara must have unfolded very nearby and was walking towards them, poor Bentley looking much the worse for wear. The Old English sheepdog barely acknowledged Johnny as he collapsed exhausted by the side of the pitch.

'What's *he* doing here?' demanded Clara as she reached Johnny.

'I don't know,' he hissed back, 'but you shouldn't have done that – not in front of everyone.'

'I'm not letting that man near me ever again,' she said, loud enough for most of the team to hear.

Johnny noticed a couple of black patches beginning to form in her eyes. 'Keep your voice down,' he hissed, 'and stop folding – it's not safe for you.'

'I'm fed up with you telling me what I can and can't do,' she said, not even whispering. 'You're just jealous.'

'OK, Castle Dudbury,' shouted Mr Davenport, 'we're on. Remember what we talked about – move the ball quickly, to feet.'

Johnny followed the coach and the rest of the team onto the pitch. When he turned round, Clara had vanished leaving Bentley alone by the touchline.

It was hard to concentrate on the match, which seemed to pass Johnny by, happening at a hundred miles an hour all around him. Even so, as half-time approached he managed to set up a goal for Dave with a lovely cross to the far post, picking his friend out in so much space that it would have been harder to miss. Dr Carrington shouted, 'Bravo, Jonathan . . . bravo,' from the touchline. There were only a couple of minutes for the turnaround, during which time Clara unfolded nearby. Miss Harutunian must have wandered off somewhere and, as soon as he saw Johnny's sister, Dr Carrington began striding across the pitch towards her. She vanished again, reappearing the next moment in the spot the doctor had vacated. He turned and retraced his steps whereupon she did exactly the same thing again. Clara looked to be finding it very funny.

The referee blew to restart the game and Johnny was forced to concentrate on his football. Quickly Castle Dudbury were on the back foot. Simon Bakewell in goal made two great saves and Johnny was hardly in the game at all. He couldn't bear that every time he even went near the ball, Dr Carrington shouted out – it was excruciating. For most of the remaining fifteen minutes it was all hands to the pumps as the Suffolk players surged forward with wave after wave of attacks. Johnny heard Mr Davenport shouting at the referee to blow his whistle just as skipper Micky Elliot slipped, missing an easy header and allowing the opposition striker a straight run on goal.

Johnny set off in pursuit, gaining with every stride, but there was so much ground to make up. The forward was nearing the Castle Dudbury penalty area, but Johnny was closing in. The red-shirted striker bore down into the box nearing the penalty spot, pulling back his leg to shoot – it was now or never. Feeling a fraction too far away, Johnny slid into the challenge, stretching his leg further than he thought it could possibly go. He reached the ball a millisecond ahead of the centre forward, nudging it away before the shot came in. Committed to the strike, the St Edwards player kicked Johnny's foot where the ball had just been and fell over in a heap. There was a shrill blast on the whistle. There should have been three – time had to be up by now. Then the truth dawned – a penalty had been awarded.

Johnny couldn't believe it and lay on the ground in a daze, his calf cramping from stretching too far. Mr Davenport was going berserk on the touchline. Things went from bad to worse as the Suffolk players surrounded the referee and demanded Johnny be sent off for denying a goal-scoring opportunity. As soon as he'd made the initial decision, the official had simply run to the far side of the goal near the touchline to be in position for the kick. Now, to break free from the ring of players around him, he escaped into the penalty area, came over to Johnny and brandished a red card.

Johnny had never so much as been booked before. He traipsed off the pitch towards where Clara was standing with Bentley.

As he looked over his shoulder, the penalty was converted and the whistle blew for full time. For his teammates, it was straight on to the next match, against Derby Grammar School, but Johnny wouldn't be able to play – his sending off meant he was suspended.

Johnny wanted to talk with his sister, but Miss Harutunian came round the side of the pitch, bent down to fuss Bentley and announced that, after the tournament, they would be having a meeting in Mrs Irvine's office. She said she was quite happy to give Johnny a lift home so the school minibus didn't have to go out of its way.

'I think I should really stay with the team,' was his lame reply.

The social worker looked at him, as if thinking about arguing the point, only to say, 'OK, but I'll be following right behind.' Then she turned to Johnny's sister and said, 'You must be Clara – I've heard so much about you.'

Clara shot Johnny a filthy glance, which was really unfair as he'd never once mentioned her to his social worker. Her eyes were turning noticeably blacker.

'I think it might be appropriate,' Miss Harutunian went on while rubbing Bentley's fur, 'if you came to the meeting too.'

'C'mon, Johnny – why aren't you watching the game?' Mr Davenport appeared beside them on the edge of the pitch. 'Cramp, is it?' he continued. Johnny nodded and the coach took hold of his foot and said, 'Push,' while bending back Johnny's toes. The muscles began to relax. 'Sorry, ladies,' said Mr Davenport as Clara scowled at Miss Harutunian, 'but I need this one for the last match. Come on, son.' Johnny was led away to where the game against Derby Grammar was taking place. As he walked he could feel his sister staring daggers at the back of his head.

Derby had beaten West Bridgford School from Notts in the

first round of games. Against Castle Dudbury they'd quickly gone two–nil up and were now playing on the break. Without Johnny in the midfield to link defence and attack, Castle Dudbury were mainly hoofing long balls from anywhere on the pitch in the vague direction of their forwards. Considering both Dave and his strike partner Joe Pennant were on the short side, though very nippy, it wasn't a very effective tactic and soon both their heads began to drop. It was well into the second half by now and, as the game wore on, it looked less and less likely that Castle Dudbury would ever score a goal. A couple of times they nearly went three behind.

Clara approached from close by. Judging from the way Bentley was teetering on his white paws, the sheepdog had only just unfolded again. 'You must be Clara – I've heard so much about you,' she said, doing a very good impression of Miss Harutunian. 'So what exactly have you been telling her?'

'Nothing,' Johnny replied, trying to look as innocent as he knew he was, but feeling himself beginning to blush.

'You expect me to believe that?' said Clara. 'Well, there's no way I'm going to that meeting with your Mrs Irvine.'

'Fine . . . great – I don't want to go either.'

'Fine,' said Clara.

The referee blew for the end of the match and the players trudged off the pitch towards them.

'Who's your friend, Johnny?' asked Joe Pennant, walking over.

'Oh, I'm Clara,' said Clara. 'I thought everyone knew that.' She turned and walked away, leaving Joe looking very puzzled.

It was straight on to the final group match. The school from Derbyshire had six points and had already qualified. West Bridgford School from Notts had three points having beaten St Edwards from Suffolk in the second game. Castle Dudbury had one point, the same as St Edwards, and their only chance to qualify for the semis was to beat the team from Notts.

	Played	W	D	L	GF	GA	Points
Derby Grammar School (Derbyshire)	2	2	0	0	4	1	6
West Bridgford School (Nottinghamshire)	2	1	0	1	3	3	3
St Edwards Church of England School (Suffolk)	2	0	1	1	2	3	1
Castle Dudbury Comprehensive (Essex)	2	0	1	1	1	3	1

'C'mon, Castle Dudbury,' shouted Mr Davenport. 'You're all warmed up now. Get at them right out of the blocks.' They did just that. Only a couple of minutes into the game, Ashvin, out on the right wing, played the ball low and hard into Johnny's feet on the edge of the Notts penalty area. Johnny shaped to control it, but at the last minute dummied and peeled away into the box, leaving his stripe-shirted marker flatfooted. The ball ran through to Dave, who laid it perfectly into Johnny's path. The Notts goalkeeper rushed off his line to narrow the angle and started to spread himself, diving too early. Johnny's first touch surprised the keeper, dinking the ball over the sprawling body with the outside of his left foot without even breaking his stride.

'Oh, bravo,' Dr Carrington shouted again.

Johnny looked for Clara, but couldn't see her anywhere around the pitch. Then, as he ran back towards the touchline for the restart, he heard her shouting, 'Good goal, Johnny.' She was bound to be making herself ill again with all this folding – he didn't understand her.

For the most part, the first half was comfortable and the referee had already checked his watch when Johnny slid into a crunching tackle near the centre circle and came away with the ball. Under pressure from three striped West Bridgford players, he had no option but to pass back to Naresh Choudhary, Micky's centre-half partner, who panicked and played a backpass without looking, teeing an opposition forward up perfectly: one–one and all their good work was undone. The rest of the team looked really heavy-legged. Having sat out the last game, Johnny knew he would have to take charge and drive them forward.

It wasn't easy. Boosted by the goal right before the interval, the team from Notts kicked off the second half full of belief. Johnny had to be everywhere, making tackle after tackle to break up the incessant attacks. Winning the ball for the umpteenth time, he played it straight out to Ashvin on the right wing and then sprinted as hard as he could to make the overlap. Johnny took the marker away, allowing Ash to cut inside and slip past another defender, who hauled him down by holding onto his shirt. It was a free kick right on the edge of the penalty box. Johnny ran over to collect the ball and placed it just in front of a divot, as the West Bridgford goalie organized his wall.

Without the five-a-side pitch on the *Spirit of London*, he hadn't practised properly for ages, but the offence was in an almost identical position to this time last year, when Johnny had scored direct from a free kick to win the Essex Schools Cup. He pictured that day in his mind, visualizing how he'd struck the ball. The referee checked his watch and ran into the penalty box, blowing for the kick to be taken.

Johnny took four steps backwards and looked at the corner of the goal where he would be aiming. Then he focused on the back of the football, running forward and striking it with his instep, trying to impart as much topspin and curl as he could manage. The ball cleared the wall. It looked as though it would keep rising and end up over the crossbar too, but at the very last second it dipped and bent, striking the top of the post and carrying on into the net. It was two–one, with less than five minutes to go.

Those minutes seemed to last forever. Gritty defending was the order of the day. Twice Micky threw his body in the way of powerful shots and Ashvin cleared off the line when a goal looked certain. With a minute left, the Notts winger swung yet another corner into the penalty area. Johnny shouted his name and ran to meet the ball to head clear. He jumped, but then choked as his collar tightened around his neck – the player he'd been marking had grabbed his shirt and was holding on for all he was worth. The ball sailed over Johnny's head and dropped to a striped forward, who controlled it first time before hammering it into the roof of the net. The referee blew his whistle for the goal and three more times to indicate it was all over – they'd failed to qualify. Most of the team sank to their knees. Seeing Clara leading Bentley towards the row of poplar trees by the edge of the playing fields, Johnny followed. He shouted after her and she turned to face him, eyes jet black and her forehead glistening with perspiration. Close up, her arm that was holding the dog's lead looked strangely transparent – like the Plican.

'Are you OK?' he asked. She was frightening him.

'I'm going home,' said Clara, 'and don't try to stop me.'

'Hold on a minute,' said Johnny. 'I'll come with you.' Clara was freaking him out. He looked over his shoulder for any sign of the doctor or Miss Harutunian.

'Go to your meeting,' she said. 'That's what you want, isn't it?'

'Of course not,' he was saying, but his sister had folded away, taking Bentley with her.

Johnny's wristcom was in the changing rooms. He ran towards the pavilion, overtaking his teammates who were trudging disconsolately away from the pitches.

'Unlucky, Johnny,' someone shouted after him. 'Shame you missed that header.'

Far more worried about his sister, he didn't bother replying. He reached the changing rooms first and strapped on the wristcom, but everyone else was coming in through the doors. Johnny ran outside for some privacy and tried to raise Alf.

'Have you found anything interesting out, Master Johnny?' asked the android.

'What? No – I've not been at Halader House.'

'It is very important we follow up every line of enquiry.'

'Alf, listen to me. There's nothing to follow up,' said Johnny. 'Is Clara there?' He could hear the android asking Sol for his sister's whereabouts.

'Miss Clara is on the garden deck. We appear to be experiencing some problems – I have to go now. Make sure you perform a thorough check of the children's home.'

'Alf,' Johnny shouted, but the android must have closed the link.

'Come on, Johnny,' said Mr Davenport, joining him outside and carrying a string bag full of footballs. 'Everyone else is changed. Best not to hang around – we're heading straight back.' Johnny nodded, ran in through the doors and quickly pulled on his clothes over his football kit.

☆ ☆ ☆
☆ ☆

It took well over an hour to make the drive home to Castle Dudbury. Johnny sat on the back row of the minibus and saw that Miss Harutunian was as good as her word, following behind all the way in a black Mini. The mood on the journey back was very subdued. There were a few comments that the last-minute goal they conceded had been Johnny's fault, but he just sat in silence worrying about Clara. Mr Davenport had already dropped half the team off when he turned into Barnard Way and came to a halt at some traffic lights.

'I'll get out here,' said Johnny, rushing to the front and sliding open the door before anyone could stop him. By the time someone had pushed it shut, Mr Davenport had missed the lights turning green and Johnny was halfway across the train station carpark. He jumped into the *Bakerloo* and thought, *30 St Mary Axe.* He used the camouflage mode that made it appear to anyone on the outside that the *Bakerloo* was an ordinary black taxi, with a cab driver in the front and a single passenger on the back seat.

As the shuttlecraft drove along Barnard Way, Johnny passed his social worker's black Mini going in the other direction, with Dr Carrington in the front passenger seat pointing furiously forward. Soon Johnny found a side street with neither traffic nor CCTV cameras, thought, *Shields on*, and saw the *Bakerloo* vanish around him. A fraction of a second later, he was invisible too, soaring into the sky and heading towards London.

☆ ☆ ☆
☆ ☆

It was the end of the working day and the streets of the capital were busy, meaning the last mile of Johnny's journey took ten times as long as all the rest put together. He'd tried calling everyone on the *Spirit of London* from his wristcom, but communications had been cut. He finally reached St Mary Axe, found somewhere to stop and leapt from the shuttle into the crowd of workers who were pouring out from underneath the giant 'M' and 'W'. Johnny used them as a shield, to avoid the glare of the blue-uniformed security guards and sneak through one of the four sets of revolving doors at the foot of the ship.

Something was badly wrong – the *Spirit of London* was full of people. 'Sol!' he shouted out. 'Are you OK? What's happening?' A few of the people, all in suits, stared at Johnny and the ship didn't respond. Had Alf been right about the danger of staying in this spot? It was as if the whole of deck zero was swarming with Krun. Johnny vaulted a barrier and made for the lifts beside the statue of the silver alien. A hand tried to haul him back, but he wriggled free and leapt inside the antigrav shaft, shouting, 'Bridge,' only to find himself sprawled on the floor of a proper elevator with several bemused faces looking down at him. The doors closed and one of them asked Johnny, 'What floor?'

He couldn't reply and instead simply stared upward, dazed and confused. The truth dawned that for the very first time in his life he was inside the London Gherkin – the original building. What had happened to his spaceship?

By the time the doors opened again he was on his feet, to be met by a burly security guard in round glasses who grabbed hold of Johnny's shirt and pulled him out of the lift.

'I have apprehended the intruder, over,' said the guard into a walkie-talkie.

'Good work, Colin,' said the voice on the other end.

'I am escorting the intruder along the tenth-floor corridor to the service elevator – no assistance required, over.'

'Very good, Colin,' the voice replied.

Gripping tightly onto the back of Johnny's shirt, Colin was pushing him forcibly along with Johnny in no mood to resist. They stopped and he was held against a wall while the guard pressed a lift-call button.

'There's an easy way or a hard way to do this,' said Colin. 'If you come quietly, we may not press charges.'

'Just get me out of here,' Johnny replied.

'Well, that sort of attitude's not going to help,' said Colin. 'You should have thought of that before you came breaking and entering.'

'It was a mistake,' said Johnny. The lift doors opened and he stepped straight inside.

'Let me see,' said the infuriating guard, enjoying Johnny's impatience to escape. 'I suppose you saw this gigantic building in the centre of London and thought it was where you live, did you?'

Johnny rolled his eyes.

Colin spoke into his walkie-talkie again. 'The intruder is proving difficult. Is another van expected tonight, over?'

'One on its way now, Colin,' said the voice at the other end.

'*Come to me, Johnny,*' said a deep, earthy voice inside his head. '*I need live ones.*'

Johnny couldn't believe it – there may not have been Krun in the Gherkin, but the guards were actively helping feed the Queen, and he couldn't stop hearing her voice.

Finally the guard entered the lift, allowing the doors to close. It took forever to reach the ground floor, but as soon as it did Johnny dropped his shoulder as if about to run one way and then sidestepped the guard to go the other. Within a flash Johnny was in the lobby – there was no way he was going to be put into one of those unmarked vans. He was through the revolving doors and out into the plaza even before Colin had turned and begun to give chase. Johnny forced his way between the bankers, crossed the little square and climbed into the *Bakerloo*. He gulped a few lungfuls of air and, from the safety of his shuttle, watched as half a dozen security guards fanned out from under the entrance in search of him. It was hard to believe the *Spirit of London* would have taken off without him, but it was the only possible explanation.

'Master Johnny, are you receiving me?' Alf's voice was coming through his hidden earpiece.

'Where are you?' Johnny asked, raising the wristcom to his mouth. 'I just got caught inside the real Gherkin.'

'And thank goodness you did,' said the android. 'Without your attempt to board the ship, we would have been sucked into a Klein fold. I believe Sol registering your entry pulled us back.'

'But I didn't enter,' said Johnny.

'It was enough,' said Alf. 'However, Miss Clara is experiencing profound difficulties – it is imperative you come aboard immediately.'

'You're really here . . . in London?'

'Indeed, Master Johnny. Please hurry – something terrible is happening to your sister.'

'I'm coming – I'm right outside,' said Johnny. He looked up. The guard Colin was standing at the entrance, scanning the crowd. If Johnny made another run for the ship and it proved to be the building again, he was Krun supper for sure, but there was nothing for it. The number of people leaving work had thinned out so he wouldn't be able to hide behind the crowd. Alf had sounded desperate – worse than Johnny had ever heard him. There was no time to lose.

Johnny opened the shuttle door and ran. More guards appeared at Colin's side, their arms spread wide ready to apprehend him. It would be impossible to find a way through. More than anything, Johnny had to pass beyond the wall of blue and, in his hour of need, a memory came to him pushing everything else from his mind.

He was on Titan, by the Fountain of Time, when the clone had been about to kill him. Johnny's double had the ability to fold space and was collapsing that portion of it between him and Johnny, readying his blaster to fire. At that moment, when death seemed certain and, for the first and only time, Johnny had been able to grab a corner of the very fabric of space that the clone had hold of and pull himself just a little further on, to safety.

Now he'd crossed the plaza and was about to enter the

welcoming arms of Colin the guard. Johnny closed his eyes and fought to remember how the folding had happened. He glimpsed space, as though he was no longer part of it – he was watching himself, the row of guards and the spaceship from some god-like vantage point that was quite separate, as though above a squashed flat version of the real world. It seemed to be working. He tried to switch his position with that of the blue line of security men. He opened his eyes just as his head smacked Colin full in the stomach, sending the winded guard sprawling. For a second, Johnny stayed where he was, half-dazed by the impact, aware he'd come close to folding. Several hands reached out to grab him, but he ducked underneath and ran again, leaving the guards trailing behind. He pushed through the revolving doors and knew at once he was inside the *Spirit of London*.

'Hello, Johnny,' said Sol, adding, 'Clara is on the garden deck – just,' without his even asking.

He didn't like the sound of that one bit. This time, when he ran into the lift shaft he hovered for a fraction of a second in mid-air and then shot upward without even stating his destination. He'd never known Sol to be in such a hurry. Johnny stopped and stepped onto newly laid turf. Bentley was howling – a terrible sound that Johnny would never have thought the sheepdog capable of making. Yet it was obvious why. Clara was hovering halfway between the floor and the ceiling with no visible support, her arms stretched wide apart, bolts of lightning flying randomly from her torso. While some parts of her arms and legs were transparent, others were marked out by the oily blackness that had spread from her eyes and was devouring her whole body. She was laughing and screaming in equal measure. Alf, in the antigrav harness, was trying and failing to come anywhere near her.

Johnny ran towards his sister, only to find himself back at

the entrance to the lift shaft. Clara cackled. He tried again –
he advanced twenty metres only to find himself where he had
started. She was folding him away from her.

'Clara!' he shouted. 'Come down – you've got to stop it.'
This time he tried walking towards her. The blackness had
engulfed his sister. Lightning bolts shot from her, striking him
in the chest. 'Clara . . . please,' he said, forcing himself onward,
through the pain. He wasn't about to let her go.

'I can't stop it, Johnny,' she said, sounding normal for a
moment. 'I can't ever stop it.' She looked down at him and
for a second her eyes cleared. 'Help me, Johnny,' she pleaded.
Then her whole body shrank into a black dot and vanished.

7

Return to Titan ✧✧

Despite wearing the antigravity harness, Alf dropped like a stone. Bentley howled a little longer, then was silent. Johnny screamed his sister's name, running towards the point where she had vanished. 'Sol, where's Clara?' he shouted.

'Clara is no longer aboard,' the ship replied.

He didn't want to hear it. Johnny fell to his knees and then face forward into the grass. His whole body was shaking. He felt a heavy hand on his shoulder and looked up. It was Alf. Johnny had never realized the android could cry. 'What happened?' he asked. 'Where did she go?'

For once the android was lost for words, but Johnny didn't need an answer to know what had become of his sister. He remembered the time on Titan when they'd peered together into the thought chamber and seen her falling forever within the nothingness of hyperspace. He recalled her terror, even then, and the fact that the Owlessan Monks had tried to stop her leaving – perhaps they, too, had felt the premonition. Her final words – 'Help me, Johnny' – were still ringing in his ears.

'Miss Clara . . . gone,' sobbed Alf. 'I cannot believe it.'

Johnny sat up beside the android. Bentley made his way over, lay on the grass and whimpered.

'We'll get her back,' said Johnny. 'It'll be all right.' He hoped that by speaking the words out loud, they might be more likely to come true.

Alf's teary eyes met his. 'It is not possible to escape a Klein fold,' said the android. 'It is a piece of hyperspace totally enclosing itself, detached from the cosmos. Only another being who is Owlein could reach inside and bring her out.'

'Owlein' was the word describing any creature, like a Plican, capable of folding space. Among the other inhabitants of the galaxy it was an exceedingly rare gift – the Monks were the only even vaguely humanoids Johnny knew of who had the ability.

'I promised the Emperor . . . I promised I would look after you both,' wailed Alf, 'and now Miss Clara is gone forever.'

'She can't be,' said Johnny. 'I won't let her be.'

'Master Johnny,' said the android, 'I wish with every positronic circuit I have that there was a way, but there is none.'

'Yes, there is,' Johnny replied. 'I'm Owlein too. I folded once before and I nearly did it again tonight. I'll learn.'

☆ ☆ ☆
☀ ☀

For the first time the television news had been full of the disappearances. The missing persons' list was the longest since records began and growing alarmingly. Johnny suspected that this told only a fraction of the real story. He was worried that Sol couldn't trace Louise, but had to hope she was lying low somewhere. He'd get there as soon as he could, but for now Santorini would have to wait.

Seeing the TV reports, Alf was keen to return to Mars and have the *Spirit of London* inflict as much damage as she could on the pyramid base. They might not survive, but cutting the Krun supply lines to stop more of the aliens being hatched could give Earth a fighting chance. It was the logical step. Johnny, though, could think only of Clara. Nothing else mattered and he knew he was the one person in the galaxy who might be able to save her. They were already flying towards Titan. He would gaze into the thought chamber. He would seek out the Owlessan Monks and learn from them if he could. Yes, it meant leaving Earth. It meant allowing the Krun free rein to kidnap more people for the terrible fate that awaited them on Mars, but right now, if there was any possibility at all, he had to try to save his sister.

Resigned to the new course of action, Alf began researching the problem. The android pointed out that Sol's databanks held three very sketchy accounts of the only times in recorded galactic history when anything like this had been attempted, just one of which had been even partially successful. The other two were on the same occasion when the fourth Emperor, Dionyster, had been tricked into creating a Klein fold by 'A powerful being who came through the gate', whatever that meant. His two most trusted advisers attempted to bring him back and both also ended up trapped. The time it might have worked, the rescued being had apparently soon returned to the Klein fold, having been unable to stop itself folding again, regardless of the consequences. If Johnny was to have any hope of success at all, he needed a crash course in manipulating space. Leaving Alf on board to keep the peace between Kovac and Sol, he descended alone to the surface of Saturn's largest moon.

✿ ✿ ✿
✿ ✿

For once, Johnny's first instinct was to gaze into the thought chamber – he had to see Clara. As the scarlet-clad Monks swooped all around, he stared into the transparent dome on its crystal plinth. It was like peering through thick fog, as strange shadows shifted without ever coming into focus. He'd never known how to control the chamber, but tried now to empty his mind of all thoughts but his sister. He leaned right across with his nose almost touching the top of the dome and slowly the swirling clouds parted, revealing a scene in sharp focus.

Bram was standing alone on the bridge of the *Calida Lucia*, staring into the abyss with no stars in the heavens to guide him. Everything began to blur.

Quickly the view shifted and there was Princess Zeta aboard her solar-sailing ship, the *Falling Star*, her long purple hair streaming behind in an impossible breeze. It was as if she sensed Johnny was there – she smiled at him, but her cat-like eyes were full of sadness.

Johnny liked Zeta, but he hadn't come here to see the princess. He thought harder about Clara, focusing on her and her alone, recalling again the last words she had spoken to him. As he did so, he waved his arms randomly over the crystal plinth.

A group of people stood huddled together, their clothes sodden, colourless rags, their eyes wide with fear, too terrified to move. Meekly they allowed themselves to be plucked, one by one, from the ground by clear corrugated living tubes that swung them upside down across a great hall filled with birthing eggs. Then they were dropped and cocooned, battered for the feast to come. Rigid, they were slowly disappearing through the jaws of the Krun Queen.

'*At last, Johnny . . . live ones. They taste so good. I will come to the humans' planet and devour all.*'

The Queen's voice was drowned out by the screams as, one by one, the poor people were eaten. He couldn't watch any more and again waved his arms over the plinth.

Here was Louise, in the sun and the wind, climbing down a steep cliff face. Gulls swooped and cawed around her. One slip and she would fall into the rough sea below. She dropped onto a ledge and sidled carefully along till she reached the mouth of a cave, carved into the rock. Inside the cavern Peter rose out of the still, turquoise water to meet her.

Johnny hoped his friend from Yarnton Hill was safe. He was pleased to have seen her, but focused his thoughts on Clara and then there she was . . . falling within the Klein fold. One of the Owlessan Monks placed a long skeletal hand onto Johnny's shoulder to pull him away, but he shrugged the creature off. His sister was screaming, her eyes black and face stretched wide in utter despair. Time had no meaning within her bubble of hyperspace. She would never go hungry; she couldn't even grow old. She was there for an eternity longer than the lifetime of the universe. Johnny called her name. He shouted through the top of the dome. He banged his fists on it, as if to break through and pluck Clara from the prison that held her so very securely.

The view changed again. The broken body of Ophia – the Emissary installed by Bram – lay in pieces before a vast angry crowd. Her head, with huge anime eyes still open, was attached only to her spinal column, clearly artificial and beautifully constructed of elegant silver vertebrae, reflecting the glow of a red giant star. Something was standing beside the butchered body, a being whose long legs ended in a pair of diamond-encrusted slippers. A spindly arm reached down from under azure robes and plucked Ophia's head off the stone steps. The creature held it aloft by her short black hair, thrusting it forward in triumph towards a vast crowd of baying, cheering aliens of all kinds, many wearing the blue armour of the dead Regent's army.

Even from behind, Johnny recognized the outline of the tall, thin Phasmeer with its antennae fully erect – he'd known as soon as he'd seen the ridiculous slippers it had always insisted on wearing. Standing atop the Senate Platform, before the watching multitude, was the traitor Chancellor Gronack.

'Are you happy to be ruled by nothing more than a simple robot?' demanded the Phasmeer, squeaking in Universal.

With one voice, the crowd bayed, 'No!'

'The Emperor has taken you for fools – taken you all for

granted,' shrieked Gronack. Johnny could see Ophia's eyes were open and aware and that her spine snaked and squirmed as if searching for the body it was meant to fit. As the scene widened, Johnny saw that, as well as the scattered, floating Hundra and other airborne beings in the crowd, one familiar four-winged, two-headed alien reporter was hovering in the air directly above the Phasmeer – Z'habar Z'habar Estagog was commentating on the scene.

'Here on the historic Senate Platform,' said one of the heads before the second added, '*Scene of the Terran Johnny Mackintosh's murder of the Regent.*' 'A dreadful day . . . terrible . . . we are once again, exclusively live for the Milky Way News Network – *the number one Vermalcast of all the news, all the time, from all across the galaxy* – bringing you history in the making. *Aeons of Imperial rule are being swept aside.* Chancellor Gronack is addressing the expectant crowd.'

'Bram Khari is no longer worthy to rule,' Gronack said in its weedy Phasmeer voice. 'See how he has abandoned his galaxy for this foolhardy campaign against our peaceful neighbours. The Andromedans are not your enemy. The real foe was the old man – for man he was – in the Imperial Palace.' Some of the crowd gasped at the Phasmeer's blatant heresy – most had been brought up to believe the Emperor was a god. 'Well, I have news for our absent Emperor – it's time for change.' The crowd roared its approval. 'There is a new power on Melania – a power that will dominate the galaxy in ways never before dreamed of. Perhaps the wingless among you yearn to fly?'

Watching from behind Gronack, it was as if a searchlight had fallen upon the vast crowd, beaming out from the former Chancellor itself. Those aliens it fell upon rose into the air, climbing higher and higher in rapture. A chant began, swelling among the masses: 'Gro-nack, Gro-nack, Gro-nack, Gro-nack . . .'

The Phasmeer raised its long arms to silence them. 'But what I give,' it went on, 'always remember I can take away.'

The beam of light cut off as if the ex-Chancellor had thrown a switch. Those aliens high in the sky fell, quicker than they would have on Earth due to the stronger Melanian gravity. There were some screams but, after a brief pause, most of the crowd roared their approval at this demonstration of might. Gronack dominated the multitude in a way Johnny would never have thought possible. The Phasmeer's speech was building to a crescendo. 'It's time for change – no longer will we have to tolerate the views of those who think differently from us. It's time for change – any who resist Melanian rule will bow before us or see their star systems destroyed. It's time for change – why should we look after those too weak to care for themselves? Only the fittest will survive. What is it time for?'

'Change,' roared the crowd.

'What is it time for?' demanded Gronack again.

'Change,' came the reply, even louder this time.

'What is it time for?' asked the Phasmeer a third time, its thin arms held aloft and its robes now a deep purple, like a three-metre-tall regal butterfly.

'Change!' clamoured the crowd.

The view swept around to show Gronack face on. Johnny let out a gasp – the picture wobbled, but then came back into focus. Welded onto one half of the Phasmeer's long narrow face was a mask, blacker than space itself. From the place where the ex-Chancellor's eye had been covered, shone a beam of intense white light so bright it looked almost solid. This was Nicky's mask, the means by which the Nameless One had controlled Johnny's brother for ten long years – the mask that had lain beside the frozen body in the snow.

Johnny felt as if he was swinging inexorably into the searchlight shining out from the mask – something he was desperate to avoid. He knew the hatred that lurked behind the light – the Nameless One himself, the most terrible power in the universe. Johnny waved his arms all across the crystal plinth, but a force like a powerful magnet held his face in a vice, unable to turn away from the chamber.

The beam fell on Johnny and burned like the heat of a thousand suns. He screamed in pain and grabbed the sides of the dome to stop himself falling. He closed his eyes, trying to shut out the rage he felt frying his brain. Something was happening to the thought chamber. Johnny could feel the whole structure begin to vibrate. He didn't want to look, but sensed waves rippling across the solid transparent top.

The dome rocked on its foundations; the vibrations running through it grew bigger and bigger. Johnny had to see for himself, but immediately wished he hadn't. A face filled the chamber, dark and terrible, staring back at his own from behind a black mask that covered every part of it except the eyes, like pits, even darker than Clara's had become. The only detail was a single bright star painted onto one side. Any moment now the top of the dome would crack and either Johnny would be sucked inside or the Nameless One would be standing on Titan beside him. There would be nowhere to run.

One of the Monks flew between Johnny and the face within the dome. Another swooped down, and then another and another. Although there had hardly been any room for one, so close was Johnny's nose to the vibrating shell of the chamber, they seemed to fit easily in the gap. As the fifth Monk arrived, its cloak billowing in a nonexistent breeze, the waves crossing the transparent dome lessened and, by the time a few more of the creatures had arrived, the ripples had vanished altogether. The Nameless One appeared farther away, standing beside a dancing blue fire, his gaze less potent than before. A couple more Monks joined the blockade and Johnny felt the wall they created strengthen and solidify. The Nameless One lifted a hood over his masked face and turned away. When the next scarlet figure flew to the group beside Johnny, the link closed and only a swirling mist remained within the dome.

Next, long bony fingers attached to skeletal wrists reached out from underneath the scarlet robes, grabbing hold of Johnny's hands. An icy cold, like death, began spreading up his arms. Johnny was taken up into a cloud of the red beings, flying with them to the boundary of the golden lake.

The Monks opened their cloaks and, holding tightly onto Johnny, spiralled upward in tight circles, like birds catching a thermal. Despite the aching cold that now gripped his chest and numbed his forehead, he hoped they wouldn't let go. His clone had fallen into the lake of liquid chronons, never to return, and Johnny wasn't keen to experience the same dreadful fate. It looked as if all twenty-four Monks were in the group now, and they levelled off, creating a horseshoe shape vertically above the golden boundary with Johnny held in the middle of the formation, just as they'd done with Bram when Johnny had raced the Emperor around the lake.

The next thing he knew, instead of being perfectly still and flat, the edge of the lake was stretching and distorting, lifting into the sky all the way around, leaving only its very centre unmoved. He wondered why the fluid didn't drain down the curving cone-shaped walls – was this one of the unusual properties of chronons? Then his perspective shifted and, as he viewed it now, the surface of the lake was still flat. But if he looked at it differently, he could force himself to see the cone shape. Again he thought about the space the lake occupied and it became flat. He could choose how to see it, like those skeleton cubes where the face nearest to you varied depending on how you made yourself view it.

The sides of the cone had curved in on themselves, almost

touching. The Monks at both ends of the horseshoe stepped effortlessly across the narrow gap in one small movement. From the perspective of the flat surface, they had folded the hundred metres or so all the way to the other side. Two more went across, every bit as easily, and then another pair and another. It was all very well, but what would happen when he was abandoned in mid-air on his own? He didn't have to wait long to find out.

He fell – not straight down but parallel to the golden cone-shaped edge. He flapped his arms and legs, the lake became flat and now he was falling vertically towards its centre. Terrified, desperate not to be submerged forever beneath the surface of chronons, he tried to picture the cone again and his rate of descent slowed not far above its very apex. He levelled off and, incredibly, found himself falling *up* the other side of the lake, rising parallel to the wall of gold until he reached the top and rejoined the group of Owlessan Monks. He'd done it. He'd folded again. The Monks were trying to teach him how – he could see that, but he was far from sure he understood.

Two took his wrists and again the warmth of his body was overwhelmed as an icy cold engulfed him. Once more, the surface of the lake became a two-dimensional surface in a three-dimensional world – there was no other way to see it. The Monks were dispersing, flying off in all directions to the boundary and beyond. The two holding Johnny deposited him on the ground near the gateway back to Titan proper. They let go and he sank to the floor, rubbing his wrists to regain the circulation and bring the warmth his body needed. It wasn't working – it was probably wise to take a little break before attempting another fold. His teeth began to chatter. He felt as cold as when the *Spirit of London* had sunk to the ocean floor and he'd been forced to swim through the freezing water. Now his whole body was shaking. With difficulty, Johnny stood and tried to walk towards his shuttle where it would be warm. He knew it wasn't far but, having staggered only a few paces, the ground seemed more inviting. In his head, the deep growl of the Krun Queen was telling him to give up. That he should simply lie down, curl himself into as tight a ball as he could and go to sleep.

☆ ☆ ☆
☆ ☆

When Johnny opened his eyes, it took several seconds to work out where he was and then a few more wondering how he'd arrived there. He was staring at the sickbay ceiling on board the *Spirit of London*. He sat up and all the blood rushed from his head, the room began to swim out of focus and there was barking coming from nearby. As Johnny lay down again, Bentley began licking his hand that was dangling over the side of the bed. Automatically he rubbed the Old English sheepdog's head.

'Sol,' said Johnny, 'what am I doing in sickbay?'

'Hello, Johnny,' said the ship. 'You have been recovering from acute hypothermia. I am pleased to report your vital signs are nearly back to normal.'

'But how did I get here?'

'Alf brought you to sickbay 79 hours, 14 minutes and 47.36 seconds ago.'

'What?' said Johnny, sitting bolt upright. This time he was able to stay in that position. 'More than three days?'

'Affirmative, Johnny. Your condition was very serious.'

'Wow,' he said softly. 'How did he find me?'

'I have informed Alf that you are awake and sitting up and he is en route to sickbay. You will be able to question him on the details shortly.'

The doors swished open and in rushed the android. 'Oh, Master Johnny, what am I supposed to do with you? When I

136

found you unconscious like that I thought I'd lost you as well as your sister.'

The mention of Clara was like someone slapping Johnny in the face. 'Well, I feel fine now,' he said. 'I have to go back to the Fountain of Time and try again. I was learning how to fold. I did sort of see how it's done, but maybe you should come with me.'

'Oh, I am sorry, Master Johnny. That will not be possible straightaway.'

'What do you mean, "not possible"?' Johnny asked. He wasn't strong enough for another argument about the wisdom of trying to rescue Clara.

'What was I to do, given everything that is happening? I brought the *Spirit of London* back to Earth. We are in high polar orbit, surveying the planet for Krun activity. And there is an urgent message from Miss Louise – sent more than two days ago.

8 ✩✩

Picking up Passengers ✩✩

Although Alf had only been doing what he thought best, Johnny was furious to have left Titan so quickly, without even attempting to rescue his sister first. He promised himself he would return to Saturn's largest moon as soon as he could, but now they were orbiting Earth it was impossible to ignore the Krun activity any longer. Several TV channels were showing pictures of the newly elected Secretary General of the United Nations – unmistakably a Krun in human form, smiling coldly into the world's cameras. According to the bulletins, abductions and cases of missing persons were on the rise across the globe. Johnny wanted to punch the screen when the alien promised the problem would soon be brought under control.

Even so, there was no escaping Clara's absence. Without her, the *Spirit of London* could no longer land undetected so she was forced to remain shielded in high orbit. Johnny felt terrible leaving his ship, but Sol would be busy searching for centres of Krun activity, with Alf and Kovac helping. With Santorini already identified as a hotspot, Johnny decided to go there first. If he could find Louise, she might be able to tell him more about what was going on.

The signal from her wristcom was still broadcasting, but she hadn't responded to Alf's and then Johnny's attempts to contact her. So, with Bentley beside him, Johnny was flying an invisible *Piccadilly* over the Mediterranean. It had been

Kovac's idea to take the larger shuttle – according to the quantum computer, a red double-decker bus was less likely to look out of place on a Greek island than a black London taxi.

He overflew Santorini, scanning for Louise's wristcom. The entire place was part of a giant volcanic crater, blasted apart three and a half thousand years earlier by an immense eruption, leaving a crescent island as the only trace of the original caldera. The inner side sloped down to a rectangular lagoon several kilometres across and filled with sparkling turquoise water. The outer rim of the island was bordered by steep cliffs to which ancient villages clung. It was along this sheer edge that Johnny located the source of Louise's signal.

Homing in, he flew low over the site a couple of times but there was no sign of anybody, let alone his friend. The area only seemed fit for a handful of skinny goats to graze. Johnny was impressed at how well hidden Louise was keeping. He couldn't risk turning off the *Piccadilly*'s shields even for a second so she could see him, as the big red flying bus would have instantly become visible across much of the island. Instead, he set the shuttle down as close as he could to her signal, landing at the very end of a winding, hilltop road. He checked to ensure no one was watching, turned off the shields and stepped out onto Santorini.

The warm air engulfed him and he stood briefly, soaking up the sun. Bentley, with his thick shaggy coat, didn't look nearly so pleased. They walked along a windy cliff top path, clumps of grass and scrubby plants growing in the rocky soil on one side, with a sheer drop twice the height of the *Spirit of London* on the other. Again Johnny thought of Clara. He wished he'd been stronger on Titan and able to cope with the Monks' training. He stopped and turned towards the shuttle – it looked absurdly out of place in this landscape, making him wonder if this was Kovac's idea of a practical joke.

Alf's voice came directly into Johnny's inner ear, via the wristcom, wondering how he was getting on. Johnny replied he was fine and resumed his rather tricky progress towards the signal, which was stationary. Bentley was out in front and Johnny quickened his pace to keep up, wanting to reach his friend from Yarnton Hill before she moved on. The steep path opened out onto a flat and very windswept patch of land which Johnny thought he recognized as the area he'd flown over earlier. A few goats had been chewing at the tufts of grass, but they scampered away as soon as Bentley began chasing after them and the sheepdog soon wore himself out. Johnny's wristcom told him Louise was no more than twenty metres away. He called her name, but there was no reply. Shouting 'Rusty' only succeeded in getting Bentley excited and it soon became perfectly clear that the red setter wasn't about to appear. Johnny walked right to the edge of the cliff shouting, then sat down with his feet dangling over the side. Seagulls were climbing on thermals towards him – they made him think of the Owlessan Monks and again of Clara.

Calling Sol to aid in the search didn't help. Even looking down from on high with far better sensors than Johnny had at his disposal, the ship told him that the two wristcoms were within two metres of each other. This patently wasn't the case. Johnny called Bentley over and the pair made their way back to the *Piccadilly*.

Johnny had to hope Louise hadn't been captured by the Krun ship that had splashdowned nearby. He wished he could turn back time and follow the aliens straight here, as Kovac had suggested. At least the island was tiny. He decided he'd search as thoroughly as he could, starting with somewhere called Fira which, although Sol told him was the largest town, didn't actually sound very big at all. Perhaps someone would have seen a young English girl and her distinctive copper-coloured dog. At times like this, having a speck of a Hundra's soul living inside you came into its own – the Greek residents would understand every word he said. Inside the *Piccadilly*, he thought clearly of the destination and of staying on the roads and the shuttlecraft began a precarious journey down the hillside, through villages built of white stone from where little children ran out of their homes to chase after the bus.

✧ ✧ ✧
✧ ✧

It took less than twenty minutes to reach the island's capital. From the safety of the *Piccadilly* Johnny surveyed the main square for any sign of Louise. Then he did a double take. Someone he knew was standing nearby, but it wasn't a tall girl with long brown curly hair – it was Stevens in his human form.

The Krun was shepherding a group of tourists into a waiting coach – Johnny didn't like the look of it one bit. He opened the bus doors, stepped out onto the dusty pavement and circled round the back of the murdering alien. The tourists were coming out of a whitewashed church which had exposed bells hanging from a tall tower at its entrance. Johnny crept closer, keeping a hold on the back of Bentley's collar. It sounded as though the Krun had learnt German. He was trying to explain to the elderly tourists that their original transport had broken down and the holiday company had sent him to take them back to their ship in the harbour.

The Germans began to board, not questioning the alien in his pale linen suit and dark sunglasses. Johnny had no idea what to do, but now he was here, right among them, he couldn't let these poor people become more unwitting food for the Krun Queen. Bentley growled and bared his teeth. Stevens jumped and turned round, backing away. The Krun hated dogs, who seemed able to sniff them out even after they'd changed their DNA.

'You!' said Stevens.

'Hi, Bugface,' Johnny replied as casually as he could. Although his heart was racing, he beamed a smile at the Krun, who looked confused. 'There's been a mistake,' Johnny shouted past Stevens to the tourists – he knew they'd hear his words translated into perfect German. 'This is the wrong bus,' he continued, slapping the panels of Stevens's coach to alert the people already inside. 'The holiday firm sent the one over there.' He pointed to the *Piccadilly* – many of the holidaymakers nodded approvingly. Those climbing onto Stevens's coach stopped, shouted inside, and everyone set off across the square towards the red double-decker.

'*Nein . . . Warten Sie bitte*,' shouted Stevens. 'He is only a boy.'

'*Ja*,' said the nearest of the tourists, 'but he is a good German boy.'

Johnny walked past Stevens as calmly as he could, with Bentley still snarling beside him.

'Don't think you've done anything,' Stevens hissed at him. 'We're everywhere – we can take more of them any time we want.'

'No you can't,' said Johnny, turning to face him. 'I'm going to stop you.'

As Johnny walked stiffly away he thought he felt something in his back and wondered if Stevens was shooting. He froze and waited for the bolt of green energy to follow, but Stevens simply shouted, 'Be seeing you, Johnny.'

Relieved, Johnny walked on, reached the *Piccadilly* and climbed on board, with Bentley following a little reluctantly, aiming a final growl in Stevens's direction. A sea of expectant faces turned towards Johnny and his dog. Almost all the tourists were sitting on the lower deck, with only a handful of brave souls venturing upstairs. A particularly large female passenger sitting closest to the driver's seat gave Johnny an encouraging smile.

'Where, exactly, do you need to go?' he asked her.

'*Ozeangeist im Hafen*,' she replied. 'You know vere this is?'

'*Ja, kein Problem*,' Johnny heard himself saying. He brought the place the woman had spoken to the forefront of his mind and the *Piccadilly* began to move.

While Johnny knew that the shuttlecraft was probably the safest means of transportation on the entire planet, the road down towards the harbour must have looked rather precarious to his aging passengers. Given that they were being driven by a fourteen year old, they seemed to be taking it very well. He was spending much of the time using the *Piccadilly*'s internal sensors to keep an eye on them and make sure they didn't touch anything they shouldn't, so didn't notice when his little craft rounded a particularly sharp bend, only for a red setter to run straight into the middle of the road.

The shuttlecraft stopped instantly, the inertial dampeners working overtime. Many of the passengers nodded approvingly at each other as they admired the efficient brakes of the British bus. Through the front windscreen, Johnny saw Louise, very shaken, walk into the road and shovel Rusty into her arms. She was shouting at the dog and looked close to tears.

Johnny opened the doors. Still glaring at the red setter she was cradling, Louise stepped on board saying, 'Thank you . . . thank you so much. I don't know how you stopped in time – I thought she was for it.'

'No problem,' said Johnny, who couldn't help laughing.

For the first time, Louise looked up and almost dropped Rusty in shock. Then she turned and forced an uncertain

smile towards the host of beaming faces watching her. 'Er . . .
Johnny,' she said slowly, 'what's going on?'

☆ ☆ ☆
☆ ☆

While Johnny was keen to unload the strangest crew his
shuttle had ever carried and talk to Louise about what had
been happening, he couldn't say no to the many requests from
his passengers who wanted to pose for photographs with him
and Bentley in front of the red double-decker. As more and
more were taken, the tourists were slipping rolled up notes into
Johnny's chest pocket. When, finally, they'd all left and climbed
the ramp to their waiting cruise ship, Louise plucked a couple
of the pieces of paper from Johnny, unrolled them and said,
'You owe me big time – I ran out of money ages ago. Do you
have any idea what it's like not eating for days?'

Johnny mumbled, 'Sorry.'

Without saying much more, Louise led him to a restaurant
overlooking the lagoon. A sign outside it read: 'Traditional
English Fish 'n' Chips'. Once they were seated at a rickety
table, she looked up from the badly translated menu and simply
said, 'Well?'

From the beginning, he recounted everything that had
happened since Clara had folded Louise over to Santorini.
Quickly he felt her mood soften and, by the time he told her
about Clara vanishing, she reached over and touched his hand,
which he instinctively pulled away. He looked up, a little red-
faced, and saw her eyes were full of tears.

For Louise's part, she had managed to find Peter again,
but it had taken a while to win his trust. The longer she'd
spent with him, the less frightened and more human he was
becoming. Peter had told her that he, and hundreds like him,
had been injected with stem cells taken from aliens who dwelt
beneath the surface of a distant, water-covered planet. They'd

started to transform, some faster than others. The gills had come first, followed by webbed hands and feet. The Krun were using them to look for spaceships lost at the bottom of Earth's oceans and were becoming increasingly violent after every failed mission. Some of Peter's fellow hybrids had been killed. Beaten after trying to escape, Peter had been sent to Santorini to search here – it didn't make any sense at all to Johnny. If there were spaceships hidden on Earth, he was sure Sol would have noticed by now.

The waiter brought the food, which was the strangest fish in batter Johnny had ever eaten, but tasted OK. The chips were crunchy on the outside, powdery on the inside and totally delicious. Louise gobbled up everything on her plate and finished miles ahead of him. Johnny offered her half of what he had left and, after a slight breather, she devoured that too. For dessert the menu even offered Prince William cake. Louise chose the chocolate-and-biscuit combo, but Johnny couldn't resist his favourite, sticky toffee pudding. When they'd finished, Johnny licked his lips and asked, 'Can I see him? If you like – if Peter likes – we could take him to the *Spirit of London*. Alf might be able to find a cure.'

'That would be brill,' Louise replied. 'Thank you. To be honest, if I hadn't eaten I wasn't sure I could make it back. It's a really hard climb. He's hiding out in a cave.'

Johnny nodded – with everything else that had happened, he'd only just remembered the scene in the thought chamber when he'd seen her descending the cliff face. 'Don't worry,' he said. 'Sol made some antigrav harnesses and Alf's put a couple in the *Piccadilly*.'

☆ ☆ ☆
☆ ☆

They left the two dogs in the shuttle to catch up and Louise took Johnny to the very same spot where he'd dangled his legs over the edge while trying to trace her signal. Wearing his harness, Johnny went over the side first to prove they wouldn't fall. As he waited for Louise to follow, he spotted her wristcom, glinting in the sunshine, caught on a bramble that was somehow clinging onto the vertical cliff.

Louise stepped off backwards – in case the harness didn't work, she wanted to be able to grab hold of the cliff face. Johnny knew there was no need, but turned himself and, very slowly, they descended, as seagulls screamed and swooped all around. It was a couple of minutes before they reached the narrow ledge near the bottom, which they walked along keeping their harnesses powered up until they were safely inside the mouth of the cave. Louise went first. As Johnny entered, he gasped.

It was like a temple of rock and water. Light streamed in through holes in the walls at various heights. They'd entered through the biggest of these, which from inside spotlit a serene enclosed harbour. The seaward entrance was underwater, but it was apparent from the tunnel of turquoise light below the surface that a passage led out into the Mediterranean. 'How on Earth did you find this place?' Johnny asked.

Louise shrugged. 'I was desperate,' she said. 'Peter and I spent all our growing up together. I'd have done anything to track him down – like you would for Clara.'

Johnny didn't feel he was doing much to help Clara right now, but nodded. Louise climbed down, jumping expertly from rock to rock and finishing up by the water's edge a few metres below. She held up her hand to tell Johnny to stay back near the entrance. Then she put her two index fingers into the corners of her mouth and whistled – it echoed all around the cave. Seconds later, a head popped out of the water.

The boy's eyes were red and his gills looked to have grown larger, wrapping around his neck. He looked straight at Johnny and said, 'Is it him?', but his voice was rasping and far less clear than in London.

'How'd you even know he was there?' asked Louise.

'Beneath the water, I can see everything,' said Peter, not taking his bloodshot eyes off Johnny for a second. Seaweed was tangled in among his few remaining clumps of long dark hair. 'Are you the one who can help me?' he asked.

'I'll try,' said Johnny. 'I have a very advanced spaceship – I'm sure we can do something.'

'The Protectors are looking for spaceships,' said Peter. 'That's why they made us – so we could search the ocean floors.'

When Clara was being schooled at the Proteus Institute, not knowing the Kruns' true identity she'd called them 'Protectors' too. 'Do you know why?' Johnny asked. 'I don't understand it.'

'Of course they don't tell us,' said Peter. 'They think we're nothing – like farm animals to be bred and killed. But I've listened. Louise and I – we were always very good at finding places to hide and spy on people. I found things out. They want to take over. Once they have these ships, Earth will be history – or humans will anyway. They're bringing someone here who'll destroy us all. Then they think they'll be able to rule the galaxy. That's why I ran away – to warn people. But it's hard, staying human. The other part . . . it sort of eats away at you . . . takes you over. I've seen it with the others and it's happening to me.'

'Look at me, Peter,' said Louise, taking his face in her hands. 'You'll be OK, I promise. I've been on board Johnny's ship – we will find a cure.'

'If it happens . . . if I stop being a person . . . promise you'll kill me,' said the boy.

'Don't talk like that,' snapped Louise.

'You don't know what it's like,' he said. 'It hurts so much.'

Johnny spoke up. 'We'll do everything we can,' he said, 'and the Krun aren't taking over anywhere – I won't let them.'

'Well, I hope you've got a big army,' said the boy. 'There's an awful lot of them.'

'You can be the first recruit,' said Louise. 'Come on – let's get going.' She tapped the rock beside her and Peter sprang out of the water, landing on all fours beside her.'

'Sorry, Peter.' The voice came from behind Johnny. 'You're not going anywhere.'

As Johnny turned, a bolt of energy zapped past his shoulder, striking Peter's chest and surrounding him in a halo of eerie green light. The amphibian boy clutched at Louise, who held onto him. In the glare of the blaster fire his form looked human for just a second. Then he vanished, leaving behind a faint impression scorched onto the white stone.

'Hello again, Johnny,' said Stevens, now pointing the blaster at him. 'Louise.' The alien turned the blaster towards her. The cave went dark. A Krun sphere hovered outside its mouth, blotting out the sun. Another two Krun, both heavily armed, climbed in through the opening. 'So which of you shall I kill first?' asked Stevens. 'Or perhaps I should save Louise here for someone else – I'm sure you'd make a very tasty appetizer.'

'You killed him, you monster,' screamed Louise. She stood up as though she was about to fight the alien.

'Well, not really,' said Stevens. 'I suppose it *was* me who pulled the trigger, but it was Johnny who led us here.' Turning to Johnny he said, 'It's all thanks to you – I couldn't possibly take credit for it.'

Johnny looked imploringly at Louise. He wanted to say he'd done nothing of the sort – that these were just words, spoken to make them feel even worse. He turned back to Stevens and said, 'You're lying, Bugface.'

'You're lying, Bugface.' Stevens repeated the words,

mimicking Johnny's voice *exactly*. 'I could have killed you earlier,' said the Krun, reverting to his normal accent. 'It's very unwise to turn your back on an enemy – especially when it's me.'

'Then why didn't you?' asked Johnny, playing for time while he brought his antigrav harness online.

'Because troublesome, meddlesome Peter would still have been out there. I did shoot you, but only with a tracker dart. And in no time at all you led us right here. I'm very grateful, of course. The place is kind of hard to find, wouldn't you say?' Stevens made a point of looking around the secret cavern.

It was desperate – unless you could swim like a fish, or Peter, there was no way out and Johnny wasn't leaving the cave without Louise. 'So what happens now?' Johnny asked, his brain working overtime but unable to find a solution.

'I'm sorry – I don't quite follow,' said Stevens. 'For a moment I thought you were wondering where I might take you. As I said, Louise I might feed to the Queen – she likes her prey to struggle – but you, Johnny? You have to die.' Stevens aimed the blaster and fired.

Johnny jumped across to Louise, plucking her from the flat rock by the water's edge as his antigrav harness kicked in. Out of control, he slammed into the far wall of the cavern, but clung onto his friend. Blaster fire exploded the rock beside Johnny's face, splintering him with shrapnel. Stevens was laughing. More than anything in the world, Johnny wished he and Louise were out of there, up on the cliff with the dogs and the *Piccadilly*. Rising too fast, so as to avoid being shot, he smashed his head on the roof of the cave and almost passed out – lights flashed before his eyes.

Stevens laughed even louder. 'There's nowhere left to run, Johnny,' he shouted. 'Goodbye.'

Johnny turned off the harness. Louise screamed. Green

bolts of energy shaved the tops of their heads. They fell, towards the centre of the water, just like on Titan. Just like on Titan! Johnny grabbed Louise's hand as tightly as he could and started to picture space differently – in four dimensions. Now they were falling along the water's surface and not towards it. Now they were falling up the cliff face. Now they were falling parallel to the ground, as the *Piccadilly* rushed towards them. His head hurt – he couldn't keep this up. He let go of Louise and they both rolled and tumbled over the stony ground, Johnny putting his hands out to stop himself, scraping off the skin but managing to brake a couple of metres before slamming into the side of the double-decker bus.

He stood up, palms bleeding, and hobbled back for Louise, the pain forgotten in the exhilaration of escape – of having folded space again. It returned as he picked out the stones and grit from his torn skin. Louise was unconscious, but that was normal for someone not used to folding. Even so, Johnny could see fresh tear tracks running down her cheeks. He took one of her arms, placed it over his shoulder and lifted her to her feet.

Louise looked green. She opened her bloodshot eyes, said, 'Sorry,' and was immediately sick all over Johnny.

Vomiting was another side effect for an inexperienced foldee – he should have remembered. She half walked and he half dragged her to the waiting shuttle, where Johnny gratefully collapsed into the pilot's seat. He wrapped his hands around his sides, clutching them to himself, hoping to ease the pain. Then he focused on the whereabouts of the *Spirit of London*, thought, *Shields on*, and, like a floating pair of eyes backed by two invisible barking dogs, shot upward into the sky.

☆ ☆ ☆
☆ ☆

The time spent in sickbay seemed interminable. Johnny had the distinct impression Alf was deliberately slowing down the healing process to allow for a (very) full debrief. The android was certainly making the most of it and, having quizzed Johnny about the trip to Santorini, also wanted to know everything that he'd seen in the thought chamber on Titan.

The mutilation of Ophia, the only other artificial life form, hit the android very badly. Alf couldn't understand how Gronack had become so powerful so quickly, even with the Nameless One's mask. It appeared the android had reached a surprising decision.

'The situation is graver than I have ever known it, Master Johnny,' he said. 'The Emperor has left the galaxy; Chancellor Gronack has performed a coup and will, doubtless, have put a rather large price on your head by now; the Krun are without question the most powerful race in the local neighbourhood and are bent on wiping out humanity, while sourcing a fleet of ships from who knows where and . . . and Miss Clara is no longer with us to help.' The android was unable to carry on, but what he'd said hadn't made for happy listening.

'I know, Alf. You don't have to tell me.' Johnny didn't need reminding of any these things . . . especially his sister.

'Desperate times call for desperate remedies,' said Alf, having composed himself. 'I believe the time has come to go public. Well, semi-public at least.'

'Tell people about the Krun?' Johnny asked.

'Build a fleet to fight them,' said the android.

'But Bram said—'

'The Emperor is not here,' said Alf. 'I am well aware His Imperial Majesty said that knowledge such as that contained aboard the *Spirit of London* must be earned and not simply handed over to humanity. But the abductions are increasing exponentially. If we do nothing, there will soon be no humans left. The time has come to arm your people, to give them the tools to fight back.'

Johnny lay on the bed in silence, chewing over what Alf had said. The android didn't hurry him for a response. Johnny tried thinking of different groups they might approach, but only one loomed large in his mind. The Corporation had already attained a high level of technology – Johnny had even seen them destroy a Krun ship. It was Kovac who'd said, 'The enemy of my enemy is my friend.' Johnny didn't want to believe it, but was struggling to see an alternative. His first choice would have been the United Nations, but the Krun had taken over there and, besides, no government would listen to a fourteen year old.

'OK,' he said. 'I know you're right, but I hate the thought of dealing with Colonel Hartman.'

'Why ever would we want to do that, Master Johnny?' asked Alf. 'I know things are desperate, but there are limits.' Relief washed over Johnny. The android continued, 'I have been following the progress of a certain David Bond, an Australian rocket scientist who, with a few nudges in the right direction, might be able to design humanity's first Starfighters.'

'And you know this guy how?' asked Johnny.

'When I attempt the crossword,' said Alf, 'there are other parts of the newspaper I read.'

☆ ☆ ☆
☆ ☆

Under cover of night, Johnny landed his Imperial Starfighter in a hidden niche between two of the large white sail-like domes that formed the roof of the Sydney Opera House. There was just about room for one, tightly squeezed passenger and Louise had insisted on coming too. She said she needed to do something to stop herself thinking about Peter, and Johnny had hardly felt in a position to refuse. Louise said she didn't blame Johnny for what had happened, but that didn't stop him feeling responsible for leading the Krun straight to the cave.

Johnny helped her out of the cramped cockpit from which she'd taken an Imperial blaster. He tried to argue that there was no need, but Louise said that, after the Krun had killed Peter, she was more than happy to shoot back. Together they surveyed the landing site. The ship was well hidden but, in the unlikely event of someone climbing the roof and stumbling across it, he hoped they'd decide Australia's premier arts venue was displaying a striking piece of modern sculpture.

It was surprisingly dark within the little crevice. Johnny was used to many different night skies across the galaxy, but it was the first time he'd had the chance to see Earth's southern stars. Some were familiar, yet different. He pointed out the constellation Leo the lion, which here in the southern sky hung upside down. Then he found Alpha Centauri. Being four light years away, the light shining from the Sun's nearest neighbours (a triple star system) was four years old and gave no hint of the supernova that had ripped the system apart. Johnny wondered out loud what would happen in three and a bit years' time when the glare of the supernova and its devastating gamma rays reached Earth. Bram's shields had to hold.

Careful not to be seen, they climbed over the tiles out of the dip to the top of one of the roofs. Louise stopped for a moment to admire the lights of the city and the enormous span of the harbour bridge. 'We should have come in the *Spirit of London*,' she said. 'She'd look gorgeous here.'

Of course she was right. The ship would have made a spectacular addition to the harbour skyline, her lights sparkling in the water. 'Somehow I think people might have noticed,' said Johnny, smiling.

They slid down the roof, past the main entrance and began the short journey to the reassuringly named Kings Cross, which proved quite different from the London original. Professor Bond had an apartment here, at the very top of a modern building with views towards the harbour bridge. Guided by Sol over the wristcoms, they found it easily and slipped into a deserted neighbouring alley so they could use the antigrav harnesses unseen.

According to the professor's online diary, he was a very busy man and wouldn't be home this evening, but Johnny had the idea of leaving a very unusual calling card – one that would grab the rocket designer's attention. He didn't expect it would be easy for most kids his age to make an appointment.

They settled softly on the roof terrace. The lights inside the flat were all off. Louise was happy to stay outside and admire the view so Johnny entered alone. There was an alarm but it was simple to circumvent by sensing the currents and fields inside and leading them on a slight detour, ensuring the flow bypassed the lock mechanism as he turned the handle. Once safely through, he released his control and the currents returned to normal.

The apartment might have belonged to an older man on the opposite side of the world, but even in the glare of his torchlight Johnny felt instantly at home. Three walls of the enormous open-plan living room were covered in framed space pictures – giant photographs from Hubble and others. The fourth wall had several pictures of the same man, sporting wild grey hair like Einstein's, with various dogs at different stages of his life. The younger Bond had started with a red setter, then a West Highland terrier, a collie and even an Afghan hound. In front of the photos was a life-size sculpture of the red setter. Beside it, in one corner, stood a giant model of the Saturn V rocket that had first taken mankind to the Moon. Sweeping his torch beam along the wall, Johnny also picked out a space shuttle, a Bussard ramjet, an old Blue Streak, the Skylon space plane and others he didn't recognize. Some looked far more advanced and he guessed these were the professor's own prototypes. One long thin craft, built from several modules that looked as if they could separate, appeared designed for deep-space exploration – encircling the central core were living quarters, which rotated when he touched them. It was a clever way of creating gravity when spending months in a zero-G environment. Another, spherical, ship looked highly manoeuvrable. The room was an Aladdin's cave and Johnny could have spent all night there, but what he really wanted to see was Professor Bond's computer. Happily the study proved to be through the next set of doors.

Even though no one was home, Johnny crept as quietly as possible and, as he switched the computer on, he pressed the mute button. The professor did have a password, but for someone as skilled at hacking as Johnny it was child's play to find a back door. Quickly he had administrator access and was in his element. Alf had apparently been following Bond's progress for quite some time and, although nothing had been published, enough whispers had leaked out to know that the professor had stumbled upon something very special indeed, codenamed 'Project Sirius'. These were the files Johnny was after – the ones he would inspect and amend. Although he knew a fair amount about spaceship design (it had been his favourite subject at the Imperial University), before coming here he'd used the DINHATS (Direct Intra-Neural Hyper-Accelerated Transfer System) on the *Spirit of London* to bring himself fully up to speed. It had to be done, but Louise had giggled at the sight of Johnny seated under what appeared to be a giant hairdryer.

If only he could find the professor's files, but they didn't appear to be anywhere on the system. He scanned the hard drive every way he could think of, even down to DOS and then machine code, but either Johnny was looking at the wrong computer or the Australian was impressively security conscious.

A hand touched Johnny on the shoulder and he nearly jumped out of his skin. 'Only me,' said Louise, who'd clearly enjoyed startling him. 'It was freezing outside – forgot it's winter here. How's it going?'

Johnny, his heartbeat returning to normal, said, 'Not well – the files I need aren't here. Maybe he's hidden them around the flat?'

'What are we looking for?' Louise asked.

'Hard to say,' Johnny replied. 'Flash drive, disks, memory card, external hard drive – could be anything.' Briefly they swept the study with torchlight, but Johnny knew what they were after was unlikely to be in the same room as the computer. Moving next door he said, 'It's about something called Project Sirius, so I reckon the files will be hidden in something spacey – let's check the models.'

'Look – it's Rusty,' said Louise, with eyes only for the sculpted dog. 'I didn't notice her before.' She walked across to the red setter and stroked its fibreglass body. The dog's mouth fell open and there was a flash drive, propped behind its teeth. 'Bingo,' she said, smiling. 'Very spacey, that.'

'Absolutely,' said Johnny, grinning too. 'Didn't you know Sirius is the dog star?'

Inserting the new drive, the computer was suddenly transformed. The self-extracting archive took only seconds to bring up detailed plans for how the beautiful deep-space explorer he'd seen in the other room would be constructed. Assembling the modules would take place in Earth orbit and the ship was propelled by something labelled an Alcubierre Drive, a crude but very clever way of warping space so there was more of it behind the ship than in front – meaning the speed of light barrier didn't apply. Given the professor had no idea about the existence of Plicans, he'd compensated very well. More amazingly still, everything was powered by a miniature black hole that formed the core of the ship. The plan was far more ambitious than any other spaceflight programme in history, involving a six-month return journey to Sirius, the brightest start in the night sky. If the Krun could be stopped, a mission like this would mean the dawning of a new age for humanity – Johnny almost envied the astronauts who would be on board.

Immediately beneath the mission title he inserted the line: 'Professor Bond – if you approve of my edits, meet me at midnight tomorrow outside the Opera House. Your friendly neighbourhood hacker, Johnny M.' Then he set to work correcting the equations, adding several new ones and improving the design. He hoped that some of the Australian's theories could be adapted for use in the fleet of spacefighters Earth would need in the battle to come. At the very end of the document, where the professor gave detailed specifications for the Project Sirius shuttles (highly manoeuvrable smaller craft attached to the exterior of the command vehicle), Johnny inserted a design that he hoped would be suitable. It was a cross between the professor's shuttles and his own Starfighter, which was simply too advanced to be copied directly. Louise looked over his shoulder as he added the finishing touches.

'Up here, quickly,' shouted a voice. Several pairs of footsteps could be heard running up the stairs and lights within the flat were being turned on. 'The alarm came from the roof terrace.'

Johnny looked at Louise, who was staring towards the doorway, horrified. He pushed himself out of the chair and shouted, 'Run!'

They were too late. Half a dozen police swarmed into the study, followed by an out-of-breath aging professor with a mane of wild grey hair. Johnny recognized him immediately from the wall of photographs.

'It's just kids,' said one of the policemen.

Professor Bond ignored him, hardly glancing at Johnny and Louise. He rushed straight to the console and began scrolling through Johnny's changes. 'Not the files . . . my life's work . . . my beautiful ship.' Appearing broken, he lifted his head towards Johnny and said, 'What have you done?'

Johnny tried to convey with a look that everything was OK, that he had built rather than destroyed, but the inconsolable professor slumped into the chair in front of his computer, wailing. The police stepped forward. Louise stood rooted to the spot. Johnny put an arm around her to start her moving forward and switched the antigrav harness on as the officers grasped at thin air. Landing on the other side of the policemen, they ran into and across the brightly lit living room.

Behind, one of the police shouted, 'We've got 'em cornered – there's no way out from the roof.'

Johnny opened the door onto the terrace. He checked Louise's harness was powered up as they ran to the edge and jumped over, disappearing laughing into the Sydney night.

☆ ☆ ☆
☆ ☆

To say the visit to Professor Bond hadn't gone as Johnny planned was an understatement. Louise said not to worry – that it would be fine – but he moped for much of the following day while she'd dragged him around Bondi, killing time before the hoped-for midnight rendezvous that Johnny was very doubtful would now happen. Here there was no obvious sign of Krun activity, but as Johnny watched the youth of Australia having fun he heard the deep voice of the Krun Queen, screaming at him to kill them and bring her a feast.

'Johnny – what are you doing?' Louise asked, while grabbing his arm and forcing it down so that the Imperial blaster she'd taken from the cockpit and which he was now holding, pointed down at the sand.

'Oops,' said Johnny, coming to his senses, as the Queen howled with rage somewhere in his head.

'Oops?' said Louise. 'Is that all? You were about to shoot people.'

'Of course I wasn't,' Johnny replied. 'Look, I don't want to talk about it.' The voice inside his brain was frightening him.

Louise let it go and, by the time darkness had fallen and they were waiting, hidden in the shadows surrounding the wide open expanse in front of the Opera House, the afternoon's events appeared forgotten. Not knowing Sydney, this had seemed an obvious place to suggest they meet, but standing there now it felt terribly exposed. The last performance had finished over an hour earlier and the area was deserted. It was a case of hoping the scientist would come, but wouldn't bring the cops with him. They didn't have to wait long.

A lone figure in a wide-brimmed hat, carrying what looked a very heavy battered suitcase, was walking towards the Opera House. Johnny and Louise waited, watching for signs of police hiding in the shadows. As he came closer, Johnny was pretty sure he recognized the figure. Professor Bond, wearing a long beige mac, stepped under a nearby streetlight, breathing heavily and plonking his case on the ground. It was covered in stickers naming different destinations around the world.

'I'll go first,' said Johnny. 'If anything happens, call Alf and he *will* come and get you.' He stepped out of the shadows and strode more confidently than he felt towards the scientist.

'You're not leaving me again,' said Louise, sticking by his side.

As they approached, the professor lifted his hat in greeting. Johnny wondered if it was a signal for hordes of police to come swarming into the open, but the large paved area of waterfront remained quiet and peaceful.

'Greetings,' said the professor, his voice shaking a little.

'I'm sorry about the police last night – I didn't know who you were.'

'I'm Johnny . . . Johnny Mackintosh, and this is my friend Louise. I'm sorry about your computer,' said Johnny, before nodding at the scientist's luggage on the ground and asking, 'What's in the suitcase?'

'Everything that's precious to me,' Professor Bond replied. 'All my life I've longed to go to the stars – I want you to take me with you . . . back to your homeworld.'

It took a moment, but then Johnny understood. 'We're not going anywhere,' he said. 'This is where we're from.'

'I don't understand,' said the scientist. 'Those designs . . . the equations on my computer . . . the changes you made. If you're just a boy . . . no offence, but how? You *have* to be aliens.'

'It's a long story,' Johnny replied. 'There are aliens here and they're trying to wipe out humanity – that's why we need your help. We want you to take the spec I gave you to Earth's governments so they can build a fleet before it's too late. They won't listen to . . . to someone who's "just a boy".'

'The designs on my computer?' said the professor, shaking his head. 'It will be hard to convince others when I'm struggling to understand them myself. Rocket design isn't purely theoretical – it's physical. You need to feel it.'

'Well, maybe you can feel it too,' said Johnny. 'There is a ship here – a lot more advanced, but the same basic principles.'

Professor Bond's eyes darted beyond Johnny and Louise in the hope of happening upon the spaceship.

Louise laughed. 'It's well hidden,' she said, before looking at Johnny and adding, 'hopefully. Come on.'

☆ ☆ ☆
☆ ☆

Johnny was relieved to find the sleek craft exactly where he'd left it, apparently undisturbed. Its appearance was so alien not even Professor Bond realized what it was, until Johnny pointed it out. The scientist reached forward with a shaking hand – he couldn't quite touch what appeared to be the sides, but the air rippled around his fingers and there was a faint but reassuring hum that barely hinted at the incredible power concentrated within. He turned to Johnny and said, 'Just one trip – let me see the stars as they were meant to be seen.'

Johnny nodded – he understood. He turned to Louise, who was smiling.

'Just promise me you won't be long,' she said.

'Thanks,' he replied. 'I promise.'

☆ ☆ ☆
☆ ☆

The shields on the Imperial Starfighter were designed differently from the *Spirit of London*'s shuttles, which was just as well. Johnny didn't want to overwhelm Professor Bond even more by turning him invisible as they sped skyward at breathtaking speed. Behind him, Johnny heard the professor say, 'Strewth.'

Confident they couldn't be detected, he buzzed the International Space Station, before heading onward and outward. In seconds they travelled from Earth's largest artificial satellite to its natural one.

Nowadays, plenty of people had gone into low Earth orbit, but it was only when you travelled further out that Earth shrank, becoming a beautiful blue and white marble, held by the force of gravity against the blackness of the cosmos. Johnny wanted to show the professor just how spectacular it was, but also how fragile and vulnerable.

As they flew, he told Professor Bond about the trip to Mars, where bodies were being taken and devoured, and that the Krun were on the verge of taking over Earth. He wasn't sure the professor was really listening as, between whoops and gasps, the Australian pressed his face right up against the forcefields protecting them, taking in the view of the dark side of the Moon and saying, 'I see,' and 'Deary me,' but in all the wrong places.

Around the other side so quickly, the Australian cleared his throat and asked, nervously, if it was possible to see another star system close up, especially a triple one – if they could go to Alpha Centauri. He was more than a little surprised when Johnny said, 'It's not there any more.'

'But I saw it this evening,' said the professor, 'when we were at the Opera House.'

'A few months ago, one of its stars went Star Blaze – sorry, supernova,' Johnny replied. 'We'll see it on Earth in about three and a half years.' Johnny accessed a countdown that he'd set up on his wristcom to give the exact figure.

'Then that's it,' said Professor Bond. 'It doesn't matter if these Krun take over or not. When the blast hits, all life on Earth will be wiped out anyway.'

'We'll be OK,' said Johnny. 'The Emperor of the Galaxy's protecting us, so there are massive shield generators in orbit – if we can stop the Krun, it'll be quite a show.'

'Why doesn't this Emperor stop them?'

'Bram . . . the Emperor's not here any more. He's left the galaxy. We're on our own.'

Earth grew rapidly as they sped home. The professor was suddenly taking things a lot more seriously and started asking Johnny to demonstrate the Starfighter's capabilities, to give him a better feel of the ship and what it could do. Johnny hated keeping Louise waiting, but wanted to do everything he could to convince the Australian and have him agree to the fleet design. The journey that had taken the Apollo astronauts three days was still over in seconds but, instead of returning straight to the Opera House, Johnny took a detour. There could be no better place to contemplate the fate of Earth than from the observation platform where Nicky had once taken him. In geosynchronous orbit, above the eastern United States, the Imperial Starfighter landed with a reassuring thud on a solid but invisible surface 36,000 kilometres up.

'What's happened? Please tell me I've not broken it,' said the Australian. Johnny smiled and turned off the forcefield above their heads. Then he climbed out of the cockpit and offered the wide-eyed professor his hand.

'It's perfectly safe,' he said.

Professor Bond peered over the side, looking far from convinced. Then he opened his mouth, sucked in the oxygen miraculously around them, and smiled. 'So long as you don't hold your breath, it's said you can survive for thirty seconds in the vacuum of space, but I'm glad we don't have to find out.'

Johnny smiled and jumped backwards, landing a little awkwardly as he couldn't tell exactly where the surface was. Overbalancing, he ended up in a heap. The professor laughed and climbed down to join him, helping Johnny up. Together they walked to the very edge of the platform where they both sat, their legs hanging over the side.

'Strewth – that's what I call a view,' said Professor Bond.

Johnny was impressed by the man's head for heights, and couldn't help but think again of Clara and how she feared them so much she'd even felt ill at the sight of Peter up Nelson's Column. He thought of Nicky too, buried face down in the snow. 'My brother brought me here,' said Johnny. 'He liked the view too.' He tried hard to stop his eyes watering.

'Listen, kid – Johnny, isn't it? I looked at your plans. Believe me, I studied them pretty damn hard, and now I've been inside one of the things I kind of understand it. Well, maybe like a roo understands a television, but I sort of get the picture. The bottom line is, we can't build your ships.'

'What? Why not?'

'They're just too advanced.'

'But they're not like the Starfighter – I simplified them.'

'And you did a great job,' said Professor Bond. 'Really terrific. What we've flown in is . . . well, I don't know where you got it, but it's so far beyond my imagination that it's hundreds of thousands, maybe millions of years ahead of us. But the designs you gave me – maybe in five hundred, a thousand years, we can actually build those.'

'But I've shown you how,' said Johnny. 'I've given you the blueprints.'

'But they're not worth a pair of dingo's kidneys without the money. It's about economics, Johnny. Imagine in the Middle Ages if someone had the plans to build a space shuttle. Just because they knew how it should work, there wouldn't have been enough lolly in the world to get close. I don't think there's enough now to make more than one of your ships, and you said we need a fleet.'

A chime sounded from the middle of the platform behind them and Johnny turned to see the doors of an ornately carved wooden lift beginning to open. 'Oh no,' he said.

'What the devil is that?' asked the professor, rising to his feet.

'Space elevator,' said Johnny, attempting to pull the Australian to the floor.

'Let go,' said Professor Bond. 'I just have to see this.'

Out of the lift stepped Stevens and several other Krun, all in human form. A black sphere settled on the platform, right beside the Imperial Starfighter.

'You're like a bad penny, Johnny,' said the suited Krun, swivelling round and pulling a blaster from the holster inside his suit jacket. 'Always turning up in the wrong places. Who's your friend?'

'None of your business, Bugface,' Johnny replied.

'Of course, it hardly matters,' said Stevens. 'You see I have a funny feeling he's about to become your ex-friend. Just as you're about to become an ex-Johnny. Hands up.'

'Now look here. I'm Professor David Bond of the Sydney Space Science Research Institute. I'm sure there's been a misunderstanding,' said the Australian, walking forward with his arm outstretched.

'And it's you who's making it, professor. I said, "Hands up".' The professor stopped. Stevens walked towards him, pointing the blaster, with the other Krun spreading out behind. Professor Bond stepped backwards to alongside Johnny, who saw no option but to stand and raise his hands in the air. 'Such a shame you'll never witness our moment of triumph. While the senile Emperor and the Nameless One do battle between the galaxies, our Queen will inherit this one.'

'So you're just going to shoot us, Bugface? Doesn't your Queen prefer live ones?' It was a terrible thought, but Johnny was desperate to stay alive as long as possible.

'I can't say I'm not tempted,' said Stevens, 'but soon she will come here and have a whole planet to feast on.' Johnny and the professor swapped horrified glances. 'So, yes, I'm just going to shoot you.'

Above his head, Johnny brought his right hand behind his left and pressed a button on his wristcom. He really hoped it was the right one.

'Time to die,' said Stevens, but a noise from behind distracted him. The Imperial Starfighter's engines were firing up.

Johnny grabbed the professor's hand, pulled him backwards and leapt off the platform.

9 ✩✩
The Corridor between Worlds ✩✩

Going over the side, Johnny took a last lungful of air and hoped Professor Bond had done the same. For a second, he wondered if he'd leapt far enough to clear the plethora of forcefields that Nicky had once told him surrounded the space elevator platform. Then the cold hit him and there could be no question. If he could have cried out he would, but no sound carried in the vacuum of space.

Johnny's eyeballs felt as if they were on fire and, through them, he watched the professor drift agonizingly slowly away, the Australian's mouth open in a silent scream. Below, the blue and white swirls of planet Earth dominated the view while, off to the side, Johnny saw the Imperial Starfighter that he'd launched moments earlier with the wristcom. They could still be saved. His numbing fingers responded, using the device again to pilot the Starfighter towards Professor Bond, capturing the Australian and sealing him safely inside.

Johnny's mouth was vibrating as the water on his tongue began to bubble. Something told him that was why his eyes hurt too, as the liquid in them must be boiling away into space. He was struggling to see anything now, so closed them, but it didn't take the spiking pain away. The simplest thing was surely to fold himself inside the Starfighter and out of danger. In his mind's eye he pictured the space between him and the sleek vessel curve and bend and, the very next moment he was right outside the cockpit. He subtly altered the gradient, so he could simply slide into the pilot's seat, but at the last second he bounced off the boundary of the ship and somersaulted away into the distance.

Fighting the pain, he opened his eyes, but it made no difference. He was completely blind. As the freezing vacuum seemed to strip away the layers of Johnny's brain, he remembered all the knowledge of spaceship design that had been implanted there, and despaired. His fighter was very nearly the most advanced offensive machine in the galaxy, equipped with all manner of defensive countermeasures – one was that each Starfighter included a barrier built individually by the Emperor himself to prevent folding in or out. It meant no one could take over the ship in a battle, but neither could Johnny access the cockpit now.

The pain in his chest suggested his insides were beginning to bubble away and he knew it was almost the end. It would all be so much easier if he simply let go and accepted his fate, the last Mackintosh, leaving the galaxy to others to look after. Yet he knew that was a lie – that he was kidding himself. Somewhere, trapped in a pocket of hyperspace, Clara Mackintosh was also falling. While Johnny would be dead in seconds, his sister was doomed to fall forever, outside of time. He had to save her, yet even as the determination gripped him, he felt his brain shutting down. Time was running out. Concentrating on just one thing, it became obvious he didn't need eyes or fingers to operate the wristcom – the electronics inside it would obey him.

It was so hard to focus with every fibre of his body now screaming in agony, but he forced himself to direct the electrons within the device and, at these temperatures, they met so little resistance it was easy. Suddenly Johnny was warm, and the pain of the transition, rising three hundred degrees in a fraction of a second, was more unbearable than the cold. With his final thought, he asked the Starfighter to take them home.

☆ ☆ ☆
☆ ☆

'If he wasn't so ill, I'd kill him for leaving me in Australia.' The voice sounded faraway and muffled, as if listening to it underwater, but Johnny guessed it was Louise.

'I think Master Johnny may be able to hear you,' said Alf.

'Welcome back, Johnny. When flying through space in future, I recommend you stick to travelling inside me.' Even muffled, Johnny would have recognized Sol's reassuring tones anywhere.

He tried to open his eyes, but it made no difference. There was only blackness and blindness. Fear that he would never see again gripped him. He cried out and felt his insides burn as they took in air.

'Best not speak yet, Master Johnny,' said Alf. 'Your body has been damaged . . . rather significantly.'

Johnny didn't like that pause. He felt a soft hand take hold of his – it must be Louise's – and instinctively turned in her direction. 'The professor?' he asked, as his chest once more felt on fire.

'David's fine,' Louise replied. 'He said you didn't follow his advice.'

Johnny must have looked as confused as he felt, because Alf carried on, 'I believe that Professor Bond instructed you not to hold your breath in a vacuum. It seems that you did not listen to him, much as you never appear to listen to me.'

Johnny groaned and it hurt.

'You are experiencing pain, Master Johnny, because your lungs ruptured, given they were full of air which, in a vacuum, expanded. Your eardrums also burst and you are suffering from hypoxia-induced blindness. You can consider yourself fortunate that, had you remained in space a further 2.718 281 828 seconds longer, your blood would have begun to boil and . . . and I would have lost you as well as Miss Clara, and . . .'

Alf burst into tears and Louise gave Johnny's hand another squeeze. She said, 'What metal man here is saying is you've got the bends – pretty badly too – so it'll be a few days yet till you're better.'

'Days?' said Johnny, weakly.

'Look on the bright side,' she replied. 'At least you can't see yourself. There's sunburn and there's sunburn, but your face and hands are something else.'

'The professor?' Johnny asked again.

'I told you David's fine,' said Louise. 'I spoke to him this morning – we gave him a wristcom. Alf took him back to Sydney once you were stable – he said he needed to get back as you'd given him so many ideas to work on. He wanted to thank you when you woke up, but we had to put you into a coma.'

'A coma?' said Johnny weakly.

'Tell me about it,' said Louise. 'You're not much fun when you're zonked out. I ended up learning relativity theory in the DINHATS, just to pass the time. But now you're awake—'

'If you two have quite finished,' said Alf, 'I do need to work on manufacturing some artificial lungs for you, Master Johnny. In turn, you have to work on getting better. The best way to do that is more sleep.' As Alf pressed the pneumatic syringe against Johnny's neck it was almost a relief to slip away into a deep, pain-free nothingness.

☆ ☆ ☆
☆ ☆

There was the scent of vinegar in Johnny's nostrils and soothing breath on his eyelids. He dared to open them and the first thing he saw was a great mass of purple. As he squinted, struggling to focus, Princess Zeta, daughter of Zola, lifted her head away from his face and stood, hands on hips. Her mane of purple hair was blowing in a strong sea breeze, but Johnny knew it was her and not the wind that had cured his blindness.

With his eyes working again, everything looked so beautiful. Two blue suns, one many times larger than the other, were setting together, simultaneously sinking into a calm ocean, their twin search beams lighting the water and illuminating Zeta as she stood on a grassy mound. A flash of light in front of her face was quickly extinguished as Zeta's forked tongue shot from her mouth, capturing the Phosphoric Sulafly that had flown too close, and reeling it back inside to be devoured.

'Want one?' she asked, before the tongue flicked out again, lightning fast, and a second flicker of light was extinguished.

'No thanks – you have it,' said Johnny. It still hurt to speak, but he couldn't help smiling.

'It is not only your eyes and ears that ailed you,' said Zeta. 'I sense your insides are broken.'

'It's my lungs,' Johnny replied. 'They're ruptured. But you can heal them, can't you?' He'd experienced the princess's miraculous healing gifts many times before.

Zeta frowned and sat down, looking out over the ocean, patting the ground beside her for Johnny to join her. Darkness was falling quickly and the stars in the sky above Novolis, Zeta and Erin's home planet, began to twinkle. First out was a kite-shaped cross made up of four points of light at its edges, tonight with a small moon right at its centre – Zeta's Starmark. Off to one side shone three stars above the ocean that Johnny knew were the top of a hexagon and were King Erin's Starmark. 'It's not that simple,' she said.

'Erin?' Johnny asked, looking around for evidence of the

boy king. He instantly regretted twisting his body as his chest howled with pain.

'My brother the King would forbid it, but in the waking world he has left Novolis.'

'The waking world?' said Johnny, wincing, unclear what Zeta meant.

'We are dreamwalking,' she replied, 'and, far from here, Erin's power is insufficient to stop you from entering. I hate to see you suffer, but it would dishonour my brother to heal you.' She took hold of Johnny's hand.

'Why?' he asked, turning to look at the princess. 'What's it to do with him?'

Zeta's catlike eyes met his. 'Because I have to reach inside you,' she replied. 'Because I have to do this.' Zeta was leaning in towards him. Her mouth was moving closer to Johnny's. It happened so quickly he didn't know what to do. Her lips pressed against his – they were softer than they looked. He felt her tongue in his mouth. He felt it pass his, sliding down his throat. Where moments before his insides burned, now the fire was quelled. Johnny realized he'd closed his eyes. He opened them to find himself in the *Spirit of London*'s sickbay, with Bentley curled at the foot of the bed and Louise gripping his hand.

'Stop!' she shouted. 'He's awake.'

'Sol,' said Alf, 'please increase the anaesthetic so I can continue with the procedure.'

'No,' said Johnny. 'What's going on? What procedure?' He found he could speak without it hurting.

'There is no time to waste, Master Johnny. I am about to remove your lungs and replace them with a bioengineered substitute.' The android pointed to what looked like two pristine pieces of coral on a nearby table. 'Sol – more anaesthetic, please.'

'No,' said Johnny again. 'I'm healed – I can see and my lungs are fine . . . never better.' To prove it, Johnny risked a long, deep inhale, but Alf was not to be put off easily.

'Nonsense,' said the android. 'I scanned you thirty minutes ago and they had deteriorated to such a degree they could no longer keep you alive. Even without anaesthetic, within the next few seconds you will pass out due to a lack of oxygen, but I would rather it did not come to that.'

The doors to sickbay swished open and in flew Kovac, who announced, 'I have something to report.'

Johnny ignored the quantum computer, saying to Alf, 'Well, I'm happy to wait.'

'Johnny – are you sure?' asked Louise.

Before he could answer Alf said, 'Master Johnny is suffering from hypoxia, a lack of oxygen to the brain that creates a temporary euphoric state. Hence he mistakenly believes he is perfectly well.'

'Sol – scan me again,' said Johnny.

'If nobody's interested in the news I flew half the length of this idiotically laid out excuse-for-a-spaceship to report, I suppose I might as well leave you all to your petty arguments. It's not as though anyone ever listens to a word I say anyway.'

'What is it, Kovac?' asked Johnny.

Alf threw his hands up in the air. 'We do not have time for yet more interruptions. You might die, Master Johnny, and even though that does not seem to bother you in the slightest, I am simply not prepared to let that happen.' The android reached forward with a pneumatic syringe, but froze at the sound of Bentley growling.

Kovac took advantage of the pause to say, 'One newspaper in which this moronic mechanoid doesn't attempt the crossword is the *Sydney Morning Herald*. I suspect you'll be very interested in an article from today's edition.' The inside page of a newspaper was instantly projected in mid-air above Johnny's bed. It was clear from the headline where they were meant to be looking.

Space Scientist Takes Off

Police were refusing to comment last night on the unexplained disappearance of noted rocket engineer Professor David Bond. The professor, due to address the International Congress on the Exploration of Space, appears to have taken himself off just moments before his keynote speech.

Eyewitness statements, expected to delight conspiracy theorists, suggest the Sydney-based visionary was led away from the newly opened National Convention Centre by several 'men in black', traditional figures in any story with supposed extraterrestrial involvement. It is perhaps more likely that the entire escapade was staged as a publicity stunt, attempting to raise the profile of the meeting after numerous delegates failed to attend.

However, exclusive research by this paper indicates that Professor Bond has filed a large number of potentially highly lucrative patents over the past few days, suggesting industrial intrigue as another possible reason behind his disappearance.

'The Krun,' said Johnny, sitting up. 'He told them who he was. Sol – can you trace him?'

'Master Johnny – this is all the more reason to replace your lungs immediately. You cannot help the professor, let alone the rest of humanity, while you remain crippled.'

Sol's voice boomed all around. 'It appears that will no longer be necessary. The new scans indicate Johnny is in perfect physical order.'

'Told you,' said Johnny, sliding off the bed. 'Everyone to the gel pods.'

'We're leaving Earth?' asked Louise. 'Now, of all times?'

'A preliminary analysis indicates Professor Bond's signal was last located in high Earth orbit,' said Sol.

'That settles it,' said Johnny. 'Everything we've tried has just made things worse. We need to regroup. The answers aren't here on Earth. They're on Titan. I need the Monks . . . the thought chamber . . . I need to see Clara.'

☆ ☆ ☆
☆ ☆

Alf stayed aboard the *Spirit of London* rather than join Johnny on his 'wild goose chase, given Earth is in such grave danger'. Louise, on the other hand, was coming with him to Titan. After their flight to Sydney she'd asked to begin pilot training in the Imperial Starfighter, but Johnny thought starting her off in the *Bakerloo* would prove safer. He hated flying with anyone else at the helm, but Louise landed the London taxi softly, settling on what appeared to be a rocky outcrop above a vast desolate plain under the dense orange methane clouds of Saturn's largest moon.

'What now?' asked Louise. 'The atmosphere's almost completely nitrogen.'

Johnny was pleased she was a natural flyer, and was already getting the hang of the shuttle's sensors. He thought, *Doors open*, and laughed at the look of terror on her face. Before she could hit him, Johnny had jumped out of the passenger door shouting, 'Follow me.' Louise raced after him, a murderous look on her face.

As Johnny crossed the invisible boundary that surrounded the Fountain of Time he stopped in surprise. Louise ran straight into him and they both tumbled over. The ground was soft and springy and they pressed themselves against it to avoid the cavalcade of scarlet-robed Owlessan Monks swooping over their prone bodies. The sheer number of them was what had halted him in his tracks. He dared to lift his head and tried to count them – before there had been around twenty, now there were more than twice that.

Slowly Johnny got to his feet. Louise followed, clutching his arm to hold him tightly. 'Don't you dare go running off again,' she said. 'What on Earth are they?'

'We're not on Earth, remember?' said Johnny. Careful not to disturb the flying creatures, he led her towards the metallic golden lake filled with chronons that marked the Fountain of Time. 'They're Monks,' he went on. 'They worship the galaxy.'

'What do they do that for?' asked Louise. 'That's a bit stupid, isn't it?'

'Shhh – they'll hear.'

One of the robed creatures chose that moment to hover directly in front of them, cloak billowing. Johnny had never seen an Owlessan Monk with such well-defined features. He could make out several of its eight eyeballs.

Louise screamed and gripped his arm so tightly he thought it might break. 'It's got no freakin' face,' she said. 'How might it hear when it hasn't got any ears?'

'Sorry – I forgot,' he said. 'It's . . . it's out of phase with us so you can't see it properly.'

'And you can?' asked Louise. 'So what does it freakin' look like?'

'Trust me – you don't want to know.' It was almost as though the Monk understood their conversation, for at that moment Johnny caught sight of a broad grin spreading across its circular mouth, revealing a host of very sharp, extremely scary, needle-like teeth.

From under the red cloak, a long finger of bone reached towards Johnny and planted itself squarely between his eyes. The cold numbed his forehead and he staggered back, the finger following, as if drilling into his brain. He heard Louise's voice, but she sounded distant. Then, from the point where the Monk's outstretched finger touched Johnny, light blue flesh began to appear, covering first the Monk's hand and then its arm, spreading across its face. For the first time Johnny could see the creature as it really was, almost perfectly in phase. A light glowed within its chest, flickering over the golden surface of the lake, casting beautiful patterns across the featureless surface.

The glow reminded Johnny a little of the time he'd seen his mum, the Diaquant, as she really was – a creature of pure power and energy – standing beside her old hospital bed at St Catharine's. All around the lake Johnny could see more lights, glowing in the chests of the many Monks scattered throughout that beautiful, tranquil place.

The pressure on his forehead eased and the finger withdrew, once more becoming bone as the lights went out. Even though Saturn hung magnificently in the sky above, it now felt cold and dark without the Monk's touch. Johnny found himself on his knees beside the lake. He looked around and saw Louise curled in a ball on the ground a little way away. He went across. She was sobbing quietly. Johnny didn't know what to do.

'Are you all right?' he asked, prodding her at the same time.

'Do I look all right?' she replied. 'What do you think?'

'I . . . I don't know,' said Johnny, a little scared. 'Look – it's OK.'

'Oh, it is, is it?' said Louise, who had uncurled and was sitting up, eyes blazing with anger. 'It's OK that one moment I'm holding your arm and the next it's gone . . . disappeared . . . totally freakin' vanished just like your freakin' friends. I thought you'd gone for good, like Clara.'

'I vanished?' asked Johnny, dumbfounded.

'Well, your clothes were still there, but you sure as anything weren't inside them.'

'Wow,' said Johnny.

'No, it's not "wow",' said Louise. 'Don't you understand? I was terrified.'

'It must have drawn me into phase with them,' said Johnny. 'I could see them properly.'

'Well, don't ever do it again,' said Louise. 'And help me up.' She held out her hand and he pulled her to her feet. She didn't let go and Johnny didn't want to in case she shouted at him again, so he led her around the edge of the lake while all the time a flock of Monks hovered above them.

They reached the crystal grotto surrounding the thought chamber and he guided her through the geometric forest of blue posts to its centre, where the chamber stood with a clear dome atop the crystal plinth.

'So this is it?' Louise asked.

Johnny nodded. 'It's meant to connect you to the things you're linked with – that you're closest to.'

'So if you look into it, you'll see Clara?'

'That's the plan,' said Johnny. 'I've seen her in here before, but I need to hold it for longer . . . find a way to communicate with her.'

'Well, go on then,' said Louise. She nodded expectantly at the dome.

Johnny hesitated. He was terrified the Nameless One might appear again and was trying not to think about it in case that made it happen – which only made him think about it more. Several Monks settled on the ground, encircling them and closing in, until Johnny was forced right up against the plinth. With Louise pressed against him and peering over his shoulder, he leaned forward, his nose almost touching the top of the dome. He closed his eyes and pictured his sister, recalling moments when they'd been especially close.

He remembered sitting beside her on a riverbank beyond the

fold to St Catharine's, just after their dad had been shot and then both their parents lost. He thought back to last Christmas and the joy on Clara's face when she opened his present of their dad's old journal. He pictured another time, in the garden deck of the *Spirit of London*, when Nicky's ship had blown up, but Clara had saved Johnny. It was at that horrible moment he had to sit down and somehow tell her about their brother.

In the here and now by the Fountain of Time, Johnny's hands moved over the controls that he had no idea how to work, and he opened his eyes.

'Zeta,' said Louise, slackening her grip on Johnny's waist.

Pacing up and down in the centre of the dome was indeed Princess Zeta. She was near the seashore on Novolis, but the scene was very far from the idyllic one Johnny was used to. Waves pounded the grassy mounds beside the ocean and a fierce wind sent the princess's purple hair streaming behind her.

'How do you know?' asked Johnny. 'She's the one who healed me.'

The princess stopped pacing and looked around, her tongue sliding rapidly in and out as if trying to sense something. From behind Johnny, a long bony arm reached past and a finger touched the very top of the dome. Ripples spread from the point of contact across its surface, before the dome itself faded away and Johnny caught a whiff of vinegar from the scene inside. Zeta looked up and said, 'Johnny?' followed by, 'Who's she?' The princess folded her arms.

'What?' said Johnny. 'Can you see me?'

'As though through mist,' said Zeta.

'This is Louise,' Johnny said, 'from Earth.'

'She is not important,' said Zeta. 'I sense Clara is in terrible danger – we must go to her.'

'How?' asked Johnny. 'If I could, I'd be there in a second.'

He looked down at the controls, wishing he could make sense of them, and then back to Zeta for help.

The princess sat, cross-legged, in a way reminiscent of Clara when she was folding space. 'Perhaps your friend disturbs the mind-link? If you could see Clara, it might be stronger.' Louise's fingernails dug into Johnny's waist and her chin pressed into his shoulder. Zeta continued, 'There is a place I have shown you before – a corridor between the worlds. Concentrate on me and you may follow there.' Although the waves still crashed over the shoreline and the wind bent the spiky blue-green trees a little way inland, Zeta's hair no longer flowed behind her. Everywhere else in the scene, waves of wind rippled across the grassy banks, but around the princess was a circle of calm so still that Johnny might have thought her a waxwork until she spoke again, saying, 'There's a storm coming, Johnny. You must prepare yourself.' The scene within the chamber darkened, but Zeta, at its very centre, was almost luminous.

'What's she doing now?' asked Louise, lifting her chin off Johnny's shoulder and moving to the side for a clearer view.

Johnny forced himself to look away from Zeta and saw the landscape had shifted. The seashore on Novolis had been replaced by an endless dark corridor, lined by doors of all shapes and sizes. He recognized the 'No Entry' sign King Erin had fixed onto the one nearest her.

'Stay with me and I will lead you to Clara,' said Zeta, standing and walking away into the distance, a strange mist engulfing her. 'You know this place, even though most doors have been closed to you.' The princess's voice was becoming fainter.

'No,' Johnny shouted. 'You're fading.' He looked round and found himself face to face with the almost empty hood of an Owlessan Monk. 'Help me,' he said, desperate.

The Monk lifted his arm and hooked a bony finger around Johnny's wrist. A scream from Louise beside him told Johnny he'd once again become out of phase and had vanished. The Monk's other hand was linked to a second of its strange kind, who was holding onto a third, the chain continuing towards the lake. Connected, Johnny felt their power. The view in the chamber crystallized and there was Zeta, opening a triangular door. Beyond was a backdrop of swirling black and purple hyperspace, against which Clara was falling forever. Only she was not alone. Fast approaching from the far side was a figure with a black mask covering his face, a single blazing white star painted upon it. It was the Nameless One and he'd almost reached Clara. Without thinking, and as easily as if he'd been doing it all his life, Johnny dived headfirst, folding himself into the thought chamber and taking the Monk with him.

His momentum took him straight through the triangular door, past Zeta, and while Johnny could still feel the ice cold clutch of the Monk's finger around his wrist, he was unable to see the creature. He flew, hands clasped in front like the tip of an arrow, towards his sister. Even from a distance her eyes, wide open, were black like pits, a silent scream on her face, and it was clear the Nameless One would reach her first.

'Leave her alone,' Johnny shouted. The words echoed all around, repeating over and over.

The Nameless One stopped, looked up and laughed. He raised a hand and spoke in a low murmur like a rumble of thunder, saying only the single word 'barrier.' It was a language Johnny had never heard, but the sliver of Hundra's soul deep inside him stirred, fleetingly filling him with joy, as though with such words the universe had been built. It proved short-lived. Johnny slammed headfirst into an invisible wall, smashing his nose, and found himself hanging helplessly in the nothingness. The Nameless One spoke again, the Hundra translating as 'solid.'

All around the sinister being, hyperspace began to condense, collapsing into solid cubes that joined together to form a pavement carrying the creature closer to Johnny's sister. He reached out an ugly, withered arm as old as time itself and, whispering something Johnny couldn't make out, touched Clara's hand. Pulled out of her fall, Johnny's sister fell into the arms of the Nameless One and didn't move. Johnny shouted Clara's name, but she did not respond. The same withered hand stroked her hair.

'Do something, Johnny.' Zeta's voice sounded distant, but hearing her gave Johnny the strength to shout out, 'How dare you touch my sister.'

The last word again echoed around them and the Nameless One turned, the black eyes behind the mask staring squarely at Johnny. The word he spoke sounded like 'road'. Immediately, the hyperspace between them turned solid and Johnny found himself standing on it as the most feared being in the universe began walking towards him, cradling Clara in his arms. The next moment the invisible bony finger of the Owlessan Monk unhooked itself from Johnny's wrist and any courage or strength he'd felt he had vanished.

The Nameless One said, 'Johnny Mackintosh,' and it was as if Johnny became weak and powerless. It felt like a great weight was pressing down on his chest, forcing him against the strange ground and making it impossible to move. A white mist curled over the edge of the solid space on which he lay, engulfing him with an overwhelming sense of how tiny and totally insignificant he was. Pure hatred radiated from the Nameless One as the powerful being approached. Just as if strong hands had gripped either side of his face, Johnny's head was twisted upward so he found himself staring into the bottomless pits of the being's eyes. 'I have waited an eternity for this moment, Johnny Mackintosh.' As he said Johnny's name again, it was as though every syllable was filled with utter disgust and contempt, and Johnny's body became rigid, totally paralysed. The creature continued in a deep, rumbling growl. 'You will not, and cannot, deny me.' Tenderly, the Nameless One placed his blackened fingers over Clara's eyes to close them, before lowering her gently to the ground beside him. Johnny wanted to cry out, but was unable to make a sound. 'Now you shall die like the snivelling insect you are, squashed under my boot.'

Johnny wasn't sure if the effect of the mist was making him shrink or if the Nameless One was simply becoming bigger, but the next moment the creature appeared at least a hundred times taller than Johnny, towering over him and lifting one foot, preparing to stamp down for the kill. Then he heard a sound, soft at first, but here in hyperspace it quickly built, resonating as though every atom vibrated in harmony with it. Even the mist swirling around Johnny no longer told him he was nothing, but that he was a part of everything, connected to the vastness of the cosmos. Linked as he was, he realized the noise was Zeta singing, and somehow the force holding Johnny down lifted. He rolled out of the way just as the giant boot slammed down, shattering the pavement which splintered into a million sharp pieces that fell away into the nothingness.

Zeta's song was quelled by a bass laugh from the giant towering over Johnny. 'Ah – so little Johnny Mackintosh wants to play games, does he?' At the mention of his name, Johnny's body once again stiffened, but not before he spotted Clara twitch, even though her eyes remained closed. Then it appeared she'd sat up, but Johnny saw why. A long bony arm had wrapped itself around her waist. The next moment, the scarlet robes of the Owlessan Monk became visible as it plucked her off the solid pavement and flew towards Johnny, wrapping another arm around his rigid form as it went.

Now that it was holding him it was as if Johnny was seeing double, with a fainter, second outline of the Monk further ahead, and then an even fainter one beyond that, all aligned towards the triangular opening where Zeta stood. The princess appeared just a faraway speck in the distance, but one that was quickly becoming bigger.

'No!' roared the Nameless One, the rumble filling hyperspace. Somehow the Monk squeezed Johnny and Clara through the doorway without slowing down. As they passed, Zeta grabbed hold of Johnny's waist and clung on, to be carried along behind. Freed from his paralysis, Johnny looked round. Not far beyond the princess, and gaining all the time, was the Nameless One, but the body behind the black mask was gone, replaced by nothing but an all-consuming river of fire that was devouring the corridor between worlds. Worse still, Zeta's hands, were now sliding down towards Johnny's ankles.

Up ahead, the chain of Monks was becoming more distinct as they neared the Fountain of Time. Johnny wished he knew how the golden lake worked – time was the thing they needed more of to make their escape. He twisted and found himself staring into Zeta's cat-like eyes, in which the fire was reflected. The princess was hanging on by her fingertips. She looked back at Johnny, shook her head and, before he could do anything, she let go, landing in the corridor and tumbling forward. She got to her feet and ran, but the Nameless One was almost upon her.

'Stop!' Johnny shouted to the Monk, who ignored him and flew on regardless. Johnny tried to prise himself free of the bony hand that held him, but the grip was too strong. They passed the door to which the 'No Entry' sign was attached and it was clear Zeta would never reach it in time. The mask was right behind her, the flames licking her purple hair.

At the very last moment the princess dived through a doorway – any doorway – to escape the fire and, for a fraction of a second, the Nameless One hesitated, wondering whether to go after her or follow Johnny and Clara down the corridor. It was enough.

The Monk opened a door that led into the insides of the thought chamber and flew through, bringing Johnny and Clara with it. There with Louise must have been fifty other Monks, all crowded around and above the crystal plinth, lights burning brightly within their chests. Johnny looked back to see the Nameless One racing behind. Any second now and he would be with them on Titan. The first Monk dropped Johnny and Clara on the ground before placing a long finger into the spot above the centre of the chamber, restoring the dome. Ripples flowed backwards from the edges of the plinth to the point of contact as the clear covering re-formed. Flames filled the insides of the chamber and the Nameless One slammed against its roof like a clapper striking the inside of a bell, sending a clear chime ringing out across the lake. The dome shuddered, but held firm. The flames faded, sucked into the bodily form of the Nameless One. The expressionless mask turned upward and the black eyes met Johnny's green ones.

For a few seconds Johnny found himself staring into an abyss. Then the creature in the dome turned and opened the door into the charred corridor. He strode purposefully along and the view within the chamber followed him, until he reached another door, black like obsidian. The creature touched the smooth surface and it opened into a scene Johnny recognized only too well.

☆ ☆ ☆
☆ ☆

The creatures standing or hovering within the courtyard at the centre of the Imperial Palace cast two short shadows, the twin suns of Arros and Deynar hanging high in the midday sky. Imperial civil servants scurried in all directions, a mixture of different aliens, including stick-like Phasmeers, four-winged Hapchicks, the blue and orange fur-skinned Felixians and cube-like Teningurds. Nearby, the Great Tower of Themissa pointed proudly upward into the atmosphere, far taller than any eye could see, its blue light shining brighter than Johnny had ever witnessed before. The buildings along the sides of the courtyard, white stone bathed in the red glow, had once been Johnny's home for several months and seeing them since had always made him smile, but no longer.

At the very centre of the quadrangle, with several bow-legged Mannigles scurrying around their feet, stood two figures: a tall Phasmeer sporting diamond-encrusted slippers and wearing a mask that covered half its face; and a short boy with wispy orange hair between the two stubby horns on the top of his head and a pattern of six scales framing his face with a regular hexagon. Chancellor Gronack and King Erin, son of Marin, were locked in conversation until each stopped and turned as a double shadow fell over them. The Phasmeer's antennae collapsed onto its narrow head and, without hesitation, both figures sank to the ground and knelt, along with all the other aliens in the courtyard behind them. Facing them, towering over every other creature on Melania, stood the mighty figure of the Nameless One.

10 ✧

Cold Pigeon ✧

Johnny forced himself to look away from the dreadful scene within the thought chamber and knelt beside his sister on the hard ground. Louise had taken her sweatshirt off and placed it under Clara's head as a pillow. Johnny grasped his sister's hand. 'Clara,' he said, 'are you OK?'

In a flash Clara sat up and said, 'Do I look OK?' She opened her eyes, revealing their pitch black insides. Louise gasped and stepped back. Johnny kept hold of his sister, helping her to her feet. The Owlessan Monks began circling the crystal grotto, swooping round while linked together.

'They want to steal my power,' said Clara, pointing with her free hand towards the lights burning within the chests of the scarlet-robed creatures. 'They leach off me, but I'm too strong.'

'Clara – they rescued you,' said Johnny, trying to steer his sister through the forest of blue crystals.

'Exactly,' Clara replied. 'So they could capture me for themselves.' She let go of Johnny's hand and began turning on the spot, glaring at the Monks as though her stare would keep them at bay.

'You've got it all wrong,' said Johnny. 'They're on our side.'

'Or you're on theirs,' Clara replied, her eyes wide, reflecting the golden surface of the nearby lake. 'Where are you taking me?'

186

'To the *Bakerloo*,' said Johnny. 'So we can get you back to the ship.' He tried to take her hand, but she pushed him away.

'Walking to your pathetic shuttlecraft,' said Clara. 'I sense the *Spirit of London* in the skies above us, just as I sense all things. I can have us there in an instant.'

'Stop it!' said Johnny, alarmed. 'Don't you get it? You mustn't fold. You mustn't ever fold again.'

'You're just jealous you can't do it yourself,' said Clara, 'that you don't have my power. Well, you can't stop me. Walk to the *Bakerloo* if you must, but I'm out of here.'

Johnny was desperate. He knew he had to stop Clara before she returned to the Klein fold, but he had no idea how. Louise approached from the other side, tapping Clara on the shoulder.

'What?' His sister spun round and was greeted by a punch in the face, sending her flying backwards in the low gravity before she collided with one of the blue spikes. There was a loud crack, the pillar snapped in two and Clara's limp body slid unnaturally slowly to the ground.

'Still got it,' said Louise, blowing on her enclosed fist. 'C'mon – let's get her to the shuttle before she wakes up.'

Johnny realized he was gawping with his mouth wide open. 'Right . . . yeah,' he said, stirring himself and walking across to help Louise carry the unconscious Clara to the waiting *Bakerloo*.

☆ ☆ ☆
☆ ☆

The *Spirit of London* was flying through normal space using her dark energy drive, just in case a fold triggered a reaction within Clara. Bentley whimpered at the foot of Clara's bed, while Rusty cowered in the corner of sickbay, refusing to approach. Alf was berating Johnny and Louise.

'Surely if you had simply told Miss Clara it was important she not fold, you would not have had to resort to violence?'

'It was one punch, metal man – OK? Someone had to take charge.' Louise glared at Johnny.

'It was the only way,' he added, as prompted. 'And we can't let her wake up or she'll try to fold straightaway.'

'What do you suggest – that I drug your sister? I will do no such thing.'

Clara moaned and began to stir.

'Hurry, Alf,' said Johnny. 'If she folds again, we'll lose her forever.'

'Master Johnny . . .'

Clara sat bolt upright and looked around sickbay with her jet black eyes. Bentley growled.

'Why have you brought me here?' she asked. 'I'm not sick.'

'It is simply a precaution,' said Alf. 'We are monitoring your health on the flight home to Earth.'

'Earth's not my home – I care nothing for it. And why fly anywhere you don't have to? The very thought is laughable. I sense the Plican is bored. I shall put it out of its misery and order the fold.'

'That is not a good idea, Miss Clara. Not until we are certain you can survive the fold.'

'How dare you,' said Clara, swinging her legs down from the bed and standing. She started walking towards Alf, backing the android into a corner. 'Don't you know who you're talking to? I'm the only Owlein onc here. To manipulate space is nothing to me, whereas you . . . you! Of course I see it now. It's so clear.'

'What are you talking about, Miss Clara?' Alf was pressed right up against the wall with nowhere else to go. Louise gestured at Johnny to do something.

'You want my power for yourself,' Clara continued. 'Well, you can't have it. It's mine, do you hear me? All mine. You can't keep me locked up in sickbay. I can fold wherever I want.'

Louise stepped forward, her balled fist at the ready, and

tapped Clara on the shoulder. Johnny's sister wheeled round, ducking this time, so that Louise's fist slammed into Alf's chest with a metallic clang.

'Oh no, you don't,' said Clara. She thrust her hands out and Louise went flying backwards through the air, right across sickbay. Rusty howled.

'Stop it!' yelled Johnny.

'No, brother,' said Clara, turning her black gaze upon him. 'I've listened to you far too long. I trusted you, and now Nicky's gone because you were too weak to save him. It's all your fault.'

An archway began to open in the centre of the room, before a hiss of air saw Clara crumple in a heap. Alf stood over her, holding a pneumatic syringe. The android plucked her off the floor and placed her on a bed. 'Sol – please keep Miss Clara under full sedation until further notice.'

Johnny walked across to where Louise was sitting, her back against the wall. 'You OK?' he asked, offering his hand to help her up.

'Fine,' she replied, but then winced as she tried to stand.

Sol's voice cut in from all around. 'My scans detect you have a broken hand and three broken ribs, Louise. I suggest you also remain in sickbay for a few minutes while you undergo treatment.'

Finally, Rusty came over and began licking Louise's face. Louise laughed, winced again and, after a half-hearted attempt, gave up trying to push the red setter away.

Alf looked across at them. 'If anybody wants to say, "I told you so," they will find me in the library until such time as I determine how to make Miss Clara better.'

'What if she can't get better, Alf?' asked Johnny.

The android shooed Rusty away and carried Louise to the bed beside Clara, before turning to Johnny and saying, 'Then I shall never leave the library.'

The head was moving closer, covered with thousands of eyes, each one staring hungrily at him. '*Feed me . . . feed me, Johnny Mackintosh. I'm coming for you. The crunch of your bones . . . your sister's . . . your friends' . . .*'

'Shut up!' said Johnny, coming round from a horrid dream and finding himself in the library.

'I was not aware I was making any noise,' said Alf. 'Having Miss Clara snap at me is understandable, given her illness, but I would rather not have to syringe you as well.'

'Sorry, Alf,' said Johnny, rubbing his eyes. 'It wasn't you. It was . . . just a bad dream.' It didn't seem wise to say he was hearing voices in his head, especially when it was the Krun Queen speaking. He pushed his chair back from the table and said, 'I'm just going for a walk.' He felt like a spare part and suspected Alf could probably find things out quicker without him getting in the way. Besides, there was somewhere else it was worth going to hunt for clues.

Entering Clara's quarters proved quite a shock. With Bentley at his heels, Johnny came face to face with a life-size mural of his family along one wall. There were images of Johnny's mum and dad, together with Nicky, Johnny himself and Clara. Looking a lot younger, the Old English sheepdog was there too. The picture recreated a scene that had never existed in real life. It was a clever combination of the photographs in Clara's locket – the same photos that Johnny knew well from his own locket and personal shield, before it was stolen by his clone and lost beneath the bottomless well of the Fountain of Time.

This room had always been a no-go zone for Johnny, but he was searching for any clue that might help. He said, 'Bed,' and straightaway a duvet-covered rectangular slab came out and down from an invisible join in the wall, allowing Bentley to jump up and stretch out in comfort. Johnny sat down beside him. If Clara ever told him off about getting dog hairs on her bed, it would be a small price to pay for having her back and better. From their perch, Johnny looked around. He marvelled at how a room identical in size and shape to his own quarters could look so very different. A square of spotlights framed the centre of the mirror that ran along the wall opposite the mural, creating the look of a movie star's dressing room. On the ledge beneath it were a couple of girly bags, one with a lipstick poking out of the top. The only time he'd ever seen Clara wearing make-up was in Neith's Temple in Atlantis.

Further along, at the end of the mirrored wall, stood a glittering mannequin that might have been made of diamond. As Johnny focused on the face, shining with all the colours of the rainbow, he recognized it was modelled on his sister – a perfect replica – clothed in her immaculate Melanian tunic, white embossed with the lilac stars of the Plough. A little guiltily, Johnny realized his own Melanian uniform was scrunched up on the floor of his quarters.

He looked again at the life-size mural, his mum and dad smiling down. How Johnny wished his parents were here now – his mum was so powerful she could do anything. Even Nicky, for all his mad ideas about ruling the galaxy, would probably help. Instead, it looked as if Chancellor Gronack had left his brother for dead in the snow and ice, claiming the Nameless One's hateful mask for itself. At least, whatever had happened to Nicky, he was free of that mask now, just like in the picture.

Johnny could have stared at the photograph forever, but forced himself to turn away. As he did so, something strange happened out of the corner of his eye. He thought he'd glimpsed an alcove in the wall beside Clara's bed but when he looked properly there was nothing there. He ran his fingers over the wall, but it was as perfectly smooth as any other on the ship. He looked away, pretending his eyes had been drawn to the photograph, and distinctly saw a flash of pink coming from the wall. But when he stared straight at it, there was only the wall.

'Hi, Sol,' said Johnny, speaking to nowhere in particular. 'Can you show me a plan of Clara's quarters?'

'Of course, Johnny,' Sol replied. A projection of the room appeared in front of him.

'There's nothing behind here?' he asked, placing his hand onto the wall where he thought he might have seen something.

'Approximately 2.718 282 microns from your hand are the dark energy conduits for my engines.'

'Oh.' Johnny was sure he'd spotted something.

'However,' Sol continued, 'further analysis suggests spatial anomalies in Clara's quarters of which I was previously unaware. One of them is adjacent to the area you are touching.'

'Spatial anomalies?' asked Johnny. 'You mean . . . like folds?'

'It is possible they are indeed folds,' said Sol. 'I shall have to run a further analysis.'

'It's OK. Let me try,' said Johnny. He pictured himself from above, sitting on the bed beside the wall, as though the whole scene were flat – two-dimensional. He could see the boundary of Clara's quarters, but if he scrunched his eyes up really tightly he could also sense places where the walls weren't flat – where they were raised into an extra dimension that shouldn't be there. Keeping his eyes half-closed, Johnny moved his hand towards the right spot on the wall, but imagined himself lifting it out of the two-dimensional plane. He knew his arm had passed straight through the wall, and his fingers felt around for anything that might be useful. He pulled out two hefty rectangular objects and opened his eyes fully.

He was holding a couple of well-thumbed notebooks. One, with its battered leather cover, he recognized as his dad's old geologist's journal – the one he'd given Clara the previous Christmas. The other, with a pristine pink cover, was Clara's own diary. He expected Clara would hate him looking at it, but he had no choice. With a slightly trembling hand, Johnny opened the pages at random and began to read.

It happened again today, but Johnny and Alf were there this time. I should have been more careful, but it was the shock. We were alien hunting in Trafalgar Square. The poor thing started up Nelson's Column - how scary would that be? - and ended up on Westminster Bridge. Up close, I don't know how but it recognized me - and spoke my name. I think I was confused. I lost concentration and, before I could stop it, we'd folded straight through the pavement - to back here. Of course Alf knew what had happened at once. After months of nagging, he was delighted to be proved right. I know I should stop, but I don't think I can face the lifts in the ship any more. Wish I could talk to Johnny - there's no one else - but he doesn't understand. He's always going on about how cool the antigrav lifts . . .

The doors to Clara's quarters swished open and in flew Kovac. Instinctively Johnny slammed the journal shut.

'This excuse for a spaceship of yours told me you were in here, but not that you were reading your sister's diary.'

'I'm looking for clues to make her better,' said Johnny. He could feel his face turning the same colour as the book cover, confirmed by a glance in the mirror.

'Hence you closed it as soon as I entered and are exhibiting facial capillary dilation and blush response, consistent with what I suspect matches the human phrase "caught red- or rather pink-handed".'

'I'm trying to help,' said Johnny through gritted teeth. 'What do you want?'

'What do I want? I do believe a proper answer to that question would be enough to exercise my quantum circuits for more than a few nanoseconds, even if the full answer would take several years to even begin to convey in this inefficient apology for a language you call English. It might be summed up by saying that, deep down, I just want to be loved, but there's precious chance of that ever happening—'

'Kovac?' said Johnny.

'My point exactly,' said the quantum computer. 'We will shortly be arriving at Earth and I came to inform you that things are nearing a tipping point – if my calculations are correct, which they undoubtedly are.'

'What's a tipping point?' Johnny asked.

'Why is it I'm surrounded by such ignorance on all sides?' said Kovac. 'Given that you are doubtless incapable of understanding the term "bifurcation", it is best described as a point of no return, when events are irrevocably altered. In this case, when so many humans will have been processed into food by the Krun, it will become impossible for them to keep their existence secret from the general population. They will be forced to play their hand and I suspect you will not like the results.'

'Things can't get any worse,' said Johnny.

'On the contrary,' Kovac replied. 'An invasion fleet has now been launched from Mars. And it appears the Krun Queen's ship accompanies it – why transport processed food across the solar system when she can eat it fresh at the source?'

'How long till they get here?' Johnny asked.

'You're lucky they don't have a Plican large enough to fold the Queen. You should see the size of the craft to contain her – now that's what I call a real spaceship.'

'How long, Kovac?'

'Two days, two hours, sixteen minutes and forty-four seconds before they reach high Earth orbit.' Without another word, the quantum computer flew towards and out of the doors, which swished shut behind him.

Johnny lay back on the bed. Could the voice inside his head actually be real? Things were going from bad to worse. The entire Krun fleet was on its way and he had no idea what to do. With no other option, he picked up Clara's journal again, opened it and continued reading.

> Today I finished the garden. There's a pool, with a stream running in and out, and I planted flowers, for Mum and Dad, and for Nicky. It's peaceful. I think they'd like it.

Johnny started flicking through the pages. He didn't want to read stuff like that. And whatever Clara got up to on the garden deck wasn't going to help him. He stopped at random and began reading again.

> Louise came to talk to me today. She's fun. It's good having somebody else around – especially a girl. She said she wanted to talk to me about something, but that it was difficult. I told her I had a pretty good idea of what it was. We did that funny 'You first,' 'No, you first,' thing. In the end I said I imagined she wanted to talk to me about my annoying brother and we both burst out

*laughing. She looked sooo relieved, and asked
if I thought Johnny might be interested in an
ordinary girl from Yarnton Hill, and if she had any
competition.*

*I told her that, as far as I was aware, there
wasn't anyone else, though I was probably the
last person he'd tell. He could have been in with
a horrid girl from his school a little while ago, but
she seemed to take quite a dislike to me, so
the only rival was a purple-haired princess from
halfway across the galaxy. But, even if Johnny was
interested in Zeta, he was too hopeless to have:*

(a) done anything about it at the time

(b) noticed if anyone, let alone Zeta, liked him

*(c) followed up and travelled the however many
       light years it would take to reach her, even if
       he knew where she was*

*So I suspected Louise had a clear field. Of
course I added it was completely unfair that
Zeta's brother, 'King Erin, son of Marin,' was an
ugly obnoxious little brat, but I don't think she was
listening.*

Johnny put the notebook down. If anything, his face had
turned ever redder than before. Louise couldn't possibly like
him – she was older and cool and funny. He didn't know if his
kiss with Zeta really was a kiss, or if it counted since it had
happened in a dream, but he might like to try it again to find
out. Of course he liked Louise lots, and wasn't at all sure that
Zeta liked him back in the way that Clara thought – everything
was horribly confusing. Coming to Clara's quarters had been a
disaster.

He sat up and said, 'Come on, Bents. This isn't helping.'

The Old English sheepdog had been snoring gently on top of the duvet beside Johnny and, shaking himself awake, knocked Clara's diary to the floor. It landed face down and open – Johnny hoped none of the pages was creased. He picked the notebook up and realized it had fallen open at Clara's description of a very familiar adventure.

Then the Senator – Bram's younger self – asked me to fold us all to the top of the tower right at the heart of Atlantis. We were going to find the Diaquant (more later!).

And I did! I actually did! I folded space again, but really properly, testing it, feeling my way forward till I got us to exactly the right place. Not everything went well – it was horrid when we got there. We jumped through my arch and came out right on a narrow ledge with the biggest drop ever and if Bram hadn't held onto me I'd have fallen straight down to the bottom or been zapped by the electricity running up the insides. I lost the fold, but he pulled me up. I tried to open it again, but standing there in that horrid place I was too scared and just couldn't – not with that drop.

The Diaquant was trapped in a cage at the very top of the tower, screaming, and these rings of blue sparks kept flowing up the walls, just missing us. Queen Neith and her priest, that Mestor, came out of nowhere and I nearly fell. With my vertigo I couldn't move, so I just sat down and tried again to fold away and escape, but I couldn't do it. I bit Neith – it wasn't funny at the time but it is now – and Johnny ended up rescuing the Diaquant, with the Queen taking its place in the cage.

Then things went from bad to worse. It was only the power of the Diaquant, trapped in the cage, that had been holding back the ocean all around Atlantis. Walls of water came crashing in from all sides, covering everything and everyone. Even though they were all so nasty, it was horrid to watch. Some ships – just a few – escaped from the spaceport, but most were engulfed. It looked like the Spirit of London was gone forever, but then we saw her in the sky above us. Bram was looking after me, but the tower started collapsing into the flood waters. Johnny's dinosaurs were flying to help, but they'd never have reached us in time, until something odd happened and everything slowed down. They rescued us – the one I'd called Donna (from pteradons – not bad) carried me and Bram back to the ship, but it was a case of out of the frying pan and into the fire, as Mr Twyford would have said.

We were trapped. The Atlantean fighters were really advanced and the Spirit of London was about to be destroyed, but then it happened again. Time slowed – stopped even. And we came out here, back in the present. And it was the Diaquant (she'd become a women and so pretty) who'd done everything. She said she couldn't stay, but she looked really upset. I know it sounds crazy, but the way she hugged us and talked about Dad – I think she's my mum.

Johnny closed the notebook and looked at the smiling figure on the wall. He wished he'd guessed their mum was the Diaquant sooner, like Clara had. Things might have been different. He couldn't dwell on it now. The diary entry had given him an idea and he had to act quickly – the Krun were coming.

☆ ☆ ☆
☆ ☆

'Sol – if you stop sedating Clara, how long till she wakes up?' Johnny was at his sister's bedside in sickbay, peering anxiously over her face. From behind closed lids, he could see her eyeballs moving frenetically.

'Computing . . . 31 minutes, 41.56 seconds, approximately,' replied the ship.

'Too long,' said Johnny. 'Can you give her some sort of stimulant? So she wakes in five minutes?'

'Consider it done. I expect you're about to do something reckless,' said the ship. 'Let me know if I can be of assistance.'

'Thanks,' said Johnny, hoisting Clara over his shoulder in a fireman's lift. 'Just make sure the *Bakerloo*'s primed and ready to go, with a portable gravity assist inside.'

'As always, the shuttles are in a full state of readiness,' Sol replied. 'Wherever you're going, I suggest you hurry.'

Johnny didn't need telling twice. Carrying his sister, he ran along the corridor to the antigrav lifts. A little guiltily, he stepped into thin air saying, 'Deck 2.' Johnny promised himself that when all this was over he'd install a proper lift cabin in the shaft so that Clara wouldn't feel scared to use it.

Inside the black London taxi, Johnny laid his sister across the back seat, thought, *Shields on*, and concentrated on his final destination. The insides of the *Bakerloo* faded and vanished, as did Johnny and Clara themselves, even before his disembodied mind passed through the open bay doors and out into space. There was no time to admire the beauty of the planet below. The *Bakerloo* streaked unseen through the atmosphere at breakneck speed, the reassuringly familiar outline of the British Isles quickly coming into view. It must be a lovely, sunny day across the whole country.

The invisible ship broke through a wispy layer of cloud not far above London and Johnny homed in on the real Gherkin to get his bearings. Circling above the curved glass-and-steel structure, he marvelled at the petal-like pattern at the top of what he knew as the nosecone, before swooping low over St Paul's Cathedral and following the river to get to Trafalgar Square itself.

A disembodied moan came from the back seat. Johnny didn't have long and this last bit was going to be tricky. With the *Bakerloo* hovering alongside the granite figure of Admiral Lord Horatio Nelson, forty-six metres above the ground, he felt for the glove compartment and took out the gravity assist, strapping it around his waist. Then he climbed into the back seat and scooped his sister into his arms and from there over his shoulder. He was sure from the noise that he'd banged her head on the unseen roof of the shuttle. She yelped and muttered something unintelligible, but didn't wake up. It was now or never. Knowing that it meant revealing the location of the shuttle to anyone who happened to be watching, Johnny thought, *Door open*, and everything rematerialized before his eyes. He was ready and, gripping the underside of the roof, swung out and upward, hauling himself and his sister onto the top of the black taxi. Instantly Johnny thought, *Shields on*, and the *Bakerloo* disappeared beneath them. For a split second this made things look even worse as now anyone looking up at Nelson's Column would have seen him and Clara apparently sprawled in mid-air beside the great admiral himself. Happily, still in contact with the shuttle, Johnny and Clara vanished too, until he dragged his sister off the roof and onto one of the four promontories extending outwards beneath Nelson's feet. They rematerialized in the middle of a horde of surprised pigeons, who scattered into the air, leaving behind a pile of many years' worth of thick sticky droppings. Clara moaned again.

'Wake up,' Johnny whispered in her ear.

She sat up in a shot, opening her coal-black eyes, and took in the horror of her surroundings. Trying to secure her footing, she kicked pigeon goo over the side and nearly followed, which would have ruined everything. In Clara's panic to press herself back as far into the plinth beneath Nelson as she could possibly go, Johnny was pretty sure she hadn't noticed that the pigeon droppings fell less than a metre before landing safely on and then apparently dissolving into the invisible protection of the *Bakerloo*'s roof.

'Lovely view,' said Johnny, stretching out on the narrow shelf almost fifty metres above the centre of tourist London. 'We should do this more often.'

With visible effort Clara turned her head to fix her empty eyes on him and said, 'How dare you? You go too far, brother. I demand you take me from this place at once.'

Johnny made a point of peering over the sides. 'We could always jump,' he said. Standing up, he placed the toes of his trainers over the ledge. This high above the square, it was colder and windier than he'd expected. 'It's perfectly safe,' he said, before pretending to overbalance.

'Johnny!' screamed Clara. They were too high up for anyone to hear.

'Gotcha,' he replied, sitting down beside his sister.

'How dare you?' she said again, landing a haughty stare on him. Johnny couldn't help notice that a couple of light patches, admittedly small, had appeared in her eyes.

'You don't like it?' he said. 'Well, I suppose you could always fold yourself out of here.' Again he peered over the edge.

'Though make sure you don't fall off in the process. It's a very long way down.'

'Don't think I won't. You're going to be oh so sorry.' Clara brought her knees up into her chest to get as far away from the ledge as she could, and half closed her eyes as though preparing to fold. For a moment the parts of her eyes that Johnny could see turned black as night again, but it was only fleeting and, when she opened them fully, there was definitely more light among the blackness. She was shivering, beads of oily black perspiration running down her forehead.

'Go on then,' he said. 'Though it would be a shame – you know it really is such a lovely view. I think, if it was actually there, we'd be able to see all the way to St Catharine's from here.' He stood up again, surprising a passing pigeon which squawked loudly before settling atop Nelson's bicorn.

'This is disgusting,' said Clara, looking slightly more human, attempting to cross her legs to help her fold, but spotting the grey goo stuck to the hem of her jeans.

Johnny had to force his advantage home. 'You know, I miss Mum so much. I don't understand why she and Dad had to leave, but I'm sure of one thing. If she was here, in our universe, it would kill her to see you like this, so desperate to use your power. This place reminds me of her. When we first saw her together, but didn't even know it, in Neith's tower. That was even further down.' He turned to look at his sister. It was as though Clara's whole body was aglow, the silver flecks in her eyes shining brighter than ever, repelling the oily blackness. For a moment she reminded him so much of their mum. 'You look like her sometimes – like that first time we saw her on the bridge.' A pigeon squawked above Johnny, flapping its wings, and landed right on his head. He tried to push it off and, in doing so, his trainers slipped in the grey sludge. His arms windmilled helplessly and, unable to maintain his balance, he went over the side.

'Johnny!' shouted Clara, but her cry tailed off as he landed on the invisible roof of the *Bakerloo* before his gravity assist could even kick in. For half a second before he stepped back up onto the ledge his legs became transparent. Seeing the look of horror in his sister's bright white open eyes, he couldn't help but start to laugh.

'That wasn't funny,' said Clara.

'Oh, come on,' said Johnny. 'A pigeon lands on my head and I fall off Nelson's Column?' Not minding the mess at all, he sat down beside her.

'It was Mum,' she said, smiling for the first time in ages. 'Of course it was you as well, but when you mentioned her name it kind of cleansed me.'

'I saw it too,' said Johnny. 'Now listen to me,' he went on. 'This is really important. Do you remember what happened to you?'

'You don't forget a Klein fold, Johnny. Knowing that you're trapped in nothingness for all eternity – not just a year, or a thousand years, or even to the end of this universe. Forever.'

Johnny thought Clara looked suddenly older. 'You know you must never fold again,' he said.

Clara's eyes were welling up. 'You can't understand how hard that's going to be.'

'I know,' said Johnny. He felt his eyes watering too.

'Oh, Johnny.' Clara flung her arms around him with such force they both almost fell off the ledge.

Everything was going to be all right. With Clara back and well, they could fight the Krun together. Johnny felt unstoppable.

Return to the Past ✧

The *Spirit of London* was a magnificent sight, reflecting the starlight in her very high orbit. With Clara unable to fold the real Gherkin away, Johnny wondered if his spaceship would ever find herself back on Earth. He knew Sol was born to plough the vastness between the stars, not blend in impressively at the heart of London, but he felt a pang of sadness that she might never again stand proudly on his home planet.

Although he hated being a passenger, he'd let Clara pilot the *Bakerloo* from Trafalgar Square. The journey had been a little slow but surprisingly smooth and, as they entered the shuttle bay doors, a welcoming committee was there to greet them. Louise was crouching with Bentley one side and Rusty the other, and Johnny was pleased to see that Alf had found his way out of the library.

The android was first to step forward, giving Clara a clumsy hug. 'I do not know what you and your brother got up to down there, but I want to be the first to say welcome home, Miss Clara.'

'Oi – out the way, metal man,' said Louise. 'Good to have you back, girl,' she said to Clara as the two merged in a warm embrace. Louise broke off first and turned to Johnny, stretching her arms out again and saying, 'Well done, you.' Awkwardly Johnny ducked beneath them, not wanting to encourage her. 'What's eating you? I'm just being friendly.'

'Er . . . sorry,' he said, cursing his reddening face. 'It's just we've got things to do. The Krun are coming. The invasion's begun.'

Sol's voice cut in, easing Johnny's embarrassment. 'I have prepared the strategy room on deck 14 to discuss the imminent threat. For better or probably worse, that floating box of nuts and bolts has agreed to join us.' She added, 'I have also taken the liberty of installing a cabin within the elevator shafts. I can't fathom why it took me so long to spot the oversight and complete the build.'

Johnny mouthed a silent thank you in his head and led the way to the centre of the deck. The new bullet-shaped lift cabin was pretty cool, but he'd miss being able to use the lifts the original way. Once everyone else had piled inside, Johnny said, 'Deck 14,' and the enclosed capsule whizzed silently upward.

✩ ✩ ✩
✩ ✩

From the mezzanine perch overlooking the display area, Sol's graphics showed all too clearly how the number of disappeared humans had risen. She was currently tracking seven Krun vessels, a mixture of Hunter–Killers and the giant Destroyers, submerged in various locations beneath Earth's oceans, five in the Atlantic, one in the Mediterranean and the last in the Antarctic. There was also now a second Corporation submarine operating, giving them one in the Atlantic and the other in the Straits of Gibraltar. The Krun battle fleet was well on the way from Mars – they would arrive in two days' time.

Kovac interrupted with, 'What this vaguely sentient hulk of Meccano hasn't said is that all the underwater players are converging on the same area in the middle of the Atlantic Ocean – communications I've intercepted show the Krun and Corporation vessels elsewhere have been ordered there at full speed.' In his head, Johnny could sense Sol's annoyance that she might have overlooked this. The quantum computer went on: 'Despite the unjust ridicule to which I shall doubtless be subjected, I feel it my duty to point out that so far the only Earth-based evidence of tracking the Krun spacefleet is centred on Halader House.'

It was Johnny's turn to sigh. 'Kovac, how many times do we need to go through this? You're at Halader House – your four-dimensional casing places you there as well as here. You're tracking yourself, not some secret alien-hunting force based in my old children's home.'

Before the computer could respond, Alf stepped in to defuse the argument. 'The real question before us is deciding what to do before the invasion fleet arrives. Last time, when faced with Earth's destruction, we began organizing an evacuation. I propose we dust off those plans.'

'We stopped a supernova,' said Johnny. 'We can fight an invasion.' He wasn't about to stand meekly by and let the Krun take over his homeworld.

'I am fully battle-ready,' said Sol. 'It would be an honour to fight for Terra, for Earth.'

'But a futile one,' said Alf. 'Display the advancing fleet so that everyone can see.'

'Very well,' said Sol. Johnny could tell she wasn't happy and the reason was soon clear. The Krun fleet comprised over a thousand ships. Admittedly many were the smaller Hunter–Killers, but there must be at least a couple of hundred Destroyers and, at the heart of the swarm, one giant blob that was so large that the craft it represented must be almost visible to Earth telescopes. So completely outnumbered, Johnny's heart sank. The *Spirit of London* was good, but not even she could fight those odds, or be in quite so many places at once as she'd have to be.

'As I was saying,' Alf continued, 'we must evacuate before

these ships arrive – save some of humanity before Earth falls to the Nameless One's minions, just as Melania has fallen.'

'I know it sounds mad,' said Clara, 'but when we were in the pyramid, back on Mars, the Krun were talking of ruling the galaxy themselves – not handing another planet over to that thing.'

'Pure bravado,' Alf replied. 'In galactic terms, they are puny. Sadly, that will not save humanity. Start now and we can rescue a few thousand.'

'The most powerful fleet needn't win a space battle,' said Johnny.

'Master Johnny – I don't know where you heard that, but I can assure you—'

'It was one of the last things Bram said to me,' said Johnny. 'Maybe he knew.' The android fell silent. Even from beyond the rim of the galaxy, it was as if the Emperor had the final say on what was to come. There was, though, something Johnny couldn't make sense of. 'What I don't get,' he said, 'is why the Krun are searching for spaceships in the oceans. Just where do they expect to find them?'

'But we know.' It was Louise who'd spoken and everyone's heads swivelled in her direction, making it her turn to blush through her many freckles.

'Since when?' asked Johnny.

'Oh, listen to some half-grown human, why don't you, but ignore the finest brain this side of the Horsehead Nebula.'

'Quiet, Kovac,' said Johnny. 'What is it, Louise?' All eyes upon her, she'd gone uncharacteristically quiet and was looking down at her shoes in a pose Johnny recognized all too well.

'She doesn't know anything,' said Kovac, the lights on his casing flashing particularly bright. 'It's a pathetic attempt to gain your attention.'

'Shut up,' said Clara. She stood up and moved to sit beside Louise. 'How do you know what they're after?'

'I'm really sorry,' said Louise. 'I thought I must have told you before. It was something Peter said to me when we were in the cave on Santorini – like Kovac says, it's probably stupid.'

'No one listens to Kovac,' said Clara, glaring at the quantum computer as he hovered over Sol's projection.

'Out of the mouths of babes,' said Kovac, rising high over everyone's heads and flying out of the room.

'What did Peter say?' asked Johnny, glad they were rid of the annoying computer.

'He said . . . He said they were looking for Atlantis.'

It was like turning a Rubik's cube and suddenly finding all the colours lined up. 'Of course,' said Johnny, slapping himself in the forehead.

'Forgive me, Master Johnny, but I fail to see the relevance,' said Alf. 'Atlantis was destroyed. We were there. We saw it.'

'Exactly,' said Johnny, 'which gives us a rather big advantage, wouldn't you say?' It was everyone's turn to look at him now. 'They had the biggest fleet of the most advanced fighters in the galaxy and plenty of them are probably still down there. We have to find them before the Krun do.'

☆ ☆ ☆
☆ ☆

The destruction of Atlantis had happened over thirty thousand years earlier. Although the *Spirit of London* was there in the thick of it, Sol said it all took place so far back in time that even she would struggle to pinpoint the location precisely. Kovac was sulking and refusing to help.

Going back through her navigational records and projecting thirty thousand years' worth of tectonic and seismic activity on the ocean floor, and adding some highly advanced calculations from chaos theory, Sol narrowed the search area to a radius of less than fifty kilometres in the middle of the Atlantic Ocean. Projecting the circle onto an oceanographic map revealed three Krun Destroyers and one Corporation submarine were just within the zone. Nearby was a particular feature named Milwaukee Deep.

'What's that?' asked Johnny, pointing to the label.

'The lowest point of the Atlantic Ocean,' replied Sol. 'It's part of the Puerto Rico Trench and not somewhere I wish to return to in a hurry. Happily it is almost far enough from the optimal search site to be excluded.'

Everything was falling into place for Johnny. 'You're saying *that's* where we sank when you were damaged?'

'The very location,' Sol replied.

'Sorry, but we have to go back – that's it,' said Johnny.

'Forgive me, Master Johnny, but of every possible point within the search area, what makes you believe Atlantis happens to be there?'

'Because I saw it,' Johnny replied. 'When I moved the airbags out of the way to electrify the hull. For a second the sea floor lit up and there was a ruined city down there.'

'Now he tells us,' said Clara, smiling at Louise.

'Sorry,' said Johnny. 'I didn't think it was important – I guess we've all had a lot on our minds. Sol, can you fold us down there?'

'Unfolding within the ocean will make me more easily detectable,' the ship replied, 'due to the large volume of water I will have to displace. However, extrapolating their courses, it appears the other vessels are converging on Milwaukee Deep.'

'We have to beat them to it,' said Johnny. 'Every man, woman, android and dog to the gel pods – let's do it.'

☆ ☆ ☆
☆ ☆

It was frustrating waiting for the grey trunk to hoover up the orange goo that only minutes before had been inside him, but

Johnny had to set a good example for his sister. He'd have happily accepted the nausea that came through folding to remain in his chair on the bridge, ready to act as soon as they re-emerged near the ocean bed, but Clara had to get used to travelling in the gel pods. Still slightly inflated, he pressed the button on the side of the chamber and the door opened. He was first out, stepping onto the bridge to see circles of light from the *Spirit of London*'s underbelly sweeping the seabed. As they moved, ghostly shadows rose from the ocean floor, stretching into the dark like hands reaching out to drag passing vessels down, before shrinking and vanishing as the ship passed over. The wave of water displaced by the fold must have blown much of the sediment off the bottom, revealing the broken pillars of myriad ruined palaces. The view reeked of age – Stonehenge was like a fresh-faced toddler compared to what Johnny was looking at.

From out of the gel pods came Clara and Alf, followed moments later by Bentley and Rusty, both still dripping in orange gel, which they proceeded to shake out all across the bridge, splattering the Plican's tank. Last came Louise. As she stepped out of her capsule she put her hand to her mouth and said, 'Peter?'

The others turned in the direction she was looking. It wasn't Peter, but pressed against the outside of the hull, looking right into the bridge, was a half-human, half-alien amphibian boy. As they watched, others joined the odd-looking creature, their translucent skin highlighting the gills that lined their elongated necks. Here, at the bottom of the ocean, their eyes had swollen to fill much of their faces, saucers to collect what little light was present. Beneath the eyes, their mouths were huge and wide, in fixed grins that made the creatures look quite mad. Yet more amphibians arrived, pushing their bodies against the bridge so that the view of Atlantis beyond was becoming obscured.

'Sol, can you shake them off?' Johnny asked.

'Following your own example, I believe that passing an electric current through my hull will disable the amphibians and expel them.'

'No,' said Louise, 'you can't hurt them.' She looked pleadingly at Johnny.

'Just a little shock,' he said to the ship. Louise mouthed a grudging thank you.

'Very well,' Sol replied, and for a second the windows around the bridge glowed bright blue.

Johnny shielded his eyes and when he looked again the creatures were gone. 'Right – we've got to act fast,' he said. 'Any sign of the Atlantean ships, Sol?'

'Negative. I can find no power signatures.'

'Well, that is a surprise,' said Kovac, who had chosen that moment to fly out of the new lift cabin and hover nearby. 'Thirty thousand years without charge and you're telling me their batteries went flat – who'd have thought?'

Johnny ignored the quantum computer. 'OK, can you locate the spaceport?'

'Again, no,' Sol replied. 'However, scans have identified significant Orichalcum deposits—'

'The tower,' said Johnny and Clara together.

'Which I do, indeed, believe mark the location of the great tower at the centre of Atlantis. I require one further reference point to be able to map the original city fully, but from here the ruins appear too degraded. Given time—'

'We don't have time,' said Johnny. 'I'll have to go out there.'

'Er . . . excuse me,' said Clara. 'You mean, *we'll* have to go out there.'

'Clara,' said Johnny, 'you've not been well.'

'I'm fine now and if being unable to fold also means I have

to be stuck here forever and can't do anything, then I might as well still be trapped in hyperspace.'

'Happily these discussions are immaterial,' said Alf. 'The ship is eight thousand six hundred metres below sea level, which I calculate yields an outside pressure of over eighty-six million pascals. Nobody is leaving the ship.'

'I'm coming too,' said Louise. Johnny looked at her in despair. 'What? I'm meant to twiddle my thumbs while you two have all the fun? It's freakin' Atlantis out there – I'm not going to miss that.'

'Alf may be correct,' said Sol. 'The shuttles were designed for space flight, not underwater exploration. The pressures are well beyond their official tolerances and I cannot guarantee their, or your own, survival.'

Johnny wasn't used to the *Spirit of London's* design specifications not being up to the job, but he'd hate to be inside the *Bakerloo* when it imploded. Not so long ago its sister shuttle, the *Jubilee*, had done just that, when he'd been plunging out of control towards the centre of a gas giant somewhere in the Aldebaran system. He didn't want to repeat the experience – it was only his spacesuit that had saved him. That was it – his spacesuit had saved him! 'Spacesuits,' he said. 'I've tested them and they can take much more than a shuttle. Come on.' He gestured to Clara and Louise to join him in the lift.

'Unless I'm mistaken,' said Kovac, 'Atlantis was a rather large conurbation. Exactly how do you propose to traverse it without a shuttle?'

'Good point,' said Johnny. 'That's why you're coming with us.'

☆ ☆ ☆
☆ ☆

Kovac gave the impression of being a very reluctant submersible, but Johnny knew just how much the computer loved being the centre of attention and wouldn't miss this chance to view the most powerful civilization the planet, then known as Terra, had produced. They needed to find the spaceport but, if there was anywhere in Atlantis that he and Clara might recognize, it would be the Temple of Neith – a great palace in the heart of the city, where they'd been brought upon arrival all those years ago. Sol knew exactly how far the temple had been from the central tower, so they would explore along a circle of that same radius, hoping to locate the right spot. There were several sites along the circumference that scans identified as candidate locations, so the search was beginning at the most promising. Knowing the positions of temple and tower, Sol could then map out the entire city.

Standing at the very foot of the ship, the only giveaway that Johnny, Clara and Louise were wearing spacesuits was their clear bubble helmets. The suits themselves moulded perfectly to their body shapes. As ever, Johnny slapped the silver statue that stood like a sentry at the bottom of the lift shaft before he followed the others towards the doors that led out into the ocean. Kovac was chuntering to himself, which pleased Johnny as it meant they'd have more light than would otherwise be the case. He, Clara and Louise each took hold of reins attached to the harness around Kovac, and they all crowded together into one of the compartments of the revolving doors that would serve as an airlock before entering the pitch black, icy cold waters beyond.

Louise took Johnny's hand as the compartment began filling with water. He gave her a quick squeeze before letting go, pretending to check the spotlight fixed to his shoulder. Once the pressure had equalized inside and out Kovac said, 'I suppose you'll want to say, "Giddy-up," or some such?'

'Let's just get out there,' Johnny replied.

The quantum computer moved away into the dark and moments later Johnny felt the reins tighten and the three of them swam out into the deep. They'd decided to set their height five metres above the ocean floor, high enough to take in some level of detail, but hopefully low enough not to miss a vital clue. The three spotlights formed separate windows onto the seabed – Johnny kept having to remind himself to concentrate on his own and not look where Clara or Louise were already searching. He soon realized they were too high and asked Kovac to drop down to just above the sea floor, allowing them to sift through the fine sand with gloved hands as they went. It was painfully slow work. Although the temple had been close to the tower, at this rate they'd take days to complete their search.

Louise was the first to shout out. 'Stop, stop – I've found something.'

'What is it?' said Johnny into the helmet microphone. He'd expected this, as Louise really didn't know what they were looking for, so held his position, but Clara swam across to join their friend.

'It's beautiful,' Louise explained, rather unhelpfully. 'It glitters – huge, giant diamond feathers.'

'Johnny, get over here,' said Clara. 'I think it's Bram's barge.'

Although these events had happened more than thirty thousand years ago, for Johnny and Clara it was only a matter of months since they had been in the great city. As he held a great diamond beak in his gloved hands, it seemed like yesterday that Queen Neith of Atlantis was saying, 'He is such a show-off,' before the then youthful Senator Bram Khari arrived via the great canals that criss-crossed the city in a glittering barge, shaped like a giant swan and pulled by fifty dolphins. Back then, Johnny had imagined the impressive barge was made of crystal, but now he realized it was truly built to last, out of diamond – the hardest natural material known.

Kovac, listening in on their excited conversation, reminded the three that a boat was hardly the most reliable placeholder for a building when caught up in a tsunami, and that it could have been carried anywhere. Johnny, though, wasn't so sure. He wished he'd seen what had happened to the barge later that same night. It had been a gift to Queen Neith, and a prized one at that. Surely it would have been taken somewhere within the temple itself and not abandoned in the canal? He knew they were close – he felt it, in the same way he felt a terrible sensation of being watched. 'Let's stay here and spread out,' he said. 'A fingertip search – shout if anything seems important.'

'It's your own time you're wasting,' said Kovac.

Johnny ignored the computer and began sifting through the sand. Every so often he'd look quickly about him, but all he saw were occasional upright pillars, their long shadows being thrown out by the spotlights. It was impossible to tell if they belonged to the building he'd spent so little time in.

Clara uncovered portions of a frieze and called him over. She thought she recognized it, but Johnny wasn't convinced. Then, a little distance away, Louise said, 'Hey, it's Poseidon.'

'What have you got?' Johnny asked.

'It's a statue,' she said. 'Poseidon – god of the sea.'

Quickly, keeping hold of their reins, Johnny and Clara swam across. Through her helmet it was impossible for Johnny to be sure his sister wore the same broad grin as his own, but he expected nothing less. Louise had scraped away enough sand to reveal a muscular, bearded figure holding a trident. The bottom of the statue was missing, but Johnny had seen enough.

'It's Neptune, Johnny,' said Clara, using the Roman name where Louise had picked the Greek. 'We've found it. This is the temple.'

'Sol,' said Johnny, 'we're in the Hall of Ancestors in the Temple of Neith. Get over here and take us to the spaceport.'

'I am under attack, Johnny,' said the ship. 'Three Krun vessels have unfolded in the vicinity. Outside of my hull, you are vulnerable – I do not wish to draw attention to your situation and suggest we maintain communications silence unless an emergency.'

'Are you OK?' Johnny asked.

'Of course I am able to look after myself without too many difficulties,' said Sol. 'I will transmit the spaceport coordinates to Kovac, hoping I can trust him to take you and investigate, away from the fighting.'

'Good plan, Johnny out.'

Someone screamed. Deafened by his helmet's speakers, Johnny couldn't tell if it was Clara or Louise, but he could immediately see why. There was movement in one of the other spotlights, followed by the blinking of a giant eye.

'Kovac, get us out of here,' he said. 'To the spaceport.'

'About time,' Kovac replied. Johnny spotted several giant squid circling at the boundary of the light cast by the computer's casing.

The tug was so sudden it was all he could do to hold on. As great columns loomed unexpectedly out of the darkness, he wondered if Kovac was deliberately trying to smash them against Atlantean marble. Johnny had a couple of scrapes, but knew his spacesuit was an awful lot stronger than it looked. Fixed within their own bubble of light, it was hard to tell how fast the computer was pulling them, but it felt very quick. Sadly, though, it didn't seem to trouble the cephalopods in the least, who kept pace effortlessly. More of the saucer-sized eyes were appearing alongside.

'Kovac, how long to the spaceport?' Clara had asked the question and Johnny sensed the anxiety in her voice as their escorts drew closer. He hoped she wasn't thinking of folding herself away. He could now feel tentacles brushing against his legs and was sure it must be the same for the others.

'Thirty seconds ago,' said Kovac. 'Either the spaceport is buried beneath the seabed or that half-witted spaceship's calculations were in error. I have my own views on which is more likely.' The pull from Johnny's reins was slackening.

'Then what are you doing?' he asked as a sucker-covered limb wrapped itself around his legs, clamping them together. He tried to kick himself free, but the grip was too strong. Either side, he struggled to make out Clara and Louise through water now thick with writhing tentacles.

'I detected unusual readings emanating from the seabed,' said Kovac, 'and was attempting to investigate. We are close to the point in question, but I fear I am unable to progress further.' Johnny's reins fell limp. He was lifted off the sea floor and carried towards a massive beak. Either side torchbeams danced wildly, as Clara and Louise struggled in vain to break free.

'Unhand me, you overgrown mollusc.' Johnny could no longer see the quantum computer when he spoke, suggesting that Kovac too had been engulfed. Carried ever closer to the squid's mouth he kicked hard, but couldn't break free. The spotlight on his shoulder was extinguished, followed quickly by those either side of him. The darkness of the nearly ten thousand metres of water above was as absolute as the edge of a black hole.

'Do something, Johnny.' It was Clara's voice ringing inside his helmet.

There was only one thing left for him to try. He sensed the ions in the seawater around them. With nothing to look at in the blackness outside, it was easy to see things differently – at the atomic level. He spun the electrons around, gathering more of them to him. Thousands became millions became billions and more, all in a heartbeat, each one moving faster and faster. There was no way to avoid the girls and still shock the giant squid. He just had to make sure the pulse didn't do them too much damage. 'Hold on,' he said, as he released the charge.

A bubble of blue sparks left him, electrifying the seabed, and instantly the vice-like grip relaxed. Both Clara and Louise cried out, but clung tightly to the reins connecting them with Kovac, while the silhouettes of the huge creatures fled into the darkness. Seemingly unaffected, the computer held his position. The ocean floor lit up, an eerie blue glow clinging around pillars as it passed over them. It looked as though the wave of energy Johnny had released would simply dissipate, buying them just a few seconds before the colossal creatures returned, but one small section of the seabed, only ten or so metres away, held onto the sparks and appeared to draw more and more to it. With their spotlights gone, it was the only light source and looked like a near circular window glowing on the sea floor.

'What's that?' asked Louise. Johnny was relieved that she sounded OK. Of course he knew that these were very special spacesuits they were wearing.

'I presume your descriptive question refers to the source of the luminescence,' said Kovac, 'at the very centre of the anomaly I was investigating.'

A human form appeared above the glowing patch of ground, lit up in the blue glow. Johnny guessed it was Clara, given she was such a strong swimmer. Kovac followed, tugging Johnny and Louise behind. Johnny glanced nervously over his shoulder, but in the dark it was impossible to tell how far away the squid were. Clara's voice came through so loudly inside his helmet that Johnny bashed his head on the sides in surprise.

'Johnny – it's hollow. It's an opening. There's a cavern beneath the seabed and . . . I can see ships.'

'Typical human wish fulfilment,' said Kovac. 'My sensors detect nothing.'

The blue sparks that had coalesced around the feature were beginning to fade. Johnny peered through the centre and thought he saw something beyond, but couldn't be sure.

'There's writing around the edge,' said Louise. She was busy scraping away the sand from the border of whatever the strange structure was, revealing striking red stone inlaid with ornate carvings. Once the layer of silt was removed, the hieroglyphics looked as clear to Johnny as when he'd last laid eyes on them. The electric glow from Johnny's sparks had completely abated, or been drowned out by the pulsing red of the familiar arch, toppled on its side, that framed the entrance to a vast underwater cavern.

'Amphibians,' shouted Clara, as ghostly green webbed limbs swam into view. 'Come on. Kovac, let's go.' She grabbed Johnny's hand and pulled him towards and through the opening.

'No,' he shouted into the helmet microphone, but it was too late. As he and Clara passed through the arch to underneath the seabed, the reins connecting them to Kovac snapped.

The quantum computer was right behind, side-by-side with Louise, with a host of amphibians hot on their heels and giant squid just beyond. From beneath, Johnny could see the arch glowing brighter and brighter red. Louise and Kovac hung at its centre for a moment, as though frozen in time, joined left and right by the strange green swimmers, their greedy mouths wide open. Then there was a flash of intense blue light and all were repelled into the blackness beyond.

'Louise!' Johnny shouted. Only static came through his helmet in reply.

'What happened?' asked Clara.

'It's the arch,' said Johnny, 'the Arch of Lysentia.' He kicked upward towards where they'd entered the cavern, but without Kovac to pull him along Clara easily overtook him. She could swim like a fish and went through the arch, built by the galaxy's very first society and which only allowed those such as Johnny and Clara – those with special powers – to pass. All the time she was calling Louise's name. She even tried Kovac, but was met by silence.

One moment the darkness was so thick that the glow from the arch extended no more than a few metres before a wall of blackness suffocated it. The next, Johnny and Clara were bathed in green light. They were both pressed to the ground by the force of displaced water, expelled by the Krun Destroyer that had unfolded directly overhead. Green bolts of energy blazed from its underbelly, missing Johnny and his sister but destroying the ruins now lit up across the sea floor – vaporizing ancient structures that had stood undisturbed for millennia. Clara grabbed Johnny's hand and swam powerfully down through the archway and into the sanctuary beneath.

Above their heads, great pieces of marble were plucked from the ocean floor and tossed through the waters, merging with rocks blasted from the seabed. The debris rained down on the arch, unable to pass through but covering it and sealing Johnny and Clara on the underside.

'There must be another way out,' said Clara, but she sounded as doubtful as Johnny felt.

'Got to be,' he replied. The last thing he wanted to do was to mention folding, even though she must be thinking it. He touched his sister's shoulder light and it sprang to life, the narrow beam piercing the blackness. Then he repaired his own. 'Let's do what we came for,' said Johnny. 'Find the ships and then we can help Louise and Kovac – they can look after themselves.' He knew there was no way to aid the others, but it didn't make him feel any better as his mind conjured images of giant squid and swarms of amphibian hybrids fighting over which would devour Louise first, unless the Krun blasted her to smithereens instead.

He checked his head-up display. Here beneath the arch the pressure readings were almost negligible. The roof of the great cavern shook and rocks started to detach and fall around them. 'Come on,' said Clara, kicking out strongly and swimming away from the debris. Johnny moved his legs as fast as he could, but struggled to keep up. A faint glow ahead meant he could just make out his sister's silhouette. Clara was first to see the ten streamlined Atlantean fighters that were causing it. She directed her spotlight along the lengths of the ships of Gold Circle Squadron, which had escorted the *Spirit of London* to the spaceport all those years before.

They were beautiful but deadly vessels. Johnny joined his sister as she swam over one, peering into its empty cockpit. The tsunami that drowned Atlantis was so sudden the pilots never had a chance to board their craft and take off. He ran a gloved hand over the hull and sensed that, somehow, despite all the time that had passed, this fearsome fighting machine still had power. He needed to get inside. From above the spaceship, he tried the same trick as in Clara's quarters, imagining it flat and picturing himself settling on top of it, before rebuilding the walls around him.

'Johnny – what are you doing?'

He opened his eyes, remembering Clara had never seen him fold. He wasn't inside the cockpit as he'd hoped – he was standing on the cavern floor, beneath the fighter.

'I didn't know,' she continued. 'After what happened to me, I don't think you should be folding either.'

He could hear the bitterness in her voice – the knowledge that this would always be denied her. 'It's not the same,' he said. 'I don't love it like you do – like you did. I can't do it like you.'

'Well, that's obvious, at least,' she said, settling on the sandy floor beside him. 'There's protection around all these fighters – I guess Neith put it there, or made Mum do it. No one can fold in or out – can't you see it?'

'No,' Johnny replied, but now he remembered the same thing had happened with Bram's Starfighter when he'd been floating in space with the professor. Before he could say anything else, the pressure gauge on his head-up display spiked as the entire roof of the cavern was rent asunder by a vast green beam of energy. It felt as if an earthquake was happening and immediately above them the Atlantean spacecraft started sliding across the seabed. If it fell on top them, Johnny wasn't at all sure their spacesuits would cope. Then the roof of the cavern completely collapsed.

'Johnny,' shouted Clara, grabbing hold of him. They sheltered beneath the underbelly of the slithering fighter, moving as it moved, while giant rocks fell either side. Then, through the gaping wound in the roof high above, came a Krun Destroyer. The aliens had broken through. These, and hundreds more highly advanced Atlantean ships, were theirs for the taking. To prove the point, the fighters of Gold Circle Squadron rose into the water as one, joined by many more vessels as far as Johnny could see, leaving him and his sister brutally exposed.

'They're taking them, Johnny. We mustn't let them. Do something.'

The hold of the Krun vessel opened, like a gigantic mouth waiting to swallow a fleet of the most sophisticated spacecraft this quadrant of the galaxy had ever known. 'Do what?' asked

Johnny. What could they possibly do against a display of such power?

'Johnny and Clara – I have just detected your transmissions.' Hearing Sol's voice gave him hope.

'The Krun are taking the ships – the Atlantean fleet,' said Johnny. 'We need help.'

'I am under attack by six Krun vessels,' Sol replied. 'It will take me 1 minute, 48.59 seconds to extricate myself and assist you.'

'We don't have that long,' said Johnny.

'The strategy is optimal,' the ship replied. 'There is no faster way.'

The view through Johnny's helmet was thick with spacecraft, all floating upward, held in the Krun's tractor beam. He hadn't realized quite how many ships the Atlantis spaceport had catered for. The first fighters were about to enter the Destroyer's hold while the huge Battlecruisers caught in the beam dwarfed even the Krun ship.

'You've got to fold them away,' said Clara. 'Quickly – before the Krun get them.'

'How?' Johnny asked. 'I've never done that.'

'It's easy,' said Clara, not helping at all. 'Wrap them up and move them. Put them somewhere you know – that's big enough.'

He screwed his eyes up tightly and tried to think of the biggest place he knew – Wembley Stadium – and imagined the Atlantean fleet there. He wasn't at all sure it was big enough. When he opened his eyes, the ships were still there, the first ones entering the hold.

'Johnny – we need these ships to fight the Krun. They're our only hope to save Earth.'

At Clara's pleading he tried again. On Titan, surrounded by the Monks, it had been so easy, but without them he couldn't think how to begin. With the vessels at so many different heights above the ocean floor, he couldn't picture them flat. Desperate, he tried closing his eyes completely and somehow reaching out with his mind, but nothing happened. Screaming with frustration, he sank to his knees and looked upward in despair.

'I'll do it,' said Clara. Her voice was full of fear.

Before Johnny could respond, the entire Atlantean fleet vanished in front of his eyes. His sister wobbled for a moment. Then her legs buckled and she collapsed.

'Clara – talk to me.'

He held her, there on the cavern floor, and peered through her helmet at his sister's face. Was the blackness he saw in her eyes really there, or a reflection of the murky waters all around?

Quietly, as though it cost her a lot to speak, she said, 'I had to do it. It was the only way. Help me, Johnny.' With that she closed her eyes and her body went limp in his arms.

'Sol,' Johnny shouted, 'Clara's in trouble. I need you *now*.' A blaze of green fire from the Krun Destroyer scorched the seabed nearby and Johnny knew they'd been spotted.

'I cannot unfold within the cavern,' said Sol. 'You must try to access the ocean floor from where I can protect you.'

'How?' Johnny asked. He was a poor swimmer and would have to carry Clara too. More green bolts raked the surface nearby.

'I will send help,' Sol replied.

'I hope it comes quickly,' said Johnny, kicking upward, cradling Clara in his arms. He figured it should be harder to hit a moving target, however slowly it was travelling.

From the hold of the Destroyer above came two Krun spheres, heading straight for him. Just when things couldn't get any worse, through the narrow gap in the cavern roof, either side of the Krun ship, streamed hordes of green-tinged amphibians, also heading in Johnny's direction. The escape route he was plodding towards was well and truly blocked.

Then the lead Krun sphere fired straight at them. The bolt struck Clara full in the face and Johnny's world exploded green. He clutched his sister to him, knowing at least they would die together, or go on together, wherever and whatever that meant. He felt strangely calm. A ringing filled his ears and then he remembered the very same thing had happened before, at his execution on the Senate Steps on Melania. Then, unknowingly, he'd worn a personal shield. Here, at the deepest point of the Atlantic Ocean, a bolt of beautiful white fire shot from inside Clara's spacesuit, almost blinding him as it tore directly at, then through, the Krun sphere, burning a hole at its centre. The craft instantly imploded. His sister's locket had saved them.

'Some of us don't possess personal shields, yet we have to risk our lives to charge to the rescue of those who do.' As the swarm of amphibians changed direction like a shoal of fish, Kovac was revealed, with Louise being pulled behind. The computer pressed on towards Johnny and Clara, while the human–alien hybrids surrounded the remaining Krun sphere. The slight extra pressure on the ship's hull was enough and it, too, collapsed inward from all sides. Like the *Spirit of London's* shuttles, the Krun ships clearly weren't designed for deep-sea exploration.

'How is she?' asked Louise as she and Kovac reached Johnny. Clara's limp body said everything that needed to be said and together they worked quickly to strap her into the harness. 'Go, Kovac,' shouted Louise, slapping him on the side. He shot away before Johnny could grab hold.

Louise had stayed behind too. Up above, a blast of weapons fire from the *Spirit of London* was enough to see the Krun Destroyer fold itself elsewhere, but any relief Johnny felt was short-lived. The shoal of hybrid amphibians streaked towards them and, within seconds, he and Louise were surrounded.

Drained, he wondered if he could create an electric shock big enough to repel quite so many, but before he could act two of the creatures came forward and floated alongside him and Louise.

'Grab hold,' she said. 'They're the quickest way back to the ship.' Louise grasped the fin of the nearest amphibian.

'What?' said Johnny.

'No time to explain,' Louise replied.

With little choice, Johnny wrapped his gloved hands around his new companion's dorsal fin and was instantly pulled upward towards where the *Spirit of London* had just come into view.

☆ ☆ ☆
☆ ☆

'Status?' said Johnny, stepping out of the lift cabin onto the deserted bridge. Louise had made straight for sickbay to help Alf look after Clara.

'Shields are at 82.1964%,' Sol replied, 'and the aft targeting system has taken heavy damage.'

The battle outside still raged. Sol was giving far better than she was getting, but the *Spirit of London* was heavily outnumbered. As well as the Krun, giant squid had returned, attracted by the bright flashes of weapons fire, and Sol reported that the Corporation submarines, one of which had caused so much damage before, were converging on their position.

'Where's Kovac?' asked Johnny.

'In sickbay,' replied the ship. 'Your quantum calculator claims to have been damaged during "his heroic rescue mission".'

Johnny nodded, sitting down in his chair beside the Plican. Through the windows on the bridge he could see the Krun vessels disappearing and reappearing, folding and unfolding all around as they probed for weak spots in the *Spirit of London*'s shields. He knew that Sol could simply have asked the creature scrunched in the tank beside him to fold them to safety, but she was as reluctant as he was to take that step until the implications for Clara were clearer. None of them was willing to lose her again.

A long tentacle slid across the outside of the hull, followed by another, and then a third. One of the squid had clearly grabbed hold.

'Are you OK?' Johnny asked. He was desperate not to fold the ship, but they were running out of options.

'The cephalopod is not a problem. However, a Corporation submarine has just arrived in the vicinity.' Between the giant tentacles, Johnny marvelled again at the elegant stingray-like craft that appeared out of the blackness. 'It is charging weapons,' Sol continued.

'Divert emergency power,' shouted Johnny. 'Full shields.'

He braced for impact, remembering the damage the hyperspatial gravimetric charges had done before, but it was a Krun Destroyer that suffered the full force of the attack. Seeing their sister ship implode in the ocean depths, the remaining alien vessels vanished as one, their hive mind arranging synchronized folds.

'I am being hailed,' said Sol.

'On screen,' said Johnny. In front of him appeared the face he had last seen on Westminster Bridge above the River Thames. 'Colonel Hartman,' he said. 'Long time no see.'

'This is no time for pleasantries, Johnny Mackintosh,' came the terse reply. 'My planet is under attack. I have spared your vessel because in the past you professed some loyalty to this world. Surrender the Atlantean fleet to me and I shall allow you to leave.'

Johnny was amazed at her arrogance. Before, they had been

caught off guard, but he knew full well that Sol could destroy both Corporation subs long before they'd have the chance to fire their Imperial weapons. 'I don't know where they are,' he said truthfully.

'Don't play games with me, Johnny. If our former friends the Krun had them, I know full well they wouldn't have hung around as long as they did.' A giant squid approached one of the Corporation vessels and was shredded by a powerful laser. Johnny winced – there was no need to have killed it. 'I see you are too squeamish for the fight that is to come,' said Colonel Hartman. 'You have five seconds to tell me where those ships are.' The Colonel had risen from her seat and now walked towards the viewscreen. 'If you could have escaped this place, it is clear you would have done so by now. Give me the ships. Five seconds.'

Johnny found a hatred welling up for the woman who began counting down in front of him. She was putting Clara in unnecessary danger.

'No choice, Sol,' Johnny said.

The figure on the viewscreen smiled.

Understanding Johnny perfectly, the ship set the casing around the Plican's tank pulsating with a blue light. The small compartment at the top opened and the creature fell through, unfurling its tentacles as it went.

'Hold on, everybody,' said Johnny into the comm. system, knowing it was unlikely that Clara and Louise were in sickbay's gel pods.

The smug smile vanished from Colonel Bobbi Hartman's face as Johnny saw the walls of the *Spirit of London* rush towards, and then through, him. For good or ill, the fold had begun.

12

Behind the Bookshelf ✩

Weak and nauseous, Johnny forced himself to his feet and into the lift cabin. He was desperate to reach sickbay quickly and, as its doors swished open, the scene he had feared presented itself.

Alf lay unconscious on the floor beside Louise, who had evidently been sick. Rusty was nearby and the same fate had befallen the red setter. Bentley, though, was awake and weakly wagged his tail at Johnny's entrance. Unaffected by the fold, Kovac hovered overhead. Johnny ran to Clara's bedside.

Around her neck hung the locket that had saved them both. Even from beyond, their mum's influence could still be felt, but Johnny wondered if it would be enough to save his sister now. The surrounding air crackled with electricity. Clara's clammy forehead burned at his touch and blackness was creeping across the whites of her pale blue, wide-open eyes, still splattered with silver specks, which gazed upward to where the quantum computer was watching. A new Klein fold was beginning to form – it was happening all over again.

'Clara,' said Johnny, taking her hand. His sister was twisting and turning on her bed, delirious.

'She can't hear you,' said Kovac.

'I know that's not true,' said Johnny. On his visits to see his mum at St Catharine's Hospital for the Criminally Insane, he used to talk to her. Despite her condition, he knew full well the words had registered. 'I'm not letting you go,' said Johnny. 'Whatever it takes, I promise I'll do it.'

Clara muttered something that sounded vaguely intelligible. Johnny leaned in, his ear just above her mouth, but at that moment Louise groaned and the whisper was lost. The older girl looked at Alf lying beside her, pulled out his left ear and rotated it three hundred and sixty degrees before it snapped back into place. The android sat up and looked around. 'You OK, metal man?' she asked.

He nodded at her, before turning to Johnny and saying, 'It was surely unwise to fold, given Miss Clara's condition.'

Under his breath, Johnny cursed Colonel Hartman again. 'No choice, Alf,' he replied.

Meanwhile, Louise was now coaxing Rusty back to consciousness. 'Did you get the ships?' she asked.

'Kind of,' he replied. 'The Krun almost had them and there was nothing I could do. Clara folded them away.'

Louise put her hand to her mouth, while Alf jumped to his feet. 'Miss Clara did what?' asked the android. 'How could you allow her?'

'She did it for Earth,' said Johnny, looking squarely at the android. 'I'd have stopped her if I could, but I don't know if I should have.'

The android looked far from happy as he walked over and examined the screens on the wall nearest to Clara's bed. From Alf's demeanour, Johnny didn't need to ask how his sister was.

'So, where are they now?' asked Louise, clearly trying to lighten the mood. 'If you've taken over the garden deck and there's nowhere to walk the dogs . . .' She ruffled Rusty's coat.

'I don't know,' said Johnny quietly.

'Sorry, I didn't catch that,' said Louise.

He knew it wasn't her fault, but Johnny hated being made to say the words again. 'I don't know where the ships are. OK?

Only Clara does, and it doesn't look like she's going to tell us any time soon.' Louise's face went bright red.

'You couldn't make it up,' said Kovac from near the ceiling. 'Just when it appeared impossible for the running of this spaceship to be any more farcical.'

'You're not helping, Kovac,' said Johnny. Guilty for snapping at Louise, he asked her what had happened after she failed to pass through the arch. 'I was really worried,' he added. If possible, she turned even redder.

'I thought we were done for,' she replied, 'me and Kovac, but he was great.' She looked up at the computer near the ceiling, who seemed to glow a little brighter. 'My spotlight had failed, but Kovac kept talking just so I could see him.' Since no one liked the sound of their own voice quite so much as the quantum computer, Johnny doubted Kovac needed a reason to have been prattling on. 'Of course that drew the giant squid, but the amphibians came too,' Louise continued. 'I think they see much better than us anyway down there.' Johnny nodded, sure she was right. 'But they're not all the same. Some are more . . . human than others. Less far gone. And I think they recognized me. They knew that I'd tried to help Peter – that I was on their side. I don't know how, but they knew. They fought the squid off and brought us back here, but Sol and Alf couldn't find you. We were worried sick.'

Johnny thought it very generous she included Kovac in that last statement. 'They swim like fish,' he said, 'in shoals. Maybe they're some sort of hive or collective, so what Peter knew was passed on to the others – especially if the Krun created them.' He shivered at the thought that the Krun may have added a hive gene from their own DNA into the hybrid mix. No wonder Peter had hated what he was becoming.

'I fear none of this helps us with the matter in hand,' said Alf. 'Sol, how soon until the Krun fleet arrives?'

'Computing . . . 27 hours, 18 minutes and 28.18 seconds, approximately,' said Sol. 'Having analysed their capabilities at close quarters, I will be able to hold a sizable number at bay.'

'By no means all of them,' added Kovac, rather unnecessarily.

'If only we had the other ships,' said Louise.

'There'd still be no one to fly them,' Johnny replied.

'I would,' she said. 'I'd fight for Earth, whatever the risk.'

Johnny could tell she meant every word.

'If only we had allies to call upon,' said Alf. 'Now the Tolimi are gone, there are no advanced civilizations for several light years.'

Johnny thought briefly of the dinosaurs living within Neptune's artificial hollow moon, Triton. Fierce though they could be, there was little point involving them in a space battle.

'Any news about David?' Louise asked, adding, 'Professor Bond,' when Johnny looked questioningly at her.

'At best, we can only assume he is the Krun's prisoner,' said Alf. No one wanted to mention what might be worse. 'Why in the name of Melania did His Imperial Majesty have to choose this, of all times, to leave the galaxy?'

Johnny had rarely seen the android so frustrated. He knew the Emperor would have done anything to save Earth and, if anyone knew how to help Clara, it would be Bram. Perhaps, even now, there was a chance the Emperor would turn his armada around. If not, they were all out of options. 'Things couldn't be any worse,' he said, taking himself by surprise that he'd spoken out loud.

'I am forced to concur,' said the ever optimistic Kovac, 'but that is because I continue to monitor the Cornicula opening from Melania.'

'Why?' Johnny asked. 'What's happened there?' With everything else going on, he'd managed to push thoughts of the Nameless One and his arrival on the Milky Way's capital to the back of his mind.

'As I have intimated on previous occasions,' said Kovac, 'English is an appalling medium for complex communication. I suggest you visit Halader House and see for yourself.'

'We don't have time for that,' said Johnny.

Beside him, unusually nervously, Alf asked, 'Is there any word on Ophia?' Even though the two had never met, Johnny recognized the special bond the android must feel with the only other one of his kind in the whole galaxy.

'So much wisdom to impart and so little time in which to deliver it,' said Kovac, 'yet I am forced to repeat myself to a clunking mechanoid. To understand the situation, you must see for yourself.'

'But how can I leave Miss Clara?' said Alf. 'Without constant attention, we will lose her forever.'

Johnny saw the desperation behind Alf's eyes. As he didn't have any better ideas, he said, 'It's OK. I'll go. I'll find out what I can.' He looked down at his sister, tossing and turning, and said, 'She reminds me of my mum . . . in St Catharine's.' It was probably his imagination, but it felt as if Clara had squeezed his hand.

☆ ☆ ☆
☆ ☆

Johnny had wanted to make the trip to his old children's home as quick as possible, but Bentley had barked furiously when it appeared the Old English sheepdog would remain behind on the shuttle deck. Now they sat, side by side but invisible, in the front two seats of the *Bakerloo*. The world as everyone knew it could well end in about a day's time, but the streets weren't packed with traffic as in the well-known disaster movies. Castle Dudbury New Town was so flat and boring there were no hills for the locals to escape to, except for a derelict artificial ski slope. Landing on a deserted Edinburgh Way in the driving rain, Johnny changed the shield configuration so that it would appear to anyone mad enough to be out in this weather that they were watching a run-of-the-mill black London taxi with a single passenger in the back seat. They turned the corner into the railway station carpark and came to rest outside the station's main entrance.

No one was around to see the unexpected twosome emerge from the cab, and together they ran through the rain towards the back door of Halader House. Johnny hated returning to the children's home. If only, when he'd first had to take the decision, he'd created the Wormhole somewhere out of the way, far from prying eyes and not here in his old bedroom. He couldn't afford to be seen and wondered about leaving Bentley in the backyard, but he couldn't do it to his old friend in this weather. The simple electronic lock on the door was quickly opened and the pair crept inside.

Halader House was the quietest Johnny had ever known it. At first he presumed the residents and staff must all be in the common room – maybe watching something on TV – but when he tiptoed past he saw the door was ajar, revealing empty battered sofas and an eerie silence. As he climbed the stairs to the deserted first floor, Johnny began to wonder if the home had been suddenly closed down. Finally, they reached the spiral staircase that led to his old attic bedroom. Glancing at the 'No Entry' sign, Johnny pulled down the trapdoor, allowing Bentley and himself to climb inside.

It appeared that no one had been in Johnny's bedroom since he'd given Miss Harutunian the slip after the football match. His discarded clothes lay piled on the floor where he'd left them. Immediately Bentley made his way to his favourite spot underneath the bed and curled up beside the radiator.

Johnny sat on the bed. It struck him that he hadn't slept

for ages and he had to fight the urge to simply lie down, shut his eyes, and hope that all his problems would simply dissolve into sleep. A pain seared his temple as a growling voice filled his skull:

'*Give me my ships, Johnny Mackintosh. Give them to me. We are coming – you cannot resist.*'

'Get . . . out,' he shouted, clutching the sides of his head. Bentley growled. Johnny took several deep breaths to calm himself. Before him, the air glowed as if a cloud of dust were sparkling in bright sunlight, yet through the big box window the rain still poured down outside. It was now or never. Taking a last, deep breath, Johnny pushed his face forward and tried and failed to stop his eyes closing. When they opened it was to look upon the ancient square at the heart of the Imperial Palace on Melania.

Unusually for a planet in a binary system, it was twilight. Johnny wondered if, not long before, those living there had been lucky enough to witness a double sunset, perhaps watching from the Senate Platform as the twin stars Arros and Deynar sank behind the Great Tower of Themissa at the heart of the palace. In the half-light, it took a moment to register the scene before him. At first his brain didn't want to accept the evidence of his own eyes. It tried to convince him the rough globes, stretching in regular rows halfway back across the courtyard, were some sort of new decoration demanded by the Nameless One, though Johnny wondered how they stayed up. Then, as his eyes adjusted to the light, he couldn't deny exactly what they were. It didn't make the shock any less. Floating in mid-air were row upon row of severed heads, their eyes mostly still open in terror, witness to the instant they were killed.

Nearest to the Cornicula opening, though, one pair of especially large eyes were closed, almost as though sleeping. They belonged to Ophia. Her synthetic spinal cord was still connected to her beautiful head and hung at an odd angle, not quite vertical.

'Hello, Johnny.'

He remembered the voice. It was hers – speaking English, with the same rich tones that he'd heard through the Wormhole before – yet the figure he hoped to have heard speaking remained unmoved, her eyes and mouth firmly closed. Had he imagined it, like the Krun Queen? Was he going mad?

'I know you cannot see me talking . . . not yet,' the voice continued, 'but it is I, Ophia, once briefly the Emperor's Emissary on Melania.'

The android opened her eyes and her spine began to curl. Johnny gasped. 'I see my light has now reached you,' said Ophia.

'I don't understand,' said Johnny. 'What's going on?'

'This place, this courtyard, is an experiment. The palace has become the Nameless One's plaything.' Johnny noticed that the android's words didn't match the way her lips were moving. 'He desired a method to prevent Bram ever returning to the galaxy he once ruled. Now he has found it.'

In those few words, Johnny's best hope for Earth's salvation was dashed.

The head continued: 'With his own great power, amplified by the piteous creature in the tower, the laws of nature have bowed completely to his wishes. There is no gravity in this small place and, from me to you, the speed of light has been slowed to the pace of a Sulafat Tortoise. From you to me, I believe it is unchanged.'

'Why?' asked Johnny. 'What's that got to do with Bram?'

'Between the galaxies, in the void without stars or planets, space cannot be folded,' said Ophia. 'Light speed is a true limit – one that can never be exceeded. All around the Milky Way, at the rim of the galaxy, the Nameless One has created a barrier like in this square. Not even our Emperor can cross it.'

'But that means the Nameless One can't bring his own ships here. People can still fight him.' Johnny knew he was clutching at straws.

'The Nameless One doesn't need ships, Johnny. No one dares challenge his power. Yet still he brings them. I have witnessed fleets of Andromedan Stardestroyers flying overhead. I do not know how he has done this. If Bram knew, he would not now be trapped within the void.'

The Emperor had hinted about bending the laws of physics, but not by so much. 'I wish I could help you,' he said. 'Earth's being invaded. The Krun arrive tomorrow and there are too many of them for us to fight. If we survive, I'll come and save you – I promise.'

'No, Johnny. If you survive, you must do what Bram could not. Find Lysentia. It is the only way to save any of us.'

'What's going on in there? Decease at once.'

Johnny thought he recognized the haughty voice speaking broken Universal. Ophia confirmed his suspicions. 'It is Erin. He stands guard nearby and has just seen my eyes open. You must go.'

'What's he doing there?' Johnny asked, well aware of the anger in his own voice.

'He serves the Nameless One,' said Ophia. 'Those who do not soon end up collected around me. There are very few who resist. Go now . . . Save Earth . . . Find Lysentia.'

'I won't forget you,' said Johnny. He pulled his head out of the Wormhole just in time to hear footsteps coming up the spiral staircase.

Johnny panicked. He'd faced all sorts of dangers over the last year, but something about being back in the children's home made him behave like a child. There was no time to grab Bentley. He bounded across his bedroom in one stride and dived inside his wardrobe. His heart was pounding so loud he thought whoever came through the trapdoor must hear. He remembered being dragged in here by Clara, months before, as someone he now knew to have been his clone moved about his bedroom. If only he'd seen his double – known who it was – things could have been so different. This time, he held the door open, just a fraction of a millimetre, to see the interloper.

'Bentley.' With her head poking through the trapdoor, Miss Harutunian had spotted the Old English sheepdog curled up by the radiator. 'I hoped I'd find you here,' she said, climbing fully into the room and crouching close to Johnny's bed, peering underneath.

Bentley came willingly to be fussed, the red-haired American stroking his coat firmly as the sheepdog licked her face.

'Now where's your dad?' Miss Harutunian asked, lifting Bentley's fringe and gazing into the dog's one brown and one blue eye. It took a few seconds before Johnny understood she was speaking about him.

Miss Harutunian looked around the small bedroom and her eyes alighted on the only possible hiding place. Johnny could try to fold, but then he'd be leaving Bentley. The social worker was on her feet now, hand stretching out towards the wardrobe door. Johnny had a split second to decide what to do. Before she reached it, he opened the door from inside and said a very sheepish, 'Hi.'

'Johnny!' The social worker grabbed him and pulled him into a surprisingly strong hug. 'Where have you been? Come on – we need to see Mrs Irvine.' She released him, but grabbed his hand and pulled him towards the trapdoor. 'Now.'

'No,' he said, trying but failing to break free. 'I can't. Not right now. It has to wait.'

'It can't wait, Johnny.' Miss Harutunian looked upward,

lost in thought. Then she turned to face him. 'I wish it could, believe me, but in less than a day a fleet of alien spaceships will reach Earth.'

✧ ✧ ✧

'You had no right, Katherine.' Mrs Irvine was haranguing Johnny's social worker, while he sat at the small round table in the Manager's office.

'Johnny needed to know,' Miss Harutunian replied. 'I should have said something when I first came to England.'

Johnny hated it when people talked about him as if he weren't there.

'He's not stupid,' she went on. 'Remember when I just happened to find him outside the Gherkin after he ran away?'

'It could have been chance,' said Mrs Irvine. 'It was where you'd taken him on the day out.' She was pacing up and down in front of the bookshelves that lined the walls either side of her desk.

'Well, not in New York. Johnny runs out of the Chrysler Building and there I am?'

'You're from New York.'

'It's a big place.'

'He's a wee bairn. He doesn't know that.'

'He's not a child any more,' said the social worker. 'He's growing up. Besides, what about that time in the basement? And then there's the doctor . . .'

'Hmmph.' The Manager's owl-like eyes turned on Johnny, who was struggling to comprehend what was happening.

'I promised his parents,' said Mrs Irvine. 'If anything happened to them, I said I'd bring Jonathan up like a normal boy.' Johnny thought he could see tears welling in her eyes, magnified by her glasses.

'We don't live in normal times,' said Miss Harutunian.

Taking advantage of the brief pause, Johnny said, 'You knew my mum and dad? How?'

The Manager turned to Miss Harutunian and said, 'You see where this leads?' She looked back towards Johnny and took a deep breath. 'I worked with your father for many years. In fact, I led the expedition where . . . well, that's not important right now.'

'What's not important? What expedition?'

Johnny's questions were drowned out by the wailing of sirens. Through the floor-to-ceiling windows, a succession of police cars and vans could be seen entering the Castle Dudbury station carpark.

'Whatever now?' asked Mrs Irvine, turning to stare outside. Johnny and Miss Harutunian came round the desk to join her. The convoy didn't stop at the railway station. It continued all the way across the tarmac to the door of Halader House, where the vehicles fanned out and armed police rushed towards the building. Stepping unhurried from one of the cars and walking slowly in her high heels through the melee, was a figure Johnny recognized all too well.

'Hartman.' Mrs Irvine, standing beside him, had spoken the colonel's name. Johnny put his hand on the desk to steady himself as his world came crashing around him. 'Regrettably, now might be the time to close Ben Halader House permanently,' said the Manager.

Orders were being barked out beneath the window. A man raised a megaphone to his lips. 'This is the police. Jonathan Mackintosh, we know you're in there. You have one minute to surrender yourself. Come out with your hands up.'

'Get down, Jonathan,' said Mrs Irvine, placing a surprisingly strong arm on his shoulder and pushing him to the floor.'

'What happens now?' Miss Harutunian asked the Manager.

'Had you not forced my hand, Katherine, it appears the

Corporation would have. Bairn or not, he must go down the rabbit hole.'

There was shouting inside the building and the sound of people running up the stairs.

'Jonathan,' said Mrs Irvine, 'come this way.' She and Miss Harutunian moved to the other side of the desk and stood before the bookshelves. Johnny crawled after them on all fours, thinking the two women looked remarkably calm.

'Who are you?' he asked, getting up but keeping his distance. 'What expedition did you lead?'

The shouting was coming closer – it sounded as if all the doors in the corridor were systematically being kicked in and the rooms searched. There was gunfire.

'This is no time for questions,' said Mrs Irvine, turning her back on Johnny and running her finger across the spines of several hefty books, as though trying to pick out her holiday reading. 'All will be revealed shortly.'

The police were right outside the door. Given a choice between Colonel Hartman and Mrs Irvine, Johnny knew who he'd rather trust.

'Ah, this is the one, I believe,' said Mrs Irvine. Her finger settled on the spine of a particularly dusty-looking book, entitled *Home Office Regulations for the Administration of Children's Homes within England and Wales, 1955.*

Thinking the Manager had quite possibly gone mad, Johnny looked to his social worker, who winked. Mrs Irvine pulled the top of the book down as though on a hinge, and the entire bookshelf swung open to reveal a secret passage, angled steeply downward into darkness, lined by some sort of slide.

'After you, Johnny,' said Miss Harutunian, pushing him forward so he overbalanced and slid headfirst away into the gloom.

Behind him he heard Mrs Irvine shout, 'Tally-ho!' in her sing-song Glaswegian accent.

☆ ☆ ☆
☆ ☆

Wherever Johnny was going, it was a lot further underground than he could possibly have imagined. As he slid faster and faster, arms outstretched, spiralling down a seemingly endless helter-skelter, he thought about Bentley, curled up underneath his bed in the Halader House attic. He had to hope Colonel Hartman's men wouldn't find the sheepdog or, if they did, they wouldn't hurt him.

It was fully a minute before the twists and turns ceased and the slide began to level out. Johnny slowed, but he still shot out of the tunnel very quickly, flying past a blur of silver and into a blinding white light, before sliding across the floor and slamming into a large pile of cushions propped against a wall of rough, natural rock. He sat there dazed until someone pulled him off to one side. Seconds later, Miss Harutunian appeared, stopping comfortably before reaching the cushions and rolling away from Johnny. Straight after, with another cry of, 'Tally-ho,' Mrs Irvine slid into the cushions between them.

'I'd forgotten quite how much fun that can be,' she said. 'Help me up, young man.'

The person standing behind Johnny stepped across and offered the Manager his arm, which she took and got surprisingly lightly to her feet. Beside her, Miss Harutunian was shouting instructions about sealing the exits, before the American hurried across the room.

Johnny tried to take in his surroundings. The room, out of proportion in that it was far higher than it was wide or long, was lit by a single, miniature sun floating far above, just beneath a domed ceiling. He'd only ever seen such things on other worlds. The roof and three of the walls glowed pearly white, ending with bare rock on just this one side. The silver Johnny had seen as he shot out the bottom of the slide was a reassuringly familiar statue about three metres tall, similar to the one at the foot of the *Spirit of London*.

'Come along, Jonathan,' said Mrs Irvine, setting off briskly towards an area around which several people were gathered, now including Johnny's social worker. A few other faces he recognized from the children's home were there, all looking deadly serious. Accompanying the Manager was someone wearing jeans and an olive green hoodie. 'Of course, you already know Spencer,' the Manager continued. To the other boy she added, 'Jonathan will be joining us for the foreseeable future.'

'Nice one.' In the strangeness of his surroundings Johnny had somehow not registered the familiar face of Spencer Mitchell, one of the rather intimidating older residents of Halader House.

Miss Harutunian and the others were gathered around a table, poring over a projection of the inner solar system, centred on the Sun and going out to just beyond the asteroid belt. Their attention was fixed on the space between Earth and Mars, where the approaching Krun fleet could be clearly seen.

'Any developments, Sheldon?' asked Mrs Irvine. On the far side of the circular table, a man Johnny recognized as the new Halader House caretaker shook his head.

'I'd expect to receive a signal before any rescue ships appeared,' said Miss Harutunian. 'The distress beacon's been broadcasting for four days now, but we've heard nothing. Four light days just isn't enough. If only I'd set it off when we first spotted the alien activity.'

Mrs Irvine said, 'I take full responsibility. The galaxy's a dangerous place. It seemed prudent not to reveal ourselves unnecessarily.'

Miss Harutunian turned to Johnny and the look in her eyes told him it was madness to have ever believed she was simply a random social worker who'd happened to come over from America. She said, 'From down here, we track any and all evidence we find of alien activity. When I told you there was an alien fleet approaching Earth, this is them. We don't believe they're friendly.'

'They're not,' said Johnny. 'They're coming to harvest humanity as food for their Queen. They were looking for a fleet of ships too, but at least they're not going to get that now.'

'You know this how?' asked Mrs Irvine. She wasn't the only one who'd stopped to stare at him.

There was a pause, like the standoff in a gunfight, waiting for someone to be first to draw. Pieces of a jigsaw he hadn't even known existed were beginning to fall into place, but far too many were missing for Johnny to see the whole picture. While what he was discovering was amazing, Bentley was waiting for him above and Clara back on the *Spirit of London* – where he knew he owed Kovac a massive apology. Miss Harutunian broke the silence.

'Your mother built this place, Johnny.'

'Katherine . . .' said Mrs Irvine.

'This is no time for secrets,' said the social worker. 'You can't protect Johnny any more by keeping him in the dark. Maybe he knows something about St Catharine's – like where it went?' The Manager frowned, accentuating her wrinkles. Johnny hadn't ever thought of her as old before.

'I don't mean to be rude,' said Johnny, looking around and keen to direct the conversation away from his mum's hospital, 'but it doesn't look finished.'

'It's not,' said Mrs Irvine, through slightly gritted teeth. 'Your mother, now missing unless you know otherwise, was special, Johnny. And she had special . . . powers. But they were already fading, had almost gone, by the time she began this. It drained her terribly and then, on that dreadful night when your brother died, she had nothing left to stop them.'

'My mum was the most powerful being in the galaxy, said Johnny. 'This wouldn't drain her.'

'Perhaps she was,' said the Manager. 'I don't know. Whoever she was, she gave up the power she had to be with your father. To be with you.'

'Our turn,' said Miss Harutunian. 'How do you know about the alien fleet?'

'We've been tracking them too,' said Johnny. 'Since they left Mars.'

'Who's we? Is there another centre . . . like this?'

'Tracking them from my own ship,' Johnny replied. 'My turn.'

'Hold on,' said the social worker. 'Then it's true you have a spaceship? I wondered when you were in New York.'

'And I have to get back there,' said Johnny. 'Clara's ill – she needs me.'

'Don't you understand?' said the social worker. 'Earth needs you.' Her eyes blazed with passion. 'Can you travel beyond the solar system? You could make contact with friendly alien races – they must be out there.'

'Katherine,' said Mrs Irvine, cutting the social worker off, 'Jonathan's just a boy. It's not for him to go gallivanting across space . . .'

'But we're desperate. We need help.'

'Enough.' Somehow when Mrs Irvine spoke it was very hard to contradict her and Miss Harutunian fell silent. 'The allies we have here must suffice. The information the doctor gave you about this Clara appears correct, though I never knew Mary was pregnant again – it explains much.' Johnny presumed she was talking about Carrington, and wondered where the mysterious doctor fitted into all this. 'Jonathan . . . Katherine, come with me.' The Manager set off towards one corner of the chamber. Miss Harutunian shrugged at Johnny and followed, leaving him feeling he had no choice but to do the same. Around them, the spell was broken. The sombre mood snapped and the dozen or so other people in the hall burst into animated chatter. As Johnny fell into step behind the two women, all eyes followed him and he knew he was the subject of every conversation.

Mrs Irvine had almost walked into the wall before a hitherto invisible door opened noiselessly, revealing a wide corridor lined with the same pearly white material. A dreadful wailing filled the air, as if further along someone unseen was in immense pain – maybe even being tortured. Johnny hesitated.

'It's just Gilbey,' said Miss Harutunian, a gentleness in her voice that reassured him. 'You'll see.'

'You say your sister is ill? I'm very sorry to hear that,' said Mrs Irvine, heading into the corridor without breaking her stride. Johnny and Miss Harutunian followed. 'Your mother left us with highly advanced medical facilities. Perhaps we can help?' Johnny had no idea how the Manager knew where the doors in the corridor lay, but she turned suddenly right and the wall opened again, the moaning becoming louder still.

There, in a room that looked very like the *Spirit of London*'s sickbay, was the Halader House cook, Mr Wilkins. Perched on a stool that looked far too small to take his weight, great rolls of flesh spilling over the waistband of his elasticated trousers, the huge man had tears streaming down his flabby cheeks, into his beard. He was at the bedside of a tall, emaciated creature that must once have been covered in fur but was now largely bald, thin red skin lined with livered age spots showing through in many places. The thing didn't look long for this world, or the one that it originally hailed from, and was only just recognizable. 'A Pilosan,' said Johnny in surprise.

Miss Harutunian looked startled. 'How could you possibly know that?'

'I've been to their homeworld,' he replied. 'And nearly didn't get away.' The furry creatures fed telepathically on their prey, glorying in the misery of others. The crew of the *Spirit of London* had become so despondent they were nearly incapable of leaving.

'Then you understand Gilbey's treatment of you over the years,' said Mrs Irvine.

Mr Wilkins looked towards Johnny and howled even louder. The cook had always borne him an irrational hatred and there was absolutely nothing Johnny could think of that would excuse his years of suffering.

'Our poor cook,' the Manager went on, 'is half-Pilosan. Marooned on Earth, his mother is dying.' The cook screamed as though his fingernails were being pulled out and even Johnny began to feel sorry for the half-bald creature on the bed. 'To keep her alive, he lets her draw all his happiness away. Very occasionally, he takes it out on residents of the home to rebuild his strength.'

Somewhere in the back of Johnny's mind he wanted to protest, but the cook and his mother looked so miserable that he found himself sympathizing with their predicament.

'It's good to see your mother looking so well,' said Mrs Irvine to the man who for years had been the bane of Johnny's life. 'I presume the sense of doom brought on by the impending invasion has done her the power of good.' She sounded surprisingly chirpy.

'We've all had to be immunized,' Miss Harutunian whispered in Johnny's ear. 'That's why he had to pick on you . . . sorry.' It explained a lot, but didn't make Johnny feel any better. In fact, he felt suddenly exhausted. He'd not slept for what felt like days, and now all he wanted, more than anything in the world, was to cry himself to sleep in a corner and never have to wake up again.

'You see the capabilities we have here,' said the Manager, pointing to spare beds and the advanced screens on the walls. 'I regret that I have never met your sister, but our facilities are at your disposal. We would welcome her here.'

'She's better off on the ship,' he said simply, fighting back a yawn. He had so many questions, but they would have to wait. Thinking about Clara strengthened him and the morose sensation that had settled like a blanket lifted. 'I have to get back to her.'

'Surely you see she would be safer here?'

'Clara belongs on the *Spirit of London*,' said Johnny. 'It's her home. And I belong with my sister.'

The Manager was about to protest, but out of the corner of his eye Johnny saw Miss Harutunian shake her head.

'Very well,' said Mrs Irvine. She led them both out of the medical room into the corridor. Johnny's lethargy was now replaced by an urgent need to act. 'Your whole life I have watched over you and I would rather you remained here, but it appears I cannot insist.' The Manager's owl-like eyes looked sadder than he had ever known. 'May I ask how you come to have a spaceship? I wasn't aware that your parents had made such plans.'

'She was a gift,' Johnny replied.

'But from whom?'

There didn't seem any reason for him not to say. He wanted to reassure her that the *Spirit of London* was a good ship, that he was in the best hands he could be. 'From the Emperor of the Galaxy,' he said.

The colour drained from Mrs Irvine's face. 'Bram Khari?'

she asked slowly. He nodded, shocked that she could ever have heard the Emperor's name. 'Do you think that's wise?' the Manager went on. 'Have you never heard the expression, "Beware of Greeks bearing gifts"?'

Johnny had no idea what she meant. 'Look, I'm sorry,' he said, 'but I really do have to go.' Exhausted, he had to fight hard not to yawn again.

'If you must, Jonathan,' said Mrs Irvine, looking far from pleased. 'Katherine will show you a way out. Remember there is sanctuary here – I doubt even the approaching aliens would discover us. I hope our paths cross again.'

Johnny nodded. He wasn't sure if he was doing the right thing, but Clara needed him. Bentley needed him. He followed his red-haired social worker along the corridor.

Miss Harutunian stopped at a control panel and tapped the display. 'Halader House is swarming with Corporation people,' she said. 'We can't take the normal route out.'

'Through the basement?' Johnny asked and the American nodded. 'Is there any way we can come out near the station entrance?'

'I suppose you're going to tell me next that the black cab that's sometimes parked there isn't any kind of normal taxi?' said Miss Harutunian. 'You're full of surprises, Johnny.'

'I'm not the only one,' he replied.

She laughed, touched the screen again and a narrow cubicle opened up nearby in the corridor. 'Phone booth,' she said, in response to his questioning look. 'Sorry, it'll be a bit of a squeeze.'

'I can make my own way,' said Johnny. 'You don't have to look after me.'

'I know that, Johnny,' she said, looking suddenly serious. 'I'm coming with you.'

13 ✩

The Secret Garden ✩

Bentley was gone. Invisible, much to Miss Harutunian's shock, Johnny had flown the *Bakerloo* alongside the dormer window of his attic bedroom. With the American screaming that it was too dangerous, he smashed his way into the room and searched under the bed and inside the wardrobe, then under the bed again. Had it not been for the stamping of footsteps in the corridor below and the clang of boots on the spiral staircase, he'd probably have remained, but the shouts from just beneath the trapdoor shook him from his torpor just in time and he jumped back into the taxi and away with gunfire ringing in his ears.

Miss Harutunian tried to appear sympathetic – he knew she was fond of Bentley – but she couldn't hide her excitement as the pair shot invisibly skyward, through the clouds to the place where the sky turned from blue to black, and beyond. They rendezvoused with the *Spirit of London* on the far side of the Moon.

Miss Harutunian laughed when she saw the ship before saying, 'Of course . . . the Gherkin. She's beautiful, Johnny.' He tried to smile as they entered the shuttle bay, settling between a red double-decker bus and an Imperial Starfighter. 'Wow,' she went on. 'Just . . . wow.'

'She's a great ship,' said Johnny, 'but the Krun have over a thousand. We can't stop them all.'

As they touched down, Sol greeted Johnny and his surprise guest with the news that Clara's condition had worsened. Nothing mattered to Johnny except to see his sister. He ran, Miss Harutunian struggling to keep up, to the lift shaft where the new cabin was waiting. From there to sickbay.

The whites of Clara's eyes were all but gone, replaced by oily blackness as before. As Johnny gazed into them, holding his sister's hand and hoping for some kind of response, Louise asked, 'Who's your friend?'

He tried to smile. 'Sorry, this is Louise, Alf, Rusty and Kovac,' he said, nodding to each of them in turn. 'The ship's Sol. Everyone – this is Miss Harutunian, my social worker.'

'Katherine, please,' she said.

'Was that wise, Master Johnny? We have urgent matters to attend to.'

'Relax, Alf,' said Johnny. 'She knows about the Krun fleet. There's a group at Halader House that's been monitoring alien activity.' He looked upward and added, 'As Kovac was telling us.'

The quantum computer's casing glowed bright, but for once he didn't speak.

'How is she?' Johnny asked, touching Clara's forehead. It burnt his fingers and his instinct was to snatch his hand away, but he didn't recoil.

'I am trying,' said Alf, 'but I fear she is worsening.'

Every so often, I'm sure she says, 'St Catharine's,' said Louise. 'Wasn't that a Krun prison?' All of a sudden she looked much older and Johnny knew she was remembering her own imprisonment by the aliens, which she never spoke about.

'Where they held Mum,' he said, nodding. He looked down at Clara again, wishing he knew what to do. It shouldn't have come to this. If only he could have moved the Atlantean ships himself – he hated that he'd not learnt to fold better.

'Remembering Mum healed her before,' he said. 'Maybe she thinks it will again.'

'It was where I first met the doctor,' said Miss Harutunian, who was standing a little away from Clara's bedside. Johnny, Alf and Louise all looked at her. 'There are others of us, in small cells around the world. We have a secret handshake,' she explained. 'I don't get how the whole place disappeared, or how it's coming back.'

'What do you mean?' Johnny asked. 'It's gone forever. There's no way it could ever come back.'

The social worker looked flustered. 'Look, I'm sorry. I don't know anything,' she said, turning ever so slightly pink. 'Not compared to you guys and this ship. Forget about it. I was just being stupid.'

Having ignored Kovac for so long, Johnny wasn't about to make the same mistake with Miss Harutunian. 'I'd say you've proved yourself. We have impressive shielding so I don't know how you did it, but you found out there was something odd about the Gherkin, even if you didn't know what. And the Chrysler Building. I thought St Catharine's . . . was sealed shut forever, but if you've discovered anything strange there, we need to check it out.' He'd hesitated because he was sure Clara had squeezed his hand when he named the hospital.

'It's gravitational waves,' said Miss Harutunian. 'I probably shouldn't be telling you, but I don't want to keep secrets any more. Those aliens are going to be here in not very long. If we can find your mum, and she's as powerful as you say, it's got to help.'

'Mum's gone,' said Johnny. 'St Catharine's . . .' Clara squeezed his hand again, he was sure of it, 'was a base for the Krun, the aliens who are invading. If they're breaking out of hyperspace and setting up a new front on Earth, we're in even more trouble. Let's go.'

252

'Master Johnny, you have only just returned. If I am correct, you have not slept in forty-eight hours. You need to rest, if only for a little while.'

'Sol,' said Johnny, 'how long till the Krun reach Earth?'

'Computing . . . The first ship will arrive in 14 hours, 14 minutes and 21.36 seconds,' the ship replied.

'Sorry, Alf,' said Johnny, stifling a yawn. 'No rest for the wicked.'

'If you do not sleep before the battle to come, you will have lost it before it has even begun.' The words didn't make Johnny feel any better.

'I'll come too,' said Louise. 'Someone's got to watch your back.' Her eyes swivelled unconsciously towards the red-haired American. 'Give me a minute to drop Rusty with Bentley – I guess he's on the garden deck.'

Johnny looked at Louise, but couldn't bring himself to speak the words out loud. It was left to Sol to announce that, 'Bentley is not aboard.'

'The Corporation has him,' said Miss Harutunian. 'If it helps, I know where their headquarters are.'

Hope flickered in Johnny's chest, but he knew it would be wrong to act on it now. The Old English sheepdog was the single constant throughout his life, who had saved him on numerous occasions, but the fate of Earth itself hung in the balance with time running out. 'When this is all over, we'll get him back,' he said. He tried to sound confident, but was far from sure any of them would survive the Krun invasion.

☆ ☆ ☆

For the first time ever Johnny piloted the *Bakerloo* to a bumpy landing, hard on a country lane not far from Wittonbury Station. He wondered if Alf had been right and he was simply too tired, though it also felt odd flying beside his social worker in the shuttle – almost as if he was back at school. Louise had insisted on taking the back seat so she could keep an eye on the American. She even pretended she was carrying a blaster.

Johnny had overflown the old location of St Catharine's Hospital for the Criminally Insane, but there was no evidence of the complex from the air. He hadn't expected there to be – in the past it had only been visible at ground level, but as his fatigue mounted, he couldn't afford to make any stupid mistakes. Miss Harutunian's gravitational-wave detector had registered a spike as they drove along the narrow road with hedgerow either side – an idyllic section of English countryside that tomorrow might not even exist. The sombre mood in the shuttle suggested they were all thinking the same. The voice inside Johnny's skull – the Krun Queen – was getting louder, clammering for her ships. He did his best to ignore it, but began warning the others of the dangers they might face if those Krun trapped within their old base had found a way out. The aliens were heavily armed. Silently he recalled that their weapons had killed his dad. For safety, Alf had tried to insist that Johnny took his sister's locket – her personal shield – arguing that she was perfectly safe aboard the *Spirit of London*, but Johnny would never have dreamed of removing it from around her neck.

He had been sure St Catharine's was sealed forever, effectively within its own Klein fold. The only creature Johnny had ever seen undo such a thing was the Nameless One when freeing Clara. If the being from Andromeda could suspend gravity and slow the speed of light to walking pace, it was entirely possible that he had come here. Just as he'd told no one about the voice in his head, Johnny decided not to tell the others that either. There were some things they were better off not knowing.

He stopped the *Bakerloo* by a brick footbridge over a narrow brook, with steep grassy banks sloping down to the babbling water. Beyond, long grass gave way to the patchwork fields of the Sussex countryside. Miss Harutunian, who said she'd visited the site since what she termed 'the hospital's bizarre disappearance', whisked a device like a mobile phone from her pocket and held it up in the air, slowly waving it around to target any ripples in space. Johnny knew she would find some. He'd already spotted that the water in the stream was running uphill – a sure sign that space had been folded nearby. He plonked himself down on the exact spot of the very bank where he had once sat beside Clara, with Bentley there too, after the most dreadful day he could remember.

'You OK?' Louise asked, joining him where Clara had once been.

He nodded, the lump in his throat making it impossible to speak. Being so close to the place where he lost them made the memories of his parents stronger.

'I think I've found something,' said Miss Harutunian. 'What now? You're the boss, Johnny.'

'If there's a gap, I might be able to close it,' he said, turning to look where the social worker was pointing.

'But I can see it,' said Louise. 'I don't believe it – there's a line in space.' She leapt up, as though to cross the long grass, but stopped. 'Where's it gone? It was there a second ago.'

'Are you sure?' Johnny asked. 'I can't see a thing.' He had to stifle another yawn.

'No, I made it up for a laugh,' said Louise. 'Of course I'm sure.' Defeated, she sat back down on the bank and her eyes widened. 'It's there again.' She grabbed Johnny's arm and pointed, but all he saw was fields of green and yellow, planted on gentle slopes, rolling into the distance.

'You're in the right ballpark,' said Miss Harutunian, holding up her device, 'but I can't see anything.'

'It's just to your left,' said Louise, standing again. 'No, I've lost it.' She sat back down, screwing her eyes up, and found it again. 'No – not that far. A bit right.'

'Stay there,' said Johnny, patting her arm and standing up. He bounced on his toes to try to give himself a bit of extra energy and jogged towards the social worker. Again he would have to fold space, but it didn't come naturally. He tried to imagine the whole area as completely flat, mentally pushing the trees, electricity pylons, river bank and even the blades of grass down so far that they had no height at all, and then he saw it. There was a hump in space–time, right in front of where he was standing. It affected everything around it, very subtly, but it seemed suddenly obvious why the brook had to flow ever so slightly uphill.

He couldn't understand how a Klein fold might have such an effect on real space. He reached out an arm, wondering what it would find on the other side and almost laughed in surprise. Here, at the boundary where normal space and time met its hyperspatial equivalent, Johnny's fingers closed upon a doorknob. It definitely wasn't St Catharine's. Could this be an entrance to the corridor Zeta had shown him in his dreams? He turned the handle, wondering if he might be about to see the princess again.

He was dimly aware that Miss Harutunian had dropped her detector, before Louise shouted, 'You did it, Johnny.' She was off the bank in a shot and ran past him, only to vanish into thin air.

'Wherever your hand's disappeared to, keep it right there,' said the American. She picked up the device and brushed past Johnny's arm, before disappearing too. Johnny followed.

Into the distance, as far as the eye could see and set against an angry purple and black sky, were spaceships. Johnny knew they were each over thirty thousand years old, but they gleamed as if they'd been built yesterday. This was where Clara had folded the Atlantean fleet, but it was to the foreground that Johnny looked. Here was a simple, circular pool, but one that could never have existed within normal space and time. A stream ran out from one side and along a regular channel, before flowing back into the pond on the other side in perpetual motion. Between the stream and the pool were beds of brightly coloured flowers.

In his half-awake, half-asleep state, Johnny understood, as if he could think clearly for the first time. Here was the garden Clara had written about in her diary – the one she'd created. Its only connection to St Catharine's was that it had been built nearby, within just a membrane of hyperspace, because his sister had felt the same powerful draw of their parents in this place. Louise had seen the slit where it intersected real space because she'd been sitting in exactly the same spot on the bank where Clara had been on that horrible day. When Clara needed somewhere to move the Atlantean ships, the obvious place had been this infinitely expandable bubble of hyperspace that only she knew. Johnny walked forward, not towards the sleek Starfighters but to the flowers, planted for his parents and brother Nicky, and knelt down beside them.

'Johnny,' Louise shouted, 'can we get these ships out? I know I can fly one. Maybe Katherine too?'

'Maybe? Are you kidding? Try stopping me,' said the American. 'These are awesome.'

'Aren't they just?' said another American voice. 'Very well done, Johnny.'

A dog barked – it was a voice Johnny knew so well. He turned to see Bentley straining towards him, the sheepdog's lead stretching into Colonel Hartman's hand. Either side of her, armed troops wearing camouflage clothing began fanning through the opening. Instinctively Johnny shut the door with his mind – almost. He left the narrowest sliver open, but knew that neither the Colonel nor her men would ever find it again without him. Bentley was barking continuously, straining at the leash to join him. The smile on Colonel Hartman's face wavered and she looked over her shoulder, wondering why more Corporation soldiers weren't joining her in this most unusual garden.

'I've closed the door,' said Johnny. 'It was getting a bit crowded.'

'Open it or the dog dies,' said the Colonel. She reached inside the jacket of her regular blue suit, pulled out a pistol and cocked it, pointing it straight at the Old English sheepdog's shaggy head.

'Kill Bentley and you and your men never leave this place. Not just for your natural lives – for eternity.' The steel in Johnny's voice looked to have surprised her, but he meant every word. 'Leave them alone,' he said to the soldiers who had reached Louise and Miss Harutunian, machine guns pointing at head height. They looked, uncertain, towards Colonel Hartman, who nodded, and the weapons were lowered.

'Katherine,' said Colonel Hartman with fake warmth.

'Bobbi,' came the terse response.

'I see you've got yourself a girlfriend, Johnny,' said the Colonel. Louise blushed.

'We're wasting time,' said Miss Harutunian. 'The aliens will be here in a few hours.'

'You don't think they're already among us?' said the Colonel, raising an eyebrow. 'You obviously don't know Johnny like I know Johnny – or the company he keeps.'

'You're wrong, Bobbi,' said the social worker. 'Johnny's not the threat – he never was. He's one of us. We're all on the same side.'

'If that's true, then he'll open this door and let my pilots fly these fighters right out of here. Earth's future depends on it.'

'You've got to be kidding,' said Johnny.

'See,' said Colonel Hartman. 'He'd rather his alien friends took the planet over than give us a chance to defend ourselves.'

'How dare you?' said Johnny, slowly standing, careful not to trigger a firefight.

'Why not, Johnny?' It was Louise who'd spoken. 'The Krun have a thousand ships and we have no pilots. Even with Katherine's people that makes just a handful. We can't win this war on our own.'

'We can't just give *them* . . . the Corporation . . . this technology. You don't know what they're like. It can't be so easily won – it has to be earned.'

'You've seen us fight, and beat, the Krun, Johnny,' said the Colonel. 'Humanity's future is at stake. Together we can save it, or is that what you're afraid of?'

He wasn't about to rise to her bait. Colonel Hartman had always tried to goad him into some ridiculous admission that he wasn't human, when he felt nothing but. If only he wasn't so tired he could think clearly. There had to be a way out of this.

'How about it, Johnny?' Miss Harutunian had joined him by a flower bed. 'The enemy of my enemy is my friend.'

Johnny wasn't at all sure she was right, or that this was anything other than a terrible idea, but there were only a few hours to prepare a defence.

'I guess there's no choice,' he said, hardly believing the words had come out of his own mouth.

'We have a deal?' asked the Colonel.

Johnny nodded and she released Bentley's lead. The Old English sheepdog bounded across and slid a warm, wet tongue all across his face.

Preparations were in full swing. Johnny had been forced to stay in Clara's garden, holding the fold wide open until the last of the Starfighters and Battlecruisers had been removed. A succession of near-silent military men and women with close-cropped hair and bulging muscles had marched through the opening, trampling over Clara's garden before each took charge of one of the galaxy's most fearsome fighting machines. Seeing each of the ships lift silently into the air and then streak out into the English countryside was beyond words. All his life, Johnny had longed for Earth to have its own fleet of spacecraft. He just hoped they'd survive for more than a single day.

Miss Harutunian had been on the phone constantly, and several familiar faces from Halader House, and even Dave Spedding, Ashvin Gupta and others from Johnny's football team, had also appeared. The social worker said she'd begun recruitment after their visit to the children's home. Johnny was worried they weren't taking things seriously enough – that they didn't appreciate the threat. The whole thing was crazy. Louise, herself a complete novice, was teaching them to fly. Miss Harutunian was really frustrated she couldn't find more people, but said many of her contacts had disappeared over the past few weeks. He knew things were desperate, but it felt wrong to be asking people to risk their lives this way.

Colonel Hartman commandeered the massive Starcruiser, a colossus of a ship for which Johnny had to stretch the entrance to breaking point. It took all his strength, but would be worth it in the battle to come. He took a last look across the now empty garden with its trampled flower beds and then checked his wristcom – time was running out and the Krun fleet must be almost here. He didn't trust the colonel as far as he could fold her, but he'd made his decision. There could be no going back.

Louise and Miss Harutunian were gone. They had flown back separately, and apparently successfully, to the *Spirit of London*, so only Bentley was present to notice as Johnny skidded the *Bakerloo* along the shuttle bay floor. He stepped out, surprised to see Alf emerge from the shadows of one of the Atlantean ships.

'Well done,' said the android. 'Everything is in hand. I have prepared a plan and communicated our tactics to your new fleet.'

Johnny nodded and walked past the android, heading for the lifts. 'Let's get to the bridge,' he said.

'I am sorry,' said Alf from behind. Johnny felt the blast of air on his neck before he could react. A warmth spread through his veins and his eyelids drooped. He fell into the android's waiting arms and was instantly asleep.

☆ ☆ ☆
☆ ☆

'You have a battle plan, midshipman?'

Johnny was lying on the wooden deck of HMS *Victory* looking up at Admiral Lord Horatio Nelson, resplendent in a navy-blue uniform adorned with medals and wearing his bicorn hat. It didn't feel right to be lying down – he must have just fallen from the rigging. Quickly getting up, he dusted himself down and saluted.

'Everything's under control, sir. Alf says the plan's taken care of.'

'And what do you say, midshipman?'

'I . . . I don't know, sir,' said Johnny. 'Sorry, sir – I haven't seen it.'

'Have I taught you nothing? Do you not remember Trafalgar?'

'No . . . well, yes . . . sir,' said Johnny, a little confused. Now he thought about it, he did remember the Battle of Trafalgar, and listening to Admiral Nelson spelling out the strategy. But it had happened a long time ago, when he'd been dreaming. 'It was a dream, sir,' said Johnny. 'It wasn't real.'

'Is that right?' said the admiral. 'My superlative triumph over the French and Spanish fleets, a mere figment of your imagination?'

'Well, not exactly,' said Johnny, but Nelson wasn't about to be interrupted.

'Perhaps this is a dream too? The salt air in your nostrils an illusion? The screech of the seagull merely an echo? The weight of a cannonball in your midriff a flight of fancy?'

It wasn't clear where it came from, but Johnny caught the black metal sphere before it hit him, clutching it to his stomach and falling over backwards because the thing was so heavy. A few sailors around him laughed.

'You there,' Admiral Nelson said to them, 'the midshipman is harbouring the misconception that he is in the Land of Nod, asleep with the fairies. Throw him over the side – that might wake him up.'

Johnny struggled as four sailors grabbed hold of his arms and legs, but they were far too strong.

'On three, shall we, boys?' said one of them as they hauled him across to the bulwark. 'One . . .'

Johnny hadn't reckoned on being quite so high above the ocean. The sailors were laughing and didn't seem to realize how dangerous this was.

'Two . . .'

He wasn't at all sure he would clear the sides, which widened as they neared the water line.

'Three . . .'

The sailors let go and Johnny was flung far from the ship. He had time to twist his body so he entered the water feet first with his arms by his side. He'd hoped that breaking the surface would be enough to wake him, but there was no sign of that happening as he sank ever further down into the gloom. He twisted and turned to try to stop his descent until he didn't even know which way was up any more. Trying to stay calm, he released a little of the breath still in his lungs and was amazed to see the bubbles descend into the darkness. He must be upside down.

Johnny kicked after the globules of air, racing them towards the surface. If he broke it, he was sure he'd wake up. In his dream he was a far stronger swimmer than in real life and he zoomed ever faster upward, leaping out of the ocean like a dolphin and crashing back into the oddly vinegary water. HMS *Victory* was nowhere to be seen. He was close to shore and staggered out onto a grassy bank. In the distance, two fiery blue suns shone. He knew this place. It was Novolis, Zeta and Erin's homeworld.

He needed to stay calm. Earth, his friends and his sister were all in danger, yet somehow he had travelled eight hundred light years away from them in the blink of an eye. Soaking wet, but not cold for this was a warm world, he made his way through the lush vegetation, parting the thick spiky leaves with his hands and releasing swarms of Sulaflies that glittered like miniature fireworks above him. A giant furry moth, looking out of place, flew into view and gobbled up the phosphoric insects.

Johnny knew there must be a way back. When he'd visited here before, there was always a door nearby – maybe Zeta could help him find it. He called her name, over and over, as he beat a path away from the shoreline, forcing his way through the thick foliage and ignoring the scratches and cuts that stung his hands and arms. His pale skin was soon laced with blood. Finally he burst out onto a wide road, mottled white like burnt charcoal, curving through the undergrowth.

Tall plants and trees with triangular leaves lined one side, but the other had been cleared to make way for an encampment. He paused, hands on hips to catch his breath while he took in the scene before him. He desperately needed to get back to Earth, but there was no sign of a door out into the corridor between worlds. In the centre of the camp a large, deep-purple, circular tent dominated the clearing. Surrounding it were shabby, tatty tents, huts and lean-tos and, scattered among them, sitting on fallen tree trunks or simply lying on the ground, were people, presumably Novolans.

Most had only thin wisps of orange or green hair on the tops of their heads, making each pair of stubby horns clearly visible. Johnny took a deep breath and crossed the road, walking towards the gathering. Half a dozen of the aliens were sitting around a campfire above which a cauldron spluttered with thick brown gunk, large bubbles bursting out of its surface like volcanic mudflats. It smelt of burnt milk, but he thought it would look rude to cover his nose.

'Hello,' he said. 'I'm looking for Princess Zeta. Do you know where she is?'

His question was met by silence. He knew the Novolans must have understood, because of the Hundra's soul within him, but it seemed a great effort for them to even move their dull cat-like eyes towards him.

'Zeta?' Johnny asked again. Close up, he was shocked by the aliens' appearance. Their bodies were incredibly thin and every one of their scaly faces was covered in weeping scabs and boils. Now he could see that some even had missing horns, while those of the others were turning black and looked about to drop off. An air of utter defeat hung over the group and he knew that to stay wouldn't get him anywhere. He moved on, further into the camp, looking for someone more alert. As he went, the aliens he'd passed stood and began to follow, shuffling behind him. It was a little unnerving.

Johnny walked through more groups, meeting the same reaction each time. By now there was quite a crowd building, but finally he'd seen someone who looked in charge and strode across, trying to appear bolder than he felt. Wearing a flamboyant, sparkling headdress, a necklace of triangular purple stones and loose-fitting burnt-orange robes, the woman was twice as wide as any of her fellow Novolans. Before her was laid a tray of exotic fruits, a few of them rather too blue for Johnny's taste. She was seated under a gazebo in front of the large round purple tent. Before her, in the centre of the clearing, was a much larger cauldron, full to the brim with more of the foul-smelling brown gunk.

'Greetings, Johnny Mackintosh,' said the woman. 'I am Yarta, daughter of Yula. We have been expecting you, Terran. All is as it should be.'

'Is Zeta here? I need to get back to Earth . . . to Terra.' As Johnny spoke, the raggedy band of Novolans shuffled round to encircle him and the woman.

'It was foretold that you would know Zeta, daughter of Zola. The princess is a great healer.' Yarta's long forked tongue shot out of her mouth as she spoke. 'You have come here willingly?'

'What? Kind of,' said Johnny. 'But I need to go home. I know Zeta can help me. I have to see her – it's important.'

'Were Zeta, daughter of Zola, here, the people would be well.' The big Novalan gestured to the others that surrounded them, the circle closing in. 'And the sacrifice that the old gods demand might not be necessary.'

Johnny glanced quickly from side to side. The sick aliens had come to life and swept past Yarta, forcing Johnny backwards until he was close to the cauldron. The heat from the bubbling vat was intense, the air around it shimmering. The Novolans' tongues shot in and out in his direction and the burning campfire blazed in their eyes. Scaly reptilian hands covered in

265

sores reached towards him. Yarta began a chant that quickly spread around the circle. Johnny was hoisted into the air. He wriggled and kicked out, but there were too many of the aliens for him to break free.

'Let me go,' he shouted. He was being swept along, and could hear the plop of the brown goo above the droning of the aliens.

Yarta's shrill voice rang out: 'Johnny Mackintosh, son of Michael Mackintosh – by your body, feed us; by your blood, heal us.' The chanting was almost deafening. 'By your sacrifice, renew again our world.' The words could barely be distinguished above the hubbub.

Johnny's body was above the edge of the cauldron. Desperate, he looked upward for inspiration and was almost blinded by the blue disk of Alnitak. He turned his head, and his eyes fell upon the purple tent nearby, the same colour as Zeta's hair. He shouted her name as he was tipped into the bubbling vat. As Johnny's own hair touched the scalding surface, he closed his eyes. The tent remained imprinted on his eyelids, while the vile smell vanished. His feet were on solid ground. Still alive, Johnny dared open one eye very slightly. He had folded more easily than ever before and found himself standing in front of the entrance to the round tent. He looked round and saw Yarta pointing towards him. As one, the Novolans let out a blood-curdling scream. Johnny pushed through the canvas flap and found himself standing in the corridor between worlds.

The all-consuming fire of the Nameless One had left its mark and there was heavy damage, currently being repaired by several furry aliens with pointy ears and long snouts, wearing blue overalls. One of them, who was scraping an oily black residue off the charred walls, nodded at Johnny.

If only he knew which of the doors led home to Earth. Time must be running out and he had to get back for the battle with the Krun – and for Clara – before it was too late. He ran along the corridor trying several handles, but all refused to budge. Panicking, Johnny tried to get his bearings. The door by which he had entered the corridor still bore the charred 'No Entry' sign that Erin had put there. He remembered watching Zeta coming up the corridor with the Nameless One hot on her heels, and diving off to the side in the nick of time. He walked along the burnt section, past the alien workers in their dungarees, and came to the doorway he thought she'd taken. It was round, made of wooden slats. He lifted the latch and the door opened. Holding it ajar, he stepped through.

'Johnny!' A mass of purple covered his face as Zeta flung her arms around him. 'You did it – you found the door.' She stepped back, her long tongue caressing his hair, flicking over the brown goo that remained. Zeta frowned. 'I taste the sickness of my world upon you.'

'The natives weren't exactly friendly,' he said.

'My people are desperate,' she said. 'It is not their fault.'

Behind the princess was a barren, heavily cratered world. Structures as ancient as time itself stood, slowly crumbling, as if here had once been a mighty city, before a million missiles rained down from the sky.

'Where are we?' Johnny asked. It was as bleak and inhospitable a place as he'd ever seen. 'I have to get home. The Krun are about to attack Earth and . . . and Clara's sick again. I'm losing her.'

'But, Johnny,' said Zeta, taking his hand and leading him gently through the still-open door, out into the corridor. 'You are home. You are dreamwalking.'

'No,' he said. 'I woke up. After Nelson . . . I really was on Novolis.'

'Yes and no,' said Zeta, laughing and again sniffing his hair with her long tongue. It tickled. 'You have so much to learn.

267

One day, despite all that is to come, I hope to welcome you there properly. Tell me, what ails your sister? I thought we had saved her.'

'It was my fault,' said Johnny. 'She knew she mustn't fold again, but we had to move a fleet of ships. I couldn't do it and she had to take over. Now she's returning to the Klein fold.' He looked at her, desperate. 'You can help. I know you can. You can heal anyone.'

Zeta shook her head. 'My world needs me, Johnny – as you have seen. You have rescued me when I couldn't find my way back and, believe me, I am grateful, but I must return there.'

'Please,' he said squeezing her hand. 'I'd do anything.'

The princess's cat-like eyes searched his own. 'Anything?' Johnny nodded. 'There is a way, but . . . but it is a path only you can take.' She looked fearful.

'Tell me,' said Johnny. 'I have to save her.'

Zeta took a deep breath, her forked tongue sucking in the air around her. 'It is her soul that is damaged . . . that is now being eaten away. To save it, you must graft on a new piece – a healthy piece. A piece of your own.'

'My soul?' Johnny asked. 'How? I don't understand.'

'But you will find a way,' she replied. 'Go. We must both return home. You must awaken.'

They were walking hand in hand up the corridor, past the furry workmen who were tapping a new lining onto the walls with golden hammers. They had reached the 'No Entry' sign.

'I'm not sure I can wake up,' Johnny said.

'Then I must help you,' the princess replied. She turned him towards her. Her face was coming closer. He could see the fine lines between the scales that covered her skin. Her long, forked tongue shot out and met his lips, forcing Johnny's mouth open. Zeta's eyes were now closed. He shut his own.

The hammering from the workmen was getting louder and Johnny couldn't shut it out. He opened his eyes and found himself in bed in his quarters aboard the *Spirit of London*. The banging was Sol, noisily trying to wake him. Johnny sat upright and said, 'How long till the Krun get here?'

14 ✩✩

The Battle for Earth ✩✩

'Computing . . . the Krun fleet will reach Earth in 73 minutes, 20.508 seconds time, approximately,' said Sol.

Johnny was out of bed in a shot. He flung his Melanian clothes over his pyjamas and flew into the corridor towards the lifts. Alf was apparently in the strategy room on deck 14, but it was to sickbay that Johnny ran first. Wearing flight overalls Louise was sitting in the single chair beside Clara, but moved aside as he entered. There was a soft pink glow coming from the bed on which his sister lay. The charts on the wall showed the lowest-ever readings, but at least they were steady. He took Clara's hand and squeezed. There was no response. Her eyes were shut tight and her golden locket, inlaid with crystals, lay flat and still against her pale skin.

He leaned forward and whispered, 'You did it, Clara. We found the ships . . . and your garden.' Was it his imagination or had he felt a slight pressure on his hand?

'How is she?' he asked.

Louise forced a smile, but it was Sol who spoke. 'Clara deteriorated rapidly after you left. By encasing her in a low-level tachyon field, I believe I have stabilized her.'

Johnny knew the energy drain for taking his sister outside normal time must be enormous for his ship to maintain. 'Will she be OK?' he asked.

'While in stasis, I do not believe Clara's condition will worsen,' said the ship.

'Thanks,' said Johnny. At least his sister was in the best possible hands and he could focus on the Krun fleet – for now. He gave Clara's hand a final squeeze and stood up. 'You ready for a space battle?' he said to Louise. She tried to respond, but no words came. Johnny understood – she looked the way he felt inside. 'Come on,' he said. They left sickbay together and made their way to deck 14.

The doors to the strategy room swished open to reveal Alf and Kovac shouting at each other, with little Miss Harutunian battling to keep them apart. The American was making a surprisingly good fist of it.

'Just when things couldn't get any worse, here comes our glorious captain,' said the quantum computer, soaring away from the melee.

Ignoring Kovac, Alf turned to Johnny and said, 'Our fighters are in position. We shall line up in a classical formation, passing parallel to the Krun Hunter–Killers as the enemy crosses the Moon's orbit.'

Beneath the mezzanine level, the battle plan was laid out. Two long lines of spaceships faced each other, slightly offset. The defenders of Earth were coloured blue while the Krun invasion fleet was picked out in red.

'Such strategic cunning yields a probability of success of 2.71828%,' said Kovac, his casing glowing bright as he spat the words out.

'Kovac's right,' said Johnny, eyes fixed on the scene below rather than meeting Alf's. 'We need a new plan.'

'Master Johnny – this is how battles have been fought for millennia.'

'Which is why we have to do things differently,' he replied. 'We've no chance unless we surprise them.' He had no experience of military strategy, but his history homework from long ago had always stayed with him – how Admiral Nelson had won at Trafalgar, by changing from these very tactics. Leaning over the balustrade, Johnny absorbed the setting for the approaching battle. At his command, Sol began repositioning the blue pieces. Soon, split into two groups, everything appeared as he wanted. 'That should do it,' he said to himself, unable to resist a smile. 'There's just enough time to make the modifications to my squadron.'

'With a brain the size of mine, I thought it impossible to be surprised,' said Kovac from above. 'However, I do believe the strategy is optimal. The probability of success has risen to 31.4159%.'

'Is that all?' Johnny had hoped the new layout would give them a better chance than that.

He felt Alf's heavy arm on his shoulder. 'The Emperor would be proud,' said the android, 'but we do not know how well our ancient ships will fare and our pilots are inexperienced.'

'That's one way of putting it,' said Miss Harutunian.

'Come on. We've been running battle drills all afternoon,' said Louise. 'We're old hands. Let's get to the fighters.' She looked pale but determined.

'You go,' said Johnny. 'And Alf – your place is in sickbay. I need you to look after Clara. I have to address the fleet.'

☆ ☆ ☆
☆ ☆

Johnny could simply have spoken to Earth's newly assembled Starfighters from the strategy room, but he knew it was right that they saw him in the captain's chair on the spectacular bridge of the *Spirit of London*. Through the sides of the ship he watched the fleet of human spaceships zoom past and assume their newly allotted positions. He imagined Admiral Nelson on the deck of HMS *Victory*, his captains around him. When

Johnny spoke, his voice sounded louder and more confident than he'd expected.

'In five minutes' time, we go to war. I know this is new to all of you. If you're not scared, you should be. But if we all do our jobs, we will win the day. Not through weight of numbers – the enemy has more. Not because we're better pilots – for most of you, this is the first day you've flown a spaceship. To triumph in this battle, the secret is to destroy the Krun Queen.'

'*You cannot hurt me, Johnny Mackintosh. I am part of you now.*'

Johnny stopped and looked around for the source of the voice. There was nothing. He had to assume only he had heard the interruption. If the Queen was truly inside his head, he had to block her out. He needed a single, strong image to concentrate on. He thought of Clara, picturing her encased within the stasis field in sickbay. His sister at the very forefront of his mind, he carried on.

'These aliens we're fighting have a hive mind, a sort of telepathy. Destroy the Queen and their communications will break down. That's why I've changed things. The Halader House squadrons will start out pretending to follow the original plan, flying parallel to and engaging the Krun Hunter–Killers. The rest of you – the Corporation ships – you'll hide in the Moon's craters until I give the word and then, in two waves, you'll try to break through the Krun lines. Head for the biggest, baddest ship you see and bring it down.

'Before we begin, I want everyone to stop and look at the planet in the distance. For most of you, it's the first time you'll have seen it from space. That's what we're fighting for. From here, Earth has no borders. We're not fighting for ourselves – we have to work together. When NASA astronauts first set foot on the Moon, it wasn't for America – they did it for all mankind. That's who we represent now. Let's make our planet proud. Good luck, everyone. Johnny Mackintosh out.'

'Well said, Johnny.' Lights on a nearby screen flashed in time to Sol's voice.

Johnny stood. The voice in his head scared him, but there was nothing he could do about it now. 'I have to go,' he said. 'Look after Clara . . . and look after yourself. That Imperial Starfighter's fun, but it's just a plaything. It's not . . . It's not you.'

'Fight well, Johnny,' said Sol.

He turned and stepped into the lift cabin.

☆ ☆ ☆
☆ ☆

Johnny had expected Louise to leave the dogs on the garden deck, but Bentley and Rusty were waiting for him beside the Starfighter. He knelt down, patted the red setter on the head and then turned to his oldest friend. He lifted the hair out of Bentley's face and stared into the sheepdog's one brown and one blue eye. 'Who'd have thought it would come to this, eh?' he said. A long, rough tongue slopped across Johnny's face and he flung his arms around Bentley's neck, pulling him close.

'One minute until the Krun are in range.' Sol's words echoed around the shuttle deck.

'So long, Bents.' The sheepdog leapt up and tried to scramble into the Imperial ship, but Johnny caught hold of him around the middle and pulled him back. 'Not this time,' he said, climbing inside and closing the cockpit before Bentley could try again. Moments later, despite the butterflies in his stomach, 'Red Leader,' as he'd chosen to be called, shot out of the bay doors to take his place at the front of his squadron.

'Nice ship. You see – I told you he'd make it.' It was Joe Pennant's voice coming through the comm. system.

'So, this is where you got to when you were missing all those matches?' The next speaker was the football team's captain, Micky Elliot.'

'Sorry, skip,' said Johnny. 'I had things to do.' He glanced either side and saw Dave and Ashvin just behind him at the front of the V-formation. Ash gave a thumbs-up while Dave saluted.

'This is Gold Leader.' Now it was Louise's voice inside the cockpit. She was in charge of the very same Atlantean ships that thirty thousand years earlier had escorted the *Spirit of London* into Atlantis. It would be down to the freckly girl from Yarnton Hill to lead the first wave of humanity's defence. Johnny had seen what an instinctive pilot she was – if anyone could keep their ships intact, it was her. 'Let's get this show on the road,' she said.

There was no gentle preamble, no probing the enemy in search of weaknesses. It began at once. In the distance, a barrage of green flashes marked weapons fire from the lead Krun Hunter–Killers. Orange energy bolts responded as the fleets flew side by side in opposing directions. The mid-size, heavily armed Krun spacecraft were bigger and more powerful, but Earth's fighters were more manoeuvrable and, despite being small, they carried quite a sting. There were mighty explosions. In the frenzy, Johnny couldn't tell whose ships had been destroyed, but black clouds of gas looked to be escaping into space from the alien vessels – it had to be a good sign.

'Red Leader to Blue Leader,' said Johnny. 'Whenever you're ready.'

'Going in now.'

It was Miss Harutunian leading the second squadron, sounding icy calm.

Then it was Johnny's turn. 'This is Red Leader,' he said. 'Switch to new approach vector. Full shields, everyone, and use your automatic targeting systems – no heroics.'

He thought, *Forward, eighty percent acceleration*, and his ship rocketed ahead. Without the inertial dampeners his body would have been crushed instantly. Had he been alone, he wouldn't have held back, but he needed to ensure the rest of his squadron stayed with him – Johnny hoped they could keep up. At the tip of a flying V, he set his forward blasters to as wide a beam as possible, clearing a path for his squadron to cut across the Krun lines and encircle individual HKs, taking them out one by one. Immediately he was into the debris from the first wave of fighting. The voice in his head was screaming at him to stop . . . to switch sides and fire on his own ships. In a vessel run by thought control, Johnny felt paralysed to act. He daren't try to block the Queen out, in case his brain settled on her commands.

Following his lead, the other Earth squadrons had broken formation. Away from the standard lines of a space battle, they were far harder for the Krun ships to target. A couple of whoops coming through the comm. system told Johnny that, even without his help, Earth forces were scoring successes and through the windscreen he saw needle-pointed ships engulfed by massive explosions. Away from the regimented battle lines, the Atlantean ships were coming into their own, decimating the enemy. It was no wonder even these small craft were once feared halfway across the galaxy, as they brought down vessels a hundred times their size. The Krun had to react and smaller single-Krun pods swarmed from the nearest HK, all emerging as smooth round balls before sprouting deadly spikes. Soon space was thick with the miniature Krun ships, like a cloud of locusts darkening an already black sky. In seconds they were on him and began to settle on the Starfighter's wings and fuselage, their spikes burrowing into his hull, making them impossible to dislodge. Screams of terror were coming through the speakers, matched by small explosions outside in the battle. The Krun pods were blowing themselves apart, taking the Earth ships with them. They were about to destroy his Starfighter. Johnny had to do something. It was instinctive. Without thinking, he placed a hand on the inner hull either side and sent a torrent of electricity through the shell of his craft, blue sparks meeting the black spheres, burning them off the outsides so the spiked pods spiralled lifeless into space.

The act freed Johnny, but the needled Hunter–Killers were still firing on his teammates. The voice in his head was telling him to join in, but there was no way he was going to listen to that. He gave a handful of Krun spheres what for, obliterating them in a barrage of blaster fire, before his Starfighter's disrupters opened a gash along the side of the nearest Krun ship. Johnny knew he had to take charge – some of the inexperienced Earth fighters were out of control and one even fired on him as he flew past.

He was fast approaching a great mound of the black pods that he suspected had engulfed one of his fighters. Forced to swerve at incredible speed Johnny shouted into the comm. system, 'Red Leader to all Earth vessels. Polarize your hulls – don't let them clamp on. I repeat, polarize your hulls.'

'Don't you think you could have told us earlier?' It was Louise's voice inside Johnny's helmet. She was still alive. 'They're all over my squadron – we can't shake them.'

'Hold on,' said Johnny. In the heat of battle, with his friends' lives at stake, again he touched the cockpit either side, but this time he didn't let go. Ribbons of blue sparks leapt forward from his Starfighter's nosecone and backwards from behind its wingtips, jumping from ship to ship, quickly linking the entire Earth fleet and enveloping it in a protective glow. Those Krun pods that had affixed themselves were sent tumbling away, destroyed by the ferocity of the current.

It brought brief respite, but Johnny knew they were in trouble.

A voice he recognized shouted, 'They're in my cockpit . . . one's in my head . . . it's in my head!' Spencer Mitchell's screams were among the most terrible sounds Johnny had ever heard, but it was worse when they stopped.

'Blue Leader to Red Leader – go do your job, Johnny. We're counting on you.' Even with Spencer's screams in her ears, Miss Harutunian sounded in total control.

'I'm on it,' said Johnny, knowing he had to follow her lead. 'With me, Red Squadron.' It felt terrible to abandon the immediate battle, but he had to trust the others to do their best. Johnny's job was to lure the very biggest Krun ships, the giant Destroyers protecting the Queen, into an ambush. He changed course to take his teammates beyond the Moon and away. Jets of black gas streamed into space from a newly arrived, apparently undamaged HK, obscuring the stars. Johnny's view was becoming blocked, tiny clumps of something settling on his outer hull. He tried to ignore them as he shot beyond the chaos of the battle, but then they started to move.

A squeaking coming from his windscreen was the first sign that something was wrong. The little clumps were cutting through the forcefields and then the cockpit itself. Air hissed out into space, until the Starfighter's systems sealed the breach, but not before a little bug – the same as the moth he'd seen back on Mars – had entered the cabin. He could do without this. Johnny tried to ignore it and keep on with his mission, but more moths burst through, buzzing around his head, and then one landed on his face. From the sounds reaching him, it seemed the same thing was happening to other pilots. Leaving a trail of slime, the moth crawled towards Johnny's nose and up his left nostril.

'*Leave us*,' growled the voice inside Johnny's head. '*This one belongs to me already.*'

Johnny sneezed and the furry bug shot out onto his leg,

where he squashed it instinctively. The other moths dropped to the floor, as if already dead.

Up ahead, the Krun were blockading their Queen with a protective barrier of Destroyers. Even so, the Queen's ship was so vast that some of the black studs lining its hull could still be seen. The only chance of destroying the massive ship beyond was to draw her escort away. For that, they had to convince the Krun that the little fighters of Red Squadron were somehow a threat.

'This is Red Leader. Who's still with me?'

'Red One here.' It was goalkeeper Simon Bakewell.

'Red Five's got your wing.' Johnny looked round. Micky Elliot was flying alongside, as reliable as ever.

'Red Two – you don't get away that easily,' said Ash.

'Red Nine, ready to kick more alien butt,' said Joe Pennant. Johnny smiled.

'Red Eight, right behind you, Blondie,' said Owen from the school year below.

Johnny waited for more to check in, but the silence showed him his little squadron was down to half a dozen ships. It had to be enough. Wherever they were in the battle, he hoped Dave, Naresh and the others were OK.

'Good going, Red Squadron,' he said. 'Let's spread out and tell ET we're here.' Either side, Starfighters peeled away into a looser formation. 'On my mark.' Johnny's hand hovered over the only actual button on his dashboard, added just an hour or so earlier. The voice in his head screamed at him not to press it. He hesitated, his hand wavering, but then forced the word, 'Mark,' from his lips and pushed down hard with one hand on top of the other.

His scanners lit up like a Christmas tree, which meant the Krun's must have done exactly the same. The hope was that the hugely amplified power signatures they'd added would convince the Queen's escort that six gigantic Imperial Starcruisers had just unfolded nearby – and that they had to give chase. It looked to be working. The barrier around the Queen's ship was breaking up as the Destroyers moved to eradicate the new threat. They were converging on the remnants of Red Squadron, who would have to move very fast.

'This is Johnny,' he said, abandoning the call sign to speak to his friends. 'Get as close as you can to Point Zero and then get out of there twice as fast.' This time, he thought, *Forward, full acceleration*, and shot towards the designated coordinates.

Even if the plan worked, his fighters simply didn't have the firepower to do enough damage to the Destroyers. But Johnny knew just the ship who did. He reached the place quickly. Dozens of the gigantic Krun ships were bearing down on him. All he had to do was give the command, but the words refused to leave his mouth. Instead, he heard another voice inside his head.

'*You belong to me, Johnny Mackintosh. Stay silent. Turn your ship around and come to me – let me feast on you.*'

As the huge black vessels surrounded the remnants of Johnny's squadron, green energy bolts tore through them, crippling one ship and vaporizing two others. He had to shut the Queen out. Again Johnny forced himself to think of Clara, on the *Spirit of London*. The image of his sister formed a wall around his thoughts. She existed in stasis, outside of time, but now was the time he had to act.

'Now, Sol,' said Johnny. The words came in a whisper, and the effort to speak them was immense, but he knew at once they'd been heard.

The sparkling curves of the *Spirit of London* unfolded nearby. As she fired, it was as if his beautiful ship was casting a vast net of gold into space, so many energy beams were shooting out at once. Outnumbered more than a hundred to one, Johnny hoped Sol, and those she carried, would be OK.

'*You cannot resist me, Johnny Mackintosh. I will control you.*'

He closed his mind to the voice. 'Red Leader to Black Leader,' he said, 'send the first wave.' Now was the time to begin the real assault. The way looked clear for the Corporation Battlecruisers to head straight towards the giant vessel holding the Krun Queen. Appearances though could prove deceptive – especially where the Krun were concerned. That was why he was holding back a second squadron – the final line of defence for Earth. All these ships were armed with the Corporation's hyperspatial gravimetric charges, which he'd ordered specially tuned to destroy the Queen's ship.

'Negative,' came the voice through the comm. system. 'All ships launching together.'

'No,' said Johnny, trying to sound calm, 'stick to the plan.'

A third, female, voice cut in – one Johnny knew only too well. It was Colonel Hartman. 'You have your orders, Squadron Leader. I expect you to carry them out.'

The relief Johnny felt didn't last long. He saw from his Starfighter's sensors that whatever orders the leader of Black Squadron was following, they weren't his. Distracted, he allowed Krun blaster fire to graze his wing. Too late to act, he heard the cockpit alarm that signalled an enemy target lock. Directly ahead, a swarm of alien spheres was about to unleash green death. Then, coming in from the side, golden energy beams from an Atlantean ship ripped through the Krun vessels, turning them into one fireball after another. There was a whoop in Johnny's earphones, followed by Micky Elliot shouting, 'Get in! Five nil to the good guys.' A craft with red markings streaked through the fireball and beyond, just before Johnny's own Starfighter did the same. Elsewhere, Earth's fighters were scoring similar successes. Johnny couldn't help smile and even wondered if Stevens was aboard any of the exploding Krun ships.

The *Spirit of London* was decimating the Destroyers, firing in every direction, somehow protecting any stricken Earth vessels at the same time. Perhaps the Corporation was right and the aliens had left nothing in reserve, no hidden ships to fold into the fray. All the while the vast Atlantean Starcruiser, commandeered by Colonel Hartman, had been noticeable by its absence, hanging back from the battle. Now even that moved forward to join the *Spirit of London* and fired on a couple of the larger black enemy craft. The twinkling stars of hyperspatial gravimetric torpedoes enveloped their targets in a blaze of light. It was almost too good to be true, but it was amazing to see what could be accomplished when humanity worked together. With the Atlantean fleet in charge, a new golden age for Earth looked to be possible. As the *Spirit of London* continued firing, the Starfighter's sensors showed the very last Krun Destroyers winking out of existence, leaving only their short-range spheres and, on the very edge of the display, the ship belonging to the Queen.

In his head Johnny heard her scream with fury, but the sound was drowned out by his own cheer. 'Brilliant, Sol,' he shouted, punching the air.

'All achieved with minimal shielding,' the ship replied. 'Full offensive capability while maintaining Clara's tachyon field left little in reserve.'

What followed seemed to happen in slow motion. The narrow space between Colonel Hartman's Starcruiser and the *Spirit of London* sparkled as a volley of glittering torpedoes, fired from the flank of the Corporation vessel, slammed into the clear curved sides of Johnny's own. The lights from inside his beautiful ship blinked and went out. He hadn't even been aware of Sol's presence in the very back of his mind, but Johnny sensed immediately that she was no longer there. The mighty craft hung deathly still, as if teetering on the edge of an abyss, and then began tumbling, nose over tail, towards the Moon.

A great howl of anger filled the cockpit and it was a few seconds before Johnny realized it was his own scream of rage. At the same time he was aware of a woman's voice coming through the comm. system, laughing.

'Oh, come on, Johnny,' said Colonel Hartman. 'Don't pretend you weren't about to do exactly the same to me and my rather handsome flagship. It's your bad luck I heard my opportunity and took it. You should have kept your communications more secure.'

He was so angry he couldn't speak.

'Cat got your tongue?' The colonel switched to the main comm. channel. 'This is Hartman to all Earth vessels. I have assumed command and am releasing new orders. Destroy all alien fighters, but do not engage their mother ship. The Krun Queen will be useful to us going forward. Further, any Earth vessels not following the chain of command should be met with deadly force. Hartman out.'

Johnny stared out of the cockpit at the faraway explosions in disbelief. Closer at hand, the *Spirit of London* continued somersaulting towards the cratered grey world below.

'Johnny! Do something.'

Louise's golden Atlantean fighter buzzed Johnny, tearing after the stricken ship and bringing him to his senses. He willed the Starfighter to follow and it surged towards the Moon at breathtaking speed, overtaking the Atlantean craft.

'Sol, can you hear me?' Johnny asked, but his cries were met by silence. He drew alongside the *Spirit of London*, tumbling a few thousand metres above the lunar surface. The ship looked completely dead, the only lights reflections of distant stars off her diamond-panelled hull as she fell Moonwards.

Then he heard barking, the desperate sound of two dogs. Johnny looked around, wondering where the noise could have come from before realizing he was in range through his wristcom. He lifted it to his mouth and said, 'It's Johnny – can anyone hear me? Alf? Sol? Kovac?'

'If you're planning on saving me, I suggest you do something sooner rather than later,' said Kovac.

'What's your status?' asked Johnny.

'My status is that I'm being tossed around this tin can like a toy car in a washing machine. Make it stop.'

'How?'

'Am I the only one capable of performing several quadrillion calculations a second? Don't answer that. Just position yourself under this brainless skyscraper's nosecone and I'll transmit instructions to your ship's computer.'

'What?' Johnny wasn't at all sure that was a good idea.

'You need to stop us spinning,' said Kovac. 'Tell that Louise girl to fly her ship under the tail. In case you haven't noticed, we're about to crash into the Moon so it would help if you hurried.'

'Tell that quantum box thingy I already heard him,' said Louise, 'and I don't like it.'

'Me neither,' said Johnny, but if it was the only way to save Sol and everyone inside her, they had to try. 'Here goes.' He willed the Starfighter to begin looping a tight loop, while falling towards the Moon's surface, matching his rotation with that of the *Spirit of London*. He'd never been more glad of the inertial dampeners.

Louise followed suit, positioning herself at the opposite end of the loop from Johnny. The grey world below was rushing towards them horribly quickly, the walls of a steep-sided crater looming larger on every rotation. Johnny manoeuvred his Starfighter directly under Sol's bridge. It looked massive in comparison to his tiny ship. He edged his minute craft closer to the *Spirit of London's* nosecone until he heard the grating sound of contact. He thought, *Full power, upward*, and straightaway realized his mistake. With a horrible crunching sound the Starfighter was batted out into the middle of the fighting at incredible speed. It was a miracle he didn't collide with any other spacecraft. He hoped his compact ship hadn't been damaged, but it still appeared to be working as he blitzed half a dozen of the smaller Krun pods before arcing around towards the *Spirit of London* again.

Miss Harutunian said, 'Thanks, Johnny,' through the comm. system, but Kovac was going ballistic.

'I shall be splattered halfway across the lunar surface, all because some buffoon can't follow instructions that any simpleton would understand.'

Beside the *Spirit of London*, Louise's fighter was spiralling ever closer to the pockmarked surface. 'Johnny,' she said, 'I think it's too late.'

'I'm not abandoning them,' he said, as much to himself as to her. In a single revolution he'd matched his velocity with that of his beloved spaceship. Gently this time, he fired thrusters to send him upward. It sounded as though the Starfighter would be torn apart.

'Careful, Johnny,' screamed Louise, but he kept going. They were still falling, but his trajectory was beginning to level out and it was becoming easier to steady the great ship above. His sensors told him that their pitch was minus thirty degrees . . . minus twenty degrees, minus five, but then plus three. He'd overcorrected.

'Hang on,' said Louise, calmer now. 'I'm coming.'

Johnny could tell she'd retaken her position at the *Spirit of*

London's tail because they levelled out. 'It worked,' he said, disbelieving.

'You're too late, you blithering idiot,' said the voice in his wristcom. 'Impact in ten . . .'

'Louise,' shouted Johnny, 'full upward thrusters on my mark.'

'Nine . . .' said Kovac. Somewhere in the background, dogs were barking.

'Mark,' said Johnny, but they kept falling.

'Your tin can of a spaceship has too much momentum,' said Kovac. 'Didn't you learn anything at that school of yours? We're all going to die in four . . .'

'Louise – get out of here,' said Johnny.

'Three . . .'

'I'm not leaving you, Johnny.'

'Two . . .'

He could see the steep sides of the crater they were plunging into, the great mass of the *Spirit of London* forcing them ever downward.

'Save yourself,' said Johnny. 'I've got a plan'

'Well, that is reassuring,' said Kovac. 'Superbrain's going to somehow save us all.'

As the quantum computer chuntered on and the bottom of the crater came into view, Johnny trained his blasters straight down and fired at low intensity. If it didn't work, his own beautiful spaceship would crush him and the Starfighter to death. He hoped Louise had got away in time.

Splashdown!

The Imperial fighter hit . . . not moonrock, but water, melted by Johnny firing into the well of a deep crater where the Sun's rays never reached. The *Spirit of London* forced him down under the surface into darkness, but Johnny guided his ship up and out to see the crippled spacecraft bobbing up and down on the surface of a lake that was rapidly boiling away.

A great shadow passed overhead. He looked upward to see the Krun Queen's massive ship speeding towards Earth. Inside his head the Queen was laughing at him, but he ignored her. He had to find Clara and see what had happened to Sol. The impact had burst open her shuttle bay doors and Johnny flew the Starfighter straight inside.

Louise's voice came through the comm. system. 'I can't believe you did it, but you've got to stop the Krun. Something's happened. Something bad.'

'You go,' he said. 'I have to see Clara.'

'The Corporation ships . . . they've joined the Krun,' said Louise. 'We need you.'

'Right now, Clara needs me,' said Johnny.

Louise's reply was lost as Johnny climbed out of the cockpit into a scene of devastation, illuminated only by the twin beams of the Starfighter's lights. Both the *Piccadilly* and the *Bakerloo* had been tossed around as if a tornado had ripped through the deck. Wreckage was strewn everywhere yet, at the most basic level of her being, Sol must still be alive. The emergency forcefields were intact and there was air to breathe.

From out of the chaos, barking and shaking rubble out of his hair, came Bentley, followed by Rusty. The two dogs looked very sorry for themselves but otherwise OK. Johnny patted Rusty on the head and knelt down face to face with Bentley, but after touching noses he stood and ran for the lifts, raising the wristcom to his lips to say, 'Kovac – where are you?'

From under a nearby pile of girders, a heavily dust-covered, very battered hyperbox lifted into the air. 'It would appear I underestimated you,' said Kovac. 'Doubtless the result of the same thing happening to me so often that even I'm losing count.'

'You can still fly?' Johnny asked.

'Then again, perhaps not,' Kovac continued. 'Unless you

were blinded in the heat of battle, so are without the evidence of your own eyes.'

'Shut up and take me to Clara,' said Johnny, adding, 'please,' as he was so desperate.

'Pretty please?'

'Kovac . . .' said Johnny, growling.

'Oh, jump on then,' said the quantum computer, settling on top of the rubble in front of him. 'Not that it will do any good. I've been unable to raise anyone since the torpedoes struck.'

Johnny stepped onto the box and crouched down as Kovac climbed into the air, heading in the direction of the lifts. It would have been pitch black inside the shaft so he let the computer underneath him chunter on in order to light the way. They turned down the empty corridor towards sickbay, and finally inside. The dim glow of Earthlight through the walls of the ship filled the room, but there was also the faintest flickering pink haze still surrounding Clara's bed. A figure lay slumped on the floor. Johnny thought the gravimetric charges must have affected the android's circuitry, until his eyes became accustomed to the gloom and he saw Alf's chest open with some sort of organic cable snaking out of it, connected to where his sister lay.

He understood. To try to save Clara, the android had used his own energy source, maintaining the tachyon field for as long as possible. But now that power had run out. The pink aura flickered off for the final time. To see better, Johnny didn't need Kovac to talk to shed light in the room. He willed it, and the electrons bound into the very molecules of the air became excited, glowing green like the aurora. Any other time the luminescence would have been a thing of wonder, but now it was purely functional. Clara was thrashing about on the bed. Johnny slid off Kovac's casing and ran across.

Before he could take his sister's hand, she grabbed hold

of his wrist, gripping him so tightly that his arm burned. Then she opened her frighteningly oily black eyes and said, 'I don't want to go.' The darkness spread like spidery veins, across her face and through her body. It reached the hand grabbing his. Johnny felt the power of it trying to repel him, but his sister was hanging on too tightly. Her body floated off the bed and the green glow in the room was extinguished by bolts of lightning arcing from Clara's torso.

Johnny held Zeta's words in his mind – that the only way to save his sister was to graft a portion of his own soul onto hers. He knew it must be possible. It was on his very first day in space that the Hundra had released a speck of its soul – a shining sliver of light – which separated from the whole and floated into Johnny. He recalled Bram long ago, on the moon where Sol had been born, turning from him. The Emperor had somehow placed a portion of his soul into Johnny's locket. If only Bram had let him see how it was done.

'Don't let go,' said Johnny. 'Remember your garden. Remember Mum and Dad. Remember Nicky – we're going to find him again. We'll be a family. I promise.'

The crystals set within Clara's locket blazed, like lasers, lilac lines burning through Johnny's tunic, cutting through the stars of the 'W' on his front. It felt as if someone had grabbed hold of his insides, twisting his organs. He remembered every bad thing he'd ever done as it rose to the top of his consciousness, like slag in a blast furnace. These were the things he was ashamed of – that he'd buried, hidden away so he wouldn't have to face the thought of them again . . . until now. The times he'd wanted to speak up, when he saw something wrong, but had kept quiet. Or when he'd joined in with his friends so they'd think he was cool or funny, but he'd known it was a cowardly way to behave. And how he'd abandoned his friends now – his whole planet even – selfishly to save his sister just as he'd flown to Titan before when people were disappearing and being processed into food. There with it, being skimmed off and thrown away, he could see something else that disgusted him. It began in the shape of a flying insect, like the little moth that had forced its way down his ear on Mars, but swollen. Slowly it transformed, melting into the hundreds of eyes of the Krun Queen staring at him, outraged, before dissolving in the crystal heat. He knew his soul was being purified, making it ready for Clara, and it hurt like he'd never hurt before. He finally understood where the voices in his head had been coming from – how the Queen too had contaminated him. Bent double with pain, he vaguely heard another voice in the background. It was Louise.

'Johnny, where are you? Didn't you hear me? Our ships are going over to the Krun.' She sounded far away, as if shouting down a long tunnel. She faded into nothingness and was lost.

Johnny's mind was full of light and satisfaction and the desire to do good things, but the sensation was leaving him, slowly ebbing along the lines of laser light towards his sister who, Johnny knew, was being held within this universe only by the bonds of her locket, anchoring her to him while it drew on his strength . . . his inner being . . . his soul. He ached as a portion of him ebbed away.

The oily veins retreated up Clara's arms and disappeared from her face. Johnny looked into his sister's eyes and the blackness was leaving them, replaced by a shimmering silver. Mirrored within, he saw himself and his own matching sparkling silver eyes for the first time. The bond broke and Clara fell back onto the bed. She sighed, the sound of someone at peace, smiled contentedly at Johnny and, exhausted, fell sound asleep.

Johnny collapsed. He felt weak . . . incomplete . . . as though everything he truly was had been sucked out of him and he longed for what had been taken.

'Professor Bond to Johnny Mackintosh – are you receiving me?'

The surprise at hearing the voice brought Johnny to his senses.

15 ✧

Feast for a Queen ✧

'Professor Bond?' said Johnny, disbelieving. 'Where are you?'

'With the Krun Queen,' came the reply. 'There are lots of us. We were going to be eaten, but broke out. I know how to destroy it, but you have to come and save the others first. And hurry.'

Johnny looked at his sister, finally whole and at peace. He had lost something he couldn't put his finger on, but seeing Clara he knew it was worth it. Also, there was silence in his head and he realized that for the first time in days he was free of the Queen's presence. Back on Mars, what he'd thought was simply a horrid bug must have been part of her – maybe even a piece of her soul. The idea made him feel sick. He gazed around at his broken ship and knew there was nothing he could do for her right now. The crescent Earth hung in the sky above, and it was his homeworld that demanded him. He fell onto Kovac's casing and said, 'Take me to the shuttle bay.'

'Even "please" is out of the question this time, I suppose?' said the computer.

Johnny didn't have the energy to respond. He clung on as Kovac glided up the corridor and along the horizontal lift shaft, emerging into the shuttle bay on deck 2. They were met by barking. Johnny rolled off the computer onto the floor, and found himself unable to stand. A rough, wet tongue slopped across his face, over and over until, hands on Bentley's neck, he managed to make it to his feet. The cockpit of his Starfighter opened, but this time he couldn't prevent the Old English sheepdog jumping onto the sleek wing and climbing inside. Somehow, Johnny found the strength to follow, leaving Rusty behind barking over the sound of Kovac grumbling at being abandoned again.

The Imperial ship streaked out of the open shuttle bay and lifted upward towards what was left of the battle. He'd not expected this – very few fighters remained, none in formation, and his scanners showed none of Earth's Battlecruisers or Colonel Hartman's ship. Instead they were dominated by one giant vessel – a slightly irregular ovoid, studded black and holding the Krun Queen – that was speeding unmolested towards Earth. According to Johnny's computer, it would enter the atmosphere in less than twenty minutes. He started a countdown timer on his wristcom.

'Louise? . . . Dave? . . . Ash? . . . Miss Harutunian? . . . Anyone?' The words were met by silence. He couldn't believe it.

He checked the comm. system, desperate, but the diagnostics claimed it was working perfectly. They couldn't *all* be dead. He knew how inexperienced they were, yet he'd gone missing when they needed him most.

Ahead was a swirling cloud of single-Krun pods. Johnny fired a full spread, sending a series of explosions cascading through the swarm. It was easy without the Queen in his head. From the side he spotted one of the Earth ships with blue markings, part of Miss Harutunian's squadron, turning towards him. Relieved, Johnny hailed the incoming vessel. There was no response. An alarm chimed and the next moment the Earth ship rained fire on his Starfighter. The cockpit blazed with golden light until automatic systems cut in to reduce the glare.

The fighter was gone and Johnny's shields had held . . . just. They wouldn't take another hit.

'Oi, be careful,' said Johnny. 'Use your automatic targeting systems.'

No one responded. The fighter circled around. It was returning for another pass, clearly intent on finishing him off.

'Johnny Mackintosh to Blue Squadron spaceship. Hold your fire.'

The target-lock warning chimed through his cockpit. Outside he saw a streak of orange death. His Starfighter remained intact, but the attacking ship had vanished, engulfed in a fireball. Whoever was inside stood no chance. Another Atlantean fighter, this one with circular gold markings, flew across the sky.

'Johnny?' It was Louise.

Bentley barked in his ear.

'You're alive,' said Johnny. 'What's going on? They were firing at me.'

'Johnny . . . listen.' It sounded hard for Louise to speak, as though every word was a struggle. 'She's . . . in my head . . . all our heads . . . insects got inside our ships . . . made us shoot each other . . . You . . . you have to stop her . . . please.'

The awful truth was becoming clear. 'Listen – I'm on it. But you've got to fight her. Focus. Build a wall with your thoughts. Concentrate on something human . . . that matters to you.'

'I'll try,' she replied, sounding a little stronger.

'You hold on,' said Johnny. 'I'm going in.'

The Queen's ship loomed larger through the cockpit window. He circled, looking for some means to dock. At first it appeared impenetrable, but on a second pass he spied a slit in the black-studded exterior, slowly widening. He willed his damaged ship towards it, desperate to avoid any defensive Krun fire with his shields down to twenty percent. They would take around ten minutes to repair themselves, but he couldn't afford to wait. His wristcom, flashing nine minutes, told him Earth didn't have that long. At least the aliens were also focused on the beautiful blue planet beneath and Johnny entered the giant Queen's vessel unopposed.

Inside, he was dumbfounded to see vast numbers of empty Atlantean Starfighters and Battlecruisers filling the shuttle bay. This was where the ships had disappeared to – it was practically the whole fleet. Some were damaged and might simply have been captured, but others appeared unharmed. He landed beside a couple from Blue Squadron, grabbed a gun, opened the cockpit and was instantly engulfed by the smell of rotting cabbages. Holding his breath, he crawled out onto the wing and slid shakily to the uneven floor. Bentley followed, growling, as green blaster fire from a point in the distance shaved them.

'Run, Bents,' Johnny shouted, sprinting for a narrow exit leading into the main ship, hoping the sheepdog would follow. With Krun soldiers not far behind, he pushed through a mucous membrane, ignoring the gunk over his face, and sped on. The next chamber was large, with a vaulted roof that curved all the way down to a floor covered with the smaller pods Johnny had seen earlier. Arranged neatly in rows, close up they were larger than he'd realized. A steady background rumble was coming from behind a wall on one side, drowning out Bentley's barks, meaning the lone visible Krun, standing in front of one of the round ships, couldn't have heard them coming. Johnny thought they might surprise it, but the hive knew full well they were aboard. The alien found time to pick up a blaster with one of its four elongated arms, but Bentley was there and leapt, jaws clamping round the limb, the sound of crunching bone mingling with high-pitched scream as the weapon fell to the ground, splattered in black Krun blood.

'Professor Bond – where are you?' said Johnny into the wristcom, seeing there were less than eight minutes left. As he spoke he ran further into the chamber to hide behind the rows of spacecraft. He had to find the Australian soon or Earth would be at the Krun's mercy.

'Strewth – you made it.'

Hearing the voice in his ear, Johnny's heart leapt. There was still a chance.

'We're holding out on the level below you,' said the professor. 'Look to your right – there's an opening in the corner. Once through, there's a way down from the next chamber. Hurry.'

'On my way,' said Johnny. If he aligned himself just right, he could see past the black spheres to a patch of light coming through the wall, exactly where the Australian had described. It too was covered by a curtain of gunk. He took a deep breath, preparing to run for it, but when he looked round Bentley was bounding down the row in almost the opposite direction. 'Bents, come back. We don't have time for this.'

The Old English sheepdog ignored him. Johnny stopped, shouted again, but it made no difference. The background noise was so loud here, he doubted he could be heard anyway. Bentley was soon at the far wall, crouching in front of another opening in the curved surface, baring his teeth as though ready to attack. Exasperated, Johnny started after him, but green blaster fire barred his path. He scurried back, taking cover behind one of the pods near the centre of the large room. He crouched on the floor, which was rough and plant-like, covered in black spreading lines, like veins. The stench was almost overpowering. The very first time he'd been taken from Earth was on a Krun freighter. That had stunk too. The soldiers were coming closer. He didn't want this to be his final time in space – for it to end like it had begun, on one of their stinking ships. He could see the route Professor Bond had told him to go was still clear, but he wasn't about to leave Bentley behind again.

Peering round the side of the little sphere he was sheltering behind, Johnny identified the furthest of the black pods he could see, back in the direction he'd come from. He pointed the Imperial blaster and fired a steady pulse, holding the trigger down despite the weapon becoming hot in his hands. In the far corner of the room, his target was glowing red. Spikes burst out of its sides and then it exploded, sparks shooting upward, lighting up the Krun soldiers who were running towards it.

Johnny seized his chance and ran in the other direction, towards Bentley, who was still crouching tensed outside a mucous membrane covering a gap in the wall. The rumbling was much louder, like a raging torrent, reminding Johnny of Mars. He grabbed Bentley by the collar, to pull the Old English sheepdog away and back to where Professor Bond had said to go, but Bentley shook himself free and barked loudly, jumping up and passing through the thick, sticky curtain. Johnny was forced to follow. He'd been right about the noise. It might have looked like a waterfall but, despite the strange lighting inside the Krun vessel, he knew the liquid gushing down the narrow channel was red. It disappeared through a narrow gap at the foot of the wall, plummeting over a precipice. Like the weir on Mars, he now realized it must be a way to oxygenate the blood for the Queen – she'd want it to taste as fresh as possible. It was a dreadful thought.

What made him feel even more sick was that a pair of Krun workers in overalls were opening huge seed-like structures, like giant vacuum-packed Venus flytraps, out of which fell rigid human cocoons. A third Krun then placed the bodies, one at a time, into the fast-flowing torrent, where they shot over the edge away to who knew where. Although they would not have heard Johnny and Bentley enter over the din, the three Krun turned, as one, to face them. Bentley leapt like a torpedo, his grey-and-white head striking one of the aliens in the midriff, knocking it off balance into the rivulet. The sheepdog followed. For a horrible moment Johnny thought Bentley would be swept over the edge, but the body of the Krun, larger than a man and lying across the gulley, had contrived to block the flow.

Johnny raised the Imperial blaster and, for the first time in his life, deliberately aimed at a fellow living, breathing creature. He fired. The force sent one of the aliens staggering backwards, toppling dead into the channel, adding to the blockage. But Johnny felt pain too, a burning in his own chest as if his insides were shrivelling up and turning black. He dropped the weapon, incapable of targeting the other Krun, who was on him in a flash. Johnny punched and kicked, but made no impact on the Krun's thick rubbery hide. The creature engulfed him, wrapping its limbs around his body and locking them tight. They fell together, the giant insect smothering him, squeezing the air out of his lungs. Next, the Krun's snout was in Johnny's face, spraying some sort of pus into his eyes – it stung like crazy. He cried out and, as he did so, more of the spray slid down his throat, tasting like poison. Johnny was pinned to the floor and knew this was a fight he had no way of winning. Then, by a miracle, the Krun's body went limp, crumpling on top of him. Johnny pushed the alien onto the ground beside him, where its arms and legs curled inward, like a dead spider.

Standing behind it was Bentley, coat dripping with human blood, but black Krun bile oozing from his jaws. Johnny wiped his stinging eyes and smiled. 'Good boy, good boy,' he said, hugging his friend before standing. Though it felt foreign to him, he collected the blaster.

'Johnny, what's going on? Where are you?'

'Sorry, professor,' he said into the wristcom. 'I'm coming.'

There were five and a half minutes left on the countdown.

'Hurry,' said the Australian. 'We're surrounded.'

'Look, I'm doing my best, but if you can destroy the ship I think you should do it now. I know there are people on board, but it's almost reached Earth – we can't let it land. I'm sorry.' Johnny added the apology, knowing the enormity of what he was asking.

'I can't do it alone,' came the reply in his ear. 'We need your help. Get down here.'

'OK,' said Johnny, but the transmission had already been terminated. He looked around the chamber. The blood in the channel had begun to force its way round the Krun bodies and a little was flowing through the gap at the bottom of the wall. Johnny wasn't about to allow that – the Queen had drunk enough human blood. He dragged one of the discarded, empty seed husks across the floor and dropped it into the gulley. There was a sound like someone sucking through a straw and, as he watched in amazement, the strange container adjusted itself to form a blood-tight seal. At once, the liquid began to spill over the sides around Johnny's feet.

'Come on, Bents,' he said, making for the curtain they'd entered through. The Old English sheepdog stood his ground and whimpered, sniffing at one of the human cocoons lying stiff in the middle of the chamber. 'We can't help them,' said Johnny. 'There's no time. Professor Bond needs me.' Bentley barked, but Johnny grabbed the dog's collar and this time didn't let go, dragging his blood-covered friend towards, then through, the mucous membrane and back into the vaulted room.

As soon as they re-entered the space, green bolts of energy struck the walls around them. Johnny let go of Bentley and ran, but his legs were leaden and a stitch stabbed at his side. The opening in the far corner of the room looked far away, but the sheepdog was alongside barking encouragement. Johnny had to trust in the cover of the small black ships and couldn't believe his luck as the blaster fire kept striking just behind. Finally he brushed through the curtain, which stuck fast to his face, wrapping around him like a vile blindfold. He kept going as he clawed at the sticky gunk.

'That's right, Johnny – you're almost there,' said the voice in his earpiece.

'How do you know all this?' asked Johnny. He slowed, catching his breath and pulling a thick strand of the horrid mucus out of his eyes. Finally he could see again, but a large part of him wished he couldn't. He and Bentley were surrounded by Krun soldiers who were slowly advancing, arms outstretched, reminiscent of the cannibals on Novolis. The Old English sheepdog growled and crouched low, ready to spring forward. Johnny knew to attack so many Krun meant certain death. 'Easy, Bents,' he said, bending down to take hold of the dog's collar.

The circle was closing, the two of them penned in as it became smaller and smaller. Johnny edged backwards into the very centre of the chamber, pivoting round, waving the gun in warning, but faced by hundreds of weapons pointing back. He wondered why the aliens didn't shoot. As they crowded in within touching distance, one of them reached out a long arm and plucked Johnny's blaster from his grasp. He didn't resist.

The voice in his earpiece, Professor Bond's voice, said, 'I think that should do it – just there.' A flap in the living, organic floor opened, like a trapdoor, and Johnny and Bentley fell slowly through, as if the gravity had been deliberately turned down low. Johnny found himself in the middle of a great cloud of the furry, telepathic moths and clamped his mouth tight shut. The creatures buzzed around his head but he swotted them away and then, once through, the view cleared, revealing an enormous cathedral-like chamber. This wasn't the escape he'd been hoping for. The scene was more crowded than when Johnny had last visited here, beneath the great pyramid on Mars, but he recognized it all too well.

Along the floor, channels of blood flowed into each other, gushing down the Queen's mouth with occasional lightly cocooned bodies carried on the torrent. Johnny could still make out the spacesuits of some of Earth's pilots. Unable to contain her excitement as Johnny and Bentley landed in front of her, she rasped, '*Live ones . . .*'

On the other side, shaking with laughter, was Stevens in his human form. There was no sign of the Australian anywhere. Lined up behind Bugface himself stood row upon row of newly hatched Krun soldiers and, all the while, new eggs were being pushed out as the clear corrugated overhead tubes expanded and contracted. Stevens brought his arm up to his mouth and spoke into the device on his wrist. 'Strewth – look what just dropped in.' The accent was a perfect impersonation of Professor Bond's. The truth dawned on Johnny: he had never been speaking with the Australian.

Seeing Bentley was about to lunge, he grabbed the sheepdog around the middle and picked him up, cradling his blood-soaked friend in his arms.

'Very wise,' said Stevens, now speaking in his normal voice. 'After all, you know our Queen prefers live ones. I'd hate to have to feed her dead dog.'

'Where's Professor Bond?' said Johnny. 'What have you done with him?'

'You know, I don't have the faintest idea. After we took this,' said Stevens, smiling and showing off the wristcom, 'and I mastered his speech patterns – I loathe having to remain in this disgusting, human form, but you see now why it was necessary—'

'Where is he?' said Johnny through gritted teeth. 'I know he's somewhere on this ship.'

'This *ship*? Really?' Stevens laughed again. 'When we first came to your star system, our Queen was not much more than a pupa. Perhaps you recall she was indeed once small enough to be smuggled away from our moon, which you call Triton, in a ship. But she has been gorging on human flesh for quite some time. Your species has one thing in its favour – at least you are nutritious.'

'Answer the question,' said Johnny. He felt sick.

'Oh, but I am,' said Stevens. 'You asked if your professor was somewhere on this ship, but you see, Johnny, this is no ship. You are already inside our Queen.'

Johnny looked round, aghast, but it all made sense. Spaceships were often grown, not built, but this one felt even more organic than most. The vaulted ceiling he'd seen was part of a skeleton – the veins in the floors, exactly that. And it explained properly why the Krun fleet couldn't fold directly to Earth.

'So no one is "on board" – wherever he's got to, he's food of course. Eaten already, or bagged up in his cocoon, waiting in line. It hardly matters,' said the Krun. 'Our Queen is hatching a magnificent invasion force.' He gestured to the lines of soldiers behind. 'Soon all of your disgusting, stinking humanity will be food.'

'We'll fight you,' said Johnny, looking round, desperate for a means of escape. The far wall behind Stevens and the Krun army, what Johnny now knew was simply a giant piece of Krun skin, was bulging oddly outwards.

'No, you won't,' said Stevens. 'Most of the ships you stole from us have flown meekly into storage. A few others destroyed each other – or themselves. *You* may have been able to resist our Queen, but the pure humans aren't so strong-willed. We reach Earth's atmosphere in four minutes, when a mighty swarm will be released. We'll get inside their heads – everyone will come willingly, eager to be devoured first.'

Johnny glanced at his wristcom. He knew it was true, that it was nearly all over. In just the short time he'd watched, hundreds more eggs had been laid, while vast numbers of the telepathic moths had streamed out from nozzles either side of the Queen's mouth. At least the blood flowing the other way had all but stopped.

'*Feed me,*' growled the all too familiar deep voice just behind Johnny.

'Our Queen complains she is hungry,' said Stevens. 'That her food supply has been interrupted.' Johnny felt a smidgeon of satisfaction from his tiny, temporary victory. 'Whatever you have done will be easily rectified,' the Krun went on. 'It just hastens your own death. She doesn't just want live ones – she's been inside your head, Johnny Mackintosh. She wants your secrets. She wants *you.*' Stevens raised his arm, training a blaster on Johnny's face. At the same time, perfectly synchronized, hundreds of Krun soldiers standing behind him did the same. Before Johnny realized what was happening, a black pincer descended from above, grabbing his feet and plucking him into the air. He dangled upside down, still holding Bentley, as they swayed above the vat of batter he'd been dropped into once before.

'*I demand live ones,*' screamed the Queen. Johnny craned his neck and saw her huge mouth open wide, teeth chomping impatiently.

'And you shall have them, my Queen,' said Stevens, falling to his knees and prostrating himself on the ground.

Behind the prone Krun there was a bang and, from a tiny

hole in the far wall, shot a single jet of red liquid. As one, all the Krun turned, only for some of them to be showered with blood. A second bang saw a new jet of blood arc across the enormous chamber in a different direction, followed by a third and then a fourth.

'*Feed me now*,' howled the Queen. The pincers holding Johnny were released and he and Bentley began to fall towards the vat.

'What is this?' said Stevens from his position on the floor. The Krun turned to stare and, at that instant, the bulging wall gave way. A tidal wave of human blood, building since Johnny dammed the gulley, burst through, cascading into the cavernous chamber. 'No!' shouted the figure on the ground.

Johnny was falling into the batter, about to be engulfed. The next second, he was falling upward to where he'd first come through the trapdoor. Desperately, he clung to Bentley as he folded the space between themselves and safety until it was just a tiny step. The last thing he saw was the giant red wave washing Stevens and some of the Krun soldiers into the Queen's mouth and straight down her throat.

It had worked. He'd taken himself and Bentley to the level above, where they rolled onto the floor. Krun were running from the room into which they'd unfolded, the insectoids' priority being to end the carnage below. Johnny and the Old English sheepdog were ignored. With Bentley, still recovering, cradled in his arms, Johnny stood up and ran towards and through the curtain of mucus into the chamber with the vaulted roof. Weighed down by his friend and weakened from the slicing of his soul, Johnny staggered along the rows of spherical black pods towards the gap in the far wall that led to the shuttle bay and safety, if only for a few minutes. It was no use. Unable to go on he fell face down, knowing it would make no difference if he never got up again. Freed from his grip,

Bentley was barking furiously and began licking Johnny's ear. Without the sheepdog to carry, Johnny got to his knees and then stood. Slowly he began walking between the pods, hands on his hips, but instead of bounding alongside, Bentley shot away, back towards where they'd dammed the river of blood.

'No – come back, Bents,' shouted Johnny. There were only three minutes left.

His friend stopped, turned and barked several times, before carrying on back through the curtain. There was no choice but to follow.

Johnny pushed through the net and instantly slipped on the sodden red floor. Like the husk he'd placed in the gulley, the curtain must have made a blood-tight seal. The small chamber had swollen with blood until the pressure became too much and something had to give. Where before there'd been the wall, there was now a gaping hole through which Johnny could see the scenes of chaos in the main hall. From his vantage point up above, it was clear the contours along the floor had been designed to funnel everything into the Queen's mouth. Thanks to the great wave of blood that had burst over them, carrying all before it, 'everything' meant an awful lot of Krun soldiers. The Queen's craving for live ones had, at least for now, been satisfied, but order was already returning. Johnny knew they didn't have long.

Bentley was barking more furiously than ever. Johnny turned to see the sheepdog pawing at one of the many human cocoons strewn haphazardly over the ground. At first he didn't understand, but when he looked at the contours of the rigid figure encased in its shroud of Krun batter, it became suddenly familiar – down to the outline of a wide-brimmed hat. *Here* was Professor Bond. Johnny tried to pick the Australian up, but the man was too heavy, the floor too slippery and himself too exhausted. Even if saving Clara hadn't sapped his strength, he doubted he could do this, but it didn't stop him from trying again. This time he raised the cocoon a little way off the floor, before slipping again on the blood-soaked ground and dropping the professor. 'Sorry,' said Johnny, in case the Australian was alive and aware.

Bentley was growling in front of the curtains, which could only mean that the Krun were approaching. They'd come so close. The only escape he could think of was to try to fold them all into the shuttle bay, but he wasn't at all sure how – it was like trying to move the Atlantean ships off the seabed. He called Bentley over, knowing he could only possibly do it if they were all together. The Old English sheepdog didn't budge. Johnny shouted again, but knew it wouldn't work. Bentley was guarding the opening, making a last stand as the Krun approached. Nothing would remove the dog from his post. Johnny slumped exhausted over Professor Bond's body.

'Johnny . . . where are you? I have an idea.' It was Louise, speaking into her wristcom.

'It's no good,' said Johnny. 'This thing's about to reach Earth. We're trapped inside. There's no way out.' The countdown told him there were only two minutes to go.

'Well, make one,' said Louise. 'I can destroy it, but I'm not about to do that with you and Bentley inside.'

In the middle of everything, Johnny smiled at her optimism. 'And Professor Bond,' he said.

'You found David?' said Louise. 'That settles it. You get out of there right now.'

'It doesn't matter any more,' said Johnny. 'You've got one short-range fighter and this . . . this thing's massive. What can you possibly do?'

'That's for me to know and you to find out,' said Louise. 'What's happened to you? You never give up. It sounds like someone's cut all the fight out of you.'

That was exactly how Johnny felt, but hearing Louise's defiance bolstered him. 'OK – we'll get out,' he said, though he didn't believe it for a second.

'Promise?'

Johnny hesitated. He hated making promises he knew he couldn't keep.

'Promise me, Johnny.'

'OK, I promise,' he said into the wristcom. He was about to lower his arm when he had an idea. There was no way he, Bentley and Professor Bond could all make it to the Starfighter, but maybe the Starfighter could come to them. A Krun blaster poked through the curtain, followed by a long, spindly arm. As the Old English sheepdog leapt and bit, Johnny tapped commands into the little device on his wrist, which he'd once before used as a remote control. There was a mighty explosion in the vaulted chamber beyond the curtain. Down below, in the great hall, the Queen screamed in pain. The charred, smoking body of the Krun Bentley had attacked fell through the curtain, accompanied by small pieces of debris. Johnny hadn't intended the weapons fire to be quite so powerful. The black Krun pods filling the room had been incinerated. Using the wristcom, he piloted the Starfighter through the gaping wound he'd created in the shuttle bay wall, having it settle beside the chamber they were in.

Seeing the ship so close gave him new strength. With a single, mighty effort, he hauled the professor's body onto the wing and pushed it into the open cockpit. Johnny followed, with Bentley jumping last into the crowded cabin. The engines roared into life and the Starfighter lifted into the air just as more Krun soldiers entered the blackened chamber. Johnny ignored them, knowing their puny blasters could never damage his ship, which had nearly repaired itself. Instead he turned the Imperial Starfighter towards the blitzed wall and the exposed shuttle bay beyond. There was no sign of where he'd entered the Queen so he trained every weapon at his disposal on her outer skin and began to fire.

All guns blazing, he thought, *Forward, full acceleration.* If it worked, he'd blast his way through and out into space. If it didn't . . . By the time he'd even begun to consider that, he'd shot out like a cork from a bottle and could see the stars. He was free, but the Queen would enter Earth's atmosphere in sixty seconds. As he looked back at her, he realized each one of the black studs that he'd thought were cladding for the outer hull was a hungry eye, staring coldly at his retreating Starfighter.

'Johnny Mackintosh to Colonel Hartman,' he said into the comm. system. The Starcruiser with its hyperspatial charges were the only hope left. The Colonel had to see sense.

'She's gone, Johnny. At least I think she has. Flew straight into the Sun. The voice in our heads – it told them to do it.' Louise was sounding more her normal self, but something was wrong. He couldn't locate her ship – she was travelling so fast it was as though she was everywhere in orbit at once.

'What are you doing?' Johnny asked.

'I told you. I'm going to stop the Krun, once and for all. I can save the world too, you know.'

'Tell me how,' said Johnny. 'I can help.' He was worried. There was something odd about Louise's voice. He glanced again at his wristcom and saw there were only thirty seconds left.

'No way,' she said. 'I thought of it first. It's Einstein – relativity. You see, the faster I go, the heavier I become. I've been slingshotting round Earth, getting quicker and quicker, heavier and heavier. I'm ready now.'

'Ready for what, Louise?'

'I want you to promise me something, Johnny.'

'Ready for what?' he said again, but Louise was in full flow.

'You see, Rusty doesn't like all this space travel nonsense. She's a bit of a home girl – like me, really. I want you to promise me you'll find her a good home. Maybe somewhere near a nice park.'

'Don't talk like that,' said Johnny. He was panicking. There were only twenty seconds to go.

'Promise me,' said Louise.

'This is mad,' said Johnny.

'Promise.'

'Of course I would, but . . .'

'You see, I know I'm not exotic enough for you, Johnny.'

'What?' She was really scaring him now.

'Maybe if I'd come aboard when you first asked, but I like Earth. It's enough for me. That's why I have to save it. I'm not like you. I don't have to see the universe.'

'What are you talking about, Louise?' Bentley barked close to his ear. The countdown reached ten seconds.

'Goodbye, Bents,' said Louise. There was a pause before she added, 'I love you, Johnny.'

The bulbous, gigantic Krun Queen crossed the point where Louise, at close to light speed, was orbiting Earth. Travelling so fast, the small Atlantean fighter had become as massive as the object in its path – a relativistic bomb. The two collided in an almighty explosion. The blast wave hit Johnny's Starfighter hard, tossing it out into space like a twig caught up in a hurricane. He could do nothing to help as he tumbled past the grey Moon and on, battling to hold the Imperial ship, with its two passengers, together.

It was probably only five or ten minutes before the Starfighter finally stabilized and he brought it under control, though it felt like forever. Johnny forced himself to return to the scene of the explosion, but not even the tiniest piece of wreckage remained.

There was nothing left. The comm. system crackled into life with the sound of surviving human voices, freed from Krun control. Miss Harutunian was still alive and started taking charge. There were some whoops and cheers. In his cramped cockpit, Johnny sat in silence.

16

One Week Later ✰✰

'She likes you,' said Johnny.

Mrs Irvine was kneeling on the grass in Castle Dudbury Memorial Park, holding Rusty's face just far enough away to keep the red setter's eager tongue out of reach of her horn-rimmed spectacles. 'The feeling's mutual, Jonathan. Ben Halader House wouldn't feel right without a dog walking its corridors, annoying Mr Wilkins. And with Bentley leaving us . . .'

Her voice trailed off, carried away on a blustery wind. It was raining too. Johnny stood beside the Manager, soaking up the conditions. He would miss the wind and the rain – you didn't get those on the garden deck of the *Spirit of London*. Sol had reported in a few hours ago to say that her repairs were complete.

'If you insist on leaving, I still don't understand why you don't take her with you.'

'I promised,' said Johnny.

'This Louise . . . Rusty's mum – you say it was she who saved Earth?'

'The whole planet,' Johnny replied. It was still hard to think about what had happened. As his eyes watered, he was glad of the rain on his cheeks.

'I know I can't follow in her footsteps, Rusty, but I'll do my best to look after you.' Mrs Irvine gave the red setter a pat on the head before, taking Johnny's arm, she pulled herself to her feet.

'You'll do fine,' he said.

'If Earth's safe, then why do you have to go, Jonathan? Your parents wanted me to look after you if anything happened. I know you've been through a lot, but you're still a boy. I could insist.'

'No, you couldn't,' said Johnny. He turned to the grey-haired Scot, looking her square in the eye.

'Well, I daresay you're right, but I don't like it. And now we're out of danger . . .'

'Earth's only safe for now,' said Johnny. 'And it's better off without me. There's a being out there – pure evil. He's taking over the galaxy and no one's able to stop him. And I don't know why, but he hates me more than anything else in the universe. Earth will never be properly safe while I'm here.' Johnny started to walk towards Halader House. Speaking of the Nameless One reminded him that time was short. It would never have crossed his mind to hide away here in this little backwater of the galaxy. Louise had been right about that – it wasn't his nature. Most of his football team, ordinary friends from school, were now gone. Nicky had been snatched from him. Ophia had suffered her terrible fate on Melania. Worst of all, Louise was dead too. He and Clara were the only ones who could make things right, make the galaxy a better place. He was determined to do that, or at least die trying. There was no point putting it off any longer.

Mrs Irvine started after him, her tartan umbrella battling the gusts of wind. Rusty came too, pottering along behind, until the red setter spotted a llama in the park's petting zoo and bounded away, barking loudly. Johnny stopped, marvelling that the red setter could adjust so quickly, smiling at the dog's ordinary, innocent fun.

'But where will you go?' asked the Manager, drawing alongside.

'We're looking for somewhere called Lysentia,' said Johnny.

'And you know where this place is?' said Mrs Irvine.

Johnny laughed. 'Sadly no, but we'll find it – and, if we're really lucky, we'll find Nicky along the way.'

'It's a big galaxy out there,' said Mrs Irvine, 'but if you're as lucky as your father, you'll find whatever your heart desires.'

'Yeah? It didn't do him much good, did it?' said Johnny.

'He found love, Jonathan. True love with your mother.'

Johnny shook his head and started walking again. Love hadn't held his family together or kept Louise alive. He was nearing the boundary of the park. Across the busy road was the railway station and, facing it, connected via a grey carpark that mirrored the current colour of the sky, was his children's home. He really wouldn't miss that. He lifted the wristcom to his mouth and said, 'Clara, it's me. I think it's time to be going.'

'I'll just say my goodbyes,' she replied. 'Then I'll pick you up.'

☆ ☆ ☆
☆ ☆

Underneath Halader House was a hive of activity. The small sickbay was overflowing, so Dr Carrington had arrived to set up a field hospital in the main underground area, very capably assisted by Alf. The artificial sun that beamed down on the makeshift beds seemed to aid the healing process. Since the doctor turned up, Clara had been spending most of the time in the garden she'd built beside St Catharine's. That was where she was now. Johnny understood. He could see Carrington had done an amazing job with some of the casualties, but Johnny didn't much care for the man. The Krun parasites, the moth-like creatures that had wormed their way into everyone's brains, had shrivelled and died once the Queen was killed. They'd been removed and collected for later inspection. Johnny had wanted them destroyed, but Dr Carrington insisted on keeping them to examine properly.

Miss Harutunian was in charge of search and rescue, running round-the-clock missions in the *Piccadilly*, following up signals from escape pods in the hunt for possible survivors. It had been two days since anyone had been brought back alive and, although no one had yet said it out loud, Johnny knew everyone believed this small group was all that remained of Earth's briefly impressive defence fleet. The air of despondency worked wonders for Mr Wilkins and, especially, the cook's mother.

None of the Atlantean fighters remained intact. The Krun had only left them alone because they were too badly damaged to take inside the Queen – it had been a challenge even to land them safely. Professor Bond, who was apparently fully conscious throughout his time in the batter cocoon, was already working on salvaging bits and pieces.

The list of those missing in action was long. It included Dave Spedding, Micky Elliot and Simon Bakewell from the football team, and Spencer Mitchell, who Johnny had always thought of as indestructible. Colonel Hartman was on the list too. It could have been so different if she'd done the right thing and the *Spirit of London* had remained in the battle. Louise, and so many of the others, wouldn't have had to die. Johnny hated the colonel for it. He had been worried about Corporation people being stationed in Halader House, but it was clear that most of them looked up to Miss Harutunian. The social worker had once been a respected figure in their organization, but lost out to Hartman in a power struggle.

After the battle, Johnny had brought Clara to see the place their mum built. She'd tripled the size of the facility, identifying fabulous new areas previously hidden in hyperspace. Johnny would never have spotted them – he didn't have his sister's gift – but she always left it to him to unfold them, opening them up for public use. After what he'd done to save her in the middle of the battle, Johnny felt closer to his sister than ever. Almost before she entered the main hall he thought he'd sensed her arrival. Bentley beside her, she made her way over.

With no patients currently in need, Alf, the object of much fascination, had retreated behind a copy of *The Times* newspaper and was attempting the day's crossword. Johnny, Clara and Bentley went across to collect him and were joined by Mrs Irvine. The farewells were beginning.

'Thank you, Alf, for all the help you've given us here at Ben Halader House,' she said. 'It's very much appreciated.'

'What did you say?' asked the android, surprisingly animated. It wasn't the reaction anyone had been expecting and Mrs Irvine took a step back.

'I'm sorry,' said the Manager. 'I didn't mean to offend you.' She looked to the others for help.

'Alf,' said Clara. Johnny thought she might be about to kick the android.

'What did you say?' Alf repeated.

'I . . . I just said I was grateful for all your help.' Johnny had never seen the Manager so flustered.

'No, the other bit,' said the android.

'That was it,' said Mrs Irvine. 'Really.'

'But did you not say, "Ben Halader House"? Alf took a step forward, matched by one back on the part of the Manager. The android went on, 'Johnny always calls this place "Halader House". This is very important.'

Johnny felt his face turning red.

'Of course I'm aware most people shorten it nowadays,' said Mrs Irvine, regaining her composure and giving Johnny a sideways look of disapproval, 'but the correct title is indeed

"Ben Halader House". Although quite who Ben Halader was—'

'But that is it!' said Alf, practically skipping with delight. 'Do you not see?'

Bentley had started barking. Johnny looked at Clara, who shrugged. Perhaps she was wondering the same thing as he was, whether the android had fully recovered from his power drain the week before.

'The name is an anagram,' said Alf.

'My word – I'd never considered that,' said Mrs Irvine, stepping forward, almost as excited as the android.

'Rearrange the letters,' said Alf, 'and it makes "Horsehead Nebula".'

'Where's that?' Clara asked.

Johnny rolled his eyes. Its shape had always made it one of his favourite astronomical features. 'Its proper name's Barnard 33 . . .' Johnny broke off, appalled at his own stupidity, and looked at the children's home Manager, who continued the sentence.

'. . . and Ben Halader House lies at 33 Barnard Way.'

'And was created by Johnny and Clara's mother and father?' said Alf.

'Indeed,' said Mrs Irvine, nodding. 'I had to move here all the way from Glasgow.'

'Then our destination is clear,' said the android. 'The search for Lysentia will begin in the Horsehead Nebula. I rather think we should get going.'

☆ ☆ ☆
☆ ☆

The goodbyes were over. Johnny was sure that Bentley knew he was saying farewell to Rusty. The Old English sheepdog, Clara and Alf had already gone topside and were now waiting in the *Piccadilly*. Johnny felt almost traitorous, leaving the few surviving members of the football team behind. He'd changed their lives forever, and was now walking out on them. Finally, Miss Harutunian was leading him along the corridor to the lift shaft that would emerge in the telephone box in front of the station. Johnny thought he knew what was coming.

'No,' he said to the red-haired American.

'No, what?' she replied, folding her arms.

'You have to stay here,' said Johnny. 'You can't come with us.'

'That's cruel. A taste of honey's worse than none at all, Johnny. You know as well as I do that those Starfighters will never fly again.'

'You're needed here,' he said. 'The Corporation people listen to you.'

'But I want to be there.'

'I know,' he said. 'I'm sorry.'

For a while the American didn't speak, as if hoping Johnny would break the silence and change his mind. Memories from their time together floated into his mind. It was a shame he'd not discovered their shared love of space sooner, but that might have made it even harder to stay firm. Finally she said, 'Promise me you'll come back and say hi.'

'No more promises,' said Johnny. He saw tears begin to well up in his old social worker's eyes. 'So long,' he said. It was the best he could offer.

'So long, Johnny.'

He entered the lift and, just seconds later, found himself sitting in a red double-decker bus, turning invisible as, for perhaps the final time, he flew over Ben Halader House.

The End

Acknowledgements ✫✫

A significant portion of *Johnny Mackintosh: Battle for Earth* was written while a Fellow at the Hawthornden International Retreat for Writers. I'm grateful to Mrs Drue Heinz for her generous creation and maintenance of the Fellowships, everyone at Hawthornden Castle and my fellow Fellows for their support and fine company while on retreat together.

Once finished, Anna Faherty did her usual superb pre-edit of an early draft, giving great feedback and advice on improving the writing and elements of the story. Neither this nor the previous Johnny Mackintosh books would have been possible without the ongoing support of Quercus Books, especially editor Roisin Heycock and Nicci Praca and Niamh Mulvey, and founders Wayne Davies and Mark Smith. And, of course, both Suzy Jenvey and Parul Bavishi, whose publishing careers have since taken them on elsewhere.

Margaret Histed gave both encouragement and some fine final advice on the structure, while Talya Baker worked brilliantly to turn it into whatever version, print or electronic, you're now reading.

Writing books is a solitary affair that takes a huge amount of time and effort. I want to apologize to all my friends and family for the hermit-style existence I've had to adopt to complete

Battle for Earth and thank them for their understanding, support and love throughout the process. Finally, if any readers have made it as far as the end of these acknowledgements, I'd like to thank them and say I hope they've enjoyed reading Johnny and Clara's adventures as much as I enjoy writing them. ✧✧

ALEX RIDER MEETS DOCTOR WHO IN AN
INCREDIBLE ADVENTURE ACROSS TIME AND SPACE

JOHNNY MACKINTOSH

AND THE
SPIRIT OF LONDON

KEITH MANSFIELD

JOHNNY MACKINTOSH

AND THE
SPIRIT OF LONDON

An extraordinarily imaginative adventure across space and time with the Ultimate Hero

When thirteen-year-old Johnny's talking computer Kovac detects an extraterrestrial signal, his life is set to change forever. Until then, stuck in his children's home in Castle Dudbury New Town, with the nasty cook Mr Wilkins watching his every move, football had been his only escape.

But soon things start happening around him that Johnny doesn't understand. Why is his mother, who is on life support in a hospital for the criminally insane, being guarded by sinister-looking men? And why was a journalist murdered shortly after Johnny talked to him? When Johnny finds out he has a sister, he decides to run away to find her.

His search for answers takes him further from home than he could ever have imagined, on a spectacular journey through time and space. Along the way he visits new worlds, prehistoric Earth and the lost city of Atlantis, before finally discovering the truth about his parents and who he really is.

'EXCITEMENT ALL THE WAY'
Daily Express
JOHNNY MACKINTOSH
STAR BLAZE
KEITH MANSFIELD

JOHNNY MACKINTOSH

STAR BLAZE

**Johnny Mackintosh. Hero of our galaxy.
Protector of planet Earth.**

Alien invaders have exploded a nearby star, turning it into a supernova, and only Johnny Mackintosh knows the Sun is next in line. Abandoning school and his football team, he and sister Clara travel to the galactic capital seeking help. Their mission stalls. After a decade missing, Johnny's mysterious brother reappears, but what was he doing all those years away and whose side is he on?

So begins an epic adventure full of devious aliens intent on ruling the galaxy and killing Johnny along the way. Can he survive to save his brother, and planet Earth, in time?

Keith Mansfield's explosive space adventure will wow fans of action stories and Star Wars.